SIXTY-SIX CU

Sixty-Six Curses

Chris Johnson

Samurai West

Published by Samurai West
disappearer007@gmail.com

This paperback edition published 2025
ISBN-13: 9798294108489

Author's Note

Although the following introduction does not contain any spoilers, I strongly advise the reader to skip it anyway, as it contains comments about this author which are unflattering if not downright libellous, and has been included in this edition under protest.

Introduction

by Professor Dorothea Dupont, PhD, BSc, MSc, MILF

I've been asked by the author (actually I haven't been asked by the author, but as he freely makes use of my actual and identifiable self in his books, he didn't really have any choice in the matter) to write some introductory comments for this the new edition of *Sixty-Six Curses*.

But before I discuss the book, let's have a look at the author. What can we say about Chris Johnson, the person who has taken it upon himself (self-imposed tasks being the only kind of tasks that lazy, self-willed people like him can actually knuckle down to) to chronicle the exploits of Mark Hunter and my good self? Well, as for his mental health problems, I could write a book about those and one day I probably will, but for now let's just examine the artist in relation to his art. Chris is one of those writers who was bitten by the writing bug while he was still at primary school, and then, by the time he'd failed his GCSEs (apart from English and Art), he decided that to be a novelist was the only career for him. So it's taken him a precious long time to even get where he is today—that'll be on account of those problems I hinted at.

Formerly, to be a writer of adventure stories for the Young Adult market was what Chris aspired to: but unfortunately, at the time YA fiction was very much a niche market and dominated by teenage romance and lightweight horror; adventure stories were not in demand. But now, 'in his maturity as a writer' (his phrase, not mine) he has decided that he wants to aim his work squarely at the adult fiction market—and coming at a time when YA fiction across a wide range of genres is enjoying unprecedented popularity and being read by people of all ages, while sales of adult fiction, and especially literary fiction, are declining, I think we can all agree that this has been a very wise decision on Chris's part.

And yes, I say 'literary fiction' because Chris does actually consider his attention-seeking effusions to be 'literature'! Now, I happen to know (although he probably doesn't *know* that I know) that back when he attempted to tackle Proust's *In Search of Lost Time*, he gave it up as a bad job after the third volume—so, far being able to write literature, he can't even read it. Still, perhaps I'm being unfair to the poor darling, because after all, he can boast of having at least one important thing in common with the late, great William Golding, recipient of the Nobel Prize for Literature: to wit, a major alcohol problem.

But seriously Chris, you might as well just call yourself a science fiction writer and have done with it.

Now back to *Sixty-Six Curses*, the second book in the—actually, in the *what* series? Chris has never actually got round to giving the books a generic title, has he? I know he toyed with the idea of calling them the 'Mark and Dodo' books, but decided it sounded too informal, and then considered the 'Hunter and Dupont' and even the 'Mark Hunter' books, the latter a title which would have neatly reduced yours truly to sidekick status.

Anyway, series names aside, as I say, *Sixty-Six Curses* is the second book to feature Mark and myself (not to mention my darling honeybunch Mayumi), and the sequel to *Beautiful Chaos*, the book Chris now calls his first novel, although he had written other material before this one (all long-since consigned to the dustbin.) And it's amusing to note that when writing that first novel, he was being so careful to avoid the 'autobiographical first novel' trap, that he instead walked straight into the 'everything but the kitchen sink first novel' trap. (And I don't know why they had to get rid of the cover that I modelled for…)

Having completed the first draft of *Beautiful Chaos* (and if you think the book is shambolic now, you should have seen it before the rewrite!), Chris, drunk with his sense of achievement and the ludicrous belief that he'd actually created a work of art, launched precipitately into the sequel. And would you believe, at the time he actually conceived the plan of making these books a *numbered* series—yes, *numbered!* He even had visions of these numerals being emblazoned on the front covers of the books!—and with each volume conforming to the same number of chapters and more or less the same word count. Fortunately, Chris was forced to abandon this insane scheme when, setting to work on *Sixty-Six Curses*, he soon realised that this book wasn't going to be nearly as long as its predecessor. And along with uniformity of length and chapter-count he also dropped the idea of the numeration, thank Christ.

I call *Sixty-Six Curses* the sequel, but actually it isn't really a sequel in the true sense, because although it features the same main characters as the first book, the story covers an otherwise completely unrelated series of events. (You might be interested to know that there *is* a sequel to the events of *Beautiful Chaos*: it's called *The Delta Effect*, and it hasn't been written up yet.) However, in spite of not being a true 'sequel,' Sixty-Six Curses still manages to suffer from 'sequelitis' with the book being the predictable 'second novel that delves into the main character's backstory.' (The main character being Mark, of course, not me.)

So, is *Sixty-Six Curses* a better book than its predecessor? Well, 'better' is a subjective term; it certainly presents us with a more structured plot, while at the same time cements the author's reputation for displaying a complete lack of anything resembling subtlety and restraint in his writing, along with a tendency to overload his stories with characters.

But more importantly, my gorgeous sexpot Mayumi gets a lot more screentime in this one than she did in the first book; and it also features Yumi's assistant, the irrepressible Trina Trulove, who *was* going to appear in *Beautiful Chaos*, but ended up getting written out of it. (She was quite peeved about that.)

Returning to the subject of Chris's literary pretentions: do you know which great work of fiction is the 'key' to *Sixty-Six Curses*? The author would tell you it's Flaubert's *Sentimental Education*— but actually it's *Biggles Goes to School*. Yes: *Biggles Goes to School*.

Finally, if you're wondering why the book is actually called *Sixty-Six Curses*—well, so am I! Curses, literal or figurative, do not come into the story in any way; not a single one, never mind sixty-six of them. I did at one point think that perhaps the title might refer to the book featuring sixty-six uses of the F-word—but I've checked and there are only fifty-eight. I'm inclined to think that the title doesn't have any meaning at all, and that Chris just chose it because he thought (for some reason) that it sounded good.

Well, that's it, really. I don't want to say too much about the story in case I start bringing in spoilers; but before I sign off, I'll just glance briefly at the two books that followed this one. The first of them—in order of first drafts—was *Trouble at School*, a story in which Mark and myself are reduced to the status of supporting cast, and as for poor Yumi: nothing more than a couple of passing references! *Trouble at School* has the distinction of being Chris's longest novel—probably because it's set in a girls' school.

9

It would have been nice if Chris could have followed this by writing up one of the stories in which Yumi and me, the female contingent, get to be centre-stage (did I mention that he actually calls himself a feminist?), especially with Mark hogging the limelight in the first two, and neither of us getting much of a look-in in the third. For example, there is the *Beasts of Bellend*, the assignment where Yumi and me were the 'agents on the spot' while Mark stayed back in his office; or there's our Japanese adventure *Suicide Garden*, that Mark doesn't appear in at all. But no, instead of one of these Chris chose to make the fourth book *Mysterious Girlfriend*, yet another story in which both Mark and myself play second fiddle to a bunch of kids! (Well, at least in this one we were actually proactive in resolving the situation—something that doesn't happen very often.)

And so, what next for the chronicles of Mark Hunter and Dodo Dupont? Which will be the next of our adventures to be transformed into tragi-comic, socially-aware exploitation fiction? Perhaps one of the three I've already mentioned? Or perhaps the story of the apocalyptic advertising campaign *Countdown to Zero*? Or the epidemic of infantile humour *Only When I Larf*? Or maybe our fairy-tale adventure *The Mysteries of Primrosia*?

Well, at the moment it's sweet Fanny Adams. Chris seems to have put us on the backburner for the nonce, while he indulges his obsession with Japanese women in a series of standalone novels. When I ask him when he'll be writing up another one of our adventures, all I get are vague answers about it 'being in the pipeline.' (Sometimes I'm amazed that he ever manages to get anything done.)

So, if after reading *Sixty-Six Curses* you find yourself thirsting for more of Mark Hunter and Dodo Dupont's thrilling exploits, just contact the author and tell him to pull his finger out.

Love and Kisses

Dodo Dupont

10

Prologue
Position X

Strange things started to happen in and around the town of Market Stanford, a small town of no previous notoriety, located in the heart of Cambridgeshire's agricultural fenlands.

One night, early in July, a light appeared in the sky; a vivid ball of light. It descended vertically, never losing speed, and was lost sight of in Vernon Wood, a nature reserve situated about two miles to the north of Market Stanford. Observed by several eyewitnesses, it was no hoax or false alarm.

But what was it? A shooting star? There had been no sound of an impact when the light had disappeared amongst the trees, no explosion.

An aircraft? One witness, a farmer, declared that the falling light emitted a regular, mechanical sound, but it was a strange sound and unlike the engine of any aircraft.

Conclusion: It must have been a UFO!

Several of the eyewitnesses thought so, and had called the police saying that this was what they had seen. A search was duly made of the woods the following day. Sceptical, they had expected to find nothing, but instead had found a very definite something: in a clearing in the middle of the woods they found a circular depression, thirty feet in diameter—a perfect circle of flattened ground in which every weed, every blade of grass, had withered and died. Outside the circle the foliage was unharmed. Was this some kind of landing site? Had the alleged UFO come to rest here? Then where was the UFO? No-one had reported seeing the light take off again. So where was it? If that wasn't confusing enough, later that same day an identical circular depression had been discovered in another clearing on the other side of Vernon Wood, half a mile from the first circle, and nowhere near where the alleged UFO had been seen to descend. Had two UFOs landed last night? No-one had reported seeing more than one light. Then, were the two circles of withered vegetation related to the falling light at all, or were they the result of some other phenomenon?

11

Perhaps they were just some elaborate hoax—a new variation on crop circles. But how had they been created? Experts had examined the two circles and found no traces of any poison; they also declared that tremendous weight had to have been applied for the foliage to have been flattened like it was.

This bizarre occurrence became known as the Market Stanford Incident.

People all across the county were talking about it. It made the front page of the local weekly newspaper, and there was even a feature on the regional television news. The national news media had yet to pick up on the story—when another celebrity has put their foot in it by saying the wrong thing and people are busy clamouring for said celebrity's head on a platter, such small beer as possible visitations from beyond the stars tend to slip off the news radar.

However, the light in the sky over Vernon Wood had turned out to be only the first bizarre event of many.

The next thing to happen occurred online: Residents of Market Stanford began to experience unusual interference on the internet. At first it was just servers not connecting, not responding or taking people to the wrong sites; but then the writing had started to appear: strange alien characters, thick black shapes against a blood red background invading people's PCs, laptops and smartphones. Corresponding with no known written language, there was something about the conformation of these characters that was deeply disturbing. They just seemed *wrong*. This reaction appeared to be an instinctive one, and experienced by all. Most people, when suddenly confronted with this alien text appearing on their screens, had instinctively looked away, cleared the screen, or switched off their device. One resident of Market Stanford had not done this. Although repulsed by the writing, it seemed that this woman had become mesmerised by it; unable to take her eyes from the screen as the endless stream of bizarre text had scrolled on and on...

This woman is now undergoing treatment in a local mental institution. She doesn't talk much, but when she does, it's not in a language anyone can understand.

So much for the writing. The next phenomenon to be reported

was aural in nature. Several people out walking in Vernon Wood had reported hearing strange sounds. Variously described as 'metallic sounds', 'echoes', 'electrical sounds', or 'weird music', the people experiencing these sounds had felt a sense of extreme unease, of something strange and unknown. The sounds had seemed to fill the air all around them; they did not seem to emanate from any particular location on the ground. Nevertheless, no-one outside the precincts of Vernon Wood had reported hearing the sounds; they were confined to this specific location. No-one had any explanation to offer.

And then the little grey men had shown up.

One night, Paul Bishop—resident of Market Stanford, twenty-nine, interior decorator by trade, married, two children, one of the lads—had been driving home from an evening visit to the pub. He was alone in the car; or at least he should have been. But looking in his rear-view mirror as he turned onto Brick Road, he had been shocked to see a strange creature sitting behind him in the back seat of the car. So startled by this apparition was Bishop, he had driven his car off the road into a brick wall. In hospital, he had described the creature he saw: grey-skinned, with a domed head and black, elliptical eyes—in short, the standard 'grey alien' of abduction mythology, familiar to anyone who'd ever watched *the X-Files*. Tests had revealed that Bishop had been driving while over the drinking limit, but was not so drunk that he should start seeing pink elephants, grey aliens or anything else that wasn't really there.

Even so, Bishop's story might have been written off as an imaginative accident insurance claim; but then, only two days later there had been a second incident. A six-year-old boy had woken from his sleep in the middle of the night to find a 'funny-looking boy' sitting at the end of his bed. They had stared at each other for a few moments, the boy and the apparition, neither speaking; then the boy had started screaming and threw the duvet over himself. Awakened by the sound, his parents had rushed into the room, turning on the light. They had found their son alone; there had been no sign of any intruder. The boy's description of the creature had tallied with the one described by Bishop. Interestingly, and even though these 'greys' are usually described in any case as being small of stature, the boy insisted that the creature sitting at the end of his bed had been a child like himself.

After these two sightings, people were starting to talk in earnest. Had aliens landed in Vernon Wood? And, if so, what did they want with the inhabitants of Market Stanford? Not many more days had passed before a woman came forward claiming to have the answers.

Flora Hodgson—age forty, unmarried, a primary school teacher, and environmentalist—lived alone in a cottage very close to Vernon Wood. One night she had had a Visitation. A blinding light had appeared outside her cottage, and small grey men had appeared from the light. One of the creatures had taken Flora by the hand and led her into the light, which was of course their spaceship. Here the aliens had explained the purpose of their visit to Flora. Their tiny mouths had not moved, according to her account, but she had nonetheless heard their voices 'speaking to her mind.' They had told her of the 'harmony of the cosmos,' a resonance between all the planets, inhabited and uninhabited, in the vastness of the universe. The people of planet Earth, by polluting their world and constantly fighting among themselves, had upset this galactic harmony. Even other planets light-years distant felt the effects of the discord, with whole civilisations suffering from profound melancholia and freak weather conditions. For galactic harmony to be restored, the people of Earth needed to stop killing off each other, the lesser animals, and their environment. This was the message the aliens had brought to Earth, and Flora Hodgson was the person they had chosen to be their voice-piece (forgoing the usual diplomatic channels of the United Nations or the White House.) Flora had solemnly pledged herself to pass on this critical message. (Needless to add, the aliens, while they had her aboard their ship, had also taken the opportunity to secure their guest to the operating table and help themselves to an egg or two. We would have expected nothing less.)

When Flora had broadcast her abduction experience and its attached announcement to the world, she had, in spite of all the other recent happenings in the vicinity, not been widely believed. Flora was an eccentric spinster. She belonged to Greenpeace. She

14

wore sandals all the time. And then, when she had sold her story to one of the tabloid newspapers in order to reach out to a wider audience, all she achieved was to make herself a national laughing-stock, dubbed by the very paper that published her story as 'Flora the Fruit Loop.' The primary school she worked in had promptly given her the sack.

If things weren't confused enough already in Market Stanford, they were about to become even more so. The next reported sighting didn't seem to tie in with the others at all, and yet the source, an off-duty police officer, would generally have been considered a reliable one. (Just how reliable would depend, of course, on your personal feelings towards the law enforcement community.) This officer had been driving along the B-road which intersects Vernon Wood. It was night and there had been no other traffic. Suddenly his car had died on him; the engine cutting out, exterior lights and dashboard displays extinguishing. All the symptoms of a dead battery, and yet the car had only recently been serviced. The officer had armed himself with a torch and stepped out of the car to check the engine. Then he saw two figures emerge from the treeline; the sight of them sent him scuttling for cover. The two figures were helmeted, and appeared to be wearing spacesuits; not the cumbersome spacesuits of our human astronauts, but much more slimline versions; the helmets and boots silver, the body of the suits of some darker colour. The man could see nothing of the astronauts' faces: the helmet visors appeared to be tinted. More alarmingly, the two spacemen had carried guns: light rifles of a design unfamiliar to the policeman (who knew something about firearms.) The two figures had walked slowly across the road, taking no notice of the stalled car, and making no attempt to molest the officer, whom they surely must have seen run for cover. They just crossed the road and disappeared into the trees on the other side. The officer, unsettled by what he had seen, had waited a short while, then returned to his car. When he turned the ignition, the engine had returned to life.

When this story broke, speculation ran wild. Just who were these new players in the game? Grey aliens were generally understood to walk around naked, and besides, the astronauts seen by the policemen had been described as being of normal human height, and greys are supposed to be small. Had two sets of extraterrestrials descended on Vernon Wood? Well, there were two apparent landing-sites, after all! Some theorists suggested that the 'greys' and the 'spacemen' might be two antagonistic races, and that East Anglia was about to become the venue for an intergalactic war. Others suggested that the 'spacemen' weren't aliens at all, but the soldiers of some elite military unit, sent by the powers-that-be (generally referred to by the conspiracy theorists as 'Them') to hunt down and destroy the grey aliens. That might explain the guns, but why would human soldiers need to wear spacesuits and helmets in their native environment? Because of the radiation, of course! answered the theorists— UFOs emit the stuff like isotopes. It would have been the radiation, they declared, that killed off the plant-life at the two landing-sites. (And they declared this in the face of the fact that no radiation had been detected at either location.)

And then murder had stepped onto the stage.

The body of a young vagrant, Cully by name, had been found on the edge of Vernon Wood. He had been strangled to death; his throat crushed. The pathologist's report declared that judging from the damage to the man's neck, his assailant must have been very strong indeed. There were no other marks of violence on the body, so the unfortunate man must have been taken by surprise. Was there anything to link this crime to the lights in the sky and the other phenomena? Nothing, save for the location in which the body had been found.

Strangulation by an extraterrestrial was a new one even for the conspiracy theorists. It is hard to imagine that a race of beings intelligent enough to have mastered interstellar travel, would resort to acts of brutal physical violence. To account for this, a theory emerged that the unfortunate vagrant had actually been killed by the powers-that-be; killed because, wandering through Vernon Wood, he had 'seen too much' and therefore had to be silenced.

And that brings us up to date—this is the situation at Market Stanford, when a certain dashing secret agent and a certain beautiful TV psychologist arrive on the scene…

Chapter One
Trina Trulove is a Shameless Hussy!

Morning sunlight, cheerfully disposed, filters through the curtained window of a chintzy cottage bedroom. You can tell it's a cottage bedroom from the modest dimensions of the room and the fact that it appears to have been constructed without aid of or reference to setsquare or spirit-level. The ceiling is low, the wallpaper flower-patterned, and the furnishings all of suitably venerable appearance—tasselled lightshade, brass bed-knobs, patchwork counterpane, framed mezzotints.

Altogether a quaint and rustic picture, save for just one discordant note:

Blue hair.

Very loud blue hair, adorning the head of the bed's occupant.

Trina Trulove is the girl's name, and she's eighteen. She has just woken up, and she looks very happy. She has good reason to be happy: today is the first day of her summer holiday, and she is sharing this holiday cottage with three amazing people.

Amazing person number one is Mark Hunter, who's a real life, honest-to-goodness spy! Just like James Bond! Well, actually he isn't much like James Bond. He's only five foot nine in his socks, and he's lean rather than muscular. But he has broad shoulders. And he wears a suit. A brown suit. In fact, you never see him wearing anything else. He's handsome, has brown hair, hazel eyes, a cheerful voice and a nice smile. Yes, he is forty, but a young-looking forty, and anyway forty is just inside the acceptable age-range for a man whom Trina would consider bedding. But apparently there's not much chance of that happening; not in this particular case. In defiance of all the accepted conventions for a man in his particular line of work, Mark Hunter is not a hypersexual serial womaniser. In fact, according to Dodo and Mayumi he spends most of his time being celibate. What a waste!

Amazing person number two is Dodo Dupont. Professor Dorothea Dupont, to be precise. The well-known professor of

17

psychology who writes books and makes television documentaries. A six-foot Juno with short black hair, and a beautiful, slightly androgynous face. Trina doesn't think she's ever known a more erotic woman. Just looking at her makes you wet. And she has a perfect personality to go with that perfect body. Smart, good-natured and with a great sense of fun. Dodo often helps out Mark Hunter on his assignments. (Amongst her other accomplishments, Dodo holds a black-belt in karate, which as everyone knows, comes in handy in the spy business.) And if that isn't enough; she's also disgustingly rich!

Amazing person number three is Mayumi Takahashi, the renowned erotic photographer. Trina, a budding artist of the lens herself, is currently working as Mayumi's assistant. She stands in awe of her mentor. A beautiful Japanese woman, Mayumi is very small, and has very long hair and wears big glasses. Her age is actually thirty, same as Dodo, but to look at her, you would think she was more Trina's age. (Something to do with the pH balance of Japanese skin, apparently.) Mayumi's great fun to be with, although she never speaks more than she needs to, probably because her English isn't that great.

Dodo and Mayumi are an item. Dodo has been the model for two of Mayumi's photobooks: *Juno* and *Dodo in Bali*. The two also collaborated to produce the book *Beautiful Chaos – A Portrait of Eleven Killers*. This was a study written by Dodo on the subject of the infamous terrorist group the SEA: the Society of Evil Actions—illustrated with photography of the teenage terrorists taken by Mayumi. Dodo and Mayumi had been captured by these notorious nymphets and their time in captivity had enabled Dodo to compile her research material and Mayumi to take her photos. The book had been published to (almost) universal outrage, both on account of the erotic nature of the photography and claims that the whole book glorified a bunch of mass-murdering sociopaths. Caving into pressure, the publishers had withdrawn and pulped the book—existing copies now change hands online for ridiculous sums of money.

Mark Hunter's latest assignment is to investigate the Market Stanford Incident—which explains why they have installed themselves in this quaint little holiday cottage on the outskirts of

18

that town. Dodo has come along in case Mark needs her help; Mayumi has come along to take some pictures, and Trina has come along because she's Mayumi's assistant. They drove up from London last night in Dodo's Jaguar F-type.

The cottage has three bedrooms: one for Trina, one for Mark, and a double for Dodo and Mayumi.

In addition to the distinguished company, Trina feels that a nice summer getaway is just what she needs to get over the rather melodramatic break-up she has just had with her last boyfriend. It was Trina herself who'd instigated the split, and for the usual reasons: the guy she was dating was selfish, thoughtless, lazy, unreliable, and—apart from size, stamina and sperm-count— basically the worst boyfriend ever.

She's glad to be rid of the horny bastard.

Time to get up, she decides. She has just heard one person— Mark Hunter she assumes—go downstairs. He's probably already got the coffee pot boiling. (She knows that he's a caffeine junkie the same as Dodo and Mayumi.)

Trina throws back the duvet and jumps out of bed, frisky as a lamb. She catches her image in the cheval glass—which looks a real antique with its carved wooden frame—and pauses to admire herself. She's a good-looking girl, of average height, with a light, trim figure, and at the moment wearing a cute pyjama suit. Picking up a brush from the dressing table, she brushes out her blue locks, and then, with hair ties, ties them up in bunches, fluffing them out with the brush. This is how she generally wears her hair.

She is just thinking of going downstairs to join Mark for some light flirtation, when she hears creaking floorboards in the adjacent room, and soon after, more footsteps descending the staircase.

Dodo and Mayumi.

And then a thought, unbidden, flashes through Trina's mind.

Naked! Dodo and Mayumi—they'll be naked!

At least, going by past experience they will be. Trina had once called round Dodo's penthouse apartment at breakfast one morning, to meet up with Mayumi; and this was how she had found the two women: as naked as Adam and Eve! (Or as naked as Eve and her Japanese girlfriend.) Mark Hunter (fully dressed) had also been present, and acting as though there was nothing at all unusual about their nudity. It was like he was completely used to seeing them both starkers this like.

Another thought, a daring one, now occurs to Trina: If *they're* going to be naked… Should she…? Should she also…?

She should!

Heart pounding at her own temerity, Trina pulls off her pyjamas. Putting on her glasses—blue frames to match her hair—she takes stock of her naked form in the mirror. To go with the unorthodox blue hair, Trina also sports a number of tattoos; two on her right arm, one on her left, and one on her right thigh. Her collar and cuffs don't match of course, and Trina would like to have rectified this discrepancy, but she has taken advice and been deterred by the health risks…

Deciding that she passes muster for a naked appearance in front of Mark Hunter, she salutes her reflection with the peace sign. (A mannerism she has picked up from Mayumi.)

Trina, you devil! She throws herself back on her bed, squirming with glee, kicking her legs in the air. Inevitably, her hand wanders down between her legs, and she starts rubbing herself… No! No, no, no! She mustn't finish off! Go downstairs feeling really horny and you'll *look* really horny…

After bringing her fingers up to her nose for a quick, reassuring whiff of herself, she jumps up from the bed, and out of the room. Okay, just stroll downstairs, completely natural, like you do this all the time. It's not like you'll be the only one…

She pads down the narrow staircase. Voices in the living room. Here goes! She opens the door and walks in.

She freezes.

The three of them are sat round the coffee table, each with a mug of coffee.

She *is* the only one.

Dodo and Mayumi are fully dressed.

Mark looks up from a map he is studying.

''Morning, Trina,' he says, and looks back down again.

Dodo and Mayumi also offer cheerful greetings.

'Hi…' says Trina weakly.

20

Standing there, she feels very naked in her nudity—yet, thus far no-one has commented on it; not even an eyebrow raised in mute interrogation. What to do? Two options present themselves to our resourceful heroine: exit the room with precipitation, and come back with clothes on; or, just act nonchalant, and sit down with the others. Deciding that the former option will just make her look even more stupid, she stumps for the nonchalant option, and seats herself in the vacant armchair.

Dodo and Mayumi sit on her left, sharing the sofa; Mark on her right, in the other armchair. Between them all is the coffee table, provided with coffee pot, mugs, carton of milk.

'Coffee?' asks Dodo, leaning forward to do the honours. 'You take milk, don't you?'

'Yes, thanks…'

Dodo pours her drink, hands it to her.

'Ta.'

Mayumi silently studies Trina, her features pensive, obviously measuring her up with her photographer's eye for human flesh.

'Sleep well?' from Dodo.

'Yes. Like a top.'

'We're lucky, having the east-facing bedrooms. It's nice getting the sun first thing in the morning.'

'Yes,' agrees Mark, of the west-facing bedroom. 'There's something oppressive about getting the setting sun in the evening. Or maybe it's just that the rooms are much warmer by then.'

Trina sips her coffee. They are all acting completely naturally! Yeah, Mayumi's giving her the once-over, but it's not: 'What the hell are you doing with no clothes on?' or 'Ha, ha, ha! Did you think we were going to naked as well?' So just relax. Everything's fine.

Mayumi lights up a cigarette. That's what I need, decides Trina. She instinctively reaches for her hip pocket, and then remembers she didn't bring any pockets with her. Perceiving her difficulty, Mayumi offers her one of her own.

She takes it and Mayumi lights it for her.

'Ta.'

'So, what's your plan for today?' Dodo asks Mark. 'Straight down to business?'

'Yes, I'm going to check out Vernon Wood,' says Mark. 'I don't expect to be lucky enough to have any Close Encounters on my first day, but still, I ought to check out the venue now that I'm on the spot.'

'Do you want me to drive you there?'

'No, I'll hoof it. I know a shortcut to the woods across the fields, just down the road from here.'

'I suppose you would know things like that. It'll be quite a nostalgia trip for you, all this.'

'Nostalgia trip?' echoes Trina.

'Yes, I was brought up in these parts,' explains Mark.

'Oh, I didn't know that! Were you born here?'

'Well, I was born at the RAF Hospital in Ely, but yes, I lived in Market Stanford until I was eighteen.'

'So you're just an oik from the fens, then?' says Trina.

Mark smiles. 'Yes. But I hide it very well, don't I?'

Well, this is a turn-up, thinks Trina. She'd never imagined the dashing secret agent Mark Hunter could have been born in turnip country. 'Have you still got family here?'

'No. My folks moved out of the area a long time ago.'

'Well, while you're off on your expedition, we'll go into town and stock up with food,' says Dodo. 'And when you go, take your mobile with you; then you can call me if you need help.'

'Yes, I'll do that,' says Mark. 'I'm not sure how much help it will be, though, if anything *does* happen. I think in those Close Encounter situations things like mobile phones are supposed to pack up on you.'

'Like the engine of that policeman's car dying.'

'Yes; that's what I was thinking of.'

'So, what are you going to do? Are you just going to keep trawling Vernon Wood in the hope of finding something?'

'Well, not exactly. The idea is that I'll be on the spot in case anything new happens. The local fuzz have been told that I'm here, and they'll let me know straight away about any new incidents that are reported to them.'

'What about the witnesses to the previous incidents? Are you going to interview them?'

Mark lights himself a cigarette. 'There doesn't seem much

point doing that. They wouldn't be able to tell me anything besides what they've already reported.'

Dodo smiles. 'What—not even Flora the Fruit Loop?'

Mark smiles, exhaling a cloud of smoke. 'Well yes, I'm sure someone as inventive as her will have lots to add to her previous testimony. Mind you, I don't dismiss her completely, though. She might have actually seen something; something that sparked off these delusions of hers…'

'What about those other sightings of the greys?' asks Dodo. 'I mean, the man in the car was drunk, and the little boy might have been dreaming.'

'Yes, but then we have the testimony of that police sergeant: he wasn't asleep or under the influence; but then the aliens he described were completely different to the greys.'

'Was he the guy who saw the men in spacesuits?' asks Trina.

'That's right. Some people have suggested they might have been costumed hoaxers—but I'd very much like to know how hoaxers could have made that man's car pack up, and at just the right moment.'

'Did they choose you for this job because you've done this sort of thing before?' asks Trina. 'Or is it because you're from here?'

'The first, I should think,' says Mark. 'I always get lumbered with the outlandish cases.' He looks at her. 'And who told you I've done this sort of thing before?'

'Dodo,' answers Trina. 'She's told me about some of the cases you've worked on together.'

Mark frowns. 'Has she now? Well, you'd better keep that to yourself; a lot of that information is covered by the Official Secrets Act.'

'Is it?' says Trina, alarmed.

'Darn,' says Dodo, clicking her fingers. 'Me and my big mouth. I'm always forgetting about that.' To Trina: 'Yes, just forget everything I've ever told you about Mark's assignments. You *should* be alright.'

'I *should* be alright?' squeaks Trina.

'Yes, just make sure it doesn't filter back to my superiors in the Department,' advises Mark. 'If *they* knew that *you* know… Well, I wouldn't want to see you locked up in the Tower…'

'The *Tower*!' exclaims Trina, now seriously alarmed. 'They don't use that as a prison anymore!'

'*Officially* they don't,' says Mark. 'But they do keep a few dungeons ready for people who need to be quietly locked away— people who know a bit too much for their own good and have to be put out of circulation.'

Mark looks at her pointedly.

'Oh, *Dodo*,' wails Trina. 'Why did you tell me all that stuff? I'm gunna be in serious trouble now!'

Dodo's response is to burst out laughing. Mayumi grins toothily.

'We're only having you on, sweetheart!' Dodo assures her.

Trina looks from Dodo to Mark; he has a broad smile on his face.

'Oh, you two!' growls Trina, stamping vexed feet.

'Getting back to the point,' says Mark. 'There may well be some other explanation for all these apparently extra-terrestrial phenomena; an Earthly explanation.'

'Even for those grey aliens?' asks Trina.

'Even them,' affirms Mark. 'One theory is that all those abduction stories involving grey aliens are actually false memories, implanted in the minds of unwilling test subjects by the military. Another theory has it that those greys are not really aliens at all, but are actually time travellers from the distant future.'

'What, so those little grey things are what we're meant to be like in the future?' asks Trina, nose wrinkled.

'That's the theory. Although, that being the case, it does make you wonder why these apparently highly-intelligent descendants of ours would travel millennia back in time just to frighten small children and make people crash their cars.'

Mark pours himself a fresh cup of coffee.

Mayumi has snuggled up to Dodo and is stroking the latter's downy upper lip with a forefinger. (Dodo does depilate there, but hasn't done so recently.)

'We've got several facts to deal with,' proceeds Mark. '*Something*, emitting a bright light, descended on Vernon Wood. That's a fact. Several people saw it; it was caught on film.

24

Whatever it was, though, it hasn't been found. *But*, at roughly the point that it was seen to go down into the woods, there is a large circle of inexplicably dead and flattened vegetation. That's a fact. It's also a fact that a second identical circle was discovered at the opposite end of the woods. Those circles *could* be the work of hoaxers, but no explanation is forthcoming as to how they were created.

'And then we come to the more bizarre phenomena. Weird alien writing starts cutting in on people's internet connections in Market Stanford. That's a fact, because a number of people have experienced this. Once again, the writing could be explained as a hoax. But how could hoaxers create a stream of symbols that are so uniformly disturbing to anyone who sees them—so disturbing that one woman, who couldn't stop herself from looking at them, ended up in the funny farm, talking gibberish?

'And then we have the weird noises in Vernon Wood. Several people have heard them. All of them reported to find these sounds unsettling.

'And then the last fact—one dead man. That he was murdered is a fact. That his murder has anything to do with the Market Stanford Incident, is not.

'To sum up,' concludes Mark, smiling ruefully; 'I've got plenty to keep me busy.'

'That you have, sweetheart,' agrees Dodo. 'When are you heading off on your expedition?'

'Imminently. Just as soon as I've finished stoking up on caffeine.'

'Don't you want any breakfast first? Any toast?'

'No, I'm all right.'

'I like cereals for breakfast,' says Trina. 'But I suppose we haven't got any until we've been to the shops.'

'No, we do have breakfast cereals,' Dodo tells her. 'We brought some with us.'

'Ooh! I'll go'n get some.'

Extinguishing her cigarette, Trina gets up. She crosses the room, and, reaching the door, glances back over her shoulder—and sees Mark, eyes resting on her rear-view, a contemplative smile hovering on his lips. Elated, she passes through the door into the hallway.

Result!

Pleased with this small victory, Trina nevertheless nips upstairs to put some clothes on before seeing about that bowl of cereals.

Chapter Two
Vernon Wood

Although still early, it is already a hot day; the vast sky a rich ultramarine, unmarked by cloud. Mark pauses at the garden gate, looking back at the cottage—half-timbered, thatched-roofed, picturesque. He remembers this cottage, which stands here at the junction of a farm track and the main road; remembers it from his childhood. He had walked or cycled past it many a time. It hadn't been a holiday home back then; an elderly couple had lived here. He has memories of seeing them pottering about in their garden. (Why is it only in their gardens that you hear of people 'pottering'? wonders Mark parenthetically. You never hear of people 'pottering' anywhere else.) But the old couple will have passed on long since, and then, somewhere along the line the cottage fell into the hands of an enterprising person who decided to rent it out as a holiday home… And here is Mark now, back in his home town after more than twenty years, for a two weeks' stay in a house rendered a pleasingly feminine abode by his three companions.

He thinks of another feminine abode: a bungalow, situated at the far side of Market Stanford from this—a house that holds memories of more moment than even the family home in which he spent the first eighteen years of his life…

He will have to visit that place again…

But not now; business first!

Reaching the garden gate, Mark crosses the footbridge spanning the ditch and he sets off along the farm track. The main road behind him eventually passes through Vernon Wood, but Mark, as he has already said, knows of another way, cross-country, that will bring him to his destination much sooner. On

26

the left of the track now rises a border of elm trees, and beyond them, a paddock. Between the trees, two horses can be seen, standing like statues. On the right, cultivated fields stretch off to the horizon. All is silent and motionless beneath the sun's despotic gaze.

And the mingled scents of the countryside... these alone are enough to transport Mark back to his youth—our sense of smell is well-known for being able to trigger past memories more urgently than the other senses combined.

The squat form of a pillbox appears ahead on his right, half-submerged in vegetation, its slit window commanding the track. This pillbox is one of many such defences built in this part of the country during the early days of World War Two; built in anticipation of the German invasion that never happened. Mark pauses before the pillbox He had played here as a young child with his best friend, Clyde Waring. They had called it their 'base.'

Just a quick look inside, for old times' sake? Why not?

The low entrance to the blockhouse is round the back. Mark wades through the foliage only to find when he comes to the doorway an impassable barrier of briars and nettles filling the interior space. Clearly, no-one has been in here for years.

Clyde Waring... I completely lost touch with him when I moved away; him and the others... Does he still live here? As primary school kids we were inseparable; exploring the countryside, building camps... Things cooled off a bit at secondary school, as I recall. Clyde, he became more morose and withdrawn as an adolescent—and of course, I'd changed, too; I was spending more time with Rachel... Yes, I wonder what became of him... Is he still here in Market Stanford? And would I even recognise him if I saw him? I still picture him as an eighteen-year-old, but he'll be forty now, like me. I think I'm still recognisable from what I looked like when I was eighteen, but some people change a lot more; they get fat, they grow beards...

And what about Rachel—what's she doing? And the others he had hung around with at school? Some of them at least must surely still be living in the area. When you are born and brought up in the sticks, it's sometimes very hard to get away from them, even if you really want to. What have they all done with their lives, those schoolfriends of his? Had any of them had bold dreams for the future when they were at school? And have any of them attained those goals, or have they long since abandoned them in disillusion—resigning themselves to doing nothing more than living out the same mediocre lives as their parents...?

What would I do if I met someone I knew back then and they asked me what I was doing with myself? 'Well, actually I'm a spy!' They'd think I was pulling their leg...

A signpost appears ahead, pointing across the fields, announcing a public footpath. The signpost hadn't been there when Mark was a kid, but the path, a raised track following the course of a drainage ditch, had. Mark sets off along the path; it will take him directly to Vernon Wood. Two miles. When he had been a kid, Vernon Wood had been a sort of unattainable goal, a mysterious far-off land. Two miles! That was a preposterous distance for an eight-year-old. Vernon Wood might as well have been on the moon. (In his teens, however, Mark had become more familiar with Vernon Wood; walking or cycling to it with Rachel Farrow and other friends from school.)

Cornfields, golden in the sun, on either side Mark as he walks across the level landscape. Cambridge scholar Edward Bulwer-Lytton had once remarked that, in terms of the scenery, Cambridgeshire was the most boring county in England. And yes, to most outsiders, it probably is. For the most part, the landscape of Cambridgeshire is one huge, flat expanse of reclaimed fenland turned into farmland; a vast patchwork quilt of pasture and arable land sewn together by a network of drainage ditches. (Or 'dikes' if you prefer. Most people don't.) Apologists for the East Anglian scenery say that you get a lot more sky. Well, you can't argue with that, can you? Who wants all those picturesque wooded hillsides, rocky escarpments, etc. getting in the way of your view of the sky!

Although it does feel nice to be out in the open on a day like this, the immensity of the sky all around you... Mark can remember running through fields like these, playing hide-and-seek in them, back when he'd been not much taller than the wheatears...

Then there was that legend of the train carriage.

The story had gone that there was a field, somewhere to the north of town, a field hidden away, surrounded by trees; and lying in the middle of this field, a rusty old railway carriage... Some kids had even claimed to have visited this wonder, and Mark and Clyde had searched for it repeatedly. The prize, however, had always eluded them. Thinking of it now, Mark wonders if this story had even been true. There is something bizarre about the notion of disposing of an obsolete railway carriage in a field in the middle of nowhere.

The periphery of Vernon Wood now rises into view ahead, a green island appearing on the horizon above the ocean of corn. The path takes Mark all the way up to the treeline; and there, just as it was over twenty year ago, is the stile over the fence, giving access to the nature reserve. Mark climbs the stile. The pathway continues, well-defined, into the leafy precincts. The trees, mostly beech and chestnut, spread their crowns above the tangled undergrowth.

Mark pauses, lights a cigarette. No strong memories present themselves on returning to this place. But then, he has been in many woods since he had last been to this particular one; woods of many descriptions in many different countries—more often than not being chased through them by people with guns.

No strong memories and no sense of strangeness, either. With all the strange events that have occurred around here recently, you would expect there to be an atmosphere of *something* hanging over the place; but there is nothing; just the usual woodland sounds and smells.

Mark takes out his map; a detailed map of Vernon Wood, all the nature trails indicated, and the locations of the two landing sites marked with 'X's. Vernon Wood extends for ten square miles, with a B-road intersecting it roughly in the middle, leading in one direction back to Market Stanford, and in the other, first to the country house called Vernon Grange, and then to the straggling row of houses dignified with the name Vernon village. The first of the alleged UFO landing sites is on this, Mark's side of the road, the second on the other side.

Checking out the landing site seems a reasonable place to start.

Smoking his cigarette, Mark sets off briskly along the path.

What, he wonders, had come down in these woods that night? Little grey men or men in spacesuits? Or had the landing been that of that other cliché of UFO mythology, the secret, experimental military aircraft? That might explain the 'spacemen': they might have been the aircraft's crew in their flight-suits. But then, what about the little grey men, seen more than once now? And the other landing site? One for the spacemen and one for the greys? Yes, but then the two landing sites are identical, suggesting they were made by identical vehicles.

Ahead of Mark, the path forks. He takes the right fork; this will take him to Ground Zero, the 'first' landing site.

And what about Cully, the murdered traveller? Murdered by aliens? By the pilots of an experimental aircraft? Or killed by a fellow vagrant in a fight, or by a passing psychopath, in a completely unrelated incident?

The weird sounds reported in these woods particularly interest Mark. They are not, as far as he knows, a standard feature of these Close Encounter situations. Also, they are the only phenomenon in this particular sequence of events to have been experienced in broad daylight...

Should be coming up to Ground Zero now. About here, I think, that I need to branch off from the track.

Stubbing out his cigarette in his portable ashtray (a present from Mayumi), Mark strikes off into the deep shade of the woods, wading through waist-high ferns and growths of yarrow, a plant common in this part of the country; the sickly-sweet scent of its flowers evoking more memories of childhood.

Dock leaves. As kids, if we stung our arms or legs with stinging nettles, we were always told to rub the afflicted area with a dock leaf. Can't even remember if it actually worked or not...

The trees thin, and then, passing a recumbent moss-grown log he is there: a large grassy clearing and in the centre a perfect circle of withered yellowed verdure: Ground Zero.

Mark walks into the circle, examines the ground, looks about him. He doesn't expect to find anything new; the area has already been thoroughly examined—he just wants to see it for himself. He feels nothing, standing in the grass circle; no sense of unease or of the inexplicable. It's unnatural of course—but unnatural could just mean manmade.

A light had been seen to fall from the sky into Vernon Wood. This clearing corresponds, as far as can be judged, with the area of the woods the light had descended into. The logical inference is that something had touched down here; something with a circular base, which had flattened and withered the grass.

But where had it gone to after that?

Mark observes a well-defined pathway through the tall grass, heading off in the opposite direction from which he arrived; the track looks recent, not one of the established nature trails. It must have been made by all the officials, the experts and the sightseers who have visited the spot; in which case it will presumably join up with one of the paths leading to the main road.

Now that I'm here, I might as well check out that other 'landing site.' From all reports, it's identical to this one, but I might as well see it for myself.

He strikes off along the fresh track.

He doesn't get far.

Passing under the spreading branches of a beech tree, he steps on something. Comes a snapping noise, the twanging of a rope pulled taut, and then the ground seems to surge upwards and grab him, cocoon him, and send him shooting up into the air. He comes to rest about twenty feet from the ground, swinging gently, imprisoned by thick rope netting, his body forced into a foetal position.

A man-trap.

Mark is vaguely annoyed with himself. If he had a penny for every time he has stepped into one of these…

By all rights I ought to have developed a sixth sense to warn me about these things by now. Well, it could have been worse: at least it isn't one of those traps that leaves you hanging upside-down by the ankles.

Chapter Three
Twins of Evil!

Let's leave Mark hanging there for the time being, and take this opportunity to introduce some members of the supporting cast.

Picture a large metal barn, or more accurately a hay shed; in front of this structure a yard of sun-baked mud and fossilised tire-tracks. Golden fields of corn surround this enclosure; not another building in sight. Now we see a tractor driving into the yard from the adjacent farm track. The tractor pulls a trailer loaded with bales of straw. Three young men sit on the bales. The tractor is blue, so must be a Ford model. (Likewise, if it's red it's a Massey Ferguson, and if it's green it's a John Deere—this colour-code is well known to those versed in Rustic Lore.)

The tractor pulls up in the middle of the yard. The driver, Jack Stone, climbs out of the cab; the other three young men, Mitch, Trevor and Fergus, jump down from the trailer. The four men, all bare to the waist, wear dusty, faded jeans and battered-looking work boots. Jack extracts a tobacco tin from the pocket of his jeans, and from it extracts a roll-up cigarette, fat at one end, slender at the other—in other words a cigarette of the bohemian order. He lights it, takes a deep drag of the pungent weed, slowly exhales a thick cloud. Jack is tall and muscular, with a blond buzz-cut. The lineaments of his face would suggest to the physiognomist arrogant authority, laziness and aggressiveness. Now, I am the first to concede that physiognomy is by no means an exact science: take myself for instance; the natural expression of my features in repose is one of sullen unapproachability, but I can actually be quite affable at times. However, in the case of Jack Stone, the physiognomist would be right: arrogant, bossy, lazy and aggressive is just what he is.

The other three men are essentially Jack's minions. Jack has lorded it over all of them since they were kids. There's Mitch, who's small and wiry, and the self-appointed comedian of the group. He has a particular enthusiasm for the more 'terminal' side of livestock farming—you should see him with the meat cleaver when it's chicken-killing time: headless birds running all over the place!

Then we have Trevor; the wimpiest looking of the four farmhands, he has unkempt tousled hair, and a long face distinguished by a large mole on his left cheek, from which—apart from when he remembers to pluck them—sprout two thick hairs. Manual labour has built up his muscles to a degree, but he still looks like a lightweight. Trev is actually the only one of the four who can boast of having a girlfriend; not that this acquisition earns him any respect from the others.

Lastly, we come to Fergus. Fergus is built like the proverbial brick outhouse. He walks with bad posture, and while his knuckles don't actually drag along the ground, they give the impression of so-doing. His slack-jawed face holds a look of stolid stupidity; with his thick-lipped mouth usually set in a vacuous grin—although it can be difficult to tell if he is actually grinning at *you*, because he is also boss-eyed.

Jack sits down, leaning against the large back wheel of the tractor. The others sit down with him.

'What are you doing?' says Jack, directing the question at Trevor.

'Sitting down,' says Trevor.

'No you're not,' says Jack. 'Them bales need puttin' in the barn.'

'Yeah, but I thought we was having a rest first...' says Trev.

'No. *We're* having a rest; *you* are putting them bales in the barn.'

'Just me?'

'Just you.'

Trev stands up, looks across the yard at the distant barn.

'But ain't you gunnta park the tractor nearer to the barn?'

'No, I ain't.'

'Why not?'

'Because I've parked it *'ere*.'

'It'll only take a second to move it...'

'I've parked it *'ere*.'

Exasperated sigh from Trevor. 'But that's *stupid*. You mean I got to carry all them bales all the way across the yard to the barn?'

'Yes. That's what yer gotter do.'

Mitch sniggers.

'Fuck that,' says Trevor. 'I ain't doin' it.'

'Fergus,' says Jack, commanding.

Fergus stands up, and, as the result of long experience knowing instinctively what is required of him, lumbers threateningly towards Trevor, grinning and vacuous.

Trevor backs away from him. 'Alright, alright! I'll do it!'

He grabs a bale from the trailer, and carrying it by the binding rope, sets off across the rutted yard towards the barn, muttering under his breath. Anything is better than facing Fergus. Trevor has never actually been on the receiving end of any violence from Fergus himself; but he has seen others not so fortunate. He also retains vividly in his mind an incident from school, when Fergus had pinned him down to the ground in the schoolyard, and, looming over him, had hawked up a thick glob of mucus and dribbled it onto Trevor's face...

Oh, blissful childhood memories!

For not the first time, Trevor wonders how he's ended up spending most of his life with three people he doesn't even really like. Jack and Fergus he both fears, although for different reasons. As a kid he had always thought it was better to have them as friends than as enemies, and somehow that has stuck with him right through to the present day. Mitch, on the other hand, he reckons he could clobber any day; but the little turd possesses a weapon against which Trev is powerless: his smart mouth.

As for Jack, Trev kowtows to their self-appointed leader just like the others do, and part of him hates himself for it. But old habits die hard, and he always ends up doing whatever Jack says.

So why am I always the put-upon one? Why not that little shrimp Mitch? He wonders if it's something in his genes... At the entrance to the barn, he looks back over his shoulder. There they are, sitting by the tractor, sharing Jack's spliff. Mitch is sharing it, at any rate. Whenever Fergus smokes weed, he just falls asleep on the spot.

'Get a fuckin' move on!' roars Jack, seeing him standing there.

'You carryin' that bale or marryin' it?' shouts out Mitch. 'Give it one from me, will yer?'

Pursued by laughter, Trev enters the barn.

The bales that have already been stored are stacked at the far end of the barn. Trevor, eyes adjusting to the dim light, crosses the intervening space. The rear stacks rise almost to the rafters; those in front are still being built up. Trevor drops his bale onto the frontmost stack, wipes the perspiration from his brow.

'Look, Robert; it's a rustic fellow!'

'Acksherlly, Roberta, it's a yokel.'

Trev looks up, startled. Two children sit on one of the stacks of bales, looking down at him with amused curiosity. Aged about eight, they are identical twins, a boy and a girl. Identical chubby-cheeked faces; identical disdainful blue eyes and mocking smiles; identical blonde curly locks (albeit the girl's are slightly longer); dressed in identical dungarees, checked shirts and trainers.

Trev gawps at them for a moment. He could have sworn there had been no-one up there when he'd first come into the barn. Perhaps he just hadn't noticed them because his eyes were still adjusting to the light…?

'Oi,' he says. 'What d'you think you're doin' up there?'

The boy looks at the girl.

'Is he speaking to us, Roberta?'

'I believe that may be the case, Robert,' replies the girl.

'Hm. "What do we think we're doing up here?" A philosophical question, perhaps?'

'It could be regarded as such, Robert.'

'Indeed. By "up there" is he simply referring to our more elevated physical location compared to himself…?'

'…Or, is he p'raps referring to our superior social status? The natural envy of the plebeian towards the privileged classes?'

'Hm. Or, p'raps he might even be referring to our obvious intellectual ascendancy over himself?'

P'raps, Robert, he means all three at once!'

Trev has had enough of this. 'Get down from there, you little shits!'

The girl gasps. 'Did you hear that, Robert? Such vulgarity! To call us little… I can't even repeat the beastly word!'

'Beastly,' agrees the boy. 'Absolutely beastly. This fellow is not the noble savage I first thought he was.'

'Acksherlly,' says the girl. 'He's an *ig*noble savage.'

'*And* he smells, Roberta.'

'Stinks to high heaven, Robert.'

Trevor doesn't wait for any more. He scrambles up the stacked bales with the perfectly understandable intention of knocking the two little brats' heads together. Coming up below the two, he lunges for them.

And suddenly they aren't there.

'What the—?'

'I do believe the brute wanted to lay his rough hands on us,' comes the girl's voice.

Trev looks down. The twins are now standing on the ground, exactly where he himself had been a moment ago.

'I believe he does,' concurs the boy. 'But he fails in this endeavour, as I'm sure he fails in everything else.'

'Quite right, Robert. The way he lets himself be pushed around by those three peasants out there. Creatures even less intelligent than himself...'

'Yes; doing all the work while they just sit there smoking their noxious weed...'

'I'm almost embarrassed for him...'

Uttering an oath, Trevor dives at them. The twins vanish in the blink of an eye and he finds himself sprawling on the ground.

'He's far too slow,' says the boy, now perched with his sibling atop one of the tallest stacks.

'Yes, he practically telegraphed that last move,' agrees the girl.

Trevor stares at the twins with growing consternation.

'Jack!' he roars.

'What?' yells back Jack.

'In 'ere! Quick!'

'He's calling for reinforcements, Robert.'

'Yes, Roberta. We're clearly too much for the poor brute.'

Jack runs into the barn, followed by Mitch and Fergus.

'What is it?' he demands. 'What's wrong?'

'Them.' Trev points. The others look. The twins look back at them.

'Oi, what're you doin' up there?' yells Jack. 'This is private

36

land. Clear off out of it!'

'Is this what you called us in for?' sniggers Mitch. 'Can't you even get rid of a couple of kids? Too tough for you, are they?'

'*You* try getting them!' challenges Trevor.

Mitch shrugs. 'Alright.'

He starts climbing the bales.

'C'mere, little kiddies! Daddy's gunna show you how babies are made!'

The twins watch him impassively. Mitch climbs onto a bale just below the one on which they sit, reaches out to grab the nearest and—do I need to tell you?—*poof!* they disappear.

'What the fuck?'

'Told you, smart-arse,' sneers Trev. 'They can teleport.'

'Tele-what-the-fuck? Where are they?'

'I'm surprised that even one of these rustics is acquainted with a word like "teleportation,"' comes a voice.

The twins are now standing at the barn entrance.

'I s'pect he heard it on TV, Robert. These unimaginative types always learn the little they know from the goggle-box.'

'Who the fuck are you?' roars Jack, furious. He is confused— and he doesn't like being confused.

He lunges at the twins. They vanish. And reappear atop the bales.

'Shall we depart now, Roberta?'

'I think so, Robert. These rustics have their amusement value, but it soon begins to wane.'

'Shall we go and have ice-cream, Roberta?'

'Yes, let's! And ginger pop. I love ginger pop!'

The twins wink out.

Silence falls. And then Jack turns to Trevor, looking at him as though the whole situation has been his fault.

'Where did they come from?' he demands.

'How the 'ell should I know?' retorts Trev.

'And 'ow did they do that disappearing thing?'

'I told you: it's called teleporting.'

'I don't care what it's called; it's not fucking possible!'

'Well, it 'appened!'

A pause for serious thinking (Fergus excepted, of course.)

37

'Aliens,' declares Mitch, at length.

'You what?' from Jack.

''As to be,' says Mitch. 'All that stuff that's been 'appening round 'ere, lately. UFOs in Vernon Wood and all that. Those kids must've been aliens.'

'Oh, dream on,' scoffs Trevor. He's seen those brats teleport with his own eyes, and he can't explain it—but a couple of aliens in dungarees calling themselves Robert and Roberta…?

Chapter Four
Meanwhile, Back in the Batcave…

We left Mark hanging around.

He had expected that whoever had set this trap would appear almost immediately to see what they'd caught. They haven't. Which is a shame because then he would presumably have been set free, instead of being left up in the air; and, in addition, Mark is very curious to know just who the hell has set a trap like this in the first place, and more importantly *why*.

However, five minutes have passed and no-one has appeared. Time to do something about this. If he'd thought to bring his clasp knife, he could have cut his way out of the trap; but he hasn't brought his clasp knife. He has, however, brought his phone with him—he will just have to swallow his manly pride and ask Dodo to come along and rescue him. He can picture her reaction. She'll stop to take pictures before she cuts him down.

But now he hears footsteps approaching; advancing from the direction he had been heading in when he had stepped on the trap. The owner of the footsteps soon heaves into view; a young man, wearing what looks like a desert warfare army uniform, field-glasses around his neck, rifle slung over his shoulder.

The man—he doesn't look to be more than twenty—stops and looks up at Mark without any apparent surprise. He then—and this seems quite unnecessary to Mark considering the relatively short distance—lifts the field-glasses to his eyes to scrutinise the captive through the lenses.

And having finished this inspection, he turns and runs off without offering so much as a word.

'Oi!' yells Mark after him. 'Don't just leave me here!'

What the hell was that all about? The boy, in spite of the uniform, had looked like a skinny geek. One of those military geeks? Has Mark stumbled into the middle of a bunch of macho-wannabes' ridiculous survival game?

Mark reaches for his phone again. He has just dialled up Dodo's number when he hears more footsteps approaching. And voices this time. More than one person. Mark cancels the call and awaits events.

There are three of them this time. The boy from before, and two girls, similarly dressed in desert warfare uniforms, but not equipped with field-glasses or rifles. One of the girls, taller than both her comrades, appears to be the leader of the trio.

Hang on a minute.

'Appears to be the leader.' I feel a twinge of guilt as I write this; a definite pang. No self-respecting author should use a phrase like 'the one who appeared to be the leader.' Not ever. At least, not according to that great literary snob Vladimir Nabokov, who once declared that 'the one who appeared to be the leader' is a glaring example of the worst kind of clichéd bad writing. Now, far be it for me to dispute with my literary elders and betters; I don't doubt for one minute that old Vlad is right—but if anyone can think of another way of establishing that a particular member of a group of people evinces the characteristics of being the one holding the executive position, I would very much like to know!

One trite line seems to inevitably lead to another; now that I have made this digression, I could easily fall back on an even more hackneyed literary cliché by announcing that I will now 'resume the thread of my narrative.'

But I won't.

The three ersatz soldiers have stopped, the two newcomers scrutinising Mark. The boy salutes the tall girl.

'Prisoner does not appear to be of extra-terrestrial origin, Sir! Ma'am!'

So that's what this is about, thinks Mark.

'However, this might be a deception to trick us,' continues the

39

boy. 'He might be a shape-shifting alien bounty hunter!'

The tall girl groans. '*Nobody* believes in those! God, I knew something like this would happen! Why did I ever let you—cut him down, Pete.'

'Hear, hear,' says Mark.

'Yessir, Ma'am!'

Pete produces an army knife from his belt and commences sawing through the weighted rope holding the net aloft. Before the boy is expecting it, the rope parts and Mark drops like a stone. Peter jumps and grabs the rope, and Mark's precipitate descent is arrested a few feet from an uncomfortable, quite possibly injurious, landing. Pete, swinging back and forth like a bell-ringer in distress, is joined by the two girls, who, adding their weight, are able to lower Mark gently to the ground.

The trio now help to disentangle Mark from the netting.

'Sorry about that,' apologises the tall girl, who compared to her friends, seems almost sensible. A long strand of dark hair slanting across her face suggests a large store of this commodity piled up inside her helmet.

'So you should be,' Mark tells her. 'Anyone could have stepped on that trap of yours. I happen to be used to this sort of thing; most people aren't. What if it'd been some elderly person, out walking their dog?'

'Mind telling us who you are?' asks the girl, ignoring the reprimand.

'Mind telling me who *you* are?' ripostes Mark.

The boy—Pete—unslings his rifle, points it at Mark.

'We asked first.'

'That gun's plastic,' says Mark, unimpressed.

The girl snatches the toy gun from Pete and hurls it into the bushes.

'I'm sorry about him.'

'I imagine you are,' says Mark. 'Let's stop horsing around. I'm the injured party here, so just you tell me who you are.'

'I'm Leila,' says the tall girl. 'This is Pete. This is Jean.' (A pale, jittery-looking girl.) 'Collectively we're the Mantell Project.'

'And what's the Mantle Project?' inquires Mark.

40

'You've never heard of us?' from Pete, with disbelief.

'Should I have?'

'We've got our own website!'

'I don't go online very much.'

'We're quite well-known in UFO-hunting circles,' explains Leila.

'Oh, I get it. *That's* why you're here. But why do you call yourselves the Mantle Project?'

'*Thomas* Mantell,' clarifies Leila. 'You know who he is?'

'Yes I do, as a matter of fact.'

Thomas Mantell was the subject—and the victim—of one of the most compelling alleged UFO incidents of the late twentieth century. An American Air-force pilot engaged on a routine solo flight, he had reported seeing an unidentified aircraft, which he described as being 'metallic and tremendous in size.' Mantell had altered his course to pursue the craft. His final report had been 'It's above me and I'm gaining on it. I'm going to twenty-thousand feet.' At that point all radio contact had been lost. Mantell's aircraft had later been found crashed, the pilot dead.

'And how long have you people been here?' inquires Mark.

'We've been here since Saturday,' says Leila.

'You're staying in Market Stanford, then?'

'No, we're camping here in the woods.'

'Well, you shouldn't be,' Mark tells her. 'This is supposed to be a nature reserve. Where's your campsite?'

'Nearby,' is the vague answer. 'Well, come on; we've told you about us, so what about you? What are you doing here? You don't look like you're someone just out for a morning stroll.'

'No, I'm not. My name's Mark Hunter, and I'm also looking into this UFO business. And unlike you, I'm here officially.'

This does it. Three faces turn hostile.

'An Official?' squawks Pete. 'He's one of Them!'

'One of whom?' asks Mark.

'The Men in Black!'

Mark looks down at his brown suit. 'If I am, I'm not really dressed for the part. Or perhaps you think I'm incognito...? Well, I'm sorry to disappoint you, but I'm not a member of that fraternity. And anyway, don't they only have those Men in Black

41

in the States?'

'Okay, so you're not a Man in Black,' allows Leila. 'But who are you, then? Scotland Yard?'

'No, much worse than that, from your point of view. I'm with MI5.'

'Then you are one of Them!' from Pete.

'Shut up, Pete,' snaps Leila. 'Can you prove that?'

'Of course.'

Mark reaches into the inside pocket of his jacket.

'He's got a gun!' screams Jean. She throws herself flat.

Mark looks at the prostrate girl. 'I was getting out my ID card.'

He completes this harmless action, hands the card to Leila. Jean climbs to her feet, still regarding Mark with distrustful eyes.

'Looks genuine,' says Leila, handing back the wallet. 'Are you here because we're here?'

'Why would I be here because of you?'

'Obvious. To make sure we don't find out too much.'

'Sorry to disillusion you, but I didn't even know you existed until you introduced yourselves just now. I'm here for the same reason as you: to try and find out what's been going on.'

'Yeah, right,' sneers Leila. 'If you're with MI5 then you *know* what's going on.'

'Do I?'

'*Of course* you do.'

Mark smiles. 'Oh, I see what you mean. My department is involved in a huge cover-up conspiracy involving extraterrestrials and their spacecraft. Is that it?'

'Yes.'

'I'm sorry, but "no." I'm as much in the dark as you are. The powers-that-be are not involved with what's going on around here.'

'Then what's going on at that house?' demands Pete.

'At what house?'

'That big house down the road,' supplies Leila.

'You mean Vernon Grange? Nothing's going on there, as far as I know. It's just a private residence, isn't it?'

'Bullshit,' says Pete. 'It's some sort of government installation.'

42

'It isn't, you know.'

'Then why're there guards with guns?'

'Guards with guns at Vernon House? Have you seen them?'

'We have,' confirms Leila.

'Oh. Then in that case I don't know. I'm pretty sure it's not a government place. Isn't there any notice saying what the place is for? A sign on the gate?'

'Of course there isn't!' from Pete. 'They're not going to have a sign up saying, "Alien Spacecraft Stored Here," are they?'

Mark points a thumb over his shoulder in the direction of Ground Zero. 'If that circle over there *is* a UFO landing site, then I would say the craft that made it would be too big to fit into Vernon Grange.'

'Well, duh,' says Pete. 'Obviously there's a secret underground complex for keeping the spaceships in.'

'How do you know there's an underground complex?'

'Because they're too big to fit in the house!'

Mark turns to Leila, as being the most in touch with reality of the trio. 'Do you believe any of this about Vernon Grange?'

A shrug. '*Something's* going on at that place. They've got guards. They wouldn't have guards for nothing.'

'That's true enough. But there could be all sorts of reasons for guards, none of them to do with UFOs and aliens. And as I say, I'm pretty sure the house isn't government-owned.'

'Maybe it is, only you don't know about it,' says Leila. 'You're just a field agent, aren't you? They might not tell you everything.'

'Oh, I see! You think my own people could be keeping me in the dark about their nefarious activities. Like that Dale Cooper fellow.'

'Fox Mulder, you idiot,' says Pete.

'It's possible, isn't it?' from Leila.

'Yes, it's possible. Whatever the case, you've piqued my interest about Vernon Grange. I shall have to look into it myself.' He pauses. 'So, what's your theory about everything that's been going on here? You think there *are* actually aliens?'

'Of course we do,' answers Leila. 'The Greys. The Government has made some sort of deal with them; using their spaceship technology on experimental aircraft.'

'I see. Then those "other" alleged aliens that were seen; the ones in spacesuits: I suppose they would be the human flight-crew of an experimental aircraft made using hybrid technology?'

'That's what we think; yes.'

'And do you have any theory to cover that strange writing that people have been seeing online?'

'Yep. That would be the Greys trying to link their cyberspace technology with ours.'

'And what about that Hodgson woman and her abduction story?'

Leila blows air from her lips. 'Even *we* don't believe that story. Flora the fucking Fruit Bat.'

'Fruit Loop,' Mark corrects her. 'So, you three are just camping out here hoping to see something happen... *Have* you seen anything yet?'

'No, but we've heard something.'

'Oh! Those weird noises. When did this happen?'

'Earlier this morning; about three hours ago.'

'You all heard these sounds?'

'Yes.'

'And what did you make of them?'

Leila pulls a face. 'Those we're not sure about. Before we'd actually heard them, Pete thought they might be the sounds of an alien spacedrive being tested over at that house... But the sounds weren't coming from over there. They were in the air, all around... Like echoes, or something...'

'Like the sounds of another world...' comes the quiet voice of Jean.

'Hm. Pity you didn't record them; I'd have liked to have heard them for myself.'

'We *did* record them,' says Leila. 'We're not stupid: we brought recording equipment; that's standard for people in our line of work. But when we played back the recording we'd made, it was blank.'

'Almost to be expected,' murmurs Mark. He claps his hands decisively. 'Before I walked into your trap, I was on my way to have a gander at the second landing site. Want to come with me?'

'We've seen it,' says Pete. 'It's just the same as the one here.'

44

'But you seem to be concentrating your attention on this site. Do you think it's more important than the other one?'

'Well, no, but there are only three of us,' points out Leila. 'We can't "concentrate our attention" on both of them.'

'True enough. Look—' Once more Mark reaches into his jacket pocket. Jean squeaks, looks ready to dive for cover. Mark looks at her and pointedly produces a note-pad and pencil. 'I'm going to give you my mobile number. If you see anything out of the ordinary, don't hesitate to call me. The place I'm staying at is not too far away, so I can be here pretty quickly.'

'Why should we do that?' inquires Leila. 'We're not here to help *you*.'

Mark smiles. 'Yes, I know: I'm one of Them… But honestly, I just want to get to the bottom of what's going on here, the same as you. And there may be some danger for you, camped out here in the woods. You've heard about that murder, haven't you?'

'Yeah, but we don't think it's got anything to do with all this.'

'Unless the people at the house killed the guy because he went in there and saw something,' suggests Pete.

Mark writes his number on a leaf of his note-book, tears it out, hands it to Leila.

'Call me if you need me,' he says. 'If you don't want to come with me to check out that second landing site, I'll say goodbye to you now.'

'Yeah. See you.'

Mark sets off along the track. When he is safely out of sight, Leila tears up the piece of paper with Mark's number, scatters the fragments.

Chapter Five
Endless Summers: Scene One

The endless summers of childhood.

Each day is an adventure. A week is an eternity. The new school year seems so far off that it's not even worth thinking about. Memory paints those summer skies a brighter shade of blue than they ever look to jaded adult eyes. It never seems to rain during those endless summers of childhood recollection. Six weeks, six whole weeks of joyous freedom.

Two boys sit against the wall of a pillbox, an unused relic of World War Two. Before them, a blazing ocean of ripe corn; above them the immense blue sky. Each boy has in his hand a crumpled white paper bag with a diminishing supply of sweets. These sweets sit in tubs and boxes beneath the glass counter of the small newsagents on Beech Lane. Crouched down, face pressed against the glass, you point to whichever confection you want added to your bag. Most of the sweets are three-a-penny: liquorice laces, strawberry laces, chewy coke bottles, bonbons, fruit-flavoured chews that get stuck in your teeth, chocolate buttons that don't taste very chocolatey, milk chocolate buttons that don't taste of much at all, lemon drops, sherbet flying saucers with the texture of cardboard... The two boys have ventured out of town with their treats, to eat them at the place they call their 'base.' The two boys look to be about seven years of age. Both wear shorts, t-shirts and trainers. One boy is freckled, his hair mid-brown, the other boy's much darker. The boy with the freckles is called Mark Hunter. The boy with the darker hair is his friend Clyde Waring.

Clyde is chewing a strawberry lace meditatively.

'Girls wee out of their bums, don't they?' he ponders aloud. 'That's why they have to sit down on the loo.'

'Noooo,' says Mark, stretching the monosyllable. 'They have a hole at the front it comes out of.'

'They don't.'

'They do.'

'They *dooon't.*'

'They *dooo.*'

'Do they?'

'Yeah.'

'Just a hole?'

'Yeah.'

'Why don't they have a willy to wee out of?'

'Cuz then they wouldn't be girls.'

Clyde chews reflectively.

'If it comes out the front, why do they have to sit down to do

46

it?'

'Don't know,' confesses Mark, never too proud to admit the limitations of his knowledge. 'You know what's over there,' abruptly changing the subject and pointing across the fields.

'Fields,' says Clyde.

'*After* the fields.'

'Vernon Wood?'

'That's right. Vernon Wood. We should go there. It'd be skilliant.' (A childish amalgamation of the words 'skill' and 'brilliant.')

'But that's *miles* away,' protests Clyde.

'We could go on our bikes,' says Mark.

'But it's still miles. We'd be puffed out when we got there, and then we'd have to come all the way back.'

'My brother's been there.'

'Your brother's older.' Pause. 'We could go to the spinney; that's got trees. We could play there.'

'A spinney's not a proper woods. It's a tiny woods. Vernon Wood goes on for miles.'

'We could go to the spinney and make pretend that it's bigger.'

'S'pose so.' Mark crunches his last hundreds and thousands-coated chocolate button. 'Shall we play something?'

'Yeah. What?'

'World War Two?'

Mark and Clyde both understand the intended function of the pillbox they have made their base, and they know all about the Second World War thanks to those marvellously educational comic-strip publications *War Picture Library* and *Commando*.

But Clyde is not in the mood for World War Two. 'Nah. Let's play *Blake's 7*.'

'Yeah! I'll be Avon.'

'I'll be Vila.'

'But he's a chicken.'

'Yeah, but he's funny.'

The boys stand up, stuffing what's left of their sweets into shorts pockets. 'This'll be the Liberator,' from Mark, indicating the pillbox.

Clyde points to the doorway. 'In there can be the bridge.'

'Nah. That's the teleporter room. The bridge should be on top.'

The boys clamber up the rough sides of the pillbox onto its flat roof. Under the merciless sun the roof is like a hot-plate, but being youngsters they don't mind the heat. They take their appropriate places on the Liberator bridge, Avon in front at the main control desk, Vila behind and to the left.

'Federation pursuit ships approaching!' yells Mark.

'Take invasive action, Zen!' responds Clyde.

'It's Servalan and Travis!'

'Fire lasers!'

'Engage stardrive!'

'We've lost them!'

'No we haven't!'

'We have now!'

'Let's teleport down to the planet,' says Mark. 'Dayna and Cally need rescuing!'

The boys jump down from the pillbox and pelt along the farm-track, singing the *Blake's 7* theme tune with gusto.

Mark is the better runner, and soon takes the lead.

'Hurry up, Vila!' he yells back. 'Dayna and Cally are prisoners in the forest!'

'Where's the forest?'

'The spinney, stupid!'

Clyde lags further and further behind. Taking pity on his friend, Mark slows to a walk.

'Let's approach with stealth!'

'What's stealth?'

'It means "slowly."'

'Good idea!'

Clyde catches his breath.

Mark grabs him by the shoulder, points along the track. 'A patrol of mutoids approaching! Use stun-grenades!'

The boys know where to find their stun-grenades. Bull-rushes grow in the ditch flanking the track. They pull the heads off two, throw them, and *bam!* the heads burst open, scattering their seeds.

Two more are thrown for good measure.

'That takes care of the mutoids!' declares Mark.

Ahead of them a plank footbridge spans the ditch.

'Let's go this way!' says Mark.

They cross the bridge, enter a belt of trees. They scramble down an incline into a culvert. After heavy rain this culvert can be ankle-deep in mud, but now in summer the earth is cracked and bone-dry. They follow the course of the gully then clamber up the other side. Wading through ferns and nettles they emerge onto a narrow track bordering the back gardens of a row of semi-detached houses, hemmed in on the other side by a thorny wall of bushes. The back gardens only have low fences so you can see right into them. Most of these gardens are unkempt, many of them littered with all kinds of rubbish. The white-washed houses look equally down-at-the-heel. This is Brick Lane, in one of the scruffier neighbourhoods of Market Stanford.

This route is not actually the quickest way to the spinney, but few boys will stick to open lanes when there is the joy of a narrow side-path to follow. (And anyway, they are approaching by stealth!)

A boy stands at the end of one of the gardens. Mark and Clyde stop to greet him.

'What you doin' there, then?' asks the boy. Moon-faced, scruffy-haired, he grins at them gap-toothed. His name is Dennis and at school he has long been the designated target for victimisation on account of his being slow on the uptake, having bad personal hygiene and generally being a bit 'different.' Mark and Clyde have always taken pity on their put-upon classmate.

'We're going to the spinney,' says Clyde.

'What, you gooin' scrumpin', are ya? Scrumpin' fer apples? Ha-ha!'

'No, we're not going to the orchard,' explains Mark. 'We're going to the spinney. The one near Fen Drove.'

'Where all them trees are? You gooin' birds' nestin'? Gooin' after the birds' eggs? Ha-ha!'

'We're not birds' nesting,' Clyde tells him. 'We're playing *Blake's 7*.'

'Wh's 'at, then? *Blake's 7*? Wha's 'at?'

'It's on the telly,' says Mark. 'It's set in outer space.'

'Oh! That thing wha's on the telly, is it? That thing wha's set in space? Yeah, I know that, I do. *Blake's 7*. Tha's where they wear

49

them bird costumes, in't it? Ha-ha!'

'Nooo. *That's* not *Blake's 7*; that's *Battle of the Planets* you're thinking of,' says Mark.

'But tha's where they goo into space though, in't it?'

'Yeah, but *Battle of the Planets* is a cartoon,' clarifies Mark. '*Blake's 7*'s got real people in it.'

'Oh! I's the one where they got real people, is it? Yeah, I seen that. Ha-ha!'

'Do you want to come with us?' offers Mark. 'You can be Vila.'

'I'm Vila!' protests Clyde.

'Yeah, but if Dennis comes, I think he should be Vila and you should be Tarrant.'

'Why's that?'

'Cuz it wouldn't make sense the other way round.' To Dennis: 'Want to come?'

'Yeah, I'll come with yer; that'll be good. Play *Blake's 7*, where they're in space 'n all that. Yeah, I'll come. 'Ang on a minute. I'll just ask Mum.'

Dennis runs up the path of his overgrown back garden to the open back door of his house. The blare of a radio at full blast emanates from within; the Radio 1 Roadshow, by the sounds of things; they hear the jingle for 'Bits 'n Pieces.' Dennis stops at the kitchen doorstep, puts his head inside.

'Mum? Can I goo'n play with Mark 'n Clyde?'

'No, you can't!' responds a woman's voice.

'Oh, Mum! I won't goo far. Only the spinney on Fen Drove, in't it?'

'I said, No!'

'But, Mum...'

'En, Oh: No!'

'But, why not?'

'Cuz I said so; tha's why!'

'It's not fair!' Dennis, dissolving into tears.

'Tough!'

The tears become full-scale blaring.

'Whine all you want, but you in't gooin' out!' comes the voice of the affectionate parent.

Mark and Clyde exchange troubled looks. They silently leave the awkward situation behind.

They reach a junction in the narrow footpath. The path to the left takes you out onto Brick Lane. The boys take the other path, across an area of wasteland, wild grass dotted with scrub. At the far side of this the path emerges onto a farm track, a continuation of the same track they diverted from earlier. They follow the track to its junction with the main road leading in and out of Market Stanford. The road is a fairly busy one at this point in its history—the bypass circumventing the town and relieving the traffic flow has not been built yet.

Mark lifts his bare wrist to his mouth. 'Avon to Liberator,' he says. 'Are Cally and Dayna still being held prisoners?'

'Yes!' declares Clyde.

'You're not on the Liberator!' protests Mark. 'You're here on the planet with me! Tarrant's just told me Cally and Dayna are still prisoners.'

'I thought I was Tarrant now?'

'No, that was only if Dennis came with us; you're still Vila.'

A break in the traffic, and they cross the road. Over a ditch, crawl under a hedge and they are in another field of wasteland. At the extremity of this rise the crowns of many trees, projecting from lower ground. The spinney!

'We're getting close to the target area,' says Mark. 'There might be federation look-outs, so keep low.'

'Right.'

Bending low, they cut a swathe through the tall grass of the field. At the far side, the ground dips suddenly. The boys drop to the ground and wriggle up to the lip of the declivity. The trees of the spinney have their roots in the dell below. Mark scans the area through imaginary binoculars.

'No sign of federation troops,' he reports. 'Let's proceed with caution.'

'Who's Caution?' Clyde wants to know.

'It's not a person, you wally,' replies Mark. 'It means we've got to be careful. Come on.'

They scramble down the incline and are soon in amongst the trees, following shady winding footpaths.

51

'Guns at the ready,' stage-whispers Mark. 'There'll be federation guards guarding the girls.'

They creep forward, fingers pointed to indicate they are armed. A branch cracks audibly somewhere nearby.

'Someone's here!' yelps Clyde.

'Shhh!' hisses Mark.

They freeze, listen. Nothing but birdsong.

'Come on.'

They move forward.

A rustling sound from amongst the trees; something heavy moving.

Clyde grips Mark's arm. 'There *is* someone here!'

'So what if there is? Don't be chicken.'

Mark moves on. Clyde follows reluctantly. Ahead, the path becomes a narrow gully between two embankments from which curl the twisted roots of trees. The two boys enter the pass.

Suddenly a figure drops to the ground in front of them! Even Mark screams.

Before them looms a man with wild hair and a bulbous nose; tall and loose-limbed, wearing a donkey jacket, cords, battered-looking work-boots. It is none other than the local ne'er-do-well Dunnidge! Dunnidge is a sort of bogey-man to the young kids of Market Stanford. Just the mention of his name is enough to strike fear!

Confronting the two boys, Dunnidge glares at them.

'Whar you kids doin'?' he demands truculently.

'J-just playing,' squeaks Mark.

'An' 'oo said you could play 'ere, then?'

'It's not private property,' says Mark.

'Is if I say it is!' Dunnidge tells them. 'Clear off!'

'No!' retorts Mark bravely.

Dunnidge lumbers towards them. 'What you say? What you say?' And then, raising his arms threateningly: 'Bleeuuurrghgh!'

That does it. The terrified boys turn and run for their lives. Yes, Avon and Vila are forced to beat a tactical retreat—Cally and Dayna will just have to fend for themselves!

Chapter Six
Smalltown England

Market Stanford. (Pronounced *'Staan-fud'* by many of the locals.) An agricultural small town just like any other you might find in this part of the world; a town where life is lived on a smaller scale; an unenlightened, unprogressive environment; cut off, out of the loop, all but forgotten. Petty prejudice, petty vice and petty crime; everything on a petty, small-scale level. Few amenities, even fewer opportunities. No cultural diversity to broaden the mind. Narcotic drugs are about the only innovation to have filtered through from the big cities.

Smalltown England is a trap, a trap that its victims are born into and from which it can be all but impossible to escape...

Mark Hunter is one of the lucky ones; he *did* manage to escape from Market Stanford. But what if he hadn't...? What if he had never moved away? What would he be doing now? What sort of person would he be now? He finds it hard to conceive, and frankly so do I.

The pub is called The Four Bells. Our quartet, Mark, Dodo, Mayumi and Trina, have strolled into town this evening for a quiet pint or three. ('Strolled' so that none of them would have to be the designated driver.) Market Stanford pubs are clearly not accustomed to newcomers, and they had garnered some curious looks when they first walked into the place, especially our Mayumi, for a) being Japanese, and b) wearing a Stetson; and Trina on account of her blue hair. The Four Bells' 'beer garden' has proven itself to be a single bench in a poky high-walled courtyard, so our four friends have resigned themselves to sitting indoors and going outside usually in pairs for the occasional cigarette. They have taken an L-shaped booth with a long table, and sit drinking familiar lager brands rather than taking a gamble with any of the local ales on offer.

'So, does it bring back memories?' asks Trina of Mark.

'This pub? Well, the *outside* of it does: I walked or cycled past the place all the time. But I've never actually been inside the place before in my life, though. I left this town around the time I reached the legal pub-going age.'

'No underage drinking?' asks Dodo.

'I'll admit to some,' says Mark. 'One or two parties, etc... But never pub-drinking. This pub in particular I seem to recall had a reputation amongst us kids; if you came in here they would serve you, and then when you'd paid for your drink and sat down with it, they'd come along and turf you out for being underage.'

'What?' explodes Trina, hot with righteous indignation. 'That's gotta be illegal! Taking your money like that!'

'And that happened to you, did it?' asks Dodo.

'No. I was forewarned, so I never tried it.'

'And what about these parties? The usual secondary school "party round the friend's house while the parents are away," were they?'

'Pretty much. I can remember one or two...'

Dodo's smile widens. 'So, Mark dear, was it at one of these shindigs that you first got off with anyone?'

'"Got off with..."'

'Don't pretend you don't know the vernacular, Mark Hunter. You're not that old.'

'Yeah, my first time was at a party like that,' confesses Trina.

'Well, mine wasn't,' says Mark.

'No?' says Dodo. 'So you made it to the age of consent with your virginity intact?'

'Not exactly. There was one girl... We were never officially "going out"; we were just friends, but we did enjoy a no strings attached physical relationship... Rachel Farrow, her name was.'

'So why was she never officially your girlfriend? Were you ashamed to be seen in public with the poor girl, or something?'

'No, nothing of the sort. We hung around together all the time; we just didn't tell anyone else about the sex thing. I can't actually remember why it was... I think we just didn't want to be a part of that whole "who's going out with who" schoolyard soap opera.'

'Was she good-looking then, this Rachel Farrow?'

'Yes, she was attractive. She wasn't one of the most sought-after girls, but that was probably just because she didn't move in

54

the right circles at school. Tracey Cutter, an American girl; she was the girl all the boys fancied; the class alpha female. Personally, I never saw what all the fuss was about. I mean, she looked alright, but nothing special as far as I could see, and personality-wise I thought she was rather bland...'

'One of those passive alphas,' says Dodo. 'That's kind of annoying, that is. I mean, yeah you expect alpha males to be handsome, but it's more their personal charisma that attracts people; but a girl like that Tracey Cutter of yours: she just attracts people entirely by her exterior; her physical beauty.'

'Well, that's all boys care about, isn't it?' avers cynical Trina.

'Yes, but it's not like there's no such thing as a charismatic woman,' argues Mark. 'You're one yourself, Dodo. You must have been popular at school? Or had your personality not blossomed back then?'

'No, I was out-going when I was that age,' replies Dodo. 'And, yeah, I'd say I was popular; but then, I went to an all-girls' school. I doubt I'd have been the boys' favourite if I'd gone to a mixed school, though. I mean, I was already five foot eleven when I was fifteen; they'd have thought I was too tall.'

'But still, you had the charm, the charisma; so it's not just the alpha males who possess that quality. Same with Rachel Farrow: she was good-looking and had an out-going personality, but she was tomboyish; liked science-fiction and that sort of thing. Not one of the in-crowd.'

'So she was a geek.'

'Y'know, I don't remember the word "geek" being in general circulation when I was at school... but yes, I suppose that was what you would have called all of our crowd. The misfits; the square pegs.'

'I'm learning more and more here,' says Dodo. 'So, were you socially awkward in your teens? I can't really picture you being like that.'

Mark shakes his head. 'No, I wasn't socially awkward at all; neither was Rachel. Most of the others in our crowd were, though. Clyde, Dennis, James... I wonder what happened to them all... When I moved away, I got so wrapped up in other things, I never stayed in touch...'

'You should look them up on Facebook,' suggests Mayumi.

'Mark's not on Facebook, sweetheart,' Dodo tells her. To Mark: 'Still, it shouldn't be too hard to find out if she still lives here, your 'schoolfriend with benefits.' Do you think you'd like to see her again? Your first-time girl?'

First time girl... Rachel *hadn't* been his first. But Mark doesn't enlighten Dodo as to this, just as he'd never enlightened Rachel at the time...

Does he want to see Rachel again? He tries to imagine what she might look like now... She might have matured into a completely different woman with completely different interests to those she'd had when he had known her... If they were to meet now, would they even have much in common? Would they even have much to say to one another after so long?

'*Some* of your friends from school must still live here,' says Trina. 'They can't all have moved away. You should look them up while you're here.'

'Well, I am here on business, not for reunions,' says Mark, a shoulder-shrug in his voice.

'Yes, but there's not much you can do about that business until something else happens,' points out Dodo.

'True. I'm hoping those kids camped out in the woods will let me know if they see anything, but I'm not banking on it. I don't think they liked me very much.'

'But you a nice guy!' from Mayumi.

'Thank you for saying so, love,' smiles Mark. 'I mean that they don't like me for what I represented, from their point of view. To people like them, I'm the enemy.'

'They're bonkers, those UFO chasers,' is Trina's verdict. 'And didn't you say they were all wearing army uniforms? What's that all about?' With this, she drains her pint and emits a burp. 'Oops! Pardon my French.'

'That's usually what you say when you swear, not when you burp,' says Dodo.

'Well, pardon my English, then. Who's for another?'

'I am!' says Mayumi, who has also necked her pint.

Trina repairs to the bar.

'I suppose your only other line of inquiry is that Vernon

56

Grange place,' remarks Dodo.

'Yes, I should have heard back from headquarters about that one, when we get back to the cottage. I'm not saying I believe those kids' wild theories about the place…'

'…But you *did* see a man with a shotgun when you walked past the gate,' finishes Dodo.

'Yes, I did. Their story about armed guards was true enough.'

Mayumi has produced her cigarette packet. 'I'm going for a smoke,' she announces. 'Come with me.' The injunction is directed at Dodo.

'Okay, honey.'

'See you in a bit,' says Mark, as the two women rise to go out to the courtyard.

As they leave by one door, four newcomers walk into the pub by the other, and from the curious looks they receive from the regulars Mark concludes that, like his own party, they are not locals. A woman, who might have been either in her mid-thirties or a well-preserved early-forties, enters first, followed by a young man and two girls clearly in their late teens. The woman is tall, her dark brown hair tied back at the nape. Her features are angular but attractive. Mark's impression is that she holds some authority over the three younger people. (The one who appears to be the leader!) Their mother? No. She could conceivably be old enough, but the three youths don't look like siblings. A teacher or tutor perhaps?

One of the two girls is a Goth: big boots; a long, crinkled black skirt; a tight-fitting brocaded black velvet jacket. Hair cut short, with a long fringe, combed to one side, dyed jet-black. Black lipstick, panda eyes. She looks about her in a dreamy sort of way, as though she is lost in internal reverie, yet still vaguely conscious of her surroundings.

The other girl has the confident smile and healthy glow of a well-sexed young woman. Her face and figure, both accidents of nature, seem to emphasise the impression of voluptuous satiety in the boldness of their lines and curves. She wears a mini-skirt and halter-top; high-heeled sandals. Long chestnut hair frames those sybaritic features. As she scans the room her eyes meet Mark's, and apparently liking what she sees, directs at him an approving smile. Mark returns the smile, affable, no sexual content.

The last of the newcomers, the young man, conveys the image of a not-quite non-threatening pretty-boy. Thin-faced and skinny, his brown hair carefully styled, he wears tight black jeans, claret-coloured satin shirt, shoes with pointed toes.

As they cross the saloon, Mark wonders who these people might be... Holiday-makers? The three teens look the type who would be soon bored to tears in a dead-end town like Market Stanford—which is anyway not really much of a holiday resort, unless you happen to be a keen angler. This group of people do not look to be keen anglers. Students who are working here for the summer? That seems more likely.

At the bar, the surly landlord demands to see some ID from the youngsters.

'Oh, come on,' protests the erotic girl. 'We showed you our ID last time we came here.'

'Well, you can show me again.'

Hm. Whoever they are, they don't seem to be very popular.

Trina returns with the drinks. Mark explains Dodo and Mayumi's absence.

'I read *Sophie's World* when I was at school,' says Trina after sitting down, obviously launching into something that it has occurred to her to say while she was at the bar. 'Do you know that book?'

'Jostein Gaarder's "Philosophy for Beginners" guide; yes, I know it.'

'There's a bit in that where they're looking at books on the occult in a bookshop, and the philosopher guy tells Sophie that being into that stuff is as bad as being into porn.'

'Yes, I remember that part,' says Mark. 'I think what he meant was that being pre-occupied with the speculative supernatural starves the soul as much as pornography.'

'Yeah. Do *you* think that's true?'

Mark shrugs. 'Well, you have to remember that the author of that book was something of a snob about his pet subject. From his point of view the occult is just so much folklore and fairy-tales. He believed that people should be fascinated by the actual tangible world around them and the people in it, and not be looking to things that aren't really there to preoccupy their minds.'

'Yeah, but do you agree with that?'

'Well, not entirely. I've read a lot of the philosophers and I'm interested in the subject of philosophy. On the other hand, while I wouldn't spend my leisure time reading books on the paranormal, I do keep an open-mind on the subject. I mean, I have to, what with the kind of assignments that come my way. Look why I'm here now: chasing UFOs and little grey men.' He takes a sip of his pint. 'I seem to recall in that book, the author not taking the same line about religion. A lot of philosophers would also dismiss *that* as so much folklore and fairy-tales. We create gods because we need them, is the argument. It helps people make sense of their lives. Other people choose other things for that kind of self-affirmation, whether it's a school of philosophy or a belief in the paranormal.'

'I'm not into religion,' says Trina.

'No?' Mark regards her with a look of smiling inquiry. 'So, what is your creed then, Trina Trulove? If I had to guess, I'd say it was sensualism.'

'Sensualism?' squawks Trina. Her cheeks turn crimson. Is he thinking of her exhibitionist appearance at breakfast this morning? 'W-why do you say that?'

'Well,' still smiling, 'you're the apprentice erotic photographer, aren't you? It's an art that appeals much more to the senses than the intellect, you'd have to agree.'

'Yeah, I suppose it does...' Trina has never thought of putting a name to her outlook on life before—but if Mark wants her to be a sensualist, than a sensualist she will be.

Out in the courtyard, Dodo and Mayumi are finishing their cigarettes. They are standing by the door because, as mentioned before, the small, cobbled yard is only equipped with a single bench, and it is occupied; and occupied by none other than our four acquaintances from this morning, Jack Stone and his cronies. Well, two of them at any rate. Fergus doesn't mix well with alcohol and is happy to vegetate in front of the television of an evening. However, the number of people sitting at the bench still comes to four, because, in addition to Jack, Mitch and Trevor, there's the latter's girlfriend, Lindsey. Trevor sits next to his girlfriend; Jack and Mitch sit opposite. Lindsey might have been a pretty enough young woman, but she has a mistrustful, shifty expression permanently fixed on her thin-lipped face.

'What's that Chink doing here?' wonders Trevor, when Dodo and Mayumi have gone back inside.

'What do you think she's doing here?' retorts Jack. 'She's here for the fruit-picking, in't she?'

'I can tell you why she's wearin' those glasses,' declares Mitch. 'It's cuz she can't see properly through those slanty eyes of 'ers!'

Much chuckling at this witticism.

'An' why's she got that stupid cowboy hat on?' demands Lindsey, as though the head-gear in question is somehow a personal affront.

'Because she's a Chink,' says Jack. 'They don't know us from the Yanks and she probably thinks we all wear 'em.'

'What about that tall bird who's with her?' questions Trevor. 'Who you reckon she was?'

'Probably a Pollack,' answers Jack. 'She'll be 'ere for the fruit-picking an' all. Pollacks grab all the summer jobs.'

'Yeah, we're lucky to still 'ave *our* jobs,' says Mitch, standing up. 'I'm goin' for a slash.'

He goes inside. Two minutes later he comes running out again.

'They're 'ere!' he exclaims

''Oo's 'ere?' says Jack, seeking clarification.

'That skinny ponce and the three bitches from last time!'

Jack slams his glass down. 'Oh, they are, are they?'

'Yeah, they're at the pool table.'

'Right,' says Jack, in the tone of a man with a mission.

And a mission indeed it is. Jack has a score to settle with the aforementioned 'skinny ponce.' The grievance pertains to a political matter. Politics, you cry? What have Jack Stone and politics got to do with each other? From what we've seen of him, you may have been led to believe that Jack is just a lazy, belligerent, and bullying farm-worker. Bu, this is not the case. There are other facets to this complex character, other strings to his bow: for it so happens that Jack Stone is also Market Stanford's official representative of the British National Party. Yes, he's a political animal! (The BNP, of course, is that useful institution which exists for those citizens of our great nation who think that the UK Independence Party is just a bit too 'Leftie.')

The week prior to this, the woman and three teens Mark has just witnessed entering the pub had made a previous appearance at the same establishment. Jack had found himself in conversation with the young man of the group and had started expounding some of his party's policies, holding forth about some of the changes they would institute if they were ever elected into office. A ban on immigration and severing all ties with Europe, of course. The Islamic religion would be banned and all Muslims deported, what with each and every one of them being a potential terrorist. The death penalty would be reinstated for heinous offences such as trans- and homosexuality. These and other bold measures, Jack had poured forth, and the young man had seemed enthusiastic, appearing to agree with him, egging him on, suggesting even stronger measures. But then the cogs had slowly turned in the mind of Jack Stone and the realisation had suddenly struck him that the skinny cunt was just taking the piss out of him! Understandably, Jack has vowed that if he ever sees said skinny cunt again, he is going to kick his head in.

And now he is here!

Mason's, second-hand furniture dealer. That shop had been there when Mark was a boy. The sign is newer, the interior has been refurbished, but there it still is, across the street from the Four Bells. That's one thing that hasn't changed. But then, there used to be a toyshop next-door to Mason's. That shop has gone: in its place stands a burger-fried-chicken-and-kebab takeaway, conveniently situated for hungry pub-leavers. The modern Market Stanford seems to be crawling with fast food establishments: pizza parlours, Indian takeaways, burger places... Back in Mark's day there had only been a couple of chippies and one Chinese takeaway...

Mark is alone. He has come out the front of the pub to smoke, just so that he can have this nostalgic look at the street. When he has a spare morning or afternoon, he will have to explore Market Stanford at greater length, just to see what's the same, what has changed...

Further down the street is a thrift shop; when Mark lived here, the sign above the plate-glass windows used to read 'Market Stanford Carpets.' Mark had known the shop well, because it happened to belong to his Dad. Being the only one in town, the carpet shop had always done good business back then. Mark remembers his dad's favourite carpet fitter's joke, oft-quoted. It went like this: a carpet fitter has just finished fitting a new carpet in a woman's front room; he can't find his cigarettes anywhere, and looking around for them he sees a small bulge in the carpet he's just fitted, and realises he must have gone and laid the carpet over his fag packet; deciding it would too much hassle going to all the trouble of pulling up the carpet again just to retrieve his fags, he instead just hammers the bulge flat with his wooden mallet—but then the housewife walks in, hands him his fag packet and asks him if he's seen her pet hamster which has escaped from its cage!

Somehow Mark had never ended up following his father into the carpet trade... Life had intervened.

The short-haired Goth girl drifts out of the pub. Apparently ignoring Mark, she stands on the kerb, swaying, humming to herself, staring up at the darkening sky.

'There's something in the air,' she says at length. (Is she talking to him or to herself?) 'Currents flowing... twisting and unfolding... restless, agitating... stirring up the ocean bed of eternity...' Suddenly she spins round, facing Mark. 'Have you got a cigarette?'

'Yes, I'm smoking one,' says Mark.

'Have you got another one?'

Mark reaches into breast pocket. 'Yes, I think there's one here with your name on it.'

He proffers the packet, and the girl extracts a cigarette with black enamel-tipped fingers; Mark lights it for her.

She takes a drag, regarding Mark through those dreamy panda eyes. 'What's your name?'

'Mark Hunter. What's yours?'

'You said it was written on my cigarette… It's Lucretia.'

Mark smiles. 'It suits you.'

'I know. That's why I chose it.'

'Oh, I see. Not the name your parents gave you… I saw you and your friends come in. Are you all on holiday?'

'Sort of,' answers Lucretia, vaguely. She stretches her neck to look at the sky once more. 'Grid-patterns. If you could peel back the sky, the stars, that's what you'd see. Grid-patterns, crisscrossing infinity. The building blocks of reality…'

'And how do you know that?'

'I see things… I hear things… Things nobody else can see or hear…'

'What do you see now?'

'Disruption… Everything's out of balance in this place, out of joint… Things are going to happen…'

'Soon?'

'Tonight…'

'…Evocative words considering the current situation,' observes Mark, back at the table with his friends. 'But at the same time I couldn't help thinking about mentally ill young people's therapy groups and their "residentials."'

Dodo smiles. 'Yes, could be. That would explain the older woman with them. One of their supervisors. Those groups usually stay in hostels when they're on those residentials; have you got any hostels in Market Stanford?'

'I wasn't aware of there being any when I was kid, but that's not to say there weren't any. And even if there weren't any then, there might be one now.'

Dodo drains her pint. 'I'm off to the bar; who wants one?'

Mark does; the others are okay.

Dodo makes her way to the bar, which brings her near to the pool table where a game is in progress. The game has attracted quite an audience, but then it is quite a monumental game: Jack Stone, representing Market Stanford and political stability, versus Damien (the skinny pretty-boy), representing the outside world, anarchy and degeneracy!

Damien had been engaged in a friendly game with the sexy girl (given name: Serena), when Jack had stalked up, followed by his entourage. Jack, bellicose, had done his level best to provoke Damien, but it had been a case of water off a duck's back, and had ended with Damien affably challenging Jack to game of pool. Jack had found himself accepting, considering himself to be no mean pool player.

If Jack really is such a wizard with the ball-and-cue, then tonight is definitely one of his 'off' nights. The game had started well enough, with both players staying fairly level; but now, everything is starting to go annoyingly wrong for Jack, and annoyingly right for Damien. This, taking place in front of a large audience, is doing nothing for Jack's blood pressure.

However, things might be about to take a turn. Damien, on red, has fluffed a shot, leaving Jack, on yellow, with an easy pot into the top-right pocket. He lines up his cue, sights the ball, and makes the shot. The white strikes the yellow, and seems to be sailing straight for the corner pocket; but then it almost seems like the ball changes its mind about where it wants to go, veers off to the left, and strikes the cushion.

The audience groans.

'How the fuck did that happen?' roars Jack. ''Oo nudged the fuckin' table?'

'No-one nudged the table, my friend,' says Damien smoothly. 'You didn't hit the ball straight on.'

'I did 'it it straight on!'

'If you had it would've gone in,' returns Damien. 'I'm not disputing your skill as a pool player, Jack. We all have our bad days. This must be one of yours. I'll tell you what: I'll put you out of your misery and clear the table, and we can call it a day.'

Jack inspects the disposition of the remaining red balls. 'Clear the table? I'd like to see you try.'

True to his word, Damien proceeds to clear the table. But some of the shots he pulls off! The audience cannot believe their eyes. Dodo, having been served her two pints of beer, happens to look at the game and sees one of the shots. The red ball that has been hit clearly *describes an arc* to avoid the yellow balls, ricochets off another red, potting it, before sailing into the corner pocket! That isn't just a trick shot, thinks Dodo; that is bloody impossible!

64

Damien pots the last two reds with one shot, and then the black.

Serena lets out a cheer, sarcastically echoed by Lucretia. The older woman, who has remained seated by the wall, smiles her satisfaction. Nobody else in the audience looks amused.

Livid, Jack snaps his cue in half, throws the pieces down. 'You cheated,' he declares, facing Damien across the table.

Damien smiles. 'By reasonable, Jack. How could I cheat at a game of pool?'

'I don't know 'ow you fuckin' cheated, but you fuckin' *cheated.*'

Murmurs of support from the crowd.

'You know, I never had you down as a sore loser, Jack, my friend,' grins Damien. 'I have to say I'm disappointed in you.'

'Wipe that smarmy grin off his face,' says Lindsey. 'Fuckin' skinny faggot.'

'I'm going to,' declares Jack.

He circles around the table towards Damien. Damien makes no defensive move; just stands there, arms folded, smiling a provoking smile.

'You're not going to start resorting to violence, are you, Jack, old son? Surely that's not the BNP way?'

Jack takes a swing at him. Damien doesn't move an inch, but somehow Jack misses, staggers and almost falls under the impetus of his own swing.

'What you playing at?' demands Mitch. ''It 'im one!'

This time Jack throws a pile-driver straight at Damien's lazily smiling face. It doesn't connect; instead Jack pirouettes on the spot, lurches and ends up sprawled over the pool table. Even some of his supporters laugh at this one.

At this juncture, the landlord chooses to intervene. He walks straight up to Damien. 'You. Get out.'

'Me?' protests Damien. 'What for? I haven't done anything.'

The woman who appears to be guardian of Damien and his friends, steps in.

'That Neanderthal started it,' she says, indicating Jack.

'I don't care who started it,' declares the landlord, trenchantly. 'Jack's a regular. You lot aren't. So you can clear off. All of you.

Now.'

The woman looks like she is about to pursue the matter, but then decides it isn't worth it. 'Oh, come on, everyone. Let's get out of this dump.'

The woman heads for the door, Damien, Lucretia and Serena following. Damien stops, turns back to Jack.

'Oh, I almost forgot to say: Robert and Roberta send their regards.'

And with that parting shot, he is gone.

'Did you 'ear that?' says Trevor. ''E knows those two little bleeders from this morning!'

'Yeah,' says Jack, unusually pensive. 'I 'eard it… You know what we've gotta do?'

'No. What've we got to do?'

'We gotta find out where them freaks come from.'

'And then what?'

'And then we sort 'em out.'

Chapter Seven
Silver Space Boots

A clearing in the woods. Three tents have been pitched here. Light shines dimly from the open flap of one of the tents. Inside, Leila Foster, leader of the Mantell Project, sits cross-legged, scrolling through the day's news headlines on her laptop. Nothing relating to the incident they are investigating. Only a week ago, the Market Stanford Incident was all over the news, but now it has disappeared completely, old news, over and done with. Except that it's not over, thinks Leila; they've just lost interest: the ignorant masses with their short attention spans. The BBC's on-line news-site always displays a top ten of the most viewed news stories on its home-page, and in pole-position at the moment is the report of an attack on a schoolgirl in Wiltshire. Figures. Whenever there's a major story about a sex offence, and particularly one that involve teenage girls, it's sure to be in the top ten; in addition to the short attention spans, the ignorant masses are also very prurient; especially the guys.

She clicks on the weather to check the forecast for East Anglia. The weather is set to remain sunny, with the temperature steadily increasing; a severe weather warning has been issued for later in the week. (Leila has no way of knowing this, but what the weather will be doing tomorrow and in the days to come is going to be a matter of monumental unimportance to her.)

Leila is a veteran of these UFO-hunting camping trips. Before she started her own group, she had gone on expeditions organised by other groups; camping on moors, in forests, and on hillsides up and down the country; UFO 'hotspots' and the locations of reported sightings. They had all been wash-outs—and with the added annoyance that half of the guys on these outings had been more interested in trying to get inside Leila's sleeping bag than in watching the night skies.

Truth to tell, that had been one of the main reasons Leila had decided to set up her own group, the Mantell Project, where she called the shots. And yes, her only recruits to date are an over-enthusiastic military geek and his chronic anxiety case sister, but at least they're people she can trust. And then this time... Well, this time and this expedition it looks like they've stumbled on the real deal.

Jean crawls into the tent; like Leila she's still wearing combat fatigues, but has discarded her helmet.

'You're still up, then?' says Leila.

'I don't feel sleepy at all,' answers Jean. 'I'm all keyed up. I just feel like something's about to happen.'

Leila pulls a face and says, 'That'll be your nervous disposition, not second sight.'

'Ha ha. What were you doing?' indicating the laptop, still powered-up and providing the only illumination inside the tent.

'Just looking at the news. Where's that brother of yours?'

'I think he's out resetting his alien trap.'

'You're sure about that?'

'I think so. What else could he be doing?'

'You know how eager he is about that big house down the road; he wants a look inside; I was thinking he might just be stupid enough to try and get in on his own.'

'But they've got guards! He'll get shot!' from Jean, alarmed.

'I know. That's what I'm saying. I mean, *I'd* like to know what's going on inside that place, but we can't go just charging in, just the three of us. We need to work out a plan.'

'Have you got one?'

'Not yet. I posted that query on some of the forums; asking if anyone has heard anything about the place; any rumours...'

Leila picks up her laptop. 'Let's check out the website; maybe someone—'

She screams, dropping the device like it's a live thing. The screen has turned bright red. Bizarre characters, thick black ideograms, scroll rapidly across the screen. There is something about those forms, that blood-red background; something unknown and terrifying, and just *wrong*.

'Turn it off!' shrieks Jean.

As though she is plunging her hand into fire, Leila stabs the power button. nothing happens. She hits it again.

'I won't switch off!'

'It's horrible...' Jean, clutching her head, eyes glued to the screen.

'Don't look at it, stupid!'

Leila grabs Jean and drags her out of the tent. They collapse on the grass outside, like people who have just escaped from a burning building.

Leila stares up at the starry firmament, catching her breath. 'Well... At least now we can say we've seen it for ourselves...'

'It was horrible...'

'Alien writing from alien cyberspace... Something we're not meant to see...'

'I couldn't stop looking at it...'

'I know; it gets you like that. You know what happened to that woman who saw it and looked at it for too long: she's in the loony bin...'

And then they hear a sound. A rhythmic pulsing sound, high-pitched.

'The sounds again!'

'No,' says Leila. 'This isn't what we heard this morning: listen. That sound was in the air all around. This is different. It's coming from over there… Look!'

Above the treetops off to the right, a pale greenish glow, pulsing in tandem with the sound.

'It's coming from the landing site!' exclaims Jean.

'Looks like it.'

They scramble to their feet. Now someone is crashing through the undergrowth towards them.

Jean grabs Leila's arm. 'It's coming this way!'

'Calm down! It's probably Peter.'

It is. He comes bursting into the clearing, staggers up to the two girls, gasping for breath.

He salutes. 'Permission… to make semi-coherent report,' he pants.

'Granted, for God's sake!' from Leila. 'Spit it out!'

'Over there…!' he points. 'Landing site…! UFO…'

'Are you sure?'

'Sure I'm sure! It's there!'

'Let's go, then!' says Leila.

'Let's not,' pleads Jean.

'You can stay here if you want, but I want to see this thing. It's what we came here for—hang on a minute.'

Leila dives into her tent, emerging moments later with a digital video camera.

'I want to get this,' she says. To Jean: 'I checked the tablet; it's switched itself off.'

They tell Pete what they've just witnessed.

'It's got to be connected,' declares Pete.

'Of course it has; it's all part of the same thing.' To Jean: 'Are you coming or staying?'

'Coming,' is the reluctant answer. 'I'm not staying here on my own.'

They set off through the trees. As they approach the landing site, the pulsing sound becomes louder, the green glow brighter. They reach the fallen log near the edge of the clearing, take cover behind it.

There it is. The glow emitted is so intense you almost can't see what it is emanating from, but there it is: an unidentified craft, like an inverted spinning top, flatter underneath, conical on top.

The hull of the craft shimmers in its own radiance and it's hard to even tell if the thing is actually on the ground, or if it's hovering infinitesimally above it.

The three watchers are mesmerised by the sight.

'Did you see it come down?' breathes Leila to Pete. 'We didn't see anything back at the camp.'

'It *didn't* come down,' is the response.

'What do you mean "it didn't come down"?'

'It didn't come down,' insists Pete. 'It didn't land. It just appeared.'

'It *must* have landed. You just didn't see it.'

'I was up that tree, setting the trap. I had a full view of the landing site. And it just materialised right before my eyes; the green glow first, then the thing inside it.'

'Materialised...' murmurs Leila. 'People saw it come down from the sky the first time... Could it... maybe it never went away...'

'You mean it's been cloaked?'

'Not just cloaked; I mean we've walked all over the landing site; lots of people have—Shit! I should be recording this!'

She aims her digi-camera at the apparition, bringing it into focus on the viewfinder.

Poor Jean is shaking like a leaf. 'M-maybe we'd better call that MI5 man,' she almost pleads.

'I tore up his number, remember?' hisses Leila. 'Anyway, what good could he do?'

'They're looking at us,' quakes Jean. 'Whatever's in that thing, they can see us. I know they can.'

'You *don't* know it,' counters Leila. 'It's your imagination.' To Pete: 'Did you see anyone come out of the thing? Any door open up?'

'No,' answers Pete. 'Not while I was looking at it. No sign of movement. It was just sitting there like it is now.'

'Something could have got out while you were away,' declares Jean.

'That's true enough,' agrees Leila.

'Let's get out of here...'

'Don't be stupid. This is exactly what we came here for,

remember?'

'Leila, *please...*'

Says Leila to Pete: 'Take Jean back to the camp; I must get this.'

And then it happens. Jean must have seen something. She starts to stand up. Instantly comes a rattle of machine-gun fire and Jean is thrown violently back against the tree behind them. Leila and Pete spin round. Jean, her face and upper body drenched with blood, collapses like a broken doll.

'Run!' yells Leila, dropping the camera.

Leila and Pete spring from behind the log. The weapon roars again, bullets splintering the bark of the log. The two run headlong, dodging in and around the close-set trees. The gunfire follows them, an almost continuous fusillade. Their unseen assailant is pursuing them determinedly, murderously.

'Split-up!' yells Leila. She shoves Peter to the left, runs off to the right.

The plan doesn't have time to work. Even before he is out of Leila's sight, Pete is caught in a hail of machine-gun-fire. He screams, plunges into some bracken.

Leila stops, looking back for the assailant. She sees only a muzzle-flash; bullets perforate the foliage around her. She runs on, blundering through ferns and brambles.

Oh, Christ; oh, Christ; I'm going to die.

She bursts into open ground. She is back at the campsite. She can call for help. She makes for her tent, but her pursuer is right behind her; the machine-gun roars again, bullets tear up the canvas of the tent as they tear up Leila Foster's body.

Blood-soaked, she falls to the ground. Everything goes quiet, and Leila, lying there, strangely at ease, the last drops of life gently draining away from her ripped and useless body, dimly sees, from her worm's eye view, a figure stepping into the clearing and walking towards her, and her last conscious thought is of boots glinting in the star light, silver space boots...

Chapter Eight
The Face in the Mirror

The 1860s. Possibly the single best decade of the English novel.

Charles Dickens, of course; forever and always Dickens. *Great Expectations* and *Our Mutual Friend*, his last two completed novels were penned in that decade. And Dickens' chum, Wilkie Collins: his 'big four' novels all appeared in the 1860s: *The Woman in White, No Name, Armadale*, and *The Moonstone*. And then the man who was considered Dickens' main rival, William Makepeace Thackeray passed away in the 1860s, but not before giving us *The Adventures of Philip* and tragically only the first eight chapters of *Denis Duval*. The most notable female writer of the time, George Eliot, published some of her most famous novels, including *Silas Marner* and *Felix Holt*. Margaret Oliphant, neglected by fickle posterity, wrote many of her popular *Chronicles of Carlingford*. Anthony Trollope, the production-line writer who over the decades has veered from being underrated to being overrated, produced some of his best work in the '60s, including *Orley Farm*, and *The Last Chronicle of Barset*. Not to mention important works from other more or less neglected writers like Mary Elizabeth Braddon, Ellen Wood, Ouida, Sheridan le Fanu, Charles Reade...

And not just Britain! Those other two centres of great literature in the Nineteenth Century, France and Russia, also produced some of their best works in the 1860s. In Russia, Leo Tolstoy wrote his sprawling epic *War and Peace*. Fyodor Dostoevsky produced some of his most famous novels, including *Crime and Punishment, Notes From Underground*, and *The Idiot*. Ivan Turgenev published *his* most famous novel, *Fathers and Sons*. Ivan Goncharov's last—and longest—novel, *The Precipice* appeared...

And then in France, Victor Hugo published that *other* giant Nineteenth Century epic, *Les Misérables*. Emile Zola was cutting his teeth with early novels like *The Mysteries of Marseilles* and *Madeleine Férat*...

And then of course there was Gustave Flaubert's *Sentimental Education*...

This book had become the bible to writers of the naturalist movement in France. And it is also something of a bible to Mark Hunter. We see him lying in bed reading the book; *re*reading it in fact, and for not the first time. The copy he holds is a 1970s Penguin edition, translated into English by Robert Baldick, a detail from Gustave Courbet's 'Man with Leather Belt' as the cover illustration. 430 pages (including notes and translator's introduction), set in Monotype Fournier, pages slightly yellowed with age...

Sentimental Education. Mark acknowledges that he is being 'sentimental' himself in bringing this book with him to his childhood home, choosing now of all times to re-read it. But the book happens to be the one physical legacy he possesses of the most important summer of his early life. And this particular book couldn't be more poignant, and not just because it was on that summer that he first read it, read the same copy he is now holding; but because it is the story of a young man's love for an older woman, inspired by author Gustave Flaubert's own passion for an older woman, Élisa Schlésinger...

And then there was Mark Hunter's own 'sentimental education' that took place over that particular summer, his own first love. There is a name, a name written in blue ink on the inside cover of the book; a woman's name, Marianne Grant...

They left the Four Bells shortly after the fracas described a couple of chapters ago, Mark and his three friends. They felt that the wrong set of people had been ejected from the premises; and the atmosphere of the place seemed suddenly to have changed; or perhaps it was just that its true colours had finally revealed themselves. Either way, they had left, and with the intention of not returning. They will try out instead some of the town's other public houses on future evenings. Mark recollects a pub down by the river with ample outdoor seating; a much longer walk but perhaps a better place to go to...

Engrossed in the book, Mark has been ignoring his bladder for some time, but his bladder is becoming insistent. He needs to go the loo. Sighing, he puts his mark in the book, sets it down and gets out of bed. He is naked, but it seems frankly ridiculous to get dressed just to walk down the narrow landing to the bathroom; he might as well go as he is. A dressing gown would have been the obvious happy compromise in this particular situation; but Mark has not brought a dressing gown with him.

He steps out onto the darkened landing. The bathroom is at the far end of the landing from Mark, but a small window admits a degree of luminance; and so, as he isn't in pitch darkness, it doesn't seem necessary to turn the light on. (And regardless, he can't remember off-hand where the switch is.) The sound of languid lovemaking, issuing from Dodo and Mayumi's room, reaches his ears. Have they left their door ajar…?

Mark has only taken a few steps, and is about level with Dodo and Mayumi's door, when his lower body comes into sharp contact with something solid; something soft and alive that lets out a squeal. Mark over-balances and falls on top of this writhing impediment, and the surprised screams become suddenly muffled as by an obstruction at the source.

The light comes on in the lovemakers' room, the door opens, shedding its light upon the landing. Dodo and Mayumi appear in the doorway, expressions inquisitive and dressed as nature intended them. Mark gets to his feet and now the object he fell upon reveals itself to be a pyjama-clad Trina Trulove.

'What are you two up to?' inquires Dodo, looking from one to the other. 'And out on the landing!'

'Get a room,' says Mayumi.

'Speaking for myself, I wasn't up to anything,' says Mark. 'I was just on my way to the bathroom when I fell over Trina here. She was crouched on the floor or something.'

Trina has clambered to her feet, smoothing down her pyjamas. She looks flushed and embarrassed; her mouth is open and an inquiring tongue follows the circumference of her lips. Her eyes fix themselves on Mark's loins.

'Well?' challenges Dodo. 'What were you doing down on the floor?'

Trina meets her eyes, laughs nervously. 'Me? Ha-ha! I was… I was just looking for my contact lens…'

'In the dark?' queries Dodo. 'And anyway, you've got your glasses on.'

74

'Ah, silly me! So I have! Ha-ha, ha-ha!' is the best Trina can come up with. Still laughing nervously, she backs away from the interrogative trio, finds the handle of her bedroom door, and with a last lingering look at Mark's genitals, bolts inside.

Mark turns to the two women. Dodo smiles at him, while Mayumi studies his genitals with expressionless curiosity.

'Well, now that the corridor is free of obstructions, I'll get back to going to the bathroom,' says Mark.

'You do that,' says Dodo. 'See you in the morning.'

'Good night.'

The door closes, shutting out the light. Mark waits a moment for his eyes to adjust, then makes his way to the bathroom. He can very easily guess what Trina had been up to when he'd fallen over her: spying on Dodo and Mayumi's lovemaking! Yes, definitely a sensualist.

Pushing open the bathroom door, he pulls the light cord. It clicks but no light comes on. As you invariably do in these situations, Mark clicks the cord off and then on again several times. A pointless endeavour of course, because once a lightbulb has expired, repeatedly pulling the cord isn't going to make it change its mind and come to life again.

I'll have to sort this out in the morning, thinks Mark. Should be some spare bulbs in the kitchen. He has noticed that most of the light fittings in the cottage still boast the old filament bulbs, an indication of how long it must have been since they needed changing.

The bathroom has a window, frosted but uncurtained, so he is not in pitch darkness. He steps up to the toilet. Oh yes; seat down. Three ladies in the house! He raises the seat, takes hold of his still semi-tumescent penis and commences urinating. The splash of water in the bowl tells him that his aim is true. When he has finished, and having manipulated his penis to get rid of those last few drops, he flushes the toilet, and moves over to the sink to wash his hands.

An oval mirror is affixed to the wall above the basin. After soaping and rinsing his hands, Mark happens to glance up at the glass—and freezes with disbelief.

The eyes that stare back at him from the mirror are not his own. They are the large black oval eyes of a grey alien.

Chapter Nine
Exit the Mantell Project

'What?! Why didn't you tell us straight away?' This from Dodo.

'There didn't seem any point,' answers Mark. 'It was all over by then. When I saw the thing in the mirror, at first I froze. Then I jumped back like the proverbial startled rabbit, looking all around me. I was expecting the thing to be in the room with me; that was my first reaction. If it's in the mirror it has to be in the room. But then I realised: the thing I'd seen in the mirror hadn't been looking over my shoulder; *it's* reflection was right where *mine* should have been.'

'And then, when you looked in the mirror again it was gone?'

'Yes; only my own disconcerted features looking back at me.'

'Maybe you were half asleep and you imagined it,' suggests Trina.

'It was just after that little incident with *you*, Trina; so, no, I was not half asleep. And there's another thing: I told you the bathroom light hadn't come on; I thought at the time the bulb had gone, but I've tried the light again this morning just to see, and it worked.'

It's morning coffee-time in the cottage living room again, with this time all four of our gallant friends fully clothed.

'And it was definitely one of those grey aliens you saw?' questions Dodo.

'Definitely. Domed head, big black eyes, pointed chin, no nose, small mouth: the standard model, straight out of abduction folklore.'

'How did it appear in a mirror like that?' wonders Trina.

Mark shrugs. 'How did one appear in a child's bedroom and in the back of that man's car?'

'They must be evil spirits,' declares Mayumi.

'Maybe they are at that,' concedes Mark.

'I'm going to be scared to go in the bathroom now,' announces Trina.

'You needn't be,' Mark reassures her. 'The sightings of these greys seem to be very isolated incidents. I doubt it will manifest itself in the same place again.' He sips his coffee. 'More news. My Department has got back to me about Vernon Grange.'

'Oh! So, do you know what's going on there, now?' from Dodo.

'Not exactly. The property has been purchased by the scientific concern Vallotec, and they are using the place as a facility for quote "scientific research." My people couldn't find out anything more specific than that.'

'Vallotec. I'm sure I've heard of them…' ponders Dodo.

'You have. It was last year, during the SEA business. It was when I found myself teamed up with some of those SEA girls to raid a Vallotec lab and shut down a solanite particle-accelerator that was preventing them from getting back to their headquarters.'

'Oh, yes! And then the girls stole the solanite material from you and shot you with a tranquilliser dart.'

'Yes. Not one of my finest moments,' observes Mark drily. 'The Vallotec group, if you remember, belonged to the Wainwright business empire. Now, when Eustace Wainwright was murdered by his daughter last year, the Wainwright empire collapsed. A lot of their holdings, including Vallotec, were bought up by another faceless corporation, the Parkhurst Consortium. They purchased Vernon Grange for Vallotec to use as a research establishment.'

'So, your UFO friends from yesterday could be right,' says Dodo. 'They could be experimenting with alien spacecraft technology at Vernon Grange.'

'That's one possibility,' agrees Mark. 'I've got another one to pitch at you.'

'Go on, then.'

'Let's go, for the moment, with the theory that grey aliens are actually time travellers from the far future: well, maybe they're conducting time-travel experiments at the Grange…'

'…And time travellers from the future have come back in time to try and stop time travel from being invented in the first place?' finishes Dodo, grinning. 'Don't you think that one's been done to death in science-fiction, Mark darling?'

'Exactly! So it's high time that it happened in real life, isn't it?

Or maybe,' pursues Mark, 'the people from Grange brought these future people back in time themselves. Maybe they're cooperating with them.'

'A nice lot of speculation,' sums-up Dodo.

'Agreed. Just speculation. Which is why you and I, Dodo love, are going to pay Vernon Grange a surreptitious visit tonight. Unless you've got other plans, of course.'

'No, I'm free this evening.'

'Are we involved in this raid?' asks Trina.

'Yes, you and Mayumi will be performing the important job of waiting here at the cottage, and then raising the alarm if Dodo and I don't come back.'

Mayumi folds her arms around Dodo, nestling against her. 'You'll come back,' she affirms.

Mark lights a cigarette. 'I only hope those Mantell Project kids haven't done anything silly like trying to break-in at the Grange themselves...'

They are startled by a brisk knock at the front door. They are not expecting any visitors. Being the nearest, Trina rises to answer it. Opening the door, she finds standing on the front doorstep a smiling uniformed policewoman.

'Hello. Is a Mr Mark Hunter here?'

'Yes, he is. Come in.'

Mark rises to greet the officer. She is a small, blonde woman, neat and trim in her uniform.

'I'm Mark Hunter. I take it you're from the local station?'

'Yes, that's right, sir. I'm Sergeant Mavis Shagwell.'

Dodo splutters coffee all over the place.

'Pleased to meet you,' says Mark. 'Are you just here to say hello, or has something happened?'

'Something very much has happened. We don't know if it's anything to do with this UFO business you're here for, but we've got three dead bodies in Vernon Wood.'

'Three?' echoes Mark. He doesn't like the sound of that.

'Yes. A male and two females; they were all wearing army uniforms, but we're pretty sure they weren't actually soldiers.'

Mark's heart sinks. 'No, they weren't. I know who they are. I met them yesterday; three amateur UFO investigators... Is it

78

known how they died?'

'Oh yes, we know that alright: they were shot, and by machine-gun by the looks of it; a powerful one. You should see the bodies: riddled with bullets.'

Mark exchanges looks with Dodo.

'Machine-gunned? I wouldn't have expected that...'

'I can take you out there right now, if you want,' offers Mavis. 'My car's outside.'

'Yes, thank you,' says Mark. 'I need to see this for myself. Let me just put my shoes on.'

And with a 'see you later' to the others, Mark follows the Sergeant out to her squad car.

'How were they found?' asks Mark, as they turn onto the main road.

'A man out walking his dog in Vernon Wood early this morning,' answers Mavis. 'He was in the clearing where that grass circle is. The landing site, if you want to call it that. One of the bodies, a girl, was just at the edge of the clearing. The dog found it first. The man didn't have a phone on him, but he rushed back home and called us up. We arrived, and searching the area, we found two more bodies and a campsite, presumably the victims."

'So, the bodies weren't found close together?'

'Nope. One of them was actually at the campsite, another girl; the other I'd say roughly halfway between the other two; that one was a young man. We've sealed off the area and called in Cambridge CID.'

From the spread-out location of the bodies, it sounds like they were being pursued by whoever killed them, muses Mark. But were they running away *from* their camp or *towards* it?

'So, you know the victims' names?' prompts the Sergeant.

'Only their first names,' replies Mark. 'Leila, Jean, and Peter. They never gave me their surnames. As I say, I only met them yesterday. They were camped out in the woods investigating the UFO incident.'

'Then they got more than they bargained for,' observes Mavis.

'That they did.'

They have reached Vernon Wood. At a lay-by ahead, a number

79

of police cars, vans, and ambulances are gathered. People, in uniform and plain clothes, are milling around. They pull in and alight from the car.

'Let's go to the landing site first,' says Mark. 'The bodies haven't been moved, have they?'

'Not yet.'

They set off.

'These deaths weren't the only thing that happened last night,' reports Mavis. 'We had a number of calls from people in town saying they'd seen those grey aliens.'

'Did you?' says Mark. So I wasn't the only one.

'Yes, and also a lot of people online getting that weird interference.'

'The strange writing?'

'Yes.'

Things certainly *had* happened last night, thinks Mark. Just like that girl Lucretia said they would.

They reach the clearing. Police tape, wound around the trees, cordons off the area. Mark displays his ID, and Mavis takes him to the first body; it lies at the foot of a tree in front of a fallen log Mark recalls from the day before.

Mark recognises the corpse, encrusted with oxidised blood, as that of Jean, the nervous girl. Had she been the one to run the furthest, or had she been the first to die?

They move onto the second corpse, further into the woods. Pete, the military geek. A pathologist is crouched examining the body.

'Any idea when they died?' asks Mark.

'My preliminary estimate is ten hours,' answers the woman. 'Say between eleven and midnight last night.'

They move on to the campsite clearing, and Leila's body. The leader of the Mantell Project, now disbanded. Mark looks down at the staring-eyed corpse. They wanted to find proof of extraterrestrial life, these people; and instead they have assured themselves their own place in UFO mythology, by becoming the subjects of their very own Dyatlov Pass Incident.

Tables, shaded by awnings have been set up in the clearing, where the belongings of the three victims are in the process of

80

being catalogued.

Mark introduces himself to the plain-clothes officer in charge.

'They were running away from their killer or killers,' says the inspector. 'All the evidence indicates they were chased from that other clearing back here to their own camp.'

'So, whatever happened, it started at the landing site,' says Mark. 'Have you found anything else at that location?'

'Yes.' The inspector leads Mark over to one of the trestle-tables, indicates a digital video camera, bagged and labelled. 'This was lying close to that fallen log, not far from the first body.'

Mark picks up the bagged camera. 'I'll be taking this, inspector.'

'But that's evidence!' splutters the inspector.

'*I'll* be taking this,' repeated Mark.

The inspector acquiesces, but with bad grace.

Chapter Ten
One UFO over the Cuckoo's Nest

Back at the cottage, they have watched the film.

A glowing shape, more like a spinning-top than a saucer, and standing in the exact location of the landing site. The same craft from before, presumably returned to the same spot. It had pained Mark to hear Leila's voice saying that she had torn up the phone number he had given her. But, as Dodo had pointed out, even had they called him at that precise moment, he would never have been able to get there in time to save them. A machine-gun had opened fire. The film showed the muzzle-flash, from some shrubbery off to the left of the glowing object; but no clear view of the assailant. Then the shot had gone wild. They had heard Leila shout 'Run!' and then the picture had gone dark. This was obviously at this point at which the camera had been dropped. They could hear Leila and Pete's retreating footsteps, and an almost constant barrage of gunfire. It didn't sound like more than one shooter at work, but whoever was behind the trigger had been firing like a maniac. The sound of gunfire receded; and then silence, and nothing further until the camera had switched itself off.

Who had been behind that trigger? Someone from the glowing craft? The first shots had come from the direction of the vessel, so quite possibly 'yes.' And what was that glowing object? An experimental aircraft? An alien space-vessel? Or a time machine from the future? Unlike on that first occasion, no witnesses had reported seeing a light descending from the sky last night. But, as Sergeant Shagwell told Mark, there had been numerous other incidents in and around Market Stanford. She had given Mark a verbal resumé of these reports. One alleged incident particularly interested Mark. A group of teens, about a dozen of them, had been sat in the sunken spinney on the edge of the town, a location Mark is familiar with from his childhood. They had, they later claimed, just been 'hanging out'; but this 'hanging out' had almost certainly involved some under-age drinking and the use of illegal drugs. Either way, these youths had been sitting in a clearing, chilling and nattering, when they suddenly realised they were not alone. Standing amongst the trees on the edge of the clearing, all around them and staring in at them, had been a number of grey aliens. 'At least twenty' had been one estimate. Another thought it was more like a dozen. The creatures had made no move, hostile or otherwise, but after the initial moment of shock, the teenagers had risen as one, and fled the locality screaming.

There had been several other individual sightings of grey aliens that night (including Mark's own), but the incident with the kids was the first corroborated account, and the first time the 'greys' had been seen in any numbers. The creatures had inspired fear in those who saw them, but had made no hostile moves. But then, not far away, three other young people had been machine-gunned to death with a great deal of hostility. Mark finds it hard to imagine a grey alien wielding a weapon like a machine-gun. However, there was the case of the 'other' aliens, seen the week before by a policeman on the road running through Vernon Wood: the spacesuits. *These* creatures had been armed; they were reported as carrying weapons that resembled machine-guns, although the witness had failed to recognise the type. Could it have been one of these creatures that had wiped out the members of the Mantell Project?

Whatever the case, Mark has no intention of returning the camera to the Cambridge police. They will have to make do with his assurance that the film does not reveal the identity of the killer. He awaits with interest the results of the examination of the bullets used. Will they conform to any known type?

Mark doesn't consider it necessary to interview any of the witnesses of last night's manifestations. They couldn't tell him more than they have already reported to the police. In all of these cases—including his own—the creatures had just *appeared*. They had made no hostile moves, no attempt to communicate. (One man walking home had looked back to find a grey alien following him. It had stopped when he had stopped. Then the man broke into a run, and when he had next looked back the creature was no longer there.) There was one exception to all these accounts, all these sightings of grey aliens: the schoolteacher Flora Hodgson's story. *She* had claimed to actually have been taken on board an alien space-vessel and had held communication with its occupants. Yes, her account had been an improbable one that involved just about every abduction cliché in the book. And, yes, Flora has been psychiatrically assessed as being just the type of person who *would* broadcast tall stories. But there is just a chance, a chance that Mark cannot afford to overlook, a chance that she has been telling the truth, or if not the entire truth, that she has fabricated her story on top of something she has actually experienced...

Yes, there is just a chance; and that is why we find Mark Hunter standing outside the picturesque bungalow that is Flora Hodgson's place of abode. It is early afternoon and blazingly hot. If you're on the road that cuts through Vernon Wood, and heading away from Market Stanford, just after you pass the extremity of the woods there is a turning on the right; just a drove, a farm track. And a little way down this drove you see a single isolated dwelling, a bungalow: this is Flora Hodgson's place of residence. The front garden is a riot of carefully tended flowers and shrubs.

Mark walks up to the front door and raps on the knocker. (I know! That sounds very inelegant, but I really can't think of any

83

other way to phrase it.) He waits, but no-one comes to the door. Is she out? Perhaps she is just round the back... Deciding to check this for himself, Mark follows the quaint pathway round the side of the house, into the back garden. Yes, there she is; or at least there is a woman Mark takes to be Flora, kneeling down, tending one of the many flower-beds. She wears a flower-patterned dress, a broad-brimmed summer hat. Her long auburn hair is tied back.

Mark approaches her. 'Hello. Are you Miss Flora Hodgson?'

The woman looks up and Mark sees a frank, intelligent face, on which the lines of encroaching age look not unattractive. Altogether not what he has expected. He had pictured a more delicate face with large, slightly crazy, eyes. There's no hint of eccentricity in the pale blue eyes that coolly study him.

'Yes, I am she,' is her ungrammatical response, spoken in a crisp voice. 'If you're with the press, I'm not doing any more interviews.'

So, she isn't seeking attention anymore; that's a change. 'I'm not with the press,' Mark assures her.

'Are you a salesman, then? Whatever you're selling, I doubt I'd be interested; I haven't got much money.'

'I'm not a salesman either,' says Mark. 'My name's Mark Hunter; I'm with MI5.'

This gets her attention. She looks at him with renewed interest. 'Oh. I was wondering when you people would show up. So far I've only had sceptical policemen to deal with.'

Isn't she going to ask to see some ID? Is she trusting, or just gullible? 'I've only just arrived in the area,' explains Mark, showing her his card anyway. 'And there's a lot for me to investigate.'

Flora stands up, pulls off her gardening gloves. 'If we're going to talk, let's get out of this sun.'

A sycamore tree stands in the centre of the lawn; under the shade of its branches, a table and chairs.

'Would you like a drink?' offers Flora. 'I can do you an iced lemonade.'

'That would be very nice, thank you,' replies Mark.

'Just a tick.'

Flora heads off to the bungalow, and Mark sits himself down.

Presently, the woman returns, bearing two tall glasses of lemonade clinking with ice cubes.

Mark accepts his drink, and takes a grateful sip.

'Hits the spot, does it?' asks Flora

'It certainly does,' says Mark. 'You've got a lovely garden here.'

'Well, I've got a lot of time to devote to it at the moment,' replies Flora. 'what with being out of a job. Although of course it's summer hols, so I wouldn't be at work right now anyway.'

Time to get to the point, decides Mark.

'I was wondering if you'd had any further encounters since that first one you reported?'

'Oh, no. They haven't been back,' is the ready answer.

'Do you expect them to come back?'

'To see me again? I really couldn't say, Mr Hunter. They may want to speak to me again, but they made no definite arrangement. They don't work like that.'

'But they seem to be still in the area,' says Mark. 'You probably haven't heard, but there were numerous sightings just last night.'

'I'm not surprised.'

'But why do they keep appearing like that? Not saying or doing anything? I mean, with yourself it was different; to you they made their intentions clear.' Will she have an answer for this one?

She does. 'It's a matter of communication, Mr Hunter. It's not that simple for one species to communicate with another species that's completely unlike it in every way.'

'But they communicated with you…'

'Yes, because I was receptive. The aliens do not speak verbally, even to each other. They communicate telepathically. They can send and receive thoughts with one another as easily as human beings can exchange words. But communicating with other species is more problematic.'

She sounds so calm, so rational. She speaks as though she is just discussing basic scientific facts. 'Is it a language problem? Or do the aliens not have a language? Do they just communicate images, ideas?'

'No, they have a language. They used to speak verbally as we do, before they evolved beyond the need to do that. And no, language is not the problem. Earth languages are child's play to them, and they have mastered them all. They spoke their thoughts to me in English. How else do you think I understood them? I can't speak their language, can I?'

'I suppose not. But why can't they communicate with other people, the same way they did with you?'

'As I said, I am receptive. They can reach out to some human minds far more easily than others.'

'And that's why they chose you as the person to give their message to?'

'I would imagine so. And perhaps they knew I would be sympathetic to what they require from us.'

'Stop war, preserve the environment and give up eating meat, wasn't it?'

'Exactly. You see, I always believed very strongly in those things anyway. But now I know that we have to do those things not just to save ourselves and our own planet, but for the sake of the whole universe.'

'Oh, yes. The harmony between the planets. That's what they spoke of, wasn't it?'

'Yes. Think of the universe as a living organism; which is what it is, basically. If one part of it gets sick—and this planet *is* sick—it affects the whole body. Other planets all over the universe are suffering on account of us and what we're doing to our world.'

She's plausible; I'll give her that. She either honestly believes what she's saying, or she is a consummate liar.

'Are you a vegetarian, Mr Hunter?'

'Yes, I am as a matter of fact.'

'But, you're a spy; an agent. I imagine you sometimes carry a gun, and that you've killed people with it.'

'Sometimes I have to; to preserve the peace.'

'If you're taking human life, you're not preserving the peace, Mr Hunter.'

Mark decides not to take her up on this debate. He says: 'And what about the aliens? Do they never take life?'

'Never,' firmly. 'The idea is abhorrent to them.'

'Does that extend to human life?'

'*All* life is sacred to them.'

Mark thinks of the three bullet-riddled corpses he has seen this morning. Let's see what she has to say about that. 'And yet there have been three murders, you know. Three UFO investigators; they called themselves the Mantell Project. They were camped out in Vernon Wood. Their bodies were found this morning.'

'That's dreadful,' says Flora. She sounds sincere. 'How were they killed?'

'They were shot. A machine-gun.'

'Then they were killed by other humans, of course.'

'Yet they were filming what looked like an alien spacecraft at the time. We recovered the camera they were using.'

'A spacecraft; where?'

'That same clearing in the woods where one had already apparently landed.'

'Which clearing? The one on this side of the road, or the one on the other?'

'The other.'

'I see. Well, no-one from the spaceship would have killed those people. I'd say they were killed by the military.'

'Why would the military kill them?'

'So that they couldn't reveal what they'd just seen, of course. Part of the UFO cover-up.' She looks at Mark significantly. 'You should know all about that, shouldn't you?'

Mark holds up a hand. 'If there's any UFO cover-up conspiracy, I'm not part of it; I'm here investigating the business myself. And I honestly don't think it was the military who killed those youngsters.'

'Then who?'

'Well, you said the aliens never killed. I'm assuming you mean the grey aliens who you met. I don't know if you heard it, but a policeman saw what seemed to be a completely different set of aliens: as tall as humans, wearing spacesuits.'

'Oh, *them*. They're just one of the lesser races.'

She's got an answer for everything! 'Lesser races?'

'Yes; they sometimes accompany what you call the grey aliens on their travels. The planet of this lesser race is one of the most

87

severely affected by the cosmic disturbance. And they can't breathe our atmosphere: that's why they wear the spacesuits.'

'I see. Well maybe these other aliens aren't as non-belligerent as the greys. The man who saw them said they were carrying what looked like machine-guns.'

'They may have *looked* like machine-guns, but they weren't. *All* the other races are completely non-violent. The weapons they possess simply fire an energy beam which pacifies hostile creatures; it's completely harmless.'

'An energy beam…?'

'Yes. You see, there's a universal energy source used by all the advanced races. It powers their spaceships, their cities; and directed at an individual it can be personally invigorating or, as I said, it can pacify aggressive tendencies.'

This all sounds rather familiar to Mark. 'I see. And this energy source: does it have a name?'

'Yes; it's called vril.'

Vril. The universal energy source employed by the subterranean civilisation in Edward Bulwer-Lytton's 1871 novel *The Coming Race*. Now I know she's telling me a fairy story.

Should he confront her with this? Will she have a glib answer ready? Or, finding herself in a corner, will she reveal her true colours and fly off the handle? …No, it would be cruel to attempt the experiment, Mark decides. If she does lose her temper, someone like her, it might take her all day to recover her equanimity.

He drains his glass, sets it down on the table. 'Well, thank you for your time, Miss Hodgson. I think you've told me enough to be going on with.' He reaches into his pocket for his notebook. 'I'm going to give you my mobile number. If you do have another encounter, or if you learn anything bearing on the situation, do you think you could give me a call?'

'Certainly, Mr Hunter. I can do that. Are you staying in the area?'

'For the time being, yes.' He writes down his number, tears out the leaf, passes it to Flora. They rise from their chairs.

'Oh, by the way; do you know anything about Vernon Grange?'

'Yes.'

'What?'

'It's a big house just down the road.'

'Yes, it is. Do you know anything else about it?'

''Fraid not. What should I know?'

'Oh, nothing. It doesn't matter.'

Farewells are exchanged and Mark departs. He pauses at the end of the front garden. Across the track is a field of stubble; beyond that, Vernon Wood. Somewhere just over there is the so-called 'second' landing site, which he had visited yesterday… Had Flora seen anything at all that night? Perhaps the landing of the second spaceship… Might that have been enough to trigger her fantasy…?

Lighting a cigarette, Mark proceeds on his way.

Chapter Eleven
The Old School Tie: Clyde Waring

Captain Darma walked into the conference room and she sat down in the chairman's chair. The room became silent and everyone's eyes looked at the tall, striking blonde woman.

'Ladies and gentlemen,' said Captain Darma. 'The report has been confirmed. Admiral Dexter and his party have been captured by the Dh'Lahk on planet Grebos.'

The beings sat around the table all started exclaiming their anger.

'This is an outrage!' stated Rhomba, the reptilian ambassador from planet Centuron. 'The Dh'Lahk are defying the peace treaty!'

'They must be made to answer for their crimes!' exclaimed the fish-like Fluta.

Captain Darma thumped the table to bring the meeting back to order.

'I agree that the treaty has been broken,' she said. 'But that being the case, I don't think any official protest will do any good.'

'Then you suggest we do nothing?' thundered Twukludh, the

warrior chief of the Vishtass.

'No, I don't,' replied Darma, a smile curling at the corners of her sensuous mouth. 'I suggest we mount a rescue operation.'

There was more uproar at this suggestion.

'A full-scale invasion of Grebos?' gurgled Fluta. 'Just to rescue Admiral Dexter? How can you justify that?'

'I didn't mean a full-scale invasion,' answered Darma, coolly. 'I meant a covert operation. A small squad, in a civilian ship, in civilian disguise.'

'How could such an act be officially sanctioned?' demanded Rhomba.

'It wouldn't,' said Captain Darma. 'The rescue would be completely unofficial. If we were caught, the Galactic Federation would deny any knowledge of our actions.'

'Of *our* actions, you said. Do you mean *you* mean to take part in the attempt?' asked Twukludh.

'I intend to command the operation,' said Captain Darma, coolly

'But, Captain! You'd be stripped of your command!' said Mahoney, Darma's loyal first officer.

'Indeed. You must be either very brave or very stupid, Captain Darma,' said Fluta.

Captain Darma smiled. 'Perhaps I'm a bit of both. It wouldn't be the first time I've taken a risk. Some rules are made to be broken.'

'There's no holding you back, once you've made your mind up,' sighed Mahoney, the dour chief engineer, shaking his head.

'Ladies and Gentlemen,' said Darma. 'Any volunteers?'

'I can only take part in this rescue as its leader,' declared Twukludh. 'The warriors of Vishtass do not take orders from women!'

'There's always a first time for everything,' said Captain Darma. 'On Earth, women have become the equals of men. Perhaps it's time the same thing happened on Vishtass.'

'Outrageous!' roared the burly warrior. 'I will only take orders from you, Captain Darma, if you were to defeat me at *Zhuk' Ta*!'

'*Zhuk' Ta*?' questioned Darma.

'An ancient combat tournament of the Vishtass,' explained

90

Mahoney. 'It has long been used to settle disputes and choose clan leaders.'

'Very well, Twukludh. I accept your challenge,' said Captain Darma.

This is good! This is it! I'm cooking on gas today! Nailed it on the head! No-one's written a space-opera quite like this one! It's got everything: drama, humour, even sexual politics. This is sure to get accepted!

Clyde Waring sits back in his chair, plucks a hand-full of cheese puffs from a bag, transfers them to his mouth. It is one of those large bags of cheese puffs, 'ideal for sharing', but Clyde Waring, living alone, doesn't have anyone to share them with. Clyde's corpulent frame, and especially the bloated stomach, attest to an indifferent world that he must have munched his lonely way through a large number of these 175g snack packs over the years.

Mark Hunter wouldn't have recognised his childhood friend, if he could have seen him today, seated at his computer terminal in a very untidy front room. Aside from the drastic weight-gain, Clyde now wears glasses and sports long hair (bald on top) and a thick jungle of beard; and he wears the slob's uniform of bermuda shorts and food-stained t-shirt.

Where has Clyde Waring's life gone since those halcyon summer holidays spent with his friend Mark Hunter? Nowhere. Geographically his life has gone nowhere: he still inhabits the same house in which he has lived all his life; although these days, as said, he inhabits it alone; both his parents have died. Romantically (or 'sexually' if you prefer not beating around the bush), his life has also gone nowhere. He has never had a girlfriend and he is still a virgin. (Clyde had developed a crush on a girl around the first year of secondary school; word of this crush had managed to get out, and his classmates had all teased him about; what's more, they had teased *her* about it, and probably as a direct result of this, the girl, previously indifferent to Clyde had come to hate him, and had rebuffed him in no uncertain terms. After this crushing rejection Clyde had started to become more and more introverted and socially awkward; the belief had become ingrained in his mind that *all* girls would reject him the same way Michaela had rejected him; that he was just not someone that girls fancied and wanted to go out with. These early experiences can often affect us the rest of our lives. They have with Clyde.)

Career-wise, Clyde's life has likewise gone nowhere. After finishing school, he had got himself a job in a local cardboard box factory, and had actually held it down for a number of years. Initially, he had liked the work; had enjoyed the monotonous routine of the production-line simply because it had not required much concentration, and had allowed him to build castles in the air, work out stories, while his hands were mechanically performing the work. But then his depression had grown worse, his motivation had dwindled, he had taken more and more days off, and had eventually been fired. He has been on incapacity benefits ever since.

But Clyde still has completely given up on achieving anything in life. As we have seen from the above sample, he is busy knocking out an epic space-opera. He has written—or at least *started*—quite a few of them in his time, because like so many of his kind, he has a busy inner life, his thoughts firmly focused on science fiction and fantasy, and of course, firmly turned away from anything resembling reality. He has submitted proposals for *Doctor Who* and *Star Trek* novels. He has sent comic book scripts to *2000AD*. He has submitted story-lines to the producers of *the X-Files*.

Most recently, he has sent script proposals to BBC Wales, home of the resurrected *Doctor Who* TV series. They had responded to say that they were only commissioning scripts from experienced television script-writers. Huh! thinks Clyde. Being an 'experienced television script-writer' doesn't necessarily mean you can write good *Doctor Who*. Hell, there are script-writers who can't write for toffee, but still—through a lucky series of flukes or a good agent—end up getting a lot of work: look at Chris Chibnall.

Well, to hell with them! The new series isn't as good as the old one, anyway.

So now, Clyde has gone back to the idea of writing an original science-fiction novel that isn't part of anybody else's 'universe.' Okay, 'original' might not be an entirely accurate description: he has jumbled and recycled ideas from several of his earlier efforts into this one. But he's done it all so much better than he's done before. This time he has come up with the perfect space-opera that is sure to be accepted!

As I said, Clyde's computer desk is in the front room; the small front room of his house, a modest, two-bedroom semi-; and that the room—indeed the whole house—is very untidy and thickly coated with dust. When Clyde's mother had died, household cleanliness had died with her. Decent meals passed away with his parents, as well; Clyde subsists on snacks, takeaway food and ready-meals.

Clyde doesn't mind the mess, because it's his mess, his home, an extension of himself and the one place where her feels safe. He is alone. Of friends from school, he doesn't see any anymore. Some of his schoolfriends have moved away from Market Stanford; some have just changed as adults, changed into people Clyde no longer has anything in common with; and as for the one or two, like Rachel Farrow, Clyde still had any contact with, he has pretty much shut the door on them. (Or more accurately, he just hasn't answered the door whenever they have knocked at it.) Clyde's social skills have now dwindled to nothing and he has convinced himself that he doesn't need friends.

Clyde can still remember Mark Hunter; schooldays are always clear in the minds of people who haven't done much *since* their schooldays. But when Clyde thinks of Mark Hunter at all, he hardly ever brings to mind the pre-teen Mark, the inseparable comrade of his primary school years; he recalls only the teenage Mark, whom he resentfully remembers as the Mr Perfect who used to hang around with the outcasts like he was doing them a favour. So, yes, he remembers Mark Hunter, but he doesn't remember him fondly.

(Spoiler: a few days hence Mark Hunter and Clyde Waring are destined to pass one another in a Market Stanford street; neither man will recognise the other.)

Having polished off his cheese puffs, Clyde feels like having something sweet to balance the salt intake. Some ice-cream would hit the spot. Yes, he has an only half-eaten tub of Ben and Jerry's chocolate fudge brownie ice-cream just waiting in the freezer. Time to finish it off. He heaves himself from the swivel chair that supplies his desk, wincing as he feels a sharp twinge along the back of his neck and shoulder-blades. He's been getting a lot of pain in that area of late. He assumes it's because he sits at his computer with bad posture. (In fact, he does everything with bad posture.)

He plods through to the kitchen, with its mountain of crockery piled up in the sink, and dining table strewn with dirty plates and mugs or more recent vintage, thoughts of the impending ice-cream making his mouth water. Fudge brownie; his favourite flavour; at least when cookie dough or salted caramel aren't occupying pole-position with his taste buds. He opens the door of the freezer cabinet; he takes out the tub of ice-cream. It feels alarmingly light. With a sinking feeling of horror, he removes the lid. Empty! Apart from a few skid-marks left by the devouring spoon, nothing. This is impossible! When had he eaten it? More importantly, why had he then put the empty carton back in the freezer? Had he eaten the ice-cream in his sleep? Had he done it just to taunt himself?

He has set his heart on that fudge brownie ice-cream, and by God he is going to have some! But… this will mean having to go to the shops, and going to the shops will mean having to go outside. Clyde is not fond of going outside. For one thing it's really hot, and even when it's not really hot Clyde goes outside as infrequently as he possibly can.

Can he survive without the ice-cream? Can he reconcile himself to its absence from his freezer? He doesn't think he can. Minor disappointments of this nature easily become major disappointments to people like Clyde.

But it means going outside. It means that awful ten-minute walk to the nearest convenience store. It means passing people in the street, encountering the staff at the check-out; all of whom Clyde *knows* will be wondering why a forty-year-old man isn't at work on a weekday afternoon and will be setting him down as a sponger, a layabout and despising him for it…

But then the prospect of that Ben and Jerry's chocolate fudge brownie ice-cream… He *has* set his heart on it.

Girding his metaphorical loins, Clyde steps into his sandals, fits a baseball cap onto his balding head, slips his wallet into the pocket of his shorts.

He opens the front door and steps outside.

Chapter Twelve
The Raid on the Vallotec Building
(Fast Return)

Midnight.

Picture a brick wall, about ten feet high. Picture a dashing secret agent and his glamorous assistant (taller than he is) standing at the foot of said wall. The wall is the perimeter wall which encircles—rectangularly—the precincts of Vernon Grange. We are at the rear wall. Here, on the outer side of the wall, a pasture, currently without tenants, bovine or ovine. Beyond the pasture, a farm track, and all around, a patchwork landscape of fields. Off to the right—as you stand facing the wall—rises the gloomy mass of Vernon Wood. You can't see it, but further down the farm track just mentioned Dodo's car sits waiting, parked off the road, concealed by shrubbery. Mark's knowledge of the terrain has enabled them to drive close to the rear of Vernon Grange, avoiding the main road. (The Grange is within reasonable walking-distance of the cottage, but the transport has been considered an advisable precaution. They have no idea what is going to happen when they penetrate the grounds of the house, and they might end up needing to make a swift getaway.) Mayumi and Trina they have left back at the cottage getting stoned in front of Netflix. Dodo has changed into what she calls her 'spy costume,' the attire she usually wears when accompanying Mark on one of these sorties: to wit, black boots, black PVC trousers, black polo-neck sweater. Mark has simply changed out of his brown suit into a fresh brown suit of identical pattern. The night is sultry. On these hot summer nights it only really cools down towards daybreak.

Their plan? Very simple: climb over the wall, avoid the guards, break into the house and see if they are hiding any UFOs or time-machines in the basement.

'Getting over the wall should be easy enough,' says Mark, speaking quietly. 'There's no glass or barbed-wire along the top.'

'But there are those guards; they might be patrolling the perimeter inside,' Dodo points out. 'If we jump over at the wrong moment, we'll be caught straight away.'

'If you give me a leg-up, I can take a surreptitious peep; make sure the coast is clear.'

'Okay.'

Standing by the wall, Dodo cradles her hands. Mark, availing himself of the foothold, lifts himself to the lip of the wall. He looks. The light of the moon illumines the grounds below him. An open stretch of lawn directly adjacent to the wall; further in, stands of trees, thick shrubbery. Rising above this the chimneys and gables of the Vernon Grange.

But it is something else that grabs Mark's attention. The dark shape of a human body lays stretched out on the lawn, unmoving, a shotgun by its side. It looks to be one of the guards. Alert, Mark scans the area. No sign of movement; not a sound. He climbs up onto the summit of the wall.

'Looks like someone might have arrived here before us,' he reports.

'How's that?'

'There's a guard down here. Dead or unconscious.'

'So, do we carry on?'

'We do. There's a mystery here; I can't just walk away from a mystery.'

Mark reaches down a hand, helps Dodo up onto the wall. They jump down onto the sward, and approach the supine body. Still nobody else in sight. They stoop to examine the body. The man looks to be in his twenties, dressed in a gamekeeper's tweeds and flat-cap. He is quite obviously dead: the face livid and bloated, the neck broken, the head twisted to one side.

Mark's eyes meet Dodo's in the semi-dark.

'Strangled, and with great force,' he murmurs. 'Just like Cully,

96

the vagrant… Come to think of it, *his* body was found not all that far from here…'

'Yes, and it knocks on the head the theory that Cully was just killed by some passing lunatic. To judge by this, whoever did it is still around.'

'Yes, and possibly closer than we realise. This man's body is still warm. I'd say he was only killed a few minutes before we got here. He must have been patrolling the grounds, and apparently he hasn't been missed yet… Grab an arm. Let's drag him over to those bushes, out of sight. It'll be better for us if he's found later rather than sooner.'

Mark picking up the shotgun, together they drag the body into a clump of rhododendrons.

'And another thing,' says Mark. 'Has this man's killer broken *into* the grounds like we just have, or has he broken *out* from the house?'

'A homicidal alien escaped from his cell?'

'Well, we don't know *what* they might be hiding in there. Hopefully we'll have a clearer picture before we're done tonight.'

'On to the house, then?'

'On to the house.'

Keeping low, they weave their way through the leafy shadows towards the house. At the extremity of the garden, they come to a yard surrounded by outbuildings and close to the rear façade of the main house. Here they pause under the shadow of an elm tree to scope the terrain. Light shows through several curtained windows of the ground floor of the house. A couple of exterior lights cast their glow over the yard.

'People are still up and about, it seems,' observes Mark.

'What now?' asks Dodo. 'Take the bull by the horns and see if we can find an open door or window?'

Before Mark can answer, the rear door of the house opens, and a figure in a long white lab coat stands framed in the doorway. The figure steps out into the yard. A second figure, also wearing a lab coat, follows. They pause, seem to be waiting for something. Both are women: one with dark hair, tied back at the nape; the other smaller in stature, with fair hair long and loose.

'I think I recognise that woman with the dark hair,' whispers

Dodo.

'Yes,' answers Mark, in the same tone. 'She looks very much like the woman who was with those three youngsters at the pub last night.'

The sound of an approaching motor vehicle becomes audible.

'Here they come,' speaks the blonde women.

Headlights piercing the night, a vehicle appears round the corner of the house and drives into the yard. From its appearance, it looks to be a private ambulance. The van turns and reverses to bring its rear doors close the house, and comes to halt. The engine dies. The two women approach the vehicle. A man in an ambulance-driver's uniform emerges from the front cab. At the same time, the rear doors open, and two medical orderlies, carrying a stretcher between them, step out into the yard.

'How's the patient?' asks the dark-haired woman.

'Sedated,' is the terse answer from one of the orderlies.

'Okay. Down to the examination room.'

The orderlies and their burden disappear into the house. The fair-haired woman follows them.

'I wonder who's on that stretcher?' breathes Dodo.

'Mm. Who or *what*?'

Presently, the orderlies reappear, carrying the empty stretcher. They climb back into the rear of the ambulance.

'Okay. Thanks,' says the dark-haired woman. 'You can get back now.'

'Right,' says the driver, getting back behind the wheel.

The ambulance drives away, disappearing round the side of the house, towards the main entrance.

The dark-haired woman is about to go back inside when a newcomer hurries up to her. Carrying a shotgun, he wears the same tweeds and flat-cap as the dead man. This is evidently the uniform of the guards around here.

'What is it, Travers?' inquires the woman.

'Bailey's missing,' is the succinct answer.

'What do you mean, "missing"?'

'He was on perimeter patrol. He hasn't reported back to the gate-house.'

'Well, that's not so strange, is it? He's probably in the bushes somewhere with Serena.'

'But—'

'Don't bother denying it. I know full-well what you and your men get up to with that girl,' declares the woman. 'And what's more, I don't care. Only do it in your spare time; not when you're on duty.'

'Bailey wouldn't shirk off when he's on patrol,' insists Travers. 'He's not that irresponsible.'

'Isn't he, now?' replies the woman. 'Look, let's go'n see if Serena's in her room; if she is, *then* you can start a search for Bailey.'

Travers salutes. 'Yes, Doctor.'

They go inside. The door closes.

'Let's chance it now,' says Mark. 'From the sounds of things, those two will be going upstairs. This is our chance to sneak inside.'

'Right.'

They break from cover, and, keeping to the shadows of the outbuildings, swiftly cross the courtyard. Mark opens the rear door. A corridor, long and narrow. They traverse the corridor and then emerge into what is obviously the entrance hall of the Grange. A grand staircase, curved banisters and balusters face the double main entrance doors. Interior doors to the right and left. The walls are oak-panelled, the floor polished parquetry. Oil paintings adorn the walls. There is a profusion of potted plants, and yes, even a suit of armour. The hall is illuminated by a vast crystal chandelier. To the left of the main staircase, a pair of featureless metal doors, modern in design strike a discordant note.

'A lift,' says Mark. 'That woman said *down* to the examination room; so down's where we want to go.'

'The lift's going to make some noise,' cautions Dodo.

'Let's try that door,' says Mark, indicating a small door standing adjacent to the lift. 'Might be the emergency stairs.'

They cross the room to the door; Mark tries the handle. The door opens, and the light from the chandelier reveals a descending flight of stairs. Mark flashes a smile at Dodo. 'Just as I thought!'

Voices above them; footsteps on the staircase. They duck into the stairwell, quietly close the door. They listen in the darkness.

'...all your men and search the grounds,' comes the woman's voice. 'He might just be goofing off somewhere, but on the other hand, we might have an intruder.'

'Who'd want to break in here?' the voice of the man called Travers, sceptical.

'Why do you think we have you guarding this place, Travers?' retorts the woman, wearily. 'And with all the things that have been going on around here of late... There were three people killed in the woods not far from here last night, remember?'

The voices recede.

'Did you hear that?' breathes Mark. 'Whatever's going on here, these people didn't have anything to do with the Mantell Project kids being killed. That's something learned.'

'Yeah; but what *are* they doing here?'

'Let's see if we can find out.'

So saying, Mark leads the way down the stairs. Blindfold, they descend carefully. A switchback landing, and then below them a strip of light at ground level, indicating a closed door at the foot of the stairs and a lighted room beyond.

Pausing at the door, they listen. No sounds reach their ears. Mark cautiously opens the door. Before them a corridor, brightly lit by LED tube lights, the walls whitewashed brickwork. To their immediate left, the lift doors; further down, the corridor terminates with a pair of double doors, supplied with spherical glass panes. On the right, the corridor, with doors at intervals, extends much further. There is no-one in sight; no sound of activity.

'Let's try those doors over there,' says Mark.

'Okay.'

They progress a few steps, and then Mark pulls up abruptly, emitting a hiss of annoyance.

'What's wrong?' asks Dodo.

'Look.' Mark indicates a security camera bracketed to the wall above them.

'Oh, great. What do we do now: turn back?'

'It's a tad too late to worry about that, now. We'll just have to hope that the camera's just recording automatically and that no-one's monitoring it at the other end. Come on.'

They reach the double doors, peer through one of the glass panes. The room beyond is an infirmary. With her back to the intruders, the blonde woman in the lab coat stands over an examination table. The sheet-draped form lying on the table appears to be human; at first, the woman's starched white back prevents them from seeing the upper half of the body; but now, she moves away to examine the readings on a piece of equipment, and the uncovered head of the patient becomes visible to the two spies. It is a girl; an ordinary, human girl. She looks to be no more than in her early teens; her hair is light brown and cut in a short bob. Her eyes are closed, her breathing seems regular.

Mark and Dodo move back from the door.

'What's going on here?' breathes Dodo, perplexed. 'What are they doing to that girl?'

Mark ponders. 'Examining her for something… Youngsters… Those kids from the pub last night: I think they all must have come from here in this place. Maybe that Serena they were just talking about is the sexed-up girl who gave me the once-over…'

'You're not going to tell me those kids are aliens or time travellers from the future?' demands Dodo, sceptical.

'No, I—'

Their speculation is interrupted by a sudden sound; a heavy object falling to the ground. The sound issues not from the infirmary, but from somewhere back down the corridor.

Mark indicates a door across from the lift doors. 'I think it came from in there…'

'If someone comes out…'

They wait, expectant. No further sound follows. No-one appears.

Mark and Dodo trade looks.

'Shall we check it out?' asks Dodo.

'Yes, perhaps we should…'

They move over to the suspect door. No further sounds issue from within. Mark takes the handle, opens the door a crack. Pitch darkness. He opens the door further. Light from the corridor spills into the room, allowing them to see what appears to be a storeroom; rows of freestanding metal shelving units, stacked high with cardboard boxes. Mark gropes for the light switch;

finds it. A naked bulb lights up the room.

They step inside and Dodo closes the door behind them. They look and listen. No sign or sound of movement.

'If anyone was in this room for legitimate reasons, they wouldn't be groping around in the pitch dark,' remarks Dodo.

'Yes... I suppose it's possible that a badly stacked box could have fallen by itself...' He sounds unconvinced. 'Let's at least try and see if we can find whatever it was that fell and made the noise.'

Mark unholsters his automatic. They move cautiously along the first narrow aisle and reach the further wall.

'Here we are: look!'

The rows of shelving stop short of the wall, leaving a narrow passage. Mark indicates the far corner, where a cardboard box lies upturned on the floor, its contents—bulky ring binders—disgorged.

'That's got to be what we heard fall,' says Mark.

'But it looks like there's no-one here,' says Dodo. 'Maybe it *did* fall by itself.'

They move towards the fallen box, Mark in advance. They reach the corner. And then it happens. A sudden violent movement, a flash of colour and Mark feels powerful hands grab hold of him. Hurled violently to the ground, his gun is sent flying from his hand. Before he can even move, his assailant springs onto him, pinning him down, hands reaching for his throat.

Hands wearing metallic silver gloves.

A spaceman! An astronaut's helmet, much smaller and more streamlined than those worn by Earth astronauts, looms over Mark. He can see nothing of his assailant's face; the helmet visor, tinted to near-blackness, reveals nothing. Mark does his best to hold his attacker's wrists, but the powerful hands reach inexorably for his throat.

And then Dodo grabs the spaceman in a head-lock, dragging him from the prostrate Mark. She sends him spinning into one of the metal shelf-units. The unit topples backwards, crashing to the ground, the spaceman on top of it. Mark scrambles for his gun, picks it up, levels it at his attacker.

Sprawled over the shelves, the figure doesn't move. The

spacesuit is bright red in hue and composed of some smooth, shiny material, while the helmet, gloves, boots and a sort of girdle around the middle, are all silver.

'Well, there's our spaceman,' says Dodo.

'And our strangler, I'd guess,' says Mark.

And then, before their eyes, the spaceman starts to fade away. His body becomes translucent, and then gently fades to nothingness, and Mark and Dodo find themselves staring at a toppled shelving unit.

'What's going on in here?' demands a new voice.

A woman has just walked in; the blonde in the lab coat from the infirmary, attracted by the noise.

'Who are you?' she demands, glaring at the intruders. 'What are you doing here?'

'Actually, we're just leaving!'

So saying, Mark bounds over the fallen shelves, shoves the woman aside, and followed by Dodo, dashes out into the corridor. At that very moment, the lift doors open, and out steps the dark-haired woman. Before she has time to react, Mark grabs her wrist and sends her spinning along the corridor. Our two heroes duck into the lift just before the doors close. Mark stabs the button for the top floor.

'Why are you sending us up to the top?' demands Dodo.

Mark smiles. 'Elementary, my dear Dodo. They will expect us to get out at the ground floor; therefore, we out-manoeuvre them by going up to the top.'

'Yes, but then we'll still have to go downstairs again to get out of this place.'

'We'll burn that bridge when we get to it,' says Mark.

The lift doors open and they find themselves in a lighted corridor, panelled like the entrance hall below. They run to the head of the stairs, peer down the stairwell. The two lab-coated women, who have been joined by Travers and another flat-capped guard, appear at the foot of the stairs. Mark and Dodo retreat quickly out of sight.

'Let's try one of these rooms!'

And suiting the action to the word, Mark opens the nearest door and they duck into the darkened room beyond, closing the

103

door. They pause, senses alert. A strong scent of perfume pervades the room.

And then a light is switched on. A green light. A green bedside light. The cyan glow reveals the form of a girl sitting up in a large bed with black satin sheets; a thin-faced girl with short black hair, long strands coming down over her face. She regards the two intruders with apparent unconcern.

Lucretia. She looks different denuded of her face make-up.

'What are you doing?' she inquires.

'Remember me? I'm Mark Hunter. We met at the pub last night…'

'Yes, I remember you. What are you doing?'

'This is my friend Dodo…'

'I know who she is. I've seen her on TV. What are you doing?'

'Well, we're in a spot of bother. We sort of broke into the place and now some guards and two women in lab coats are out looking for us. I know you have no reason to ally yourself with us, Lucretia, but could you see your way clear to letting us hide ourselves under your bed? Temporarily, of course.'

'There isn't enough room under the bed,' says Lucretia. 'But you can get out through the window. There's a flat roof underneath.'

'Thank you! The window sounds admirable!'

Lucretia climbs out of bed, lithe and nude, and pulls back the heavy curtains concealing the open window.

'Why did you break in here?' she inquires.

'Oh, just nosiness,' answers Mark. 'I wanted to know what was going on here.'

'And have you found out?'

'Well, I know there is a staff of scientists, and there's you young people. At the moment my best guess is that you kids are either all alien abductees, or you're all ESPers.'

A flicker of a smile. 'Right second time.'

'I see. ESPers. Interesting. And are you being held here against your will? We saw a girl being brought in sedated just now.'

'Oh, the new girl. I dunno about her, but the rest of us are all volunteers.'

A knock on the door.

'Lucretia! Are you awake in there?'

'Let's get out of here,' hisses Dodo, one booted foot on the window sill.

With a parting look of gratitude to Lucretia, Mark follows Dodo out through the window.

Chapter Thirteen
'How Did You Guess they were ESPers?'

'Well, after I'd deduced that all those kids were at the Grange, it was what happened at the pub last night that gave me the idea. There was my conversation with Lucretia, and her claims of possessing some kind of second sight. And then what happened at the pool table: the impossible movement of the billiard balls you described, and how that lout who attacked the boy from the group couldn't land a single punch. That sounds like telekinesis at work to me…'

'So Vallotec are experimenting with ESPers. Then it looks like Vernon Grange has nothing to do with the UFO business.'

'Yes, it does seem that way.'

'What are you going to do now?'

'Well, I was sent here to investigate the UFO affair, the Market Stanford Incident; but I can't help being interested in what's going on at the Grange. Lucretia said that she and her friends were all volunteers; but that girl we saw tonight was being brought in under sedation. She may have been kidnapped.'

'Yes, but we don't know what kind of ESPer ability she might have. She might be dangerous; they might have been taking precautions.'

'Even so, it still smacks of an abduction. It's possible the Department will want me to look into this. They won't like the idea of any private concern using ESPers.'

'What do you think they're using them for?'

'They could just be conducting research, but somehow I doubt it. A corporation like Parkhurst is going to be more interested in their practical usefulness than in just broadening the horizons of human knowledge.'

'Useful for doing what?'

'The same things my people would probably use them for if they had them: espionage, sabotage. assassination…'

'Yes, that's probably what most governments would do with ESPers if they got their hands on them… But, aside from all that, we've also got the gentleman in the spacesuit who attacked you. I don't think he was one of those kids.'

'No, he was an intruder like we were. I'm sure he was. It has to have been him who killed that guard.'

'So, what did he want at the Grange?'

'I'm not sure he wanted anything. The way he attacked me, I got the distinct impression he was a raving lunatic. He just wanted to kill me.'

'A lunatic alien. Do you think he was the one who massacred the Mantell Project?'

'You know, I'm not sure about that one. Leila and her friends were shot to death. My attacker went for my throat with his bare hands. He strangled the guard. That vagrant, Cully, was killed in the same way… We got a good look at our spaceman, and it did not look like he was carrying any weapons.'

'Yes, but what he looked like matches the description of those spacemen the copper saw, and according to him they *were* packing heat.'

'Yes… You know, my busy mind is coming up with a theory here; one that might account for the presence of two UFO landing sites…'

'Go on. Let's hear it.'

'Okay. Alien number one arrives alone. He's a lunatic or a criminal, escaped from some prison or asylum. A second bunch of spacemen, armed with guns, arrive to try and recapture him. That policeman saw three of them, and they were carrying guns. The one we encountered didn't have a gun… Ergo, it was the pursuing aliens who killed the Mantell Project people—but *why* did they kill them? Unless it was simply because they'd seen the spaceship.'

'It probably was. Even if those spacemen are enforcers trying to round up a dangerous criminal, it doesn't necessarily follow that they have any concern for us human beings.'

'Agreed. One thing I don't get, though, is if we've got alien hunters and quarry in the vicinity of Vernon Wood, you would have expected those spacemen to have been seen by people a lot more times than they have been.'

'Well, we know they can make themselves scarce. We just saw that one disappear into thin air. They must have some sort of personal teleportation device...'

'That's what it looked like, yes. It's pure speculation of course, but my theory does nicely account for everything. Well, apart from one glaring problem...'

'The *other* aliens. The greys.'

'Correct. They don't fit in with the pattern... Two lots of aliens turning up at the same time... You know, something just occurs to me... Maybe the people at Vernon Grange *are* involved. Those grey aliens have only ever been *seen*; they've never actually done anything... What if one of the ESPers at the Grange has the ability to project images; to make people see something that isn't really there...?'

'Like seeing a grey alien in the mirror.'

'Exactly. It could be part of an experiment; using illusions to cause mass hysteria... It could even just be someone's idea of a practical joke...'

'I get it. After the UFO sightings happened nearby, someone might have thought it would be a good laugh to make the locals start seeing aliens...'

'Yes, and it would be valuable practical research at the same time. It all fits, doesn't it? No-one who saw those greys ever had any physical contact with them, and in most of the cases they just disappeared. They could have been illusions.'

'So, what are you going to do? Try and hunt down the spacemen and their quarry, or find out more about what's going on at the Grange?'

'I'd like to do both if I can. As I said, I'm concerned about that girl they've just brought in. If she is there against her will, that would give us a good excuse to go in and raid the place.'

'Well, getting information from the Grange shouldn't be that difficult now; you've got your Inside Woman there.'

'Lucretia?'

'Yes. You must have made a good impression there, Mark darling; she helped us escape just now without giving it a second thought.'

'Lucretia strikes me as a flighty and impulsive young lady. Yes, she decided to help us this time; but she might not be so forthcoming on the next occasion.'

'I'm not so sure about that one, sweetheart. Don't underestimate your charms... Well, here we are, back home. And it looks like they've both stayed up for us, bless 'em...!'

Chapter Fourteen
Welease Bwidget Pwice!

'Good morning, ladies!'

Thus speaks Doctor Newcome, walking briskly into the staffroom. The three women seated in the room all wear lab coats like himself—Doctor Channing; tall, with long, dark hair and a serious expression. We first saw her that night at the pub in Market Stanford. Doctor Clavering; smaller, blonde, and with a somewhat dreamy look about her. Doctor Caxton; bespectacled, clinical, her short hair is grey, although in age she is no older than her two colleagues.

The women, smoking cigarettes and drinking coffee, return Newcome's greeting perfunctorily, without enthusiasm. Newcome crosses the room, pours himself a mug of coffee, seats himself with his co-workers. Blandly handsome, Doctor Newcome is officially the head of the research establishment here at Vernon Grange. It is he who draws the larger wage packet; it is he who receives the orders from head office... It's just that he has a lot of difficulty in receiving the respect and compliance due to him in that capacity. The three women, united by their sex and their 'c' names, have erected a solid wall of contempt between themselves and their nominal chief. They never defer to him; they follow his orders grudgingly; they ignore his instructions whenever it suits them to ignore them; and they constantly ridicule him to his face, making not the slightest attempt to conceal their supreme contempt for him... And how does Newcome combat this treatment? He ignores it. In spite of every provocation, he persists in being affable to the three ladies, behaving as though there is not the slightest note of discord existing between them.

'Busy night, last night,' he observes.

'Yes. It was nice of you to surface when it was all over,' replies Channing.

'Nobody woke me. So, have you figured out how those two intruders escape?'

'There were three intruders, and two of them escaped over the wall. The other one disappeared into thin air.'

'Well, he can't have disappeared into thin air, can he? He must have just eluded us.'

'Say "it" rather than "he," and it didn't just "elude us." You've seen the security camera footage: that *thing* in the spacesuit walked into the storage room. Ten minutes later, the man and woman went in there.' Channing turns to Dr Clavering. 'You were in the infirmary and you heard what sounded like a fight, didn't you?'

'Yes, that's right. I could hear things being knocked over.'

'You went into the storeroom, and the man and the woman were in there and they pushed you out of the way and got out. But there was no sign at all of that thing in the spacesuit, was there?'

'Nope. Just the man and the woman.'

'Yes, but then everyone took off after that man and woman,' argues Newcome. 'The thing in the spacesuit may have still been in the storeroom, hiding out of sight. It could have cleared out once the coast was clear.'

'But it *didn't*, you idiot,' snaps Channing. 'It would have been caught on the security camera. That thing went *in*to the storeroom, but it never come *out*.'

'Then it's still there.'

'Don't be stupid. We searched.'

'It must have been a ghost,' declares Clavering.

'A pretty substantial ghost, if that man and woman got into a fight with it.'

109

'Ah, but we don't know that they did,' interposes Newcome. 'Clavering only *heard* the fight; she didn't actually see it. The man and woman might have been fighting each other.'

Channing shoots him a withering look. 'They were *together*. Why would they suddenly start fighting each other?'

'And if they did, they must have patched things up very quickly, because they escaped together,' speaks up Dr Caxton.

'Right. They were fighting that thing; they must have been.'

'Which then must have disappeared.'

'Well, you saw what it looked like,' says Channing. 'It has to be tied in with all the things that have been happening around here lately: those UFO sightings... We've got no proof, but I'm willing to bet it was that thing that wrung Bailey's neck as well; not the other two intruders.'

'Well, at least we should be able to find out who *they* were,' says Newcome. 'We got pretty good shots of them from the security footage, and they've been sent to head office. They should be able to tell us who they are.'

Channing looks at her watch. 'Our new subject should be waking up around now.'

'Is she still in the medical centre?' asks Newcome.

'No. She's been taken up to her room.'

'Then, I'd better go'n say hello.'

'You?' snorts Channing. 'Is that a good idea? That girl's going to be upset and disoriented. I don't think you're the best person to put her at her ease.'

'And why not, may I ask? My bedside manner's as good as anyone else's here.'

'Yes, we know all about your bedside manner, you pervert.'

'Why don't I go?' suggests Clavering. 'I'm the most mumsy person here.'

'Yes, but you'll start filling her head with all your New Age nonsense,' replies Newcome. 'The girl doesn't need to hear how her powers are a gift from Gaia the Earth mother, and all that garbage.'

'Garbage? The elemental forces—'

'*I'll* go,' announces Doctor Caxton, standing up.

110

An unfamiliar ceiling.

Bridget Price, just awake, looks up at it. Memories slide into place like jigsaw pieces, but she can find nothing in the completed picture to account for the fact that she isn't in her own bedroom.

It's Wednesday, isn't it? Not a school day because it is August, summer holidays. She had gone to bed last night in her own bed as usual... Come to think of it, she can't remember actually going to bed... She can remember playing a computer game in her room, and then she had suddenly felt very tired... Incredibly tired; and not just tired; light-headed; dizzy... After that: nothing until now.

Where is she? The bed, the room, are substantial and old-fashioned. And what's this she's wearing? Not her own pyjamas; it's more like one of those hospital gowns... What's going on?

Panic seizes Bridget Price. She can think of only one explanation. She's been sent to the loony bin! The funny farm! She knows her Mum and Dad have been concerned about her lately; looking at her in funny ways, whispering about her... Yes! That's it! They think she's gone loopy! They must have had her—what's the word?—sectioned!

Oh, gweat.

Bridget is a problem child. There's no denying that. She doesn't have any friends. She is performing badly at school. She is the victim of bullying. (The psychological kind of bullying at which girls are so adept.) Morose and introverted, wrapped in a cocoon of self-doubt, melancholy and isolation, she bears the inevitable scars of her condition on her wrists and arms.

Her alarm subsiding, Bridget sits up in bed. If this is a mental hospital, maybe she isn't so badly off after all. At least here there will be people who want to talk to her, to help her... Maybe they'll give her some of those pills that make you feel better...

Bridget possesses those teenage feelings of being apart, of being an outcast, but she has no concept of self-sufficiency. She takes it for granted that there will always be something above her—her parents, her teachers, the system—that will feed, clothe and shelter her. Some teens are thrust out into the world as soon as they finish school; many there are who find themselves in those halfway homes between nurture and independence known

111

as the Halls of Residence; some doomed unfortunates never manage to break away from the parental ties. Bridget has just never thought that far ahead. Adults are adults; she is a child.

She's a pretty girl, our Bridget Price. Of average build and height, she has mid-brown hair cut in a short bob. Her face exhibits the glow of youth, while being blessedly free of its attendant, the rampant acne of youth. Large blue eyes, tip-tilted nose, pert, full-lipped mouth. There is a sadness in those blue eyes, the only real index of her depressed state of mind.

Her clothes are neatly folded on a chair beside the bed. She has just made her mind up to get up and put them on, when the opens and a woman walks into the room. The woman has short, grey hair, and wears a white lab coat over her clothes, confirming—so Bridget thinks—her belief as to her location.

The woman smiles. 'Good morning, Bridget.'

'Hello,' says Bridget.

The woman seats herself on the edge of the bed. 'How are you feeling?'

'Alwight, I suppose,' says Bridget.

'Good. My name is Doctor Caxton. I'm sure you must be confused, waking up in this strange place; so first of all, let me assure you you're perfectly safe and amongst friends.'

'Fwiends?'

Bridget feels reassured. The woman's crisp speech and professional air inspire confidence; and her smile is friendly, sympathetic.

'I expect you're wondering where you are?'

'I think I know where I am,' replies Bridget.

Caxton's eyebrows arch with surprise. 'You do?'

'Yes. This is a mental hospital, isn't it?'

The woman smiles. The smile tells Bridget she has guessed wrong.

'I'm afraid you're off the mark there.'

Not a mental hospital? Then where is she? Bridget feels her panic returning. 'So where am I? How did I get here?'

'Don't worry. As I said, you're completely safe. You're here with your parents' permission. They know where you are.'

Then what is this place? A special school? Have her parents

112

had her transferred to one of those special schools for problem kids? But then, why would a school have a doctor in a lab coat? A science teacher? School nurse?

'This house is called Vernon Grange,' proceeds Doctor Caxton. 'It's a country house in Cambridgeshire, so you're not that far from home.' (Bridget hails from Leicester.) 'You're here because you possess special abilities. You'll be joining seven other young people who are gifted like yourself.'

Special abilities? Gifted? Then it *is* some kind of school! But how precisely, is she 'gifted'? Her grades are nothing more than average, declining of late. She doesn't excel in any subject except Art. She is good at Art. Could that be it? Is this an Art School?

'Am I here because of my dwawing?'

That smile again. Another wrong guess!

'No, this has nothing to do with your academic skills. When I said special abilities, I was referring to something else; something outside the normal curriculum. You see Bridget, you don't even realise you have this ability, but your parents have realised it, and so have we. I'm referring to Extra Sensory Perception.'

'Extwa Sensory Perception?' What is she on about? 'I haven't got that!' she exclaims. 'That's weading people's minds; making things float in the air; things like that. I can't do that!'

'Mind reading and telekinesis are just two specific ESPer abilities. There are many others. Our research has shown that people who possess ESP usually just have one specific skill, and there are a wide range of ESPer abilities, some of them more well-authenticated than others. I wonder, Bridget: now that you've been told you have ESP; can you guess what your ability is? Think about what's been happening in your life recently.'

What is she talking about? She's never done anything out of the ordinary! She'd know about it if she had! 'I've never done anything that's like ESP! You must have got it wrong. I haven't got any special power.'

'You have, you know,' Caxton assures her. 'What happened to your school science lab just before the summer break?'

'It burnt down.'

'Haven't you wondered how that fire broke out? You were there at the time, weren't you?'

113

What does she mean? Does she think *she* started that fire? But it had been an accident, hadn't it? Just an accident. Although that fire breaking out just when it had, at that particular moment, had suited her mood perfectly, and she had been grimly satisfied with the result. It had been a chemistry lesson, and they were setting up the apparatus for an experiment. The teacher had gone into the equipment room to get something, and Hayley Rice, one of Bridget's chief tormentors, had gone and dropped and smashed an expensive piece of equipment. Hearing the noise, the teacher had returned, and Hayley had promptly assigned the blame for the breakage to Bridget. Vehement denial from Bridget; but then the rest of the class had decided to back up Hayley's version of events, and the teacher, who was already in a bad mood that afternoon, had let loose with a verbal assault directed at poor Bridget, who, with cheeks burning and eyes streaming with shame and rage, had withered under the blast. The lesson had then resumed, with Hayley and her clan gloating over Bridget's humiliation. And then one of the gas taps had burst into flame. A second had followed suit. And then another, and another, until all the gas taps in the room had become geysers of flame. The fire alarm had rung; the building had been evacuated; the fire brigade had arrived as quickly as they could, but the science lab and two rooms adjoining were totally gutted before the flames could be extinguished. Bridget had felt a savage satisfaction at this disaster having happened just when it had; but, she had never, not for one minute, suspected that she herself was the cause of it. Until now.

'You mean I was wesponsible for that fire?' she asks.

'Yes. It was you. You may not have realised it, but it was you,' answers Caxton. 'There have been other instances, haven't there? What about the man who tried to assault you in the park?'

'His cigawette lighter exploded and his clothes caught fire.'

'And that time you tried to cook a family dinner and it all went horribly wrong?'

'The saucepans caught fire.'

'And that miserable family holiday in Clacton?'

'The chalet burnt down.'

'Precisely. You're a pyrokinetic. That's your ESPer ability. You possess the ability to control fire by the will of your mind.'

Control fire! She had caused all those things to happen, and she hadn't even been aware of it! 'Then I did all those things? But, I didn't even wealise it!'

A reassuring smile. 'There's no need to panic, Bridget. Now that you know you have this power, you will soon learn to control it. We'll help you. That's why you're here.'

'You'll help me contwol my powers? And my pawents agweed to this?'

'They did. We convinced them that sending you here was the best thing for you.'

'How long will I have to stay here?'

A shrug. 'That's undecided.'

'But it won't take that long for me to learn to contwol my power, will it?'

'Yes, but that's not the only reason you're here. We're a government department. People like you can be of great service to your country.'

'What d'you mean?'

'I mean you'll be given assignments. Missions. Important work for the security of the nation.'

'Secuwity of the nation? You mean I'll be a secwet agent?'

'Pretty much.'

A secret agent! ESP! Controlling fire…! It's just so much to take in! Thoughts tumble over one another in Bridget's mind. Her feelings of displacement, of abandonment by her parents, give way to something new: a feeling of importance. She, the hopeless loser, the downtrodden one at school, turns out to have special powers! And she's going to become a secret agent working for her country! That would show Hayley Rice and all those other cows!

'I know this must be a lot for you to take in,' Doctor Caxton is saying. 'But don't worry. We're all here to help you. You won't be hurried into anything… Why don't you get dressed? I'll take you down to breakfast and then you can meet your new friends.'

'You said there's seven others. Are they all the same age as me?'

'Let me see… I think most of them are a year or two older than you; and two of them are younger. But they're all very friendly; you'll get along.'

'And they've all got special powers?'

'Yes.'

'They can contwol fire?'

'No, no; you're our only pyrokinetic. The others all have different abilities.' Doctor Caxton rises from her seat on the bed. 'Get your clothes on. I'll wait for you outside.'

What was once an ornate drawing room has been turned into something more like a students' common room. There's a pool table, a music system, a ninety-inch plasma screen television… Only the upright piano standing against the wall fits in with the country house architecture of the room. A boy, fair-haired, pale and haughty looking, sits at the piano, playing Erik Satie's Gymnopédies. The twins, Robert and Roberta Morton face one another at a small table, immersed in a game of snakes and ladders. Lucretia sits on a cushion, knees drawn up, talking quietly to herself while she rocks herself back and forth. Damien and Serena sit chatting on a sofa. Another girl, in her late teens, with short hair and sharp features, sits apart, reading a book.

The doors open and Doctor Caxton steps into the room, followed more hesitantly by Bridget. All eyes turn towards the newcomer; all eyes except those of Lucretia, who is lightyears away, and the boy at the piano, who after only the briefest glance, turns back to his piano playing. Bridget is dressed in cargo pants, and a short-sleeved t-shirt over a long-sleeved t-shirt; a blue ear-flap beanie adorns her head. This hat is a ubiquitous accessory for our Bridget; apart from when in bed or the bath, she wears it all the time. (Although was never allowed to wear it in class at school, and had had it more than once confiscated from her on this account.)

'Hello everyone,' says Dr Caxton. 'Come and say hello to our newest recruit.'

Damien and Serena have risen from the sofa. 'Like the hat!' says Damien 'So, what's your name?'

'Bwidget,' says Bridget.

'Well, I'm Damien; this is Serena. Welcome onboard!'

Caxton turns to Bridget. 'See? I told you they wouldn't bite.'

'Bit nervous, eh?' surmises Damien. 'I don't blame you; new

place and everything. But don't sweat it, we'll make you feel at home. Won't we, Serena?'

'Of course will we! Take a pew, Bridget.'

Caxton turns to the door. 'Then I'll leave you to get acquainted.' Opening the door, she pauses, looks back. 'Oh, and Bridget understands that what we're doing is a *government* project.'

'Oh! That stor—I mean, right!' from Damien.

Bridget plants her bum on the sofa, Serena seating herself beside her. Damien, still on his feet, says: 'Let's introduce you to this rest of the crew. The girl there with her nose in a book is Helen.' Helen looks up from her book, utters a brief and unsmiling 'hello.' 'Oh, please, Helen; don't go overboard, whatever you do!' He waves a dismissive hand. 'Nevermind her, she's more interested in her stupid book. Well, next we have the twins there, Robert and Roberta.'

'Hello, Bridget,' chime the twins in unison. Adds Roberta: 'What's your favourite flavour of ice cream?'

'Vanilla,' says Bridget.

'That's *boring*!' declares Roberta. 'That's like plain crisps.'

'Don't you like chocolate ice cream?' asks Robert. 'What's wrong with chocolate ice cream?'

'What's wrong with vanilla?' retorts Damien. 'Back in the nineteenth century chocolate was a lot easier to get hold of than vanilla, and so for them it was vanilla ice-cream that was more of a luxury item.'

'Oh, we knew *that*!' declares Robert. 'Didn't we, Roberta?'

'Yes, we did, Robert!'

'Yeah, just get back to your snakes and ladders, munchkins… The goth chick you see sitting in the corner is Lucretia. She's gone into one of her trances, so it's no use trying to talk to her now. She'll say hello when she comes back down to Earth… And lastly, we have the boy playing the piano…' And then, louder: 'THE BOY PLAYING THE PIANO…'

The boy playing the piano stops playing, turns round on his stool. 'There's no need to shout.' To Bridget: 'My name is Edward. Pleased to meet you, Bridget Price.' And with that, he turns back to playing the Gymnopédies.

'So that's the crew,' says Serena. 'Stick with me and Damien for now. We'll show you the ropes.'

'And you've all got these special powers?' asks Bridget.

'Yep, we're all ESPers,' confirms Damien, sitting back down. 'Yeah, I suppose I should tell you who's got what! Well, starting with me: I'm a telekinetic; and in case you don't know, that means I can move objects with the power of my mind.'

'About the only thing you can do with your mind,' chips in Helen.

'And I'm electrokinetic,' says Serena. 'That means I can control electricity; the same way you can control fire. Have you met our hippy-chick, Dr Clavering? She calls people like us 'elementals.' We're harnessing the primal forces of Mother Earth, is what she says; she's into all that hippy-dippy stuff.'

'As for the rest of us,' proceeds Damien. 'The twins here are both teleporters. They can disappear from one place and reappear in another place in a flash. "Jaunting" is the technical term for it. And if you're worried about them popping up when and where they shouldn't, worry not: the munchkins have strict instructions not to teleport into anyone's bedroom or any bog or bathroom. On pain of death!'

'We know!' groan the twins.

'Helen and Ed are our telepaths. But again, not need to get your panties in a wad. They can't just read your mind whenever they feel like it. They have make physical contact to do that; they have to be touching you. They can project their thoughts and speak into your mind, though; but they won't ever do that unless they really have to; you know, if it's an emergency or something.'

'Can we speak back into their minds, then?' inquires Bridget.

'Nope. At least, not without training you can't. Helen and Ed can hold telepathic conversations with each other, because they're both telepaths. A non-telepath would have to have formed a special "rapport" with a telepath before they could speak back to them; and you have to work on that to make it happen. That was how those old music-hall mind-reading acts used to work.'

Says Serena: 'Dr Channing's working on these ear-piece things that are supposed to make the rest of us able to mentally communicate with Helen and Edward; they'd come in handy

118

when we're out on assignments.'

'What about her?' asks Bridget, indicating Lucretia, still in her corner, murmuring to herself. 'What's her power?'

'Ah! Well, she's the enigmatic one,' answers Damien. 'It might be some sort of second sight she's got, but it's not your regular seeing into the future kind of thing; she can't tell you what you'll be doing next Tuesday or anything like that. It's like she hears things. Picks things up.'

'What sort of things?'

A shrug. 'Voices on the astral plane. The collective human unconscious. The internet. Her mind's out there right now. But she comes back down to earth sometimes.'

'So that's everyone,' concludes Serena. 'We've got these laboratories down in the basement; we have to go there sometimes and do these tests. Experiments. They're to help us to use our powers properly.'

'And you go out on missions?' asks Bridget. 'What sort of stuff do you do?'

'Oh, all sorts,' says Damien. 'Spying on people. Stealing things. Eliminations.'

Bridget's eyes saucer. 'Eliminations? You mean killing people?'

'Sometimes. We only take out the bad guys, though. Enemies of the state.'

Helen has put down her book and is regarding Bridget narrowly. 'How old are you?'

'Thirteen.'

'Hm. Have you been defiled yet?'

'Defiled?' confused.

'She means have you had sex,' translates Serena. 'Helen here has a very negative view of the subject.'

Bridget turns bright red. 'No, I haven't done that,' she says, squirming in her chair.

'Hmmph,' says Helen 'But you'd like to, wouldn't you? I bet there's some guy that you fancy, isn't there? Someone you want to offer up your virginity to?'

'I like Kurt Cobain,' says Bridget bashfully. (She discovered Nirvana in her parents' record collection.)

119

'He's dead!' snaps Helen 'You can't have sex with him! And anyway, he was a rapist.'

'That was never pwoved!' hotly.

'Cut the girl some slack, for Christ's sake!' intercedes Serena. 'Poor thing's only been here five minutes and already you're asking her personal questions about her sex life and demolishing her idols.'

'Hummph.' Helen buries her nose in her book again.

Chapter Fifteen
Down Memory Lane

The bullets extracted from the bodies of the members of the Mantell Project have now been analysed. They conform to no known type. On the other hand, they are composed of a metal alloy the constituents of which are all to be found here on Earth. Of course, that didn't necessarily mean the bullets are *from* Earth; the same combination of minerals could exist on other planets. And the fact does remain that the bullets—and ergo the gun that fired them—are of an unknown type.

This afternoon, Dodo, Mayumi and Trina have gone out on a photography expedition, and so Mark, who needs some time to think things through and having nothing else that requires his immediate attention, takes himself on a nostalgic stroll through the town of Market Stanford. It is another blazing hot day. He saunters along Main Street in the town centre, observing which shops have survived from the past, which ones are new. He notes with satisfaction the presence of a camping supply shop. This is useful because he is deliberating the idea of moving from the cottage and setting up a tent in Vernon Wood, in order to be at the centre of things and on hand should anything new occur. (Not to mention being close to Vernon Grange.)

Mark stops at the newsagents they used to buy all their comics from as kids. Superhero comics, World War II comics. At the back of the shop there had been these two huge stacks of activity books, almost hidden away, and many of these books had obviously been gathering dust in the shop for years. Mark remembers once unearthing from the very bottom of the pile a *Star Trek* activity book which must have been of early 1970s vintage. The cover painting had shown the gallant Captain Kirk resolving another situation by his usual method of punching out the opposition.

Looking in through the windows, Mark sees that the shop has been completely refurbished since his day and is unrecognisable from how it used to be. They've even got the post office in there now.

Passing out of the town centre, Mark bends his steps towards the location of his former secondary school, Market Stanford Community College. Arriving there, he receives a shock. The place is now fenced in like a prison-camp, with tall gates guarding the main entrance. In Mark's time the entrance had been open to the world, with just a low brick wall running along the perimeter of the grounds. The wall is still there, but it has been topped with tall, unclimbable railings.

I should have expected something like this, really, muses Mark. Sign of the times. The kids probably feel like the gates are there to keep them *in*, but they are actually there to keep any passing psychopaths or spree-killers *out*.

Looking through the railings, the buildings still look the same, though; except that a new block has been added to the familiar group of buildings. Facing him across the schoolyard, Mark can see the great windows of the main assembly hall, venue for all those boring morning assemblies. Some of their GCSE exams had been held in that hall as well. Mark recalls a time in which the room had erupted with laughter right in the middle of one such exam; one of the supervising teachers, the clumsy humanities teacher Mr Unwin, had sat down on a chair which had immediately collapsed under his weight. Even at the time, Mark had wondered about this event. If the chair had become unsafe and was ready to collapse, presumably it would have collapsed whichever member of staff had happened to sit on it: so then why did it have to be Mr Unwin of all people, the teacher who already had a reputation from klutziness? Why did it have to be him who sat down on that chair at that moment? Was it blind chance, or had it been predestined? It had seemed more like the latter at the time.

They'd felt superior to their teachers, of course. That goes without saying. The fact that the teachers were the older and wiser ones, imparting their superior knowledge to their pupils, had meant nothing. They still always felt that in other and much more important ways, they were still smarter than their teachers. The teachers' personality quirks, their vanities, their politics, their sexuality, their affairs with one another: all of these were inexhaustible subjects of schoolyard gossip.

For Mark and his misfit group of friends, their usual meeting place during lunch break—when the weather was nice, anyway— had been an out of the way patch of grass behind the tennis courts. They would all be there, himself, Rachel Farrow, Clyde Waring, pungent Dennis Shrimpton, sarcastic David Randall, and the others, all boys apart from Rachel: there they would sit, eat their packed lunches, listen to indie music on walkmans, read *2000AD*, or gossip about TV programmes, like last night's *Doctor Who* episode, or repeats of *Mission: Impossible* and *Lost in Space*.

Mark is drawn from his reverie by the sound of a car pulling up at the curb behind him. He turns and sees that it is a police car; the driver's door opens and out steps radiant Sergeant Mavis Shagwell.

'Hello, there,' she says, treating him to her generous smile. 'Loitering outside the school gates, are we?'

'I've picked the wrong time of year for that, haven't I?' replies Mark. 'No, I'm just reliving old memories; I used to go to this place.'

'Did you? So you come from Market Stanford?'

'Born and bred. What about yourself? You don't sound local.'

'Yeah, I'm from Manchester originally,' says Mavis. 'You know they're closing down the crime-scene at Vernon Wood?'

'Yes, I know that.'

'Do you know who killed those people?'

'I have my suspicions.'

A questioning look. 'You're not going to say they were killed by aliens, are you?'

'Well… I haven't dismissed the possibility.'

122

'Gossip at the station says that it was your lot that did it.'
Mavis delivers this challenge with a smile.

'And do you believe that?'

A shrug. 'Well, you do seem like you want to hush it all up.'

'That's because I think this affair is more my business than
police business,' says Mark. 'But no, "my lot" didn't kill those
youngsters.'

'Back to the aliens, then,' says Mavis. 'Shouldn't you be there,
now? You know, investigating.'

'I *should* be. But I needed time to think, and I thought I'd do
that thinking while taking a nostalgic walk around the town…
And while I'm on the subject: when we were kids, there was this
empty old house on Fern Lane. We used to say it was haunted. Is
it still there, or have they knocked it down?'

'Fern House? Yes, it's still there.'

'And still uninhabited?'

'Yeah. I've no idea who owns the place. It must belong to
someone… Were you planning on having a look at the place?'

'Yes.'

'I can give you a lift there, if you like.'

'No, but thanks all the same. I'm enjoying the walk.'

'Right you are. Well, I'll see you around, then.'

'See you.'

Mavis climbs back into her squad car and drives away.

Mark sets off. Nice girl, our Sergeant Shagwell, he muses.
Good-natured; lovely smile… He idly wonders if Mavis does
indeed 'shag well.' Not that he has any real interest in finding out
for himself, but our minds do wander…

Memories. Every street, almost every house has them. Some of
the things he sees make him think of secondary school years;
some recall to him events from primary school life. Primary
school and secondary school: for most people, the memories of
the two are distinct; the two phases of childhood. For Mark, this is
even more true than it is for most. That summer, that stopping-
point between one life and the other, had been the summer of his
sentimental education. He had lost something, gained a lot more,
and had entered his secondary school almost a different person.
Innocence had been abandoned; he had become more

contemplative, more conscious of the world around him. In some ways he learned more in that summer than he ever learned at school; many of the habits that make him what he is, had been acquired then.

Fern Road. Yes, there's the timber yard on the corner, just as it was all those years ago. Semi-detached bungalows on the right. And here, just past the timber yard, is Fern House. Mark pauses at the front gate. Everything looks just as he remembers it: standing in overgrown gardens, a sombre grey mass; windows like eye-sockets, green paint peeling from the frames, from the front door. Gables, chimneys, slate roof… It has that look about it: old, neglected; a building with an unknown past; a building full of secrets…

Right now, Mark really feels like he has stepped into the past. He remembers… He remembers standing here as a boy, with his friend Clyde Waring at his side, looking at this house with trepidation, but also with a burning curiosity…

Chapter Sixteen
Endless Summers: Scene Two

They have been watching *Tarzan* round Clyde's house.

They're showing it every morning during the summer holidays this year. Tarzan is played by an actor called Ron Ely, which Mark and Clyde think is funny because 'Ely' is the name of a town not far from Market Stanford. The great thing about *Tarzan* is that until it starts you never know which theme tune you're going to get. Mark and Clyde prefer the more dramatic sounding one, which is actually that of the second season episodes. Last week, the boys were completely thrown when they saw an episode with yet *another* different theme tune! To add to the confusion, in this one the boy sidekick Jai had been wearing trousers and a t-shirt instead of wearing a loin-cloth like Tarzan. What they'd actually seen here was one of the earliest episodes when they had quite settled on the show's format, and Jai lived at the local settlement instead of being Tarzan's full-time sidekick.

The two friends are now on an expedition to Fern House. They have been meaning to investigate this famous Market Stanford location for some time. At least, Mark has been meaning to; Clyde has never been so keen on the project. Two summers have passed since that encounter with Dunnidge in the spinney when they were playing *Blake's 7*. The boys are growing taller, and they don't wear shorts anymore, even when it's hot like it is today; they consider themselves too big to be wearing shorts now, except for PE at school.

And now they are standing before Fern House. And it does look pretty much the same as it looks to the adult Mark Hunter, whom we just left standing on the same spot thirty years hence. Fern House has a reputation for being haunted. One story has it that a nasty old man used to live in the house, and that it's his ghost that still walks the place at night, glaring out of the windows at anyone who happens to pass by. Even Mark's big sister says she once saw a face in an upstairs window when she and her mates were walking past the place after dark. Dad said it was probably just a tramp.

But even if there is a ghost, it's well known that ghosts only come out at night; and anyway, it isn't the house itself that the boys are interested in checking out. Behind the house, in the overgrown back garden, there is—according to another local legend—a well. And this this well, so the story goes, you can climb into, because it has a ladder running down the side; and if you climb all the way down to the bottom you come to an underground stream! And there's supposed to be a small rowing boat there; and if you get into the boat and row down the underground stream, it takes you all the way to the river!

So the story goes, and Mark has long wanted to find out if it's true. Mark and Clyde, in their bucolic wanderings, have never been able to find that legendary field with the train carriage in it; so maybe they will have more luck with the well.

Mark turns to Clyde. 'Want to go in, then?'

Clyde pulls a face. 'Can't we do something else?'

'But what about the underground river? Don't you want to see it?'

'We'll get in trouble,' says Clyde. 'It's private; the owner

125

might come along.'

'They *won't* come along.'

Clyde points to the bungalows across the street. 'Someone might see us go in and call the police.'

'No, they won't,' says Mark. 'Look—if we get caught by someone, I'll say it was all my idea, then you won't get in any trouble. They'll only tell off me.'

'I dunno…'

'Oh, come on! Don't be chicken!'

'Alright,' agrees Clyde reluctantly. 'But you go first.'

'Of course I'll go first!'

With a final look around to make sure the coast is clear, the boys duck through the gateway into the overgrown front garden. They follow the pathway up to the front door of the house, both boys keyed-up and excited; they know they're doing something they shouldn't!

'Where's the well, then?' asks Clyde.

'It's supposed to be round the back. Come on.'

Skirting the angle of the house, they find themselves in the back garden, even more overgrown than the front, with grass and weeds running wild, and thickets of brambles taller than the two boys.

'I can't see any well,' says Clyde. 'It was probably just a made-up story. Let's go.'

'We haven't looked properly yet,' responds Mark. 'I bet it's hidden somewhere.'

Mark takes the lead, wading through the grass away from the house, Clyde following reluctantly.

It's like the jungle in *Tarzan*. They follow a twisting path, avoiding the brambles and stinging nettles—and then, they find it! Behind a wall of brambles, almost under the shadow of the back wall: a well; indisputably a well. A circular brick parapet, about three feet high; two wooden posts supporting a metal windlass, a handle at one end. Of the rope and bucket this windlass would have raised and lowered, there is no sign.

'We found it!' cries Mark, jubilant.

The boys peer over the rim of the well. The circular shaft soon loses itself in inky darkness, but they see can a row of metal rungs nailed to the brickwork at intervals; the story of the ladder is true.

'See!' says Mark triumphantly. 'You can get down it! There's a ladder.'

'I don't like it,' says Clyde. 'What if we go down there and can't get back up again?'

''Course we can get back up,' says Mark. 'Anyway, there's the boat down there; we can just get in the boat and come out the other end, on the river.'

'How far down does it go?' asks Clyde. 'It looks like it's miles.'

Mark picks up a fallen wedge of brick fallen from the crumbling parapet of the well, and he drops it into the well. From far below, they hear the sound of a sharp, dry impact.

'Why didn't it splash?' demands Clyde.

'Maybe it landed in the boat. Shall we go down, then?'

'Don't wanna,' says Clyde. 'It's stupid.'

Mark looks at his friend; the boy pouting and sullen, stares down into the well.

Mark relents. 'Alright,' he sighs. 'Let's explore the house instead. How about that?'

Clyde looks relieved. 'It might be locked up.'

'If it's not locked, we'll explore it.'

They make their way back to the house. Mark tries the back door. It opens.

'It's open! We can go in.'

'What if the owner comes along?'

'I told you: he won't.'

'What if there's a ghost in there?'

'Ghosts only come out at night, silly. Come on; let's explore. We can be the Three Investigators.'

'There's only two of us.'

'Alright; we'll be the Hardy Boys. I'll be Frank, you be Joe.'

They step inside. They are in a large kitchen. In the dim light filtering through the dirty windows they see cupboards, dressers, a large sink, a central wooden table, a rusty, ancient hob. The room is festooned with cobwebs, the air musty and mildewed.

'Look at it. No-one's been here for centuries,' declares Mark. 'Come on. Let's see what's through that door.'

They cross the kitchen, open the door and find themselves in the main hallway. For the first time the boys find themselves looking from the inside at that front door they've always seen whenever they walked past the house. A staircase with a banister ascends to the second floor.

'Stairs!' cries Mark. 'Let's explore upstairs.'

'Can't we just explore down here?'

'Nah. Upstairs is better.'

Mark puts a foot on the bottom step. It creaks.

'They might be rotten,' says Clyde.

'They're alright. I'll go first.'

He climbs the creaking staircase. At the top he turns and looks down at Clyde.

'See? Easy! Come on.'

Clyde tentatively starts to climb.

'It don't feel too safe.'

'Don't be a scaredy!'

Clyde ascends and joins Mark on the landing.

'Let's see what's in the rooms.'

The first two rooms prove to be empty, just walls with peeling paper and bare floorboards. The third door they come to is a lot smaller. It looks like a cupboard door, but when Marks opens it: stairs! A steep, narrow flight climbing up into the darkness.

'I bet these go up to the attic!' cries Mark. 'Let's go'n see.'

The boys climb the narrow staircase. At the top is another door; Mark opens it and they emerge into a vast open space, wooden floored, and with steepled walls. Autumnal light creeps in through dirt-encrusted dormer windows.

And there, at the far end of the attic, sits the only object in the room: a large, brass-bound wooden chest.

Treasure!

The boys make a bee-line for the chest, across the creaking floorboards. They kneel down before their prize, brushing aside the cobwebs draped over it.

'What's in it?' wonders Clyde. 'Treasure?'

'Won't be pirate treasure,' Mark tells him. 'Pirates bury their treasure in the ground, not in attics.'

'Is it locked?'

'Not sure.' After a brief inspection, Mark flips the two rusty hasps that secure the lid, and lifts. 'Blimey, It's heavy! Give us a hand.'

The boys stand up, and with their combined strength they lift the lid. A strong musty smell assails the two youngsters. Down on their knees again they peer eagerly inside in the chest. No pirate treasure, but the chest is full to the brim with bric-a-brac, all of it looking very old. The first thing they see is a tommy's metal helmet.

'A soldier's hat!'

Mark picks up the helmet, puts it on his head. It comes down over his eyes. Both boys laugh.

'Let's have a go!'

Mark transfers the helmet to Clyde's head. Same result!

'What war is it from?' asks Clyde, inspecting the helmet.

'Not sure,' admits Mark.

They turn their attention back to the chest, and start pulling out an assortment of metal objects, examining them curiously. Some of the items are recognisable to the boys: candlesticks, fire irons… Others are more mysterious.

'What's this?' asks Clyde, holding up a curious shaped object made of brass: a flat wedge-shaped implement with a long handle.

'Looks like a trowel or something,' says Mark, scrutinising it. 'I know! Maybe it goes with the soldier's helmet; maybe it's what they used to dig trenches with.'

Young Mark is at fault in his hypothesis here: shoe horns were never used by soldiers as trench-digging tools.

'There's books under here,' announces Mark, pushing aside more of the antique brass appliances. He extracts a large, heavy volume, bound in tooled red leather, and sealed with a rust-speckled metal clasp.

'Why's the book got a lock on it?' wonders Clyde, running his fingers over the elaborate pattern worked into the leather.

'Must be something secret,' says Mark. 'Maybe a diary.'

'A diary!' laughs Clyde. 'It's too big for a diary!' (Clyde always makes the most of these rare occasions when he thinks he has one up on Mark.)

'Yeah, but it might be like an explorer's diary or something,' argues Mark. 'Explorers had bigger diaries cuz they had a lot more to write about.'

'Let's look inside. Can you open it?'

'No. Look, there's this little keyhole; you need the key to open it. Hang on...' He examines the leather strap of the clasp, probing with a finger. Frayed with age, the strap gives way.

'Whoops!'

'Open it! Open it!' cries Clyde eagerly.

Resting the heavy tome against the lip of the open chest, Mark opens to the first page.

The boys immediately see that this is no explorer's journal; no quill-written text, telling tales of danger and discovery. Instead, what they see before them is a sepia print of three Victorian women. Standing with their backs to the camera, they lean forward in a huddle, shifts drawn over their hips, exposing three pairs of ripe, naked posteriors.

A stunned silence

'Wow...' says Clyde. 'That's rude, that is.'

'Yeah...'

'Naked women.'

'Yeah...'

'Is there any more?'

There certainly is—page after page of it. Ladies posing in chambers with ornately patterned walls and carpets; reclining on chairs and settees with carved woodwork; admiring themselves in full-length mirrors; women in shifts, in dresses with skirts lifted, in corsets and bloomers, in boots and stockings, and entirely nude. Breasts and pubic hair are visible in some of the images, but the emphasis is firmly on buttocks. Page after page. The boys' eyes eagerly devoir these monochrome and sepia images of Victorian-Edwardian erotica.

I strongly suspect this of being a defining moment in the life of Mark Hunter. I say this because, as Trina Trulove can attest, Mark is decidedly in the 'A' camp when it comes to the 'T and A' debate; and I cannot help but think that the sight of these pictures, burning themselves onto his impressionable nine-year-old retinas, was the original cause of this preference of his; the starting point, the prime motivator. (And younger readers need to bear in mind that Mark and Clyde as kids, belonged to a generation which did not have the benefit of the internet which in these days enables youngsters to familiarise themselves with the concept of pornography at a suitably early age; and so, what they seeing was a real eye-opener for the two boys. Of course they knew of the existence of those magazines occupying the top shelves in the newsagents, but those shelves being out of reach, they had never seen the inside of those publications.)

'Why have they got all that hair down there?' wonders Clyde.

'That's normal for grown-ups,' replies Mark. (Mark is actually in the early stages of acquiring this lower-body adornment himself; but as, judging by his puzzlement, his friend obviously *hasn't* reached that stage, he keeps quiet about this.)

'This is like those girlie magazines in the shops, isn't it?'

'Yeah, except older.'

'Are any of the other books like this?' asks Clyde.

Alas, the boys are doomed never to find out. They hear a sound below them; a heavy thump.

'What was that?' cries Clyde.

'Shh!' hisses Mark. 'There's someone downstairs!'

Floorboards creak as footsteps ascend the main staircase.

'They're coming up the stairs!'

'It must be the owner!' whispers Clyde. 'You said he wouldn't come here! He'll see we've been looking at this rude book! He'll tell our Mum and Dads!'

'Keep quiet, stupid! He probably doesn't even know we're up here, so keep quiet!'

'What if he comes up here?'

'Why should he?'

Even as he says this, Mark recalls that left the door to the attic stairs open...

The footsteps are now on the landing directly below them. Will the intruder, seeing the door to the attic stairs open, work out that someone is up here?

The footsteps stop.

The boys hold their breath.

And then they resume. The intruder is coming up the attic stairs! The footsteps sound loud and heavy on the squeaking treads.

Clyde quakes with fear. Mark, on the edge of panic himself, realises that their only chance is to conceal themselves where they are, with the open trunk between themselves and the attic door.

'Keep down and don't move!' he hisses to Clyde

The boys huddle themselves behind the trunk. And now they hear the intruder step out onto the floorboards of the attic. And then silence. They must be looking round the room, whoever it is, Mark surmises. And the lid of the chest is up! If they know that it should be closed, they'll come over to investigate!

The footsteps, now walking with slow, measured tread, start to cross the attic floor. Mark can actually *feel* the footsteps now as they depress the floorboards, feel them as they move steadily closer and closer. And then they stop. Mark has eyes squeezed shut. The intruder must be only a few feet away now. He can feel Clyde trembling beside him. Any minute now his friend is going to lose his bottle and run out screaming.

The footsteps resume—but they've turned! They're moving away! Back across the attic floorboards. And then the squeaking of the stair treads as the footsteps recede.

Silence.

Mark climbs slowly to his feet. The coast is clear.

'He's gone,' breathes Mark. 'Come on!'

Clyde stands up, still wide-eyed with fright.

'Who was it? Did you see?'

'No, I didn't look. Come on, let's get out now. We'll sneak down to the landing, and if the coast is clear we run for it.'

'Run for it?'

'Yeah. Down the stairs and out through the kitchen.'

'Won't it be better if we wait till they've properly gone?'

'No, cuz they might come back up here again. Let's escape while we can. Come on and let's walk quietly.'

Treading carefully, the boys cross the attic to the stairwell. They stop beside the door and Mark cautiously peers round the frame—and sees a pair of eyes glaring up at him; eyes in a face with a bulbous nose and surrounded by wild hair.

It's the miscreant Dunnidge! Mark springs away from the door, dragging Clyde with him.

132

Dunnidge bounds up the stairs and stands blocking the doorway with his hulking form, smiling grimly at the success of his ploy.

'I knew there was someone in 'ere,' he says. 'So it's you two, is it? What you brats think yer doin' 'ere?'

'None of your business!' replies Mark, bravely.

'Don't you answer me back!' snaps Dunnidge.

'You haven't got any more right than us to be here!' declares Mark. 'You're not the owner!'

'Oh, int I, now?' says Dunnidge. 'Well, thas as maybe… Bet no-one knows you two are 'ere, do they? No-one's gunna come lookin' for yer in this place, are they?'

'Yes, they will!' retorts Mark. 'We told our mums and dads we were coming here!'

'Don't gimme that! Yer mums an' dads wouldn't 'a let you come 'ere! They'd tell yer it was private property. Yeah, so don't tell porkies—no-one knows yer 'ere… If I was ter lock you up in a cupboard or somethin,' lock you in so's yer couldn't get out, there'd be no-one oo'd know where yer was; no-one to come an' rescue yer. I reckon you'd be stuck there until yer starved to death.' He chuckles. 'Yeah, thas a good idea, that is. Now c'mere!'

He bounds forward, arms outstretched to grab the boys. Impelled by fear, Mark and Clyde react like lightning; they swerve round him, one either side, while Dunnidge flails his arms, trying to grab both boys at the same time. And then they are past him, and barrelling down the stairs—but Dunnidge is in hot pursuit!

'C'mere yer little brats! You int gettin' away!'

Out onto the landing the boys run, and straight down the main staircase. Dunnidge thunders after them in his heavy boots. The boy's make it to the foot of the staircase, as Dunnidge reaches the top. But then comes a rending, tearing sound, a bellow of startled rage from Dunnidge, followed by a heavy crash. The stairs have caved in under him! A cloud of dust rises up from the splintered hole in the staircase.

Mark and Clyde do not stick around to inquire after their tormentor's health. They are out the back door, round the side of the house and out into the street in no time! And they don't stop there. They run and they keep on running until they've put several streets between themselves and the precincts of Fern House.

Finally, exhausted, they come a stop. Panting, they exchange looks.

Says Clyde to Mark: 'I told you those stairs were rotten!'

Chapter Seventeen
The Secret of the Old Well

Wading through the undergrowth of the long-neglected back garden of Fern House, Mark reaches the site of the well. It still stands, but is now much more inaccessible than it was thirty years ago; in fact, it has become almost overwhelmed by the unchecked vegetation.

After that encounter with Dunnidge, the young Mark and Clyde had never come back to Fern House. Not even in his teenage years, had Mark returned to check out the well. He can't remember why; perhaps as he had got older, he had ceased to believe in that story of the boat and the underground river.

And yes, it *does* sound rather far-fetched; there's no denying it. A rural legend. Apart from anything else, if it existed, the confluence of this subterranean stream with the river would have been clearly visible to all the world; there would have to have been some sort of tunnel emerging from the riverbank. Mark had walked up and down that riverbank countless times in his childhood, and he had never seen any such tunnel. But then, he recalls there was one inaccessible part of the riverbank, one spot where trees and brambles came all the way down to the river's edge. Perhaps the tunnel entrance, if it exists, lies there, concealed by the vegetation.

Either way, Mark Hunter, having returned to Market Stanford after all these years, has remembered that well and his childhood desire to explore it, and he's decided that it's high time he settled this unfinished item of business.

Standing at the parapet, Mark extracts from his jacket pocket a pencil torch he has brought with him on purpose. He smiles when recalls that neither himself nor Clyde had thought of bringing a torch with them when they had planned to go down the well, all those years ago. It wasn't an oversight as such; it just hadn't occurred to the boys that they would need a torch; film and television having accustomed them to the sight of underground tunnels and caves in which there was always plenty of light to see where you were going.

Mark shines the torch down the shaft of the well. Yes, those metal rungs bolted to the wall are still there; the fact that they are even there is itself significant. Well-shafts don't normally have access ladders; they don't need them. The fact this one does, suggests that there is something down there.

He'd thrown a piece of brick down there when he was a kid, and it had hit a hard surface. Mark rummages in his pocket for a coin, and now repeats the experiment, dropping it down the shaft. The sound of it meeting a hard surface echoes back up the shaft. When they were kids, they thought it might have landed in the fabled boat, but the sound he hears is that of the coin coming into contact with something much more solid than wood.

Climbing onto the parapet, Mark swings a leg over the edge, and finds the first rung of the ladder with his foot. He starts to descend. The metal rungs are rusty with age, and some of them feel loose, but he is undeterred. Down, down, he climbs; darkness enfolding him as the circle of daylight above him diminishes. The temperature drops noticeably.

Finally, his foot finds solid ground. He alights from the ladder, takes out his torch and switches it on.

He is standing on a concrete ledge; or rather a jetty, for beyond it lies a body water. The light from the torch catches sparks from the slow rippling movement of its inky surface. And there, right before him is a small boat; secured by a painter tied to an iron ring, it rocks gently against the landing stage. Yes, there it is: the rowing boat that according to legend will take you along the subterranean stream and all the way to its hidden confluence with the river.

Mark stands motionless, smiling, both stunned and elated; scarcely able to believe what he sees before his eyes. He feels like he has stepped into not just the world of his childhood memories, but into the world of his childhood dreams.

The tableau is perfectly arranged: the concrete ledge at the foot of the well-shaft; the dark, quietly rippling water; the glistening brickwork of the culvert; the boat with its two plank seats and two wooden paddles... Everything is as it should be. It seems impossible, yet here it is...

Recovering, and now eager to explore, he crosses to the edge of the concrete landing stage, and shines his torch all around the chamber, over the dark, glistening brickwork. This is clearly the terminus of the culvert; on his immediate left, just beyond the well-shaft, rises a solid brick wall. But on his right, the watercourse extends along a tunnel that stretches away beyond the radius of his torchlight...

And it's in the right direction, realises Mark. That tunnel, as far as he can judge, if it progresses in a more or less straight course, would finally meet up with the River Ouse! The old legend appears to be true in every last detail. Here is the underground watercourse at the bottom of the well that leads to the river, and here also is the boat that will take you there.

But wait a minute. If this stream *is* connected to the river, then whenever the river becomes swollen with rainwater, the water level in the culvert would have to rise accordingly. The jetty on which he stands is only a couple of feet above the level of the water right at this moment; any significant increase and it would become submerged... Mark directs his torch across the surface of the opposite wall... Yes! There's a clear tidemark about five feet above the current water level; the brickwork being darker below this line, and marked with growths of algae...

As a child Mark had never doubted for one minute the story of the boat and the underground stream at the bottom of the well; and now, thirty years later, he has finally made it to the bottom of the well—and it feels as though the place has been waiting for him all this time; that reality has mapped itself over his childhood expectations.

He turns his attention to the boat, shining his light into it. The craft looks just as his juvenile imagination had pictured it: an old clinker-planked rowing boat, unpainted, with two plank seats, a pair of oars lying on the floor between them. The vessel's bow is pointed towards the end of the tunnel. How long has it been here? How long since it was last used?

It looks very old. Will it even take his weight?

He steps into the boat. The planks feel damp, but the hull takes his weight, and no water starts to seep through between the planks, so the craft is still watertight. He sits himself down on the rear seat.

There's only one thing he can do, of course. He has to cast off and row the boat down that tunnel to see where it will take him; to find if the rest of the story is true. To just climb back out of the well now that he has progressed this far would be ludicrous. He'd spend the rest of his life wondering if he doesn't see this through to the end, now he has the chance.

And then something else catches Mark's eye. Hanging from a rusty iron hook in the wall is a lantern; a genuine, old-fashioned hurricane lamp, a relic conjured up from juvenile tales of ghosts and smugglers. He'd hadn't seen it because he'd been standing with his back to it before. Mark climbs back out onto the landing and lifts the lamp from its hook. The metal is rusty, the glass cage filthy, but he hears the movement of liquid inside; there is still oil in the font. And the lamp's resting place is safely above the high-water mark, so it won't have been submerged whenever the water level rose.

Will it really still work?

Mark opens the little door in the glass globe. Yes, the wick is still there. He takes his lighter from his pocket and applies the flame to the wick. It ignites!

Mark cleans up the glass surface as best he can. The lantern emits a flickering orange light, weak in its radius compared to his torch; but it's still just what he needed. Unless he wants to row down that tunnel in pitch darkness, he will need a light in the boat with him, and with both hands being employed with the oars, his torch wouldn't have been of much use to him; if he set it down on the front bench, it would just roll all over the place; the only other alternatives would have been to hold the thing between his teeth or clamped awkwardly between his knees. The hurricane lamp, with its firm flat base, is just the ticket.

Extinguishing and pocketing his torch, Mark climbs back into the boat, and sets the lamp down on the bench before him. He reaches over to untie the painter from the iron ring; the rope, rotten with age and damp, breaks off, and all but crumbles to pieces in his hand.

Throwing what is left of the painter into the bottom of the boat, he picks up the two sculls. The rowlocks fixed to the gunwales are rusty but still serviceable. He slips the oars into the grooves, and pushes the boat away from the stone pier.

Mark now turns the boat's bow to face the tunnel, the width of the stream providing ample room to perform this manoeuvre. And now he sets off, sculling through the stream at a slow but steady pace. The walls and ceiling of the culvert, which runs dead-straight, maintain their dimensions as Mark proceeds. The water laps against the walls on both sides; there is no ledge or shelf for foot passengers. The air down here is cool and moisture-laden, refreshingly so after the baking heat above.

Is it exactly thirty years? wonders Mark. When he and Clyde had stood looking down into the well, had it been exactly thirty years ago? It might have been... Perhaps a year or two more; maybe when they were eight or nine... And what would have happened if they *had* gone down the well that day? What if Clyde hadn't been too scared, or if Mark had talked him into overcoming his apprehensions? What would have happened? Well, first of all they would have found themselves in pitch darkness, and as they wouldn't have been able to light the lamp, they would have to have gone back to the surface to procure themselves a torch. But then... would they have found the rowing boat tied to the jetty back then? It seems likely. From the rotted condition of the painter, it seems fairly certain that the boat has been there for a very long time. No-one has been down here for decades... So, Clyde and himself would have found the boat down here; perhaps, with their youthful belief in local legends, they would have been less surprised than the adult Mark to find that the boat and the stream actually existed... But would they have been able to pilot the boat? Eight, nine, or ten, neither of the boys would have had much experience of rowing or canoeing, and the oars are heavy... But then, if the boys had taken an oar

138

each, they might have been able to propel the craft forward…

As to where they would have ended up, Mark has still yet to find out. Will he emerge onto the river? The confluence point must be well-hidden not to be widely known. Perhaps, at the end of the channel, he will find the exit so thick with brambles and other vegetation that he will be unable to pass through it. All things considered this possibility seems a very strong one. No-one has used this watercourse for a very long time; no-one has been around to keep the exit point free from obstructions.

And this brings Mark to the next burning question: What is this place *for*? Was it ever a simple well for supplying Fern House with drinking water that was adapted at some point, converted into an underground harbour? Or, was there always only this subterranean watercourse, and the well a blind; just a clever disguise for the entrance to the culvert? But then, *why* was it built? For what purpose? Why had the inhabitants of Fern House needed this concealed line of communication with the river? The obvious answer is smuggling. Smuggling goods was a lucrative trade back in the eighteenth century, and underground channels and storehouses were required for these activities. The River Ouse meets the North Sea not more than thirty miles from Market Stanford, and nearby King's Lynn was a thriving river port back then… Yes, smuggling could well have been the original purpose for this elaborate set-up…

He has been rowing steadily for some time, with nothing but the culvert walls and the watercourse receding before him in the radius of light from the hurricane lamp, when an obstruction appears ahead. Thrown into relief by the light of the lamp, he sees a grille composed of vertical iron bars, reinforced at intervals with crossbars, completely blocking the tunnel ahead. And in addition to this, just before the grille, and on Mark's left, the dark oblong of a large aperture in the culvert wall; a doorway. Mark pulls in the oars and allows the boat to drift towards the barrier. When the prow of the boat nudges the bars, Mark grabs hold of one of one and pulls the vessel alongside. Facing the doorway now, the light reveals a short flight of steps ascending from water level to a second open doorway. What lies beyond this doorway cannot be seen.

Mark now turns his attention to the barrier, the bars of which, upon inspection, prove to be rusty but firm; and it soon becomes evident that the grille is a solid, immovable barrier; it cannot be swung open or raised to allow passage beyond it...

This is it, then. The bars are placed just too close together for an adult man to squeeze himself through them. But perhaps, beneath the surface of the water, the bars don't extend all the way to the ground; but even to determine this, Mark would have to get into the water, and if discovers that there is a way through, he would have to swim the remainder of the culvert, and it would be a nude swimming expedition, as he did not think to bring any trunks with him...

but once again, that would involve a swimming expedition if he wants to round off this unfinished adventure from his childhood. Does he want to do this? A voice inside Mark immediately answers 'Yes!' to this question; but then, a second voice, more observant of proprieties, reminds him that he hasn't brought any swimming trunks with him, and therefore it would have to be a nude swimming expedition...

The more reasonable choice would be to remain on dry land and see first what lies beyond that doorway. Perhaps it will take him to another exit from this place. But even so... He can't help but feel disappointed that the culvert is blocked and that he can't follow the tunnel all the way to the end and discover whether the last part of the legend is true, and that it will bring him out onto the river...

Who put this barrier here? And why?

Oh, well. Let's have a look at this doorway.

Gripping the bars of the grille to propel him, Mark brings the boat to the foot of the stairs. There's an iron ring bolted to the wall beside the doorway, and so convenient for securing the boat that it surely must have been put here for that purpose... But the painter is rotten and part of it broke off when he untied it from the jetty. Is there even enough of it left to reach?

Mark picks up the frayed coil of rope—and the question becomes redundant when he discovers that the rope has parted from the ring securing it to the keel of the boat. Then the boat will just have to take its chances.

Picking up the hurricane lamp, Mark steps carefully from the boat onto the lowest step. Impelled by this movement, the boat immediately starts to drift away from the steps, towards the other side of the culvert. Oh, well. If there isn't another way out up here, he'll have no choice but go skinny-dipping now, even if it's only to retrieve the boat…

He climbs the steps. Standing in the doorway, he raises the hurricane lamp: it's a tunnel; a narrow, brick-built corridor stretching away before him as far as the eye can see, losing itself in darkness. It occurs to Mark that now he has both hands free, he can dispense with the lantern and use his torch. He gets out the torch and switches it on; and then, opening the glass globe of the hurricane lamp, he extinguishes the flame with a puff of breath and sets it down on the floor.

The pencil torch now lighting his way, Mark proceeds along the passage. The brickwork is uninterrupted on both sides; no apertures or doorways present themselves. He directs the beam of light at the ceiling. The tunnel roof is lower than that of the culvert; solid masonry and festooned with cobwebs. The ground beneath his feet is carpeted with the crumbling detritus of years innumerable. Away from the watercourse, the air, though still cold, becomes less damp, and heavy with the odour of mould and mildew.

How does this passage fit into the smuggling set-up? From the age of the brickwork it is clear that it was constructed at the same time as the culvert; it is not a later addition. Perhaps an escape route? Yes, that could be it—the smugglers may have built this passage as an escape route in case they ever found themselves boxed in, with excise men waiting at both ends of the underground stream. This seems a sound theory, and one that supports his hope that there will be another way back up to the surface at the end of the tunnel.

Mark's torch now picks out an object in his path ahead. A low mound, thickly shrouded with cobwebs and other detritus, it resembles more than anything a giant cocoon. Mark stops, shining his torch over the object from end to end; its dimensions make an immediate connection in his mind. With a grim prediction of what he's going to find, he hunkers down and starts to pull away the cobwebbing. Suddenly the whole thing comes alive! A writhing black stream spews out of the disturbed mound, and Mark falls backwards with a yelp of horror. Then he realises what the black stream is: spiders. Hundreds of spiders, fleeing precipitately from Mark's attack on their domain.

Finally, the stream subsides, the arachnid exodus is over; and Mark resumes his task. The webbing clings to his fingers as he pulls it away, and dust hangs heavy in the air. And then his hands encounter something solid. Shining the torch on the object, he sees what he was more than half expecting to see: a hemisphere of yellow bone; two blank eye-sockets.

The skull of a human skeleton.

Mark tears away the remainder of the webbing, and now the entire skeleton is revealed. They are the remains of an adult, very tall, lying at full length on its front, the skull turned sideways. The barest scraps of what was once clothing cling to some parts of the skeleton; nothing tangible enough to identify.

Mark pauses to contemplate the sight.

'So, who were you, my friend? How did you end up dying down here in this tunnel? And how long have you been here? Decades? Centuries? You didn't die any time recently, that's for sure. And you're tall; I can see that much. Well over six feet. That would mean you were most likely a man... Well, that at least is something I can confirm; let's have a look at your pelvis. Pardon the intrusion.'

Mark clears away more of the cobwebbing from the skeleton's pelvis. Ah yes, as he has surmised: the bones are those of a man. And he notices something else: glimmering in the torchlight, metal discs, strewn over the ground close to the skeleton's mid-section.

Coins! They must have been in the fellow's pockets; and they ended up on the floor when those pockets disintegrated, along with the rest of his clothing. Let's see...

He picks up a coin, directing the light of his pencil torch on its surface. A small, copper coin, encrusted with rust and detritus. Holding the torch between his teeth, he uses a fingernail to remove some of the muck. A penny piece... No, a ha'penny! A decimal half-penny piece.

'Now that narrows it down. The new half penny coin was introduced in 1971 along with the rest of the decimal system; and it was taken out of circulation in… let me see, when was it…? 1984! Yes: 1984! So, my friend, you have to have met your demise sometime between those two dates… But who were you? What were you doing down here?

'And what happened to you? What did you die here? Or were you *put* here? Did you meet with foul play?'

Mark examines the skeleton for signs of injury, and soon finds them; a broken leg; a shattered kneecap; fractured arm; broken collar bone; a couple of broken ribs.

'Well, *something* certainly happened to you. You're busted all over… You could have met with foul play, but your injuries are more consistent with a severe fall. But then how could you have ended up here…?'

He trains the light of his pencil torch on the ceiling. Solid masonry; no sign of a trapdoor.

Mark now makes a thorough search of the ground around the skeleton, in the hope of finding more clues to the man's identity. He finds nothing, just some crumbling pieces of leather around the feet, the remains of the leather uppers of boots or shoes.

No later than 1984… If Clyde and himself had actually gone down the well back then and taken this underground journey, they might have stumbled upon this man's fresh corpse; or, if there had been foul play down here, maybe even his killers. All things considered, perhaps it was just as well they hadn't gone down the well that day…

But now, to business, thinks Mark. I can't just leave this body lying here. I need to tell the local fuzz about this one. This will brighten up Mavis's day. But to do that, I need to find my way out of here, ideally a way that doesn't involve swimming. By all rights there must be a way of out here up ahead.

Mark brushes the dust from his hands and his knees, gets up and continues his way along the subterranean passage.

The tunnel finally comes to an end with another open doorway. Passing through this, Mark finds himself in a large, square, high-ceilinged chamber. The air is noticeably warmer now. This room is clearly of much more recent origin than the tunnel he has just emerged from; the walls are of smooth concrete. Mark's immediate impression is that he is in a bunker; and it looks like someone has been using it as a miniature warehouse or storeroom. Crates and boxes and junk of all sorts are piled everywhere; all of it festooned with curtains of cobwebs, for all the world like furniture under dust-covers. Mark runs the beam of his torch over the collection; amongst the junk he sees cathode-ray television sets, briefcase record players, cassette recorders; vacuum cleaners, lawn-mowers and gardening equipment; and just about every other portable household commodity from table lamps to electric toasters. Everything here looks to be of no later than 1970s or 1980s vintage; and equally it all looks to have been left undisturbed since that time—just like that poor unfortunate in the passageway.

If I had to guess, I'd say this bunker must have been built during the Second World War, probably for military, rather than civilian use. Whether by accident or design, they must have excavated their bunker over the original exit to the underground passageway; and they must have decided to incorporate the earlier construction into their bunker, leaving access to the passageway and watercourse to use as an escape route. Perhaps it was also these people who had fixed that grille across the culvert... But why would they want to limit their number of escape routes...? Unless they thought that the river exit was the one more likely to be discovered by enemy invaders...

Mark's torch lights on a metal ladder stapled to the far wall, and which disappears into a circular shaft in the ceiling. Crossing over to the foot of the ladder, he directs his light upwards, and discerns a riveted hatch-cover at the summit of the shaft.

The way out.

Forced to extinguish and pocket his torch and plunging the chamber into darkness, Mark climbs the ladder. Coming to the underside of the hatch cover, he attempts to raise it, but to no avail—it seems to be locked fast. His exploring hand locate a locking wheel. He takes hold of it, and the wheel, petrified from long disuse, turns slowly and reluctantly. Finally, and after much effort on Mark's part, there comes the satisfying click of a mechanism turning. Now able to move the hatch, Mark lifts and

144

pushes it back to its full extent.

The sudden daylight dazzles him. Blinking, he sees leaves and dappled sunlight above him. He climbs out of the bunker, and finds he that he has emerged from his underground odyssey into a pasture, neglected and overgrown. The bunker entrance is in a corner of the field, lying amidst dense vegetation, shaded by trees.

He stands surveying the view. There is something familiar about this field. Something from his past. He's been here before, back when he was a kid. He's sure of it.

At the far extremity of the field he sees a cottage roof rising above a dense thicket. He knows that roof, that cottage…

And suddenly it all makes sense. The realisation staggers him. He knows where he is and what's more, he knows the identity of the skeleton down in the passageway…

Chapter Eighteen
Endless Summers: Scene Three

'What's "two-timing" mean?' asks Clyde.

Mark and Clyde stroll along the Blackberry Trail, an overgrown, rarely used farm-track so named because of the blackberry bushes growing along both sides of it. It is an annual tradition in Market Stanford, in the first week of August when the berries are ripe, for the younger kids to go blackberry picking with some of the teachers from school supervising them. As it's now well into August, the event has passed, the thorny shrubs denuded of their fruit. Mark and Clyde have participated in the blackberry picking in years gone by, but not anymore. Mark and Clyde are Year Five boys now, and too old for that kid's stuff.

'Two-timing?' says Mark. 'That's like when someone's got two boyfriends or girlfriends at the same time.'

'Oh,' says Clyde.

'Why did you want to know?' asks Mark.

'I saw Tim yesterday,' says Clyde. 'It was outside the newsagents, and he was with Lindsey, who he's going out with. I heard her saying to Tim: "You don't mind if I two-time you with

James, do you?"'

Mark laughs. 'She said that? That's stupid. When you're two-timing someone, you're not supposed to tell them! It's meant to be a secret, until it gets found out or someone else tells him.'

'So you're not supposed to tell like Lindsey did?'

'No. I bet Lindsey was just copying something she saw on TV. You know, something off a soap opera.'

'I don't like soap operas,' says Clyde. 'They're boring.'

'I don't like them either,' says Mark. 'But my family watch them, so they're always on in my house.'

'Yeah, my mum and dad watch 'em, but I always go upstairs when they're on. All the girls like those soap operas, don't they?'

'A lot of them do,' says Mark. 'Not all of them.'

'Why is it girls don't like the things we watch?' wonders Clyde.

'Some girls like what we like. Rachel Farrow does.'

'Does she?'

'Yeah, I was talking to her about it. She likes *Charlie Chan*, *The Monkees*... That sort of thing.'

'Does she like *Magnum*?'

'Yeah, she likes that.'

(Back then, it was always just *Magnum*, never *Magnum PI*; even the ITV announcers just called it *Magnum*.)

'You like Rachel, don't you?' says Clyde. He makes it sound like an accusation of wrongdoing. 'You've been talking to her a lot.'

Mark shrugs. 'Yeah, I like her. She's good to talk to.'

'Are you going out with her then?'

'No,' says Mark. 'That going out stuff's silly. It's like pretending to be grown-ups; pretending to be like the soap operas; like Lindsey and her two-timing.'

'Do you know who I like...?' Clyde begins, hesitant.

'No.' Mark looks at his friend. 'Do you like someone then?'

'Yeah...'

'Who is it?'

'Michaela,' says Clyde, turning beetroot.

'Michaela Dawes?'

Mark is surprised, Michaela is one of their class at school, but

146

she sits at a different table and Mark has never seen Clyde so much as look at the girl, never mind talk to her.

'Yeah…'

'You mean you fancy her like her?'

'Yeah. Don't tell anyone, will you?' urgently.

'No, I won't tell anyone,' Mark assures him. 'So… Are you going to ask her out then? Or…?'

Clyde hesitates. 'I thought maybe you could ask her out for me…'

'Well, I *could*,' answers Mark. 'But I think it would be better if you asked her.'

'Yeah, but I'm shy around girls…' says Clyde, blushing some more, just to confirm this.

'Yeah, you are but… Have you ever talked to Michaela much?'

'No…'

'Have you talked to her at all?'

'No…'

'Well, how do you know you like her then?'

'I see her, don't I?' defensively. 'She's in our class.'

'You should go and talk to her,' Mark advises. 'Not to ask her out, I mean—just to be friends with. And then, if you get on with her, you could ask her out later.'

'But I'd be embarrassed talking to her…'

He would, Mark realises. If Clyde approached Michaela, he'd be so bashful that she'd work out in an instant that he fancied her. Michaela is a fairly quiet-spoken girl herself, but she's not shy like Clyde and she can be sarcastic. She's also a horsey girl (which is to say she rides horses, not that she looks like one!) and Mark can't really see her and Clyde hitting it off together; they just haven't got much in common.

But he doesn't want to discourage his friend. 'Well, just see how it goes,' he says. 'No rush, is there?'

The two boys have reached the end of the Blackberry Trail and have turned onto the lane that will take them back into town. Up ahead two younger boys, Year Three kids, are standing by the verge.

'Can you get our plane for us?' one of them asks, when Mark and Clyde draw near.

147

'What plane?' asks Mark.

'Our model plane,' is the reply. 'We threw it and it went over there into Dunnidge's field.'

He points to the barrier of trees and bushes flanking the road. Mark and Clyde know all about this particular field; all the kids do. It's Dunnage's field, situated behind Dunnidge's house. Nobody goes into Dunnidge's field; not if they know what's good for them.

A year has passed since Mark and Clyde had that run in with Dunnidge in Fern House; since then, Dunnidge has glared daggers at the boys on a couple of occasions when they have seen him in the street, but otherwise has left them alone. The boys have never ventured to return to Fern House, in spite of the lure of those 'treasures' in the attic. But then, there's a great big hole in the stairs, isn't there?

Dunnidge's place of residence is a disreputable, tumbledown cottage located here on the very edge of Market Stanford. Behind the cottage is the field that belongs to it, once pasturage for horses, but now unused and overgrown.

And it is into this field that the Year Three boys' glider has strayed. Mark can well understand that these kids (and they are kids to Mark, being all of two years below him) are afraid to enter Dunnidge's field to retrieve their property. Even though he doesn't even use it for anything, Dunnidge is notoriously territorial about his field and he always seems to be around whenever any kids have been reckless or daring enough to sneak into it—always appearing out of nowhere to chase the intruders, shouting terrible threats and curses.

'That's Dunnidge's field,' says Clyde. 'I ain't going in there.'

'But our plane's in there!' wails the first kid. 'And we only just got it!'

'Then get it yourselves,' retorts Clyde.

'Oh, come on,' protests Mark. 'I know Dunnidge chases you off if he sees you, but he can't be in the field all day long every day, can he? If he was, you'd never see him anywhere else.'

'Yeah, he's not always there!' agrees the second kid eagerly.

'If he's not there then you can go'n get it, can't you?' says Clyde.

148

The boy looks down. 'But he *might* be there…'

'Look, *I'll* go'n get it,' says Mark. 'Just me. What does your plane look like?'

The boys describe their toy, a World War Two Bristol Beaufighter, polystyrene and plastic, two dimensional in construction.

'Okay; I'll have a look for it,' says Mark.

'How are you gunna get through the bushes?' asks Clyde.

'I'll just crawl under 'em,' is the reply. 'That gap there look's big enough.'

Without further parley, Mark drops down and worms through the gap in the hedge. There's a barbwire fence just on the other side, but the wires are widely spaced and no obstacle for a boy who doesn't mind getting his clothes snagged.

The field is a jungle of weeds and tall grass, with here and there a sycamore tree rising like an islet from the green sea. Mark has been here before, a very long time ago; it must have been three years at least. On that occasion he and the friends he'd been with didn't get chased by Dunnidge, but they were so nervous about this happening that they hadn't stuck around for long.

Mark scans the area before him. No sign of Dunnidge; and he can't see the model plane. The bushes on the edge of the field here are high, so the plane must have been thrown very high into the air to make it over them. From this he deduces that it must have flown a long way into the field before it came down. He needs to go further in to find it.

He sets off, wading through the grass. Way off to his left he sees the chimneys and roof of Dunnidge's cottage rising above the shrubbery. He feels exposed now, moving further out into the open; but like he's already said: Dunnidge can't be in his field *all* the time!

On he trudges, eyes down, looking to the left and the right. Where's that stupid plane? It must be around here somewhere. Maybe under this sycamore tree…

'This what you lookin' for?' comes a voice.

Mark spins round. Dunnidge! He steps out from behind the sycamore, holding the model plane, an evil smirk on his face. No; Dunnidge can't be lurking in his field *all* the time; but he bloody is today!

Mark's heart skips a proverbial beat. He resists the urge to just turn and leg it.

'We just want our plane back,' he says, thinking it wise to claim part-ownership.

'What? This plane?' says Dunnidge, crushing the flimsy Beaufighter in his hands.

'You shouldn't have done that!' cries Mark.

"Oo says I shou'n't?' snarls Dunnidge. 'It were on my property! An' so are you! An' I got a bone to pick with you, boy! I int forgotten what 'appened last year, y'know!'

Mark decides that now will be an excellent time to remove himself from this gentleman's property—he turns and runs.

'No yer don't!' yells Dunnidge, and is hot on his tail.

Mark makes a beeline for the fence, back the way he came. But then he panics when he realises that the spot he's running towards is not the place where he came in; the bushes look different. This is bad! There might not be a way through there! He might get stuck!

This problem becomes academic when two big hands lay hold of Mark, pulling him up in his tracks.

'Gotcha!' crows Dunnidge.

'Lemme go, you creep!' struggling with all his might.

'Not likely!' says Dunnidge, and taking one of Mark's skinny young arms in a merciless grip, starts dragging the boy across the field, towards his cottage.

'Let me go!' repeats Mark, at the top of his voice, hoping that Clyde and the others will hear and realise that he's been caught.

'You been trespassin' on my property!' avers Dunnidge. 'An' I don't like kids trespassin' on my property, so I reckon I'll 'ave ter teach you a little lesson, I will!'

'I only came to get that plane!'

'Well you shou'n't 'ave, should yer? You shoulda knocked on my door an' asked me nicely instead of sneaking into me field. An' anyway, I owe you one, don't I? I nearly broke my bloody leg fallin' through them stairs! Did you know that? Did yer And that was your bloody fault! You an' that other little scrote!' shaking Mark violently.

'It wasn't our fault the stairs broke!' insists Mark.

'Wasn't it, though? It was cuz you ran down 'em so fast, wasn't it? You loosened 'em so's they broke when I come down after yer!'

'Well you shouldn't have been chasing us!'

Another violent shake. 'Shouldn't I, though! You was trespassin', weren't ya, yer bleeder? Just like today!'

'Then you were trespassing too!' retorts Mark.

'No I wasn't! 'Appens that Fern House is my property!'

'No it isn't!'

'Fuckin' well is!'

Another shake.

They are drawing near to the dreaded house. Mark throws a helpless glance over his shoulder. No-one. What's happened to Clyde?

'You're Jeff 'Unter's kid, int you?' says Dunnidge, looking at him. ''Im what runs that carpet place.'

'You know my dad?' ventures Mark.

'I *seen* 'im,' is the reply. 'An' I doon't like 'im neither. Always looks at me like I'm dirt, he does.'

'But that's how everyone looks at you!'

'Shuddup!' accompanied by another violent shake.

They reach Dunnidge's backyard. Mark sees the back of the house, a couple of rickety outbuildings, and dirt yard strewn with junk of all kinds: the wheelless rusting hulk of an old Super Dexta tractor, various dismantled engine parts and farm machinery, mouldy mattresses, a venerable clothes wringer, a rotting antique wardrobe... The cottage is in keeping with its surroundings; damp-stains climbing the roughcast, broken window panes repaired with cardboard, paint peeling from the back door.

A piebald bull terrier, sleeping in the shade near to its kennel, hearing the approaching footsteps, rouses itself, staring intently. Mark feels it is himself who is under particular scrutiny. He has heard stories about Dunnidge's dog; rarely seen but reputed to be even more vicious than its owner. And here it is; looking right at him. A growl builds up in the back of the animal's throat, and then erupts into barking.

'That's Patch, that is,' announces Dunnidge, dragging Mark

151

into the yard. 'Don't like trespassers, 'e don't. That's why 'e's makin' all that row. 'E'd just love ter sink 'is teeth inter yer, 'e would. Once he sinks 'is teeth inter something,' 'e don't let go in an 'urry.'

Patch, still barking, now leaps forward. Mark instinctively tries to retreat, but then sees that the dog is chained; a chain running from its collar to a peg in the ground near the kennel, which runs taut before the dog can reach the object of its wrath. Baffled, Patch vents his rage in renewed barking, standing up on his rear legs, straining at the leash.

Dunnidge chuckles. 'Look at 'm! 'E int arf riled up! Yeah, 'e's dead keen on meeting you, 'e is.'

He drags Mark further into the yard. A faecal odour becomes apparent, and he sees dotted around the area of the kennel evidence that Patch is left largely to his own devices.

He strains against the grasp of his captor as he is dragged closer to the baying animal.

'No yer doon't!' snarls Dunnidge, dragging him forwards. 'You ain't leavin' 'ere till Patch 'as 'ad a word with you about respectin' other people's property.'

Now, there are strict rules amongst primary school boys when it comes to fighting; a positively Queensbury-like set of dos and don'ts: no throwing stones or other missiles; no knees to the groin; no pokes to the eyes. And most of all: no biting. Mark knows these rules, and has for the most part avoided breaking them by not getting into fights in the first place. He still respects these rules and knows that any violation of them would be condemned in the school playground—but his current situation is desperate and in desperate situations sometimes the usual rules have to be disregarded.

He sinks his teeth into the tendons of his captor's hand.

Dunnidge roars with pain, releasing hold of Mark's arm—and, probably without even thinking, fetches Mark a savage cuff to the side of the head; one that sends the young boy flying, throwing him violently to the ground.

'Fuckin' little toe-rag!' snarls Dunnidge, nursing his injured hand.

Mark's senses swim. Hardpacked, dusty ground. The smell of

excrement. Frenzied barking. Pain from the blow ringing in his ear. Numbness to the side of his face. Pain from the fall in his shoulder, his side, his hip.

The barking is alarmingly loud. He looks up. Patch, straining at his chain, is perilously close, leaping and barking. The young Mark is no dog expert, and he couldn't have told you precisely what breed Patch was, but he knows that these broad-backed, bandy-legged dogs with the deceptively placid faces are the worst kind; even more dangerous than the much bigger dogs.

Dunnidge hunkers down next to Patch. The dog, still intent on Mark, pays his owner no heed.

'Yep, 'e's really strainin' at the leash. 'E doon't like you at all, Patch doon't.' He strokes the dog's back. 'You can feel the muscles in 'is back, you can. Rock 'ard they is. These dogs is all muscles an' sinews, they is. An' teeth. Yeah... Ever seen two o' these dogs fightin'? I 'ave. They int legal, these fights, but they 'as 'em anyhow. You bet on which dog's gunna win, y'see? It weren't Patch in this fight; 'e's never been in the pit. Two other dogs, it was. Really good fight, it was. Savage. Y'see, these dogs, they always goo's for the jugular. Yeah, they can use their claws when they 'ave ter, but what they really want is to get their teeth inter yer jugular. That's your throat, that is, jugular.'

'I know that!' says Mark.

'Does yer now? Smarty-pants, eh? Well, like I says, they goos for the jugular, an' once they sink their teeth in, they jus' don't let go. Cuz they know, yer see, they know that once they got yer by the jugular, they got you good. So they doon't let go; no fear; they doon't let go till they squeezed the life out o' yer. Y'either bleed ter death, or yer choke to death; whichever 'appens first. Tha's what 'appened at that fight I seed. One dog, 'e got the other one by the throat an' 'e jus' wouldn't let goo. The other dog, it was throwin' itself all over the place like mad, swipin' with its claws. But the first dog, 'e just wouldn't let goo, an' we all knoo that the other mutt was a goner.'

'Making dogs fight like that's cruel!' accuses Mark.

'Says 'oo?' retorts Dunnidge. 'Ain't no different ter a couple o' fellers in the ring punchin' each other's faces out o' shape, is it? Course not! Theys likes it, an' so does the dogs. I mean, look at

153

Patch 'ere; 'e's jus' dyin' ter sink 'is teeth into yer scrawny neck, 'e is. Comes nat'ral to dogs like Patch, it does. Instinct: tha's what it is.'

Dunnidge deliberately fingers the clip attaching the chain to Patch's collar. He looks at Mark, a malicious grin hanging under his bulbous nose.

In his sitting position, Mark scrambles backwards.

'Maybe I should just let 'im go, eh? See which of you's can run faster, eh?'

'What's going on here?' demands a new voice.

A group of peaked-capped policemen, five in number, have appeared around the corner of the cottage. Relief floods over Mark. Clyde must have called the police! thinks Mark (erroneously, as it soon transpires.)

Now it is the turn Dunnidge to take fright.

'What are you lot doin' here?' he demands, scrambling to his feet.

'We're here with a warrant to search your property,' replies the sergeant. 'But first I'd like to know what you think you're doing to this kid?'

'I weren't doin' nothin' to 'im!' fires back Dunnidge. 'He just wanted to say 'ello to Patch, 'e did! 'E wanted ter meet 'im, nice an' friendly like, that's all!'

'No, I didn't!' cries Mark.

'A likely story,' retorts the sergeant. 'No kid in his right mind would want anything to do with you *or* your mutt, Dunnidge. It looked to me more like you were about to set the thing on him!'

'He was!' confirms Mark, who has got to his feet.

'Well, you're alright now, son,' says the sergeant. 'Come over here.'

Mark joins the officers.

'I wasn't gunna 'arm 'im!' says Dunnidge. 'I was jus' meesin' around. An' why d'you wanna search my 'ouse, any'ow?'

'We're looking for stolen property,' is the reply. 'We have reason to believe you've been involved in a lot of these burglaries that have been happening around here. But before we do that, we'll just take you down to the station, Dunnidge, on suspicion of threatening harm to a minor. And there's five of us and one of you, so do yourself a favour and just come along quietly.'

Dunnidge has no intention of just coming along quietly, not when he has a way of adjusting the numerical odds stacked against him. He unclips the dog's chain.

'Get 'em, Patch!'

The dog flies at the advancing police officers.

Mark looks on with horror as the dog launches itself at the police sergeant, sinking its teeth into the arm the man raises to protect himself. He falls to the ground. The constables rush in to help, and shouting, cursing and canine growling fill the air. Meanwhile, Dunnidge takes flight, fleeing out of the yard towards the pasture.

One policeman belabours the dog's muzzle with his truncheon, and a second succeeds in re-attaching the chain to the dog's collar. Finally, they manage to force the dog to relinquish its hold.

'Where's Dunnidge?' grates the sergeant, holding his bleeding, lacerated arm.

'He ran off that way!' says Mark, pointing.

'Get the bastard!'

The four constables take off in pursuit of the fugitive—but they will find no sign of him. As for Mark, who will be made something of a school celebrity at the start of next term on account of this adventure—while he will not grow up to have an actual phobia of dogs, he will always remain firmly a cat person.

The fate of Dunnidge will remain a mystery for many years. A warrant will be issued for his arrest, but no trace of him will be found. It will be as though the earth had swallowed him up…

Chapter Nineteen
Under the Lone Ash Tree

Mayumi Takahashi, whose refined aesthetic sense is renowned across the four corners of the globe, dislikes it, and dislikes it intensely, when, in a photographic image, the soles of the model's feet are not clean; whether it is nude photography, or if the model is only naked from the ankles down, if the undersides of feet are besmirched with mud, grass-stains, or general dirt, to Mayumi Takahashi the sight is nothing less than an affront to her mind and senses. Yes, in the case of beach photography, sand-coated soles can be very aesthetically pleasing; this she acknowledges. But with that single exception, Mayumi firmly believes that any soles on display in a photographic image should be scrupulously clean.

Trina Trulove, Mayumi's current protégé and assistant, heartily agrees with this, just as she heartily agrees with anything else Mayumi Takahashi says or even thinks about saying. At this moment, we see her, with a hairdresser's neck brush, industriously sprucing up the soles of the feet belonging to glamorous model Dodo Dupont, in preparation for the next shot. They are well-cared-for feet, observes Trina; the soles smooth and without calluses; you really wouldn't have thought they'd been walked on for a good thirty years now.

Her task performed, Trina steps back out of the shot. The location is the grass verge on the edge of a field of blazing corn. A lone ash trees stands behind them, a solitary sentinel in this flat, patchwork wilderness. The meridian sun shines down upon the glistening skin of the model, who, lying on her side, hip raised, propped up on one elbow, turns her head back to face the camera. Behind the tree is a hedge and behind the hedge is the track, or drove, that brought them to this spot. This part of the world abounds with these dead-end droves, which seem especially designed to entice the unwary foot-passenger, cyclist or motorist into the middle of nowhere and then leave them there.

Mayumi, positioned on one knee, has Dodo in her camera's sights.

'Something not right,' she says. 'She not wet enough.'

'Not wet enough?' Trina is confused. Dodo's skin is absolutely glistening with liberally-applied sunblock. 'You want me to rub in some more sun-cream?'

'Not her skin!' says Mayumi, annoyed as always when her wishes are not anticipated. 'Her pussy. Should be much more wet. Make it more wet.'

'What... with sun-cream...?'

'With your finger, stupid!' replies Mayumi. 'Make her wet.'

Trina's heart kicks into overdrive. 'Me! But... but... wouldn't

156

you rather be doing that yourself…?'

'You my assistant. Is your job.'

'Mine! But I… I… I…'

'Just do it, Trina,' interjects Dodo. 'It's okay. But please get a move on. My arm's starting to go numb from holding this pose.'

Obediently, Trina hunkers down beside Dodo again. She raises her hand, discovers it is still holding the neck brush. She throws it aside. Now her arm moves in, fingers extended, to that glorious haven, fringed with raven curls, located at the junction between thighs and posteriors, and making contact she starts to manipulate the area with her middle finger. The desired goal is soon achieved, the lips are soon well-lubricated, wet to the eye.

This is a moment. No doubt at all that this is a moment. To think that she, Trina Trulove, humble photographer's assistant, is getting to actually stimulate the genitalia of the great Professor Dodo Dupont…!

'Yeah, I think you can stop now,' comes Dodo's voice.

'Yes, she ready for it,' confirms Mayumi.

Trina turns crimson, hurriedly withdraws her hand. Oh crikey! She was getting carried away there!

'Get out of shot,' instructs Mayumi.

Trina springs to her feet, retreats behind her employer and under the shade of the tree, where their bags and equipment are lying. While photographer and model are both occupied with the shot, Trina surreptitiously sucks her finger, and savours for the first time the taste of Dodo Dupont.

The camera's shutter fires off a rapid salvo. Now, Dodo raises herself onto all fours, still with her head turned towards the camera.

Seeing Dodo positioned like this, Trina has the sudden uncontrollable thought that, if she had been the owner of a penis, she would have dearly loved to take position behind Dodo right now, and give her the fucking of a lifetime.

What!?!?

Guilt and alarm! Red-faced again, she clamps both hands over her mouth as though she has just spoken these thoughts out loud. What on earth made her think something like that? She doesn't normally think things like that! Naughty things, yes! Lots of them! Her head is crammed full of naughty thoughts! (She *is* a sensualist, remember?) But not like this! Never like this. Why has she just imagined herself being in possession of a set of male genitalia? Penis envy? No; that's all nonsense—sexist psychobabble. A desire for gender reassignment? No again. Trudie is very happy with being a woman. Of course, she could always have the operation without having the gender reassignment…

No, no, no! She shakes her head to clear it. I don't want a penis!

Finally, she decides to settle the blame, as she does for everything else, on her ex-boyfriend. Yes, it was him who had gone and put that thought in her head; it is all his fault; with that over-sized member of his, and always fucking her like he was paying off old grudges.

'Hello there!'

The unexpected male voice makes Trina jump. She spins round. It's Mark Hunter! Carrying his jacket, top button undone and tie askew, handsome as always. Where did he spring from? Just popped up out of nowhere!

'Hello!' replies Dodo, equally surprised. 'How did you find us here?'

'I didn't,' replies Mark. 'I mean, obviously I *have* found you here, but I didn't know I was going to. I just happened to be strolling in this direction; I know this spot; this tree here…'

Mark sits himself down under the tree, leaning his back against it. He exhales a weary sigh.

'Do you want a drink?' asks Trina, solicitously. 'We've got water in the cooler bag.'

'I would dearly love some water, thank you,' says Mark.

Trina opens the cooler bag, and passes a chilled bottle of mineral water to Mark. Mark unscrews the plastic cap and takes a long draught.

Another sigh, this one expressing satisfaction. 'Thank you. I needed that.'

'What happened to that expedition you said you were going on?' inquires Dodo. 'Did you go down your well, or has someone filled it in?'

158

'No, the well was still there, and I did go down it, and I found a lot more than I bargained for.'

'What, was the fabled underground river actually there?'

'More of a stream than a river, but yes, it was there.'

'And the rowing boat?'

'And the rowing boat.'

Mark proceeds to give the girls an account of his recent underground odyssey, from which it then becomes necessary to follow with an account of his childhood encounters with the local ne'er-do-well Dunnidge. (The last three chapters, basically. Go back and read them again if you've already forgotten.)

'So then I had to take my story to the local fuzz and show them where I'd found the remains,' concludes Mark. 'They were obviously bemused as to why I'd decided to go down that well in the first place, and I think they had a hard time understanding that it wasn't anything to do with the UFO business I'm supposed to be here investigating. But it has to be an open and shut case. I can't see that set of bones turning out to be anyone other than poor old Dunnidge.'

'But what happened to him?' asks Trina. 'How did he die?'

'I think I can piece the story together,' answers Mark. 'Dunnidge was using the bunker as a storehouse for his ill-gotten gains. The bunker was on his land so he must have known about it. And of course, from the bunker he would have found his way to the underground stream, and thence up the well to Fern House. He probably considered it all his own private stomping ground. So, when he scarpered from the police that day, he must have made a bee-line for the bunker; it would've seemed like the ideal place to hide himself; literally going to ground. But then, what must have happened was that in his hurry, he managed to fall from the ladder all the way to the floor of the bunker; quite a drop. That would explain the skeleton's broken bones. My guess is he fell when he was turning the wheel of the hatch to lock it. The hatch was locked when I found it. Perhaps he didn't normally bother locking the hatch every time he went down his bolthole; but this time the cops were on his tail and he was in a panic. I think in his hurry to secure the hatch he lost his balance and fell.'

'And that's what killed him…' nods Trina.

159

'I wish it was that,' says Mark grimly. 'But poor Dunnidge's demise was a much more slow and painful business than that. I found his remains a fair distance from the bunker entrance, remember; right down that passageway. No; he fell; he broke an arm and a leg and smashed a kneecap; perhaps he lost consciousness for a while; but he was still alive. Alive and trapped..There would have been no way he could have got back up that ladder in his condition. All he could do was crawl along the ground. I don't know how long he waited, but he must have realised sooner or later that his only way out was to get to the underground stream. What he planned to do when he got there, we can only surmise; but then he might have been so delirious with pain that he didn't even know himself what he was doing; just obeying his instincts—the instinct to try and get out, to try and get help...

'And so he started crawling down that passage, but he never made it to the end. The pain he was in must have been excruciating. Whether it was the pain and delirium, or possibly complications from his injuries, he couldn't make it; he just wound down and died half way down that passageway. And then his body was left to rot for thirty years, with nobody to find it until I stumbled on it today.

'And so ends the story of how my childhood bogey-man Dunnidge managed to disappear without a trace all those years ago.'

'Wow...' breathes Trina.

Dodo and Mayumi feel likewise.

'And so I have successfully solved a mystery which has absolutely nothing to do with the business that I'm supposed to be here investigating,' he adds with a smile.

The story over and the spell broken, photographer, assistant and model return to their work. And Mark, lighting a cigarette and reclining against the bole of the tree, regards Dodo's naked matriarchal body displaying itself against the burnished field of corn, his mind drifts back to another time, and another paradigm female body, naked as nature like this one, and seen by himself as he sat beneath this very tree...

160

Chapter Twenty
Fool's Gallery

'They're all very friendly,' Dr Caxton had said, speaking of the group of young ESPers Bridget was about to meet for the first time. Bridget can't help but feel that she has been misinformed, if not wilfully deceived on this score. Edward and Helen are not very friendly at all; Lucretia is weird; and the twins are just annoying. Only Damien and Serena have been friendly to her. They have shown her around, explained everything about the place, and generally made her feel welcome. Helen and Edward don't seem to like her at all. Edward had found fault with her appearance. ('Do you really have to wear that hat indoors?') And Helen had even found fault with her making friends with Damien and Serena. ('Well, you've made yourself a nice couple of friends there, haven't you?') But then, Helen seems to spend all her time criticising other people. Earlier she criticised Serena because apparently Serena likes to have sex with those men dressed like gamekeepers who guard the grounds. ('I only sleep with older men; simple as that. Everyone's entitled to their preferences.') Helen said it was disgusting and Edward had called her nymphomaniac. Serena had been unimpressed. ('You know what the word for a hypersexual man is? It's satyriasis. Don't hear that one much, do you? When it's a man who's like that, they just say he's a stud.') Bridget was glad to hear that Serena only likes older men; because that must mean there's nothing going on between her and Damien; she'd been worried about that. Bridget likes Damien; she's always gone for those skinny, slightly dangerous pretty-boys.

Right now, Damien is giving Bridget a tour of the house, and they have arrived at the picture gallery. They stand before a large canvas depicting a man in a periwig and eighteenth-century costume.

'This is Sir Vernon Grange,' announces Damien. 'He's the man this house is named after; he was a notorious rake and libertine. He was notorious for the "pigeon shoots" he used to have in the

161

grounds of this very building.'

'Why were the pigeon shoots notowious?' asks Bridget.

'Well, that's because the "pigeons" they shot weren't pigeons at all; they were peasants; people.'

'No! You're not sewious?'

'I am, you know. Old Sir Vernon had these gangs of armed servants who would go out and kidnap peasants from the surrounding area. When they'd rounded up about thirty of them, they'd be herded into this kind of arena: a kind of roped-off area they set up in the gardens of the Grange.'

'In the fwont or the back?'

'I think it was in the back. Anyway, Sir Vernon, and a bunch of his fellow libertines would stand in a line outside the enclosure, and they'd all have pistols; and your peasants would be cowering inside. And then, when the signal was given, they'd start shooting the peasants: bang! bang! bang! And of course they didn't just stand there and let themselves get shot, these peasants; no, they'd be running around like headless chickens, screaming, dodging the bullets, begging for mercy. And there'd be these lackeys there to stop any peasant who tried to get out of the enclosure, pushing them back in. And there'd be other lackeys there to keep supplying the libertines with fresh pistols. (Cuz guns in those days only fired one shot, you see.) And so the competition was for them to shoot as many of the peasants as they could before they came.'

'Came where?' asks confused Bridget.

'"Came" in the ejaculatory sense. Cuz, while the libertines were blazing away at the plebs, they'd have their women down on their knees in front of them giving them blow-jobs.'

Bridget pulls a face. 'That's *disgusting*. How did they get away with it?'

A shrug from Damien. 'Cuz they were the aristocracy. The aristos could get away with pretty much anything in those days; they had the money and the power.'

They move onto the next picture. 'Now, this fellow's Sir Vernon's son, Clifford Grange, a notorious highwayman in his day.'

'Why did he need to wob people?' wonders Bridget. 'He was

162

wich, wasn't he?'

'Yeah, but he didn't do it for the money—he did it for kicks. And he wasn't one of your gallant, gentleman thieves either. Not by a long chalk. When Cliff and his gang held up a carriage, they'd always shoot the men; blow their brains out, even if they'd cooperated and handed over their goods without making any trouble; but only the men, though; they didn't kill the women.'

'Well I suppose they had some pwinciples then, if they spared the women.'

A lop-sided smile. 'They spared the women's lives, but they didn't spare them much else. Y'see, if there were any women in the carriage, they would kidnap them; they'd ride off with them to their robbers' secret base, and they'd gang-bang them. And when they'd finished with 'em, they would leave 'em lying stark naked by the roadside. They did this in the hope that whoever found them first would rape them as well.'

'That's tewwible!' cwies outwaged Bwidget. 'I hope they caught him.'

''Fraid not. Lived to a ripe old age, old Clifford did, and died a happy man... Moving on...'

The next painting is of a refined-looking woman in an elegant, low-cut gown.

'And now we come to Lady Amelia Grange, Sir Clifford's daughter.'

'She looks vewy elegant and wefined. I bet she didn't do anything bad.'

'Didn't she! Worse than the others, she was. This elegant and refined lady was a Satanist and a child-murderer. A sort of female Gilles de Rais.'

'Who was Gilles de Wais?'

'He was a man who was a Satanist and child-murderer. Just like him, Amelia here would have her servants abduct the local peasants' kids. They'd bring them back here where first she would watch some of her manservants sodomise the little tykes (that means doing them up the bum, in case you don't know); then she'd take the sodomised little kid in her arms and pretend to comfort him, kissing his tears away; and then while she was doing all that she would just get out a dagger and slit the kid's throat

163

right open,' miming the act; 'and she'd get off on letting his hot blood pour all over her naked body.'

Bridget clamps her hands over her ears. 'That's *howwible*. Don't tell me she got away with it as well?'

'Alright, I won't tell you; but she did. She killed dozens of the young pups, cuz no-one really cared about a bunch of missing peasant kids. She did it cuz she thought that the more kids she killed, the more kudos she'd earn with her master, Satan, the Lord of Darkness.'

They move onto the next picture; a man with a chinless man with vacuous expression and Victorian clothes.

'And this guy is Rufus Grange, Lady Amelia's bastard son.'

'Did he do anything howwible?'

'No; he was just a pillock.' Damien looks at his watch. 'Let's go back downstairs; it's nearly dinnertime.'

They move out of the dimly-lit gallery.

'Were they twue; all those stowies about those people?' inquires Bridget.

'Of course they were. You wouldn't believe some of the things that used to go on back then. I tell you, those aristos could get away with anything. But don't worry; the Grange isn't haunted or anything. You won't be woken up in the night by the sound of screaming children.'

'That's a weliefl'

'So, how are you feeling now? About being here, I mean. Still nervous?'

'Not as much,' answers Bridget.

'Glad to hear it! You'll soon get used to things.'

'I just don't like that they dwugged me and bwought me here in my sleep.'

'Oh, don't worry about that,' says Damien. 'It's just that you've got a very powerful ESPer ability, and you haven't learned to it control yet; there were just being careful.'

'Was evewyone bwought here like I was?'

'Not all of us.'

'What about you?'

'Well, they actually came up to me and asked me if I wanted to come here and join them. And for me, that was an offer that came

164

just at the right time, cuz I was in a pretty heavy situation right then.'

'What sort of situation?'

'Well, not to sugar-coat it, I was about to be nicked by the cops for murder.'

'You *murdered* someone?' from wide-eyed Bwidget. 'No! I bet you were fwamed or something!'

'I wasn't, you know: I did kill a guy; but it was self-defence. I don't say I'm proud of it, but this guy was a total scumbag. He'd raped a load of girls.'

'He was a wapist?'

'Yep. You wanna hear the story?'

'Yes! Tell me what happened.'

An antique ottoman happens to be amongst the furniture in the corridor they are traversing. They sit themselves down on it.

'Well, it was when I was at school, a couple of years back. There was this boy in my class; Alan was his name. He was the one. We didn't know it, but he was going around date-raping a lot of the girls in our year. He was a smooth-talker, so it was easy for him to get girls to go on dates with him; but, you see, he had this vicious streak; I mean *really* nasty. He always kept it hidden at school. Everyone thought he was a nice guy. He was good-looking, got good grades, good at Games, and the girls liked him. Only they didn't know about that mean streak. But those girls who went out with him on dates sure found out about it—they found out the hard way.'

'Because he waped them?'

'Yep; and in a really nasty way; the way he went about it, he'd really humiliate them. The girls he did this to all kept quiet about it; they had to really, cuz Alan would threaten them. Maybe some of them told each other about it, but they didn't dare tell anyone else. But then it happened to this girl I knew; we'd been friends a long time, like since Year Seven. She came up to me and she told me what had happened, what he'd done to her. And then I kind of went off the rails; I just saw red. I went looking for Alan after school; I was going to get the fucker, that's what I was going to do; I was going pound his stupid face in. I followed him and I cornered him in the park, but when I confronted him he pulled a

165

knife on me. The guy was seriously going to stab me; he wasn't just messing around. So, when he went for me, I used my telekinesis and made him stab himself instead. He dropped dead on the spot. Unfortunately for me, there were witnesses in the park; I was seen "fleeing the crime scene." The cops turned up at my house and dragged me in for questioning; they knew it was me and they about to press charges, but then who should turn up at visiting hours, but are good Dr Clavering. She made me an offer to come here, and she said she could get me off the hook if I accepted the offer. What would you have done in my shoes?'

'Accept the offer.'

'Exactly. And so here we all are. We're different to everyone else. We're the elite. We're special. Honing our abilities and using them to fight the good fight. So, cheer up Bridget Price; forget about the past and just look ahead to the future!'

Damien treats her to his best rakish smile, and Bridget blushes, perceiving her own future hopes indexed in the dancing circles of light in his dark eyes.

The dinner gong rings.

Chapter Twenty-One
Close Encounters of an Absurd Kind

The Vrilliac are the master-race of the universe. They are the so-called 'little grey men' that have visited Earth many times, and have made contact with individual humans in many well-authenticated accounts of alien abduction. The Vrilliac do not rule over the lesser races of the Galactic Collective—the other planets enjoy complete autonomy—but the Vrilliac, on account of their superior knowledge and wisdom, are always the ones turned to for advice and assistance and mediation in any dispute. The Vrilliac are also by far the oldest race in the universe. In fact they have existed since its creation, and, over the millennia, have watched over—and sometimes helped along—the evolution of other races, ensuring that they developed in peace and prosperity.

The Vrilliac have harnessed the natural power of the universe, which they call Vril. Vril can light cities, power spacecraft, and in short takes the place of the wasteful and polluting energy sources like nuclear power, electricity and fossil fuels that are used here on Earth. Directed upon a living being, Vril is a powerful stimulant. It can also be used to pacify the aggressive tendencies of hostile races.

The Vrilliac are immortal; they possess no digestive systems or reproductive organs and are unaffected by entropy. Universal beings, they live outside of time. Whenever they come here to Earth to acquire eggs or semen, it is not for their own use, as many believe, but to benefit the inhabitants of the planet Pisis, whose inhabitants have become sterile. I myself have made my own small contribution to the survival of this race. The Pisistrans breathe a nitrogen atmosphere, so whenever they come to Earth with the Vrilliac, they wear environmental suits, the helmets filled with liquid nitrogen. (The Pisistrans being able to breathe both fluid and vapour.)

But the Galactic Universe is in a crisis. The Vrilliac have long since discovered that universal harmony is maintained by the peaceful coexistence of the planets within it. An invisible thread of cosmic energy connects each and every planet in the cosmos like a vast polymer chain. And there is one planet that is disrupting this Galactic Harmony: and this is our planet, Earth. Internal strife amongst us, the dominant lifeform, the consumption of animal life, and the destruction of the environment through pollution and deforestation, are affecting not only Earth itself, but also the other inhabited planets of the universe. The cosmic thread connecting Earth with the other planets has become weakened, and is out of harmony. As a result of this, other planets are experiencing freak weather conditions, earthquakes and volcanoes, and whole populations are suffering from chronic depression and lethargy, while others, like the Pisistrans, have become unable to reproduce.

We, the people of Earth, have to be made to understand the extent of the cosmic disaster for which we are responsible. And this is why the Vrilliac have sent ambassadors to Earth, to try and remedy the situation before it is too late—carefully selecting only the most receptive and open-minded human beings to present

167

their message to in order to make it known to the whole world. I have been lucky enough to be one of the instruments they have chosen...

Flora Hodgson paces the dry sward of her moonlit back garden. Naked, she walks like the presiding deity of the fruit trees, flowerbeds and box hedges. The night is certainly warm enough to justify this naturist excursion, and living in seclusion, Flora has no neighbours either to be offended or to film her and put her up on YouTube.

I've just compared her to a goddess, but Flora is no pagan like the spiritual scientist Dr Clavering down the road at Vernon Grange. But Flora loves the natural world in much the same way, having always been a dedicated environmentalist, taking an active part in fighting for the preservation of Mother Earth. She is even in email contact with Greta Thunberg! (Hasn't heard back from the girl, though, since pitching that suggestion about replacing all fossil fuels with Vril.)

But it's not just about Mother Earth for Flora. Even as she feels the grass beneath her feet, her eyes are on the stars above her head—that centuries-out-of-date picture of the cosmos we see mapped across the night skies; the universe, of which Earth is just one tiny atom. Tonight however, there is an air of preoccupation about Flora; her thoughts are focused as much inwards as outwards.

But then, this is hardly surprising—she is writing a book.

George Meredith described it as 'leading a double life'; and so it is. The writer, immersed in the writing of his or her novel may still be getting out and about, performing the functions of daily life, interacting with other human beings; but they will have the imaginary world of their story constantly before their mind's eye; they will be sculpting, evolving and mentally reviewing their work all the time; they are, effectively, inhabiting two worlds at one and the same time, two worlds running parallel to each other; one of them unknown to the people around.

Wait a minute. I've just been talking about the art of fiction writing. What does fiction writing have to do with Flora Hodgson's work in progress? Flora is writing a factual work! It is autobiography; an account of her own personal experiences with otherworldly lifeforms, supplemented with veracious information concerning the plight of the whole universe, drawn from the most reliable extra-terrestrial sources. Yes; no citation is needed here! Flora's book is to be a revelation, a message to the world; a warning of imminent peril, but while also presenting the means of avoiding that peril.

In her conversation with Mark Hunter, Flora hadn't mentioned that she was writing a book; but if she had, Mark would not have been surprised. The book was inevitable. It was preordained. In fact, it would only have been remarkable if there *wasn't* a book. She already has a publisher for the book—which again is unremarkable in cases like this one.

At first, she had turned to the popular press to try and get her message across. She would have preferred one of the broadsheets, but they had declined; and so she had gone to the tabloids, who at least they had a wider circulation; but their presentation of her story had not been a flattering one—indeed, they had dubbed her Flora the Fruit Loop, a name which has unfortunately stuck.

(On this note, an incident had occurred today which greatly upset Flora. She had gone into town to do her grocery shopping, and a group of children from the primary school class she had formerly taught had started jeering at her, chanting out 'Flora the Fruit Loop!' over and over. And this from her very own children! Children, who only a few weeks before she had nurtured and loved as her own, and had been beloved by them in return. And now this! Oh, fickle youth! The sting of betrayal had stabbed deep inside her.)

So now Flora has given up on the printed press. Now she is writing a book. Books get taken seriously. Especially when the first edition is hardback and with a dust jacket.

At the moment, as she gracefully treads the turf, eyes ranging across the bejewelled firmament, she is fretting herself over the use of the word 'earthquake.' She was writing earlier, and she has used the word with reference to seismic disturbances taking place on other planets. Is this right? 'Earthquake'? Or should she, if talking about other planets, be saying 'planetquake' instead? Does the word 'earthquake' refer exclusively to a quake occurring on the planet Earth? Or does the word simply refer to the fact that the ground is quaking; 'earth' meaning 'ground,' the surface of the planet? Flora inclines to the latter hypothesis. When talking about the planet Earth, you would spell the name with an uppercase first letter, as you would with the name of any other planet, wouldn't you? And the word 'earthquake' is not spelt with an uppercase first letter; therefore, it must refer to the noun and not the proper name, right...? But then, on the other side of the argument, Flora has checked and found that her word-processing software does recognise the word 'planetquake' as a legitimate word. (I can vouch for this myself; I'm looking at it right now.)

Flora decides she will leave it as 'earthquake' for now. If her editor objects to it, then she will change it.

What would Mark Hunter think? Flora wonders. He is obviously an intelligent, knowledgeable man. Mark Hunter... Flora has thought of Mark a lot since he paid her that visit here yesterday afternoon. She thought of him with particularly vivid urgency last night, just before she went to sleep. He has made an impression on her. A very handsome man, he was; polite, well-spoken; she had enjoyed that conversation they had. (Mark seems to be becoming as popular as the protagonist in a harem anime; I'm going to have to ask him how he does it.)

Perhaps he will come back, muses Flora; perhaps he will want to question her some more. He had clearly believed her story. He had given her a fair hearing and he hadn't poured scorn on a single thing she had said. If she could convince him, if she could get him on her side...

Flora now stands at the far end of her garden, looking back towards her bungalow. A light now appears above the roof of the bungalow, a kind of aurora pointing its diaphanous fingers into the night sky. Flora's breath catches in her throat. That light again! Just like that other night—the night that the Vrilliac had first appeared before her. Have they returned? Have they come to pay her a second visitation...?

Galvanised, Flora races fleet-foot across the sward and around the side of her house into the front garden. Across the fields rises the perimeter of Vernon Wood. Yes! The light emanates from within the wood, from that place known as the second landing site. They *have* come back! They've come back to see her again!

Crossing the farm track, she effortlessly leaps the ditch, and makes her rapid way across the harvested field towards the beckoning light. The ground is painfully prickly to her feet, but she ignores the discomfort, driven on by her earnest desire.

And now, ahead of her, a shape detaches itself from the intervening darkness; a humanoid shape, moving towards her; a shape with a smooth round head. A Vrilliac! It must be. They draw closer to each other, and the round head resolves itself into a visored space helmet.

Not a Vrilliac, then; a Pisistran; one of the humanoid races who accompany the Vrilliac on their travels. Coming straight towards her, it appears to move with difficulty, evincing an awkward, stumbling gait. Its Vril levels must be depleted, decides Flora.

'Hello, my friend,' she says. 'It's me: Flora Hodgson, the chosen ambassador of our friends the Vrilliac. What's happened to you? Are you on your own? Have you used up all your Vril? You poor thing. Well, don't worry; I can help you. That's it; just come to me.'

Advancing towards him, she opens her arms, and the spaceman seems to mirror the action—extending its arms as it shambles towards her. Flora can see the Pisistran clearly now; the silver helmet, gloves, external underpants (sorry; girdle!) and boots picked out by the moon, glimmering in its radiance. Of the creature's face she can discern nothing; the helmet's visor an oblong of impenetrable darkness.

Only a few feet separate them now. Flora smiles encouragingly; ready to receive the poor, sterile, atmospherically-challenged, Vril-depleted alien visitor in her arms. Those silver gloved hands reach out—and closing around Flora's throat, squeeze hard. And Flora, so astonished by this completely unexpected assault, makes not even the slightest attempt to defend herself as the life is inexorably squeezed out of her.

Chapter Twenty-Two
5001: A Time Oddity

Something unusual has happened in Market Stanford this fine Thursday morning. No, not word of more alien or UFO sightings; no incidents have been reported during the night (and Flora Hodgson's body is still waiting to be discovered by the farmer whose field she lies in.) This new phenomenon has manifested itself on people's computers, on their tablets and smartphones (and no, it's not more of that weird alien text.) Many Market Stanfordians, logging on this morning to check their emails, or tell all their friends on social media what they have had for breakfast, notice—at least those who happen to look at the bottom corner of their computer screens notice—that the year being displayed is 5001. Now, this is very strange. Only yesterday the year had been 20—. (Precise year left unspecified on account of my having no idea of when this book will see the light of day.) And indeed, both on the internet and in the world around them, it *is* still 20—. So why do the clocks on their devices read 5001?

Three thousand years into the future. It's difficult to visualise. We can't quite get our heads around those kinds of figures. Most writers of speculative fiction only care to venture a few hundred years into the future, presenting various dystopian systems governing the Earth, or else depicting humanity conquering the stars, colonising other worlds, meeting strange new life, etc, etc… But thirty centuries hence…? Go backwards three thousand years and a lot of us were only just crawling out of our caves; what would we be like three thousand years from now? What sort of society would exist in that time? What sort of beings would humankind have evolved into?

Not that most people in Market Stanford give any thought to these weighty issues; they just think it is strange that their computers are displaying the wrong year.

One person who does give it more thought is Mark Hunter. He cannot help speculating as to whether this temporal anachronism is in some way related to all the other recent happenings in the vicinity. But pondering this doesn't hinder his going to the camping supply shop in town and buying himself a tent, a sleeping bag and all the other necessary paraphernalia. He has decided he will be camping out in Vernon Wood tonight.

Nor does the temporal phenomenon stop Dodo, Mayumi and Trina from setting out on their previously planned daytrip to Great Yarmouth. According to the weather forecast, today is going to be the last very hot day of the week. From tomorrow onwards it is going to be unbearably hot.

Incidentally, Mark Hunter is also the breakfast topic of conversation at Vernon Grange. Those CCTV images they had sent back to their superiors have returned with a positive identification of MI5's top trouble-shooter. The Four Doctors are discussing what is to be done about him. The report informs them that Hunter is currently staying in the vicinity, allegedly to investigate the recent UFO sightings. So why had he and his partner (identified as TV psychologist Dodo Dupont) broken into the Grange? Had they been in pursuit of that creature in the spacesuit? Or is the UFO investigation a blind, and Mark Hunter is really here to investigate Vallotec's ESPer project? They have been advised that Mark Hunter is a known interloper, and he had somehow been concerned in the death of Eustace Wainwright, head of the Wainwright Corporation, Vallotec's erstwhile owner. So, what to do about him?

Elsewhere, Trevor, Jack, Fergus and Mitch are about to start another day's desultory farm work. Nothing exciting is going to happen to them at work today, but as the quartet haven't appeared for over ten chapters, I just want to make sure that people haven't forgotten about them. We haven't seen the last of them yet.

Back in Market Stanford, popular local rockers Switchback are preparing for a gig that evening at the Boat House, a pub venue in town. A quartet of long-haired young hooligans, they play 'dumbass rock n' roll,' and their anthem 'My Willy's on Upside Down' has become a local favourite. The gig, as I say, is scheduled for this evening, and we shall be looking in on it, so don't forget your earplugs.

Elsewhere in town, Michael Standing—aged forty-three, unmarried, manager of a local supermarket, batsman for Market

Stanford's cricket team, fond of all sports, likes his pint—is lying on his stomach on his bed and in the process of defecating in this unusual place and position. Mr Standing and his coprophiliac activities have nothing whatsoever to do with our story, but I just thought I'd treat you to this little snapshot of some of the peculiar things people can get up to behind closed doors.

Another man who probably has unaddressed potty-training issues, Dennis Shrimpton, is also beginning his day… But as Dennis is one of Mark's former schoolfriends, I think the fellow deserves a fresh chapter to himself.

Chapter Twenty-Three
The Old School Tie: Dennis Shrimpton

Do you remember Dennis?

Actually, you probably don't. Cast your mind back to when primary school Mark Hunter and Clyde Waring were playing *Blake's 7*. Dennis was the boy who was standing in his back garden when Mark and Clyde were passing, and whose mother wouldn't let him go out and participate in the adventure.

Of course, Dennis isn't a boy anymore; he is now a forty-year-old man, the same as Mark and Clyde. Dennis hasn't turned out well. But then Dennis was fated from infancy to become one of society's misfits. Dennis has never enjoyed anything resembling a meaningful relationship with another human being; and the only reason he doesn't still live with his mother is because she chucked him out years ago. Dennis lives in a flat that social housing decanted him into.

Dennis is not very popular. For one thing, his childhood personal hygiene problems have pursued him into adulthood. Yes; he smells! Another black mark against Dennis, which you would discover if you were unfortunate to be button-holed by him, is that he talks nonstop. He rattles on without pause, punctuating his word with that inane, chirpy laugh of his. It drives people up the wall. Even when alone, Dennis doesn't stop talking—this man's internal monologue is spoken aloud.

But the funny thing is Dennis is actually very happy with his lonely life. Being mentally challenged has done him a favour in this regard; if he had been more intelligent, he would have been suffering from depression.

Things, however, are in the process of getting worse for Dennis Shrimpton. Rumour has been rearing its ugly head...

We join Dennis as he emerges from his flat onto the sunny streets of Market Stanford this fine morning. He is on the way to the allotments. Dennis has green fingers, and not having a job, he has plenty of time to indulge this disposition. Let's take a look at him. Dennis unavoidably reminds you of a toad; one of those upright, anthropomorphic toads like Toad of Toad Hall. Pot-bellied, he has bandy legs that are way too long in proportion to his upper body. His bespectacled face is round, with a wide mouth, and deep lines running from the corners up to his nose. He is dressed, as always, in sandals, knee-length trousers, a filthy t-shirt, a sun-hat on his tousled head.

Smiling blithely, Dennis ambles on his way, speaking to every person who passes him.

'Mr Sun's got 'is hat on today, ha ha!'

'You've gotta laugh, an't ya? Ha ha!'

'Worse things 'appen at sea, ha ha!'

Everyone ignores him.

Dennis reaches the park; cutting across this will shorten his journey to the allotments. A group of scruffy-looking men are seated on one of the benches, and carrying on a desultory gravel-voiced conversation. In spite of appearances, they are not homeless alcoholics; alcoholics yes, but they are all residents of Market Stanford living in rented accommodation. Dennis knows these men, and has even sometimes made one of their number. Seeing them sitting there reminds Dennis of something, and he ambles over to them. A stubbly, lank-haired man called Smith (dare I say 'the one who appears to be the leader'?), looks up as he approaches.

'Alright there, Smithy?' says Dennis.

'Alright,' is the surly reply.

'Nice day, innit?'

'Nice enough.'

'Wha's that you bin sayin' about me, then?' asks Dennis.

'What's what?'

'Ol' Carter; 'e says you bin sayin' thins.'

'Like what?'

'You bin sayin' that I'm one o' them paedophiles, and I like molestin' kids. Why you bin sayin' that?'

'That's because I've 'eard that you're a paedophile and you like molestin' kids,' replies Smith succinctly.

''Oo says that, then?'

'Everyone says that.'

'But thas not true. I *like* kids, I do. But I doon't do nothin' to 'urt 'em.'

'Tha's not what people are sayin.'

''Oo says?'

'Everyone.'

'But thas not true! I *like* kids. I look after 'em. I doon't do nothin' to 'urt 'em.'

'Then go'n look after 'em somewhere else.'

'Whassat? What you sayin'?'

'I'm sayin,' we don't want your sort around 'ere. Fuck off.'

A chorus of gravel voices second this proposal, and Dennis is left with no choice but to retreat, still saying to himself: 'I *like* kids. Thas all. I doon't do nothin' to 'urt 'em.'

Crossing the park, Dennis reaches Main Street, his thoughts centred on himself, mumbling under his breath. A stocky, bespectacled woman, laden with shopping bags is passing by. Dennis recognises her.

''Ullo, Rachel! Nice day for it, ha ha!'

Looking resolutely away, the woman walks past him. Then, obviously thinking the better of it, she stops and turns back to him.

'Oh, Dennis,' she says, an imploring look on her face. 'What have you been up to?'

'Whassat? I ant bin up to anythin'! Ha ha!'

'Well, I hope not,' continues the woman. 'But people have been saying things about you, Dennis. Bad things. You need to be

176

careful.'

'People bin sayin' thins? Makin' up thins about me?'

'Well, I *hope* it's all just people making things up. But people are quick to judge, Dennis; especially around here. You need to be careful. Have you seen your doctor lately?'

'I doon't need to see me doctor. I int poorly! Ha ha!'

'Yes, but your Doctor can put you in touch with people; people who can help you, Dennis.'

'What, you mean like counsellin'? I 'ad that before!'

Yes, Dennis *has* undergone counselling sessions in years past. Nothing good had come of it. Professionally trained though they may be, counsellors are still only flawed human beings when it comes down to it, and Dennis's chatter had driven the counsellor as much up the wall as it did anyone else!

'Well, maybe you should have some more, Dennis,' says Rachel. 'Where are you off to now?'

'I's gooin' to the allotments, ha ha!'

Rachel makes a show of enthusiasm. 'Well, that's good! Something to keep you busy. Just go straight there, Dennis, and don't stop to talk to any kids.'

'But I *like* kids! I ant gunna 'urt 'em, ha ha!'

'For God's sake, Dennis! I'm serious! Stay away from kids!'

With this injunction, Rachel proceeds on her way, and Dennis resumes his course to the allotments.

Both Dennis and Rachel are former schoolfriends of Mark Hunter, although I can tell you now that he's destined to meet neither of them during his stay in Market Stanford. Rachel remembers Mark, of course; but what about Dennis? Does he recall with any fondness one of the few people who had tolerated his lax personal hygiene and irritating chatter back in those days? No, he doesn't. Dennis doesn't remember Mark at all. Dennis is not one to reminisce; he does not look back upon his schooldays; and even if had attempted to do this, most likely all he would have seen would be a confused blur of incomprehensible lessons and exhausting sporting activities swirling before his mind's eye. Dennis is cursed (or blessed, depending on how you look at it) with a very poor memory. Dennis Shrimpton is a man who lives very much in the present. Never thinking of the future, never reflecting on the past, he just takes one day at a time.

He arrives at the allotments. A woman is picking strawberries on her patch.

'Ol' Mr Sun's got his hat on! Ha ha!' says Dennis to the woman.

The woman doesn't reply or look up from her work.

Dennis tries again. 'Them strawberries 'as come up nice!'

Still no response. Strange. She always used to pass the time of day with him.

Not stopping to worry about this, Dennis moves on to his own patch. Unlocking the door of his ramshackle shed (which looked as structurally sound as a card house), he goes inside and emerges with gardening gloves on his hands, and armed with pruning shears, and a bottle of insect spray.

Two young boys come up to him while he is at work on his lettuces. They look at him and snigger.

Dennis looks up at them and grins.

'What you doin' ere?' he says. 'You shou'n't be 'ere, y'know? These is private property, these allotments.'

'We're watching you,' replies one of the boys.

'Watchin' me, are ya? You 'ungry, are ya? Want some fruit and veg? Ha ha!'

'Do we have to pay for it?'

'No, you don't has to pay! I'se not the shops, is I? Ha ha! How about a nice cucumber? Go good on a salad, that would. Or cucumber sarnies.'

'Yeuurr! I hate cucumbers!' says one boy.

'Me too!' confirms the other.

'Whassat? You doon't like cucumber? 'Ow about some tomatoes, then? Got some nice, juicy tomatoes growin' over there. Ha ha!'

'Got any apples?'

'Apples? Apples grow on trees, they do! No trees 'ere! This is allotments; apples, they grow them in orchards, ha ha!'

'What do you think you're doing?'

Three pairs of innocent eyes look round. The woman from the nearby allotment has come up to them, a scowl on her face.

'Thas alright!' Dennis assures her. 'They int doin' any 'arm, ha

178

ha!'

'I'm not talking to them, I'm talking to you,' says the woman.

'What'm *I* doin'? I was just gunna give 'em some tomatoes! They sez they're 'ungry, ha ha!'

'They don't want your bloody tomatoes, so just keep away from them!'

'They come up to me, ha ha!'

The woman turns to the boys. 'Clear off, you two. And don't go near this man again.'

'Why not?' asks one of the boys.

'Just do as you're told! Now clear off, or I'll tell your mums and dads!'

Propelled by this threat, the boys run off.

'And as for you, Shrimpton, I've got my eye on you. We all have. Go near any kids again and you'll know about it!'

The woman stalks back to her patch.

Whas that? Doon't go near any kids? But he *likes* kids, does Dennis. No 'arm in talkin' to 'em, is there? People sayin' 'e wants to 'urt them or somethin'… That's daft, that is! Silly! Dennis *likes* kids; 'e isn't gooin' to 'urt 'em. 'E just wants to look after 'em, tha' all!

'E just wants to look after 'em…

Chapter Twenty-Four
The Sound of the Sky

Mark Hunter has chosen the same clearing formerly occupied by the Mantell Project in which to set up camp. The macabre element of pitching his tent in the same spot as three people who are now dead, is not lost on Mark. But he wants to be close to the landing site without being in direct sight of it; this spot is the best available location.

How long he is going to stay camped out here in the woods, he does not know. It will all depend upon what actually happens and how soon it happens. Vernon Wood is the epicentre for all the recent activity, and he would very much like to observe at least some of the reported phenomena for himself. Hoping for clear-cut answers might be too much to hope for in a case like this. He knows that these outbreaks of paranormal activity can often just peter out, leaving no-one the wiser. The incidents in the Market Stanford area have been happening for well over a fortnight now—if similar recorded cases are any indication, the phenomena can cease just as suddenly as they began.

The danger attendant on camping out in these woods is not lost on Mark. The Mantell Project had been murdered in this place by unknown assailants. And then, three people have been strangled to death in the immediate vicinity; Mark has already had one close encounter with the spacesuited lunatic who seems to be the culprit.

Yes, it is now three strangulation murders. Poor Flora Hodgson has added a name to the ranks. PC Mavis had—for the second time—brought Mark the news and had driven him to the crime scene. And then she was: a naked woman lying dead in a field, sprawled on the ground, hair splayed out around her—it bore all the hallmarks of your typical, run-of-the-mill rape and murder; but appearances can be deceptive. The forensic pathologist on the spot (the same woman Mark had met at the earlier crime scene) said there were no obvious indications of sexual assault; nor any of the abrasions and contusions that would suggest a prolonged violent struggle; nothing but those tell-tale marks of manual strangulation. And then there was the absence of the victim's clothing at the crime scene. She couldn't have just been dumped in the field after being killed in another location; the state of the soles of her feet told a different story. Discarded clothing, a summer dress, underwear, were found in the living room of the victim's bungalow, and there were no signs of a disturbance or forced entry.

So, unless Flora Hodgson had some soap opera going on in her life that Mark doesn't know about, he is sure she must have been the latest victim of that homicidal spaceman. Had this been Flora's first genuine close encounter? Certainly her last.

But why had she been walking around stark naked...?

Tent assembled, Mark crawls inside and unrolls his sleeping-bag. He has brought enough supplies with him to see him through

180

a couple of days; and if he fancies a proper meal, he can always go back to the cottage.

He hears the sound of approaching footsteps outside. Unholstering his automatic, he lifts the tent flap. A few paces away stands a girl in a black skirt and blouse; a pale girl with short hair who looks at Mark with mild curiosity. It is Lucretia.

'Oh, it's you,' she says.

'Yes, it's me,' confirms Mark, emerging from the tent and holstering the gun. 'Didn't expect to find you here. What are you up to?'

'Just out for a walk,' is the reply. 'Got a cigarette?'

Mark proffers his packet.

'They sell these things in the shops, you know.'

'Where's Dodo?' asks Lucretia, her cigarette alight.

'She's not here; it's just me/'

'Are you here to spy on us?'

'Spy on you lot at the Grange? No, I'm here about the UFO business.'

'Then why did you break into the Grange?'

'Because, before I found out otherwise, I thought that the Grange might be connected with the UFO business.'

'No. Nothing to do with us.'

'None of it?' asks Mark. 'I was thinking about the grey aliens people around town have been seeing. In every case, they appeared and disappeared very suddenly. I saw one myself in my bathroom mirror.'

'Did you?'

'Yes. It was right there in the glass, where my reflection ought to have been.'

Lucretia says 'Wow,' without an exclamation mark.

'It's not one of your lot behind those sightings, is it? That's what I've been wondering. Do any of you kids have the ability to make people see things? Cast hallucinations about?'

Lucretia shakes her head. 'No... None of us have that kind of ability.'

Are you sure?'

'Course I'm sure. There's only eight of us. None of us can make people see things.'

181

'And what about you, Lucretia? What exactly is your ESPer ability?'

A shrug. 'I sense things, hear things in my mind...'

'Telepathy?'

'No. Helen and Edward are telepaths. I can't send thoughts to other people or receive people's thoughts.'

'But it sounds like you receive something.'

'Yes. Atmospheres. Feelings. Whatever's floating in the air...' Looking upwards, she sways about on the spot, as Mark has seen her do before. 'These woods are full of atmosphere. I can almost taste it in the air... There are things here... Things overlapping... Things that don't belong here at all...' She stops swaying, looks at Mark. 'You know it's the fifty-first century today?'

'Oh, you had that one at the Grange, did you? From what I can gather, the phenomenon is only affecting computers in this immediate area; it's not happening anywhere else.'

'I wonder,' says Lucretia. 'Maybe time doesn't flow in cyberspace the same way it does in the real world. Go onto an archived website that hasn't been visited for ten years, and you've travelled ten years back in time.'

'Hmm... I think that would be like saying that if you went into a house that nobody had been in for ten years, you had travelled into the past. Poetically speaking you might say you had travelled back in time, but not literally speaking.'

'Yes, but I mean just in cyberspace; the digital universe. It's there; it's all around us; but is it moving forward in time the same way we are...? Maybe it's fixed in time.'

'The internet is a broadcast signal,' says Mark; 'several broadcast signals, in fact. It exists in the air around us, so I suppose it must be moving forward in time along with everything else.'

'Cyberspace is full of doorways; doors that take you into the past or into the future...' She pauses. 'If we could convert ourselves into data, we could really go into cyberspace and we could walk through one of those doors...and then we could come out in a different time, a different world...'

Mark smiles. 'You mean like entering cyberspace in the fifty-first century and coming out in the twenty-first? Time travel via the internet—it's an interesting theory.'

'Maybe it's already happened. Maybe that's how those spacemen got here…'

'The spacemen arrived in a spaceship,' points out Mark. 'It was seen coming down from the sky by a lot of people.'

'Maybe it's not a spaceship; maybe it's a cybership for flying through cyberspace…' She takes a drag of her cigarette. 'It's near here, isn't it?'

'What's near here?'

'The spaceship's landing site.'

'Yes, it's just over yonder.'

'I want to see it.'

'Come on, then. It hasn't been cordoned off or anything.'

Mark leads the way.

'What's your story, Lucretia?' he asks. 'How did you come to be working for Vallotec? You said you volunteered. Does your family know you're here?'

'I ran away from my family,' answers Lucretia. 'I ran away to London, where everyone runs away to. I met a man there; and he locked me up in a room in a house. There were other girls in other rooms in the house. Men came there to have sex with us.'

'Sexual slavery?' exclaims Mark, appalled.

Lucretia keeps her eyes ahead as they walk. Her voice is calm.

'Yes. Sexual slavery. I suppose it wasn't as bad for me as it was for the other girls—my mind could just drift apart from my body. While my body was being raped, my mind would be floating through the stars. The men didn't like that sometimes; they thought I wasn't paying attention… They would hit me… All those men… Sleazy men and shy men, old men and young men, ugly men and handsome men… Men… All just wanting that same silly thing…'

Mark pulls a face. 'The story's the same the world over, unfortunately. The market exists, and so do the people who'll do anything to exploit it. How old are you Lucretia?'

'Eighteen. I was fifteen back then.'

'And how did you get out of that place? Did you escape?'

'Yes. One day, I saw a way out and I ran for it. They saw me run and they came after me. I thought they were going to catch me. But then I ran in front of a car and it stopped. She saw that I was being chased, and she told me to get in. And that's how I met Dr Caxton.'

'Dr Caxton?'

'She's one of the Four Doctors at the Grange.'

'How did she come to be there? Was she looking for you?'

'No. She didn't even know who I was. Quite a coincidence, wasn't it? She took me in. I lived with her in her flat in London for a while; then we came down to the Grange...'

'You must be very grateful to her. Is Caxton that woman with long dark hair?'

'No, that's Dr Channing.'

'She's the blonde one then?'

Lucretia smiles. 'Wrong again. That's Dr Clavering. Caxton's got grey hair; she's not that old, though.'

'You said there are Four Doctors. Who's the fourth?'

'Dr Newcome. He's supposed to be in charge, but Caxton and the others never do what he tells them.'

They emerge into the clearing with the circle of flattened grass.

'Well, here we are,' says Mark. 'The landing site.'

Lucretia skips onto the grass circle, and, arms outstretched, pirouettes.

Mark had thought of those youngsters at Vernon Grange as dupes in need of rescuing... But Lucretia—she's not exactly worse off now than she was before. What did Vallotec want from her? Her rather vague and ethereal ESPer ability doesn't seem to be one that would have many practical applications... Are they just after all conducting research for the sake of research? Lucretia clearly isn't a prisoner at the Grange; she can come and go as she pleases...

'That night I paid a visit to the Grange,' he says aloud. 'Who was that girl who was brought in?'

'Her name's Bridget,' answers Lucretia, still twirling round.

'And was she brought there against her will?'

'Against her *own* will; not against her parents'. I think they were glad to get rid of her; she's a fire-hazard.'

'A fire-hazard?'

'Yeah, she's pyrokinetic.'

184

'I see. And now that she's there; is she happy with her situation?'

'She seems okay. She doesn't talk to me much.' And then: 'They've fibbed to her, though. They've told her that the Grange is a government place.'

'Why did they say that?'

'Dunno. To make us seem more official, I suppose.'

'Couldn't you do something for her?'

'Like what?'

'Like help her escape.'

'Why should she want to escape? They're looking after her; teaching how to control her powers, so she won't be a fire hazard anymore.'

She stops pirouetting, looks at Mark intently.

'What do you think about ESPers?' she asks.

'What do you mean what do I think?'

'You know. Do you think ESPers are freaks of nature? Accidents or something. Or are we the next step up the evolutionary ladder?'

'That I don't know. I've heard it said that the number of people possessing ESP is on the increase; but even that might not be true. It might just be that we have more reliable statistics than we had in the past. I mean, until comparatively recently, people just didn't have the knowledge to identify ESP; it would have been considered supernatural, evil even. Perhaps some of those poor wretches who were burned as witches in the middle-ages were actually ESPers.'

'You don't think that in the future everyone will be ESPers?'

'I'm not sure about that.'

'Seems a bit unfair. Some people having the ability and some people not. If there are enough of us ESPers in the future, we might end up dominating the normal people...'

'Yes—or you might end up becoming a persecuted minority.'

While they are speaking, Mark has been peripherally aware of a sound building up. At first he thought it was a heavy vehicle passing on the road nearby; but the sound continues to build, increasing in pitch. The sound seems to be *above* them: a heavy metallic sound. Both Mark and Lucretia look up, see only the blue summer sky. The sound now begins to reverberate, to echo around the empty sky. It is like nothing Mark has heard before.

'The sound of the sky...' murmurs Lucretia.

'But where's it coming from?' wonders Mark. 'A sound has to have a source.' He remembers the Mantell Project people saying they had attempted to record these sounds; but the recording had played back blank.

The sound increases to an alarming level, building up to a crescendo... It is the most unsettling thing Mark has ever heard. Louder and louder... And then, an abrupt termination; only a lingering echo, slowly fading from the audible scale.

And then silence.

Mark lowers his eyes from the sky, turns to address Lucretia.

The grass circle is empty.

Lucretia has disappeared.

Chapter Twenty-Five
Crossing the Bikini Line

Great Yarmouth. One of the locations featured in Charles Dickens' immortal novel *David Copperfield*; scene of the famous shipwreck chapter much-loved by Leo Tolstoy.

But all that took place one dark and stormy night a long time ago; today is a bright and sunny day, and Great Yarmouth beach is just a beach like any other, packed with half-dressed excursionists, most of them families from the surrounding inland towns and villages.

But of more interest to us, we find, under the shade of a parasol, reclining on a rug, Dodo Dupont, Mayumi Takahashi and Trina Trulove. Perhaps unconsciously, they have arranged themselves to the best advantage, with Dodo sitting in the middle, flanked by the two smaller (and bespectacled) women, Trina on her left, Mayumi on her right. They make a charming picture. Dodo, the short-haired six-foot Juno, wears a black bikini, halter-topped, thong briefs. Petite Mayumi, with the olive skin and long Yoko Ono hair, sports a yellow two-piece with black polka-dots;

both the top and the briefs are adorned with ruffles. And young Trina, with her trim figure and bright blue hair in bunches, is modelling a blue bikini (to match her hair!) with a twisted bandanna top.

Our three *bishoujo* sit enjoying the ice creams they have just purchased. Dodo has earned herself a variety of looks on account of the plenitude of pubic hair erupting from either side of the taut crotch of her thong—but Dodo a strong opponent of bikini-line shaving, and does not consider herself to be indecently exposed, and rather enjoys these mixed reactions. (Mayumi and Trina both share her bikini-line ethic, but both wearing low-legged bikini bottoms, have only a few stray curls peeping out, much less noticeable.)

The beach, as I have said, is packed: hyperactive children disport themselves noisily, while their more sedentary parents soak up the sun. The tide has receded to a grey band on the horizon, darker than the cloudless sky; on the line of demarcation between the two stands the quadruped form of an oil-platform. To the right, the pleasure-pier, with life-boat station located at its extremity, extends itself towards the sea. Behind, the ground shelves up to the promenade, and the guest houses and restaurants that look out onto the sea.

'It's like that JG Ballard story,' remarks Trina, surveying the mass of sun-baked humanity around her. 'That one where they're all on the beach.'

'Oh yes; I think I remember that one...' says Dodo. 'Weren't they turned into a singularity or something?'

'No, I thought they were harvested by aliens, weren't they?' argues Trina.

'No, I think you're thinking of *Quatermass*. Nigel Kneale. In the Ballard story they were turned into a singularity. Something to do with satellites in orbit, wasn't it? *The Terminal Beach*; that was the title.'

'The book was called *The Terminal Beach*,' says Trina. 'But that wasn't the title story.'

'Wasn't it? Oh yes, there was another story about a beach, wasn't there? A giant that got washed up on the shore...'

'That wasn't the title story either.'

187

'There was *another* story about a beach?'

'I *think* so…'

A pause. Licking of ice creams.

'I don't think Mark ought to be camping in those woods,' resumes Trina. 'It's dangerous.'

'Mark can look after himself,' replies Dodo. 'He's been walking into dangerous situations for years. That's his job.'

'Yeah, but camping out in the woods is asking for trouble,' insists Trina. 'He should just stay at the cottage.'

'You should join him there,' speaks up Mayumi. 'You might get lucky.'

A blush mantles our Trina's cheeks.

Dodo, smiling at this: 'Still got the hots for Mark, have you? Actually, I guess you'll be aching for him even more now that you've seen what he's packing down there.'

Trina, still crimson, starts to furiously fellate her ice cream.

'You've set yourself quite a challenge, though, if you want to bag Mark,' says Dodo. 'You'll find him a difficult fortress to conquer.'

Trina, white cream all around her mouth, looks at Dodo. 'Have *you* ever…?'

Dodo laughs. 'What, and spoil a beautiful friendship?'

'We could spoil it together,' offers Mayumi.

'Is Mark a dedicated celibate then?' inquires Trina. 'It kind of seems like that.'

'Maybe not a *dedicated* celibate,' replies Dodo. 'But he's not very sexually active. I think Mark's just one of those people who doesn't get that much out of sex.'

'I can't believe he's a fenny, though…' says Trina.

'Yep. Mark's a working-class boy from the sticks, and he never went to university. He just talks the way he does because he's read a lot of books.'

'I wonder why he decided to become a spy?'

Dodo snorts. 'With a name like "Mark Hunter," what else could he do?'

'If there are aliens in the woods,' pursues Trina. 'How's Mark going to stop them? I mean, he can't just slap hand-cuffs on them and arrest them.'

188

'What he can do will depend on what they're here for,' answers Dodo. 'One theory Mark has come up with is that the strangler is an escaped alien lunatic or criminal, and the other spacesuits are pursuing him. That would explain the two landing-sites, you see. It's just those grey aliens that don't fit the pattern.'

'Couldn't the other ones just be those greys wearing spacesuits?'

'No; they're too tall. Grey aliens are small.'

'Have you and Mark met any aliens before?'

'Not the kind that arrive in spaceships... We've encountered the supernatural before, though; demonic forces.'

'Demonic forces?'

'Yup. Real *Exorcist* stuff.'

'When was this?'

'Last year.'

'Tell her the story,' advises Mayumi.

'Yeah! I want to hear this!' enthuses Trina.

'Alright. Sit back and I'll tell the story of the Sternly Gables Incident.'

'Ooh! Is it going to be set in a spooky old country house?'

'Yep, the definite article. This house had been bought up by the Science Ministry and turned into a research facility. A group of eggheads were working there, but their numbers were starting to dwindle. The first casualty had been put down to accident at first; the man had received a fatal electric shock from some piece of equipment. But the second scientist was killed by an ornamental vase falling from the landing. There was no way the vase could have fallen by accident; it had to have been pushed. Was one of the scientists a traitor, a murderer? Or was there an intruder, a saboteur concealing himself in the house somewhere? That's when we were called in. Mark immediately wondered if there might not be a third possible explanation. There was an atmosphere about the whole house; you could feel it the moment you walked into the place. Maybe the place was haunted; that's what Mark thought.'

'And was it haunted?'

'Well, that's what we had to find out. We went to Sternly village looking for information. And there we met the local vicar,

189

a sweet old codger who was also a local historian. We got the whole story from him. In the eighteenth century Sternly Gables had been the home of a young aristocrat; he was a notorious rake and on top of that was also known to dabble in Satanism. He'd even set up a Satanic chapel in the place; it used to be a Christian chapel, but he had it converted. Mostly it had been used for Black Mass slash sex orgies, but one time apparently the rake and his libertine chums decided to perform a ceremony to try and summon the Devil; the whole pentagram and goat's blood business. And they got what they wanted—the summoning worked.'

'It worked? They raised the Devil?'

'Well, they raised *something*. It might not have been Lucifer the Fallen Angel, the Devil of Christian religion; but their ritual called up something, some kind of malevolent force, older than the hills.'

'It wasn't a monster you could see, then?'

'No, it wasn't tangible. Because you see what happened next was that the master of the house suddenly went on the rampage; slaughtered everyone in the house, guests and servants. At his trial he claimed to have been possessed.'

'Did they believe him?'

Dodo shrugs. 'Whether they believed him or not they still hung him. But that wasn't the end of it. The cycle of violence repeated itself with the next lot of people to inhabit the house, and the people after that, and so on. Every time, there would be one member of the household who would suddenly turn homicidal, and every time they would later claim to have been unable to control their actions, that they had been possessed. In the end, the house got itself so bad a reputation that nobody would live in it. The place was shut up; abandoned. And that's how it was for decades and decades—right up until the Ministry of Science bought up the place.'

'Didn't they know about the house's bad reputation?'

'No, because the story had been forgotten until we dug it up. And even if they had heard it, they probably wouldn't have believed there was anything in it.'

'Except that there was.'

'Right, and armed with what we now knew, Mark and I had to try and figure out which member of the team was the killer; which one was possessed by the evil force. I had my eye on the team leader, although I may have been prejudiced because he was such an insufferably smarmy git. Mark suspected another scientist, this colourless, dumpy woman. I think he was using the reverse logic of suspecting the least suspicious person.'

'And which of you was right?'

'Neither of us, as it turned out. After two more deaths, both involving the fixtures and fittings of the house, Mark arrived at the conclusion that the force wasn't possessing any of the inhabitants of the house; it was possessing the house itself.'

'The house?' exclaims Trina.

'Yes. It made sense, didn't it? The house had been empty for so long, so the evil force had had no people to possess; in the end it had made itself at home by possessing the building itself. Mark's theory had to be correct because all of the staff and scientists had had an alibi for the latest death; absolutely none of them could have done it.'

'So what did you do next? Did you have an exorcism?'

'Mark didn't think that would work; he came up with a more practical scheme. His idea was that if a huge electrical charge could be sent through the house, it would neutralise the demon. So that's what we did; we arranged with the local power station for them to send a power-surge through Sternly Gables.'

'And did it work?'

'Yes. A bit too well. When the power-surge went through, it fried the electrics, and the house caught fire and burned to the ground.'

'Awesome! So that got rid of the monster!'

'Well, yes it did; but the Ministry weren't too pleased about losing an entire research facility and a lot of expensive equipment. Poor Mark got his knuckles rapped for that one.'

'Stupid politicians,' says anti-authoritarian Trina. 'They should have been grateful that Mark destroyed the monster!'

'Should have had the exorcism,' says Mayumi.

Chapter Twenty-Six
Endless Summers: Scene Four

A hot and muggy summer's afternoon in early August. Mark Hunter, on his BMX bike (a Christmas present from last year), winds his solitary way along the droves and farm tracks. Everything is quiet and still; the sky above vast, hazy, and colourless Another year has passed since that last memorable encounter with Dunnidge (whose inexplicable disappearance has been the talk of the community), and we see a slightly older Mark; still very much a boy, but taller, his youthful freckles starting to fade. When this summer vacation ends, he will be embarking on his first term of secondary school. He will be a 'First Year' student; Mark's youth predates the advent of 'Year Seven.' But right now, he lies on the borderland—neither a primary school kid or a secondary school kid.

Mark is alone on this expedition because his usual companion, Clyde Waring, is away this week, on holiday with his parents. Mark comes to a stop at the gateway to a field of ripe corn. A solitary tree, an ash tree, stands on the margin of the field, close to the entrance. Tired from cycling, Mark decides to have a rest. He dismounts, sets his bike down on the grass verge, and sits himself under the tree—a sort of natural seat has formed itself between two projecting roots at the foot of the tree. Resting his back against the trunk, Mark looks out across the fields to the distant flat horizon where the ground meets the hazy and limitless sky.

There's a whole world out there, thinks Mark; over there, over that horizon, just out of reach...

Aside from a few sea-side holidays, Mark has seen very little of the world. And he's starting to become more and more conscious of the smallness of his native environment: the town, the cultivated land around it, the river, the spinneys and groves... He has still never made it as far as Vernon Wood... And then that field; the fabled pasture in the middle of which lies an old train carriage; this has also remained elusive to him...

Mark has just been reading another one of his Biggles books.

192

He can lose himself completely in those books; they open up to him a world of travel and adventure. In Biggles books it is rarely the flesh-pots, the glamorous capital cities of the world that are visited—it is the out-of-the-way places that provide the locations: jungles in Africa, Asia, South America; the deserts of North Africa and the Middle-East; tropical islands, frozen wastelands… Touching down on jungle airstrips, dried-up riverbeds, island lagoons… And then there are encounters with wild animals and savage tribesmen; battles against the elements: hurricanes, blizzards, monsoons, sandstorms… Of course, Mark knows that the world of Biggles books is a slightly out of date one and that a lot of those 'savage tribesmen' wear more clothing and live in houses these days, and that you shouldn't really shoot wild animals unless it's as a last resort… But even so, these books have opened his consciousness to the wider world, with all it's different environments, and different people living in different ways… It's a trite old saying that travel broadens the mind; but it's true—it really does broaden the mind, even if the travelling is only in the vicarious form of reading adventure stories. (Market Stanford, as you can imagine, neither is nor was the most cosmopolitan of places. In Mark's primary school there was an Indian girl, Hardev, in his class; she had a younger brother a couple of years below them—and that was it; all the other kids were white.)

The book he has just been reading is called *Biggles on Mystery Island*. It's set in the South Seas, and Biggles and his friends fly out to investigate a mysterious island that is rumoured to be guarded by a pack of trained dogs. They manage to get past the dogs and climb the central mountain to find a community of people living in the crater of the (apparently!) extinct volcano. It turns out the colonists were tricked into going there and they're now the prisoners of a mad king and his armed gang. The king wants to start a new race and rule over them, but the colonists just want to get out. Biggles manages to rescue the colonists, and they make their way down the mountain as the island begins to shake. After they escape in the plane, the volcano erupts, destroying the whole island.

Mark's copy of the book is a new paperback edition ('New in

Paperback' it says on the cover), with a photographic image featuring what his mum calls 'a couple of idiots pretending to be Biggles and Ginger,' dressed in safari-suits, armed with automatics, forcing their way through the brushwood. Mark's favourite Biggles book cover is of one that they've got in the school library, called *Biggles Goes Alone*; a sort of sea-side murder mystery set here in England. It's a hardback edition, and the beautiful cover painting shows Biggles, standing at the back of a cave, hands on hips, illuminated by a candle in a bottle beside him, looking towards the front of the cave, where a man has appeared at the entrance. Whenever he was in the library, Mark would like to take out that book and just admire the picture. But that was the primary school library; he won't be able to see that book anymore...

Mark's thoughts drift once again that looming milestone of Secondary School... He isn't dreading the experience (not like poor Craig is!); if anything he's looking forward to it; but it's going to be a very big change in his life. For one thing, the Secondary School is much bigger: Market Stanford Community College takes in students from the surrounding villages that only have primary schools, so there will be a lot more pupils: something like five-hundred. Another big change will be that you don't have the same teacher for every lesson like you do in primary school. You have to go from class to class, from teacher to teacher. You have a form-tutor, whose class you go to first thing in the morning; Mark supposes that your form-tutor is the one most like your teacher at primary school.

And all those different lessons. Things like Science, History, Geography, which were only occasional projects at primary school; you'll be doing them all the time. Wood-work, Needle-work, Cookery, Art; these as well will be full-time lessons... Well, it won't be too bad; his brother and sister both went there and they both say it was a doss...

Mark doesn't hear the woman approach. She is just suddenly there, a presence he is suddenly conscious of. He looks up. He keeps looking. She is the most beautiful woman he has ever seen. Tall and supple, with long, dark brown hair, and brown eyes. She wears sandals and a flower-patterned summer dress. She looks down at Mark, eyes sparkling with good-humour, the full lips of her mouth parted in a warm smile, a display of strong white teeth. There she stands, just a few feet away—a vision from out of the blue...

Who is she? Mark's sure he's never seen her before.

'Hello there,' she says, still smiling down at him. Her voice is rich, caressing.

'Hello,' says Mark, blushing.

'All alone out here, are you?'

'Yes...'

'Mind if I sit down with you?'

'Okay,' he says.

There's room for two in that natural seat between the two gnarled roots. The woman sits herself down beside Mark, her body close against his. She stretches her legs out before her, crossing her sandalled feet.

Mark can smell the woman's perfume, feel the warmth of her body next to his. A feeling of shyness comes over him. He doesn't usually feel this way, even new people, but this woman... Conscious that he's still blushing, Mark risks a glance at her, but her eyes or not on him; he sees her profile as she stares off into the distance, a thoughtful look on her face. She's tall, this woman; taller than either his mum and dad... How old is she...? Older than his sister, younger than his mum, she looks... Maybe about thirty...

'So quiet, isn't it...?' murmurs the woman. 'You really could believe it was the end of the world and that we're the only two people left...'

She looks round at Mark, and that smile lights up her face again; that warm, generous smile.

'So, Mark,' she says. 'What brings you all the way out here on your own?'

She said his name! 'Should I know you?' he stammers, embarrassed. 'I'm sorry for not remembering... Are you a friend of the family, or...?'

'No, I'm not a friend of the family,' is the smiling reply. 'We've never met before—so don't worry; you haven't forgotten me.'

Now Mark is confused. 'How do you know my name, then?'

'Yes, how *do* I know your name?' She puckers her lips in thought. 'Strange, that. What else do I know about you...? Let me see... Your name is Mark Hunter, you're eleven years old, and you've just finished your last year of primary school, so you're about to start your first year as a secondary school student. Correct?'

'Yes,' says Mark. 'How come you know all that?'

Marianne puts her arm around his shoulder, drawing him closer to her. 'How indeed? Well, since I know something about you, I'll tell you something about me: My name's Marianne Grant, and I've just moved into this neck of the woods very recently, and I happen to be a teacher by profession.'

She has her arm around him; the embrace, the contact feels very new to Mark. It makes his heart go fast, but in a good way. And she knows him...

'Are you going to be one of my new teachers at big school?' he asks, looking up at her.

She meets his gaze, holds it. Mark knows that he's blushing, but he doesn't want to look away.

'No, I won't be teaching at your school,' she tells him. 'So you don't have to call me Miss Grant. Call me Marianne.'

'Marianne...' obediently, entranced by those eyes.

'Yes, we're going to become good friends, you and I, Mark,' she says, her warm, milky voice folding around him. 'Does that sound okay to you? You'd like us to be friends, wouldn't you?'

'Yes...'

'I think we could be the best of friends, couldn't we?'

'Yes...'

And Mark finds himself starting to cry. Unbidden tears begin streaming down his face in a ceaseless cascade. Yes, of course he wants her to be his friend! *Of course* he does! Right now it feels like he's never wanted anything so much in his life as he wants to be friends with this woman. The feeling completely overwhelms him.

Embarrassed, he tries to obliterate the avalanche of tears with the backs of his hands.

'I'm sorry,' he blubbers. 'I—'

'Come here, silly.' Marianne folds him in her arms, pillowing him against her chest, her hair falling around him as she lowers her head over his. Her scent is even stronger now; not just her perfume; the smell of her skin, her hair...

'There, there...' kissing the top of his head. 'Just let it all out...'

'I'm sorry,' says Mark again. 'I don't know why—I mean I don't normally cry like this...'

'Shh... It doesn't matter, it doesn't matter. Just let it all out...'

And the tears begin to subside. He feels himself relaxing, his respiration becoming slow and regular. He looks up at Marianne.

'Alright now?' she asks, smiling, wiping the tears from his face.

'Yes...'

Mark sits back against the tree, Marianne keeping her arm around his shoulder.

Only a minute ago they were strangers, Mark and this woman—but something has happened; a bond has fashioned itself, solidified; a bond as imperishable as it is spontaneous...

Marianne kisses his cheek.

'You see, we're good friends already,' she says. 'That was all it took. Some things are just meant to be.'

'But how come you know me?'

'Don't worry about that,' squeezing his shoulder. 'Tell me, Mark: what sort of books do you like to read?'

'Books?' echoes Mark.

'Yes. I want to know all about you, Mark. I don't know everything/ So let's start with books. Books are important. What do you like to read?'

'Well, I like Biggles, Doctor Who...'

Marianne seems to ponder this, lips pouting again. 'Hmm... Yes, Biggles and Doctor Who are alright enough, but I think we can do better than that. You're a big boy now; we need to broaden your literary horizons a bit.'

'Broaden my literary horizons?' Mark chews the words over.

'Yes. A book doesn't have to be an adventure story to be interesting, you know.'

Mark *didn't* know. But he's willing to learn.

197

'Yes… I think I'll lend you some books to read,' she says. 'That's what I'll do. And then, when you've read each one, we can talk about it. Have a book discussion. How does that sound?'

'It sounds good,' says Mark, smiling.

'Good! It'll be like summer homework. A special education ahead of your high school career.'

'Special education?'

'Well, I *am* a teacher,' she reminds him. 'I'll be your special tutor for the summer. But that doesn't mean you have to start calling me Miss Grant! You call me Marianne, because we're friends, right?'

Mark concurs with enthusiasm.

'Well, that's books out of the way: what do I want to ask you about now…? I know: girls. Have you got a girlfriend?'

Mark, blushing, replies in the negative.

'But you've thought about it, haven't you?' pursues Marianne. 'I mean, you're a growing boy, aren't you? Must be getting past that stage when you think that girls are just 'sissy.' Starting to feel differently about girls now… Yes?'

Mark supposes he is.

'Good. That's something else for our summer classes. We need to address some of those gender issues.'

'Gender issues?'

'Oh, yes, my sweet. All about men and women and how they get along and how they don't get along. The never-ending cycle.' She sighs, her smile becomes sad, and she studies Mark's face, gently running a forefinger along his downy cheek.

And then, without a word, she suddenly rises to her feet. Kicking off her sandals, she moves from under the tree to the fringe of the field where the ripe corn stands, unmoving in the still air. Marianne stares off into the distance as her hands reach behind her back… Mark, watching her, hears the sound of a zipper… And then she pulls back the shoulder straps of her flower-patterned dress; it drops to the ground and she stands naked before him. Smiling, still gazing into the distance, she stretches herself, and then walks slowly along the border of the field with measured steps, turns around, paces back again, quietly humming to herself…

198

Both stunned and precociously aroused, Mark gazes at her, following her movements with his hazel eyes, completely overwhelmed by the vision, entranced... The collar bone, the broad shoulders, the full, heavy breasts; the graceful arms and long-fingered hands; the planes of her back and abdomen; the swelling of the hips; the powerful buttocks; the thick nest of hair at the junction of her thighs; the strong, sinuous legs and firm feet... She moves with an effortless grace, seeming as much a natural part of the landscape as the field of corn rising behind her... A goddess in her natural element...

She suddenly stops, turns, and smiles at Mark, and his heart performs a somersault.

She now returns to him, sits back down next to him. Sitting next to him, legs stretched out, just as she was before—but it's oh so different now!

Mark blushes furiously, endeavouring to conceal his state of arousal. Can she see it? Does she know?

'Don't be shy,' comes her voice. 'I'm not going to eat you.' He looks at her; she pats her lap. 'Lie down here with your head in my lap. Come on!'

'But, I—'

'Go *on*. I want to talk to you. This will be your first lesson. You don't have to say anything: Just lie your head down here and listen to my words...'

'Okay...'

Obedient, Mark lies down on his side, moving awkwardly on account of the aching obstruction in the crotch of his jeans. He lowers his head onto Marianne's lap.

'That's it; facing me...'

Now his head is pillowed by the warm fleshy softness of her thighs, and his nose and mouth are nestled in that exciting mound of pubic hair. Soft and thick, shampoo-scented, he feels it against his skin; and from beneath the herbal scent, rises another scent from that dense forest; sharp and tangy, urgent, suggestive of the ocean. A delicious warmth rises with the scent, a caressing heat...

'That's it. Just relax,' says Marianne, her voice low and soothing. She strokes his head with slow movements of her hand. 'You're safe here with me. Just relax... Just relax...'

Chapter Twenty-Seven
How's it Hanging?

Trevor can't honestly say that he really loves his girlfriend Lindsey. But then, has he ever really experienced the tender emotion? Yes, there had been one or two crushes back in secondary school, but that was probably just calf love. And he never ended up going out with any of those girls; at school people always used to say he had a wart on his face, no matter how often he tried to make it clear that it was just a large mole... Lindsey is his first actual girlfriend; and no, he can't really say that he is in love with her. In fact, a lot of the time he doesn't even particularly *like* her. Yes, she's good-looking enough, if you ignore that sour, shifty expression which has taken up permanent residence on her face; she's not fat or ugly, so she isn't a girlfriend he would be embarrassed to be seen with in public. (Like most people, Trevor is always thinking about appearances.) On the debit-side, Lindsey's personal hygiene habits leave a lot to be desired; she doesn't bathe nearly as often as she ought to. If she is going out somewhere, and can't be bothered to have a bath, she will just smother herself in perfume and consider that she has done her duty to society. Her feet are particularly offensive. And she's nearly always prickly from not shaving her body hair regularly. Also on the debit-side is her conversation; even if you can forgive her annoying, whiny voice, all she ever does is nit-pick and slag-off her friends; this forms the staple of her conversation. (Trevor has no illusions, and is fairly confident she also slags *him* off behind his back.)

Okay, so there is the bad personal hygiene and the shrewish disposition; but what can be said in favour of Lindsey? Come on, Trevor! You're going out with the girl, and you have been for nearly a year, there must be something else you can put in the 'credit' box!

Well, there's the sex, of course. If Trevor only stays with her for that reason, he is no worse than a lot of other people. It certainly bolsters Trev's ego to have a partner and a regular sex-life. He can even feel superior to Jack in that regard. Yes, Jack Stone, the top-dog farm hand and occasional politician, doesn't have a girlfriend! Ha! What a loser!

Ever since they were kids, Jack has been a dominating presence in Trevor's life, and this has led to Trev acquiring the inevitable ambivalent feelings towards him. Part of Trevor always wants to out-do Jack, to get one-up on him; another part of him just wants to earn Jack's approval.

Hold on; we're wandering from the point. We don't want to hear about Trev's psychological hang-ups. Back to Lindsey! Yes, Trev likes having sex with her. Well, he the likes the fact that he is having sex—he can't say that having sex with *her* in particular is especially amazing; what with the uncleanliness, laxity with reference to body-hair removal, and her stinky feet. And she makes these annoying grunting noises…

Yes, all things considered, Trevor doesn't really love Lindsey. Trevor is just one of those people who thinks that having a girlfriend is better than not having one. Nevertheless, having said all of the above, it would be a lie to say that he is unmoved when, walking into Lindsey's house that evening, he finds her engaged in having sex with Jack Stone.

Moved he is, and not agreeably!

As advertised earlier, local rockers Switchback are playing at the Boat House this evening. The band have a large local following, so the gig is going to be well-attended. Trev, Lindsey, Jack and Mitch are all going. (Final proof that morons don't only listen to dance music!) Trevor is calling round Lindsey's house to pick her up. He feels very much at home at Lindsey's house, and so he just walks in through the front door without knocking. And there they are! Lindsey bent over the sofa, her jeans around her ankles and Jack Stone unzipped and pounding away at her!

Trev freezes in the doorway.

'It's not what it looks like!' says Jack.

'Shut the door!' says Lindsey.

Mechanically, Trevor shuts the door.

'Nearly done!' says Jack.

It seems he has arrived just at the climax of the proceedings. There's the usual grunting and wincing, and then Jack extracts himself and quickly stashes away Mr Happy.

Trevor bursts into tears. 'What's going on?' he blubbers.

'Look at the cry-baby,' snorts Lindsey, wriggling back into her jeans.

'Shut up, your slag,' Jack tells her. He walks up to Trevor. 'Listen, mate; I was only doin' this for yer own good.'

'You were fucking my girlfriend for my own good?' wails Trevor, a faint suggestion of disbelief in his tone.

'Yeah! Wouldn't do it for any other reason, would I? You think I want to shag *that*?' pointing over his shoulder. 'But, y'see, Trev, if wasn't me, it'd be the whole fuckin' town.' Jack places fraternal hands on Trevor's shoulders. 'Listen to me, Trev. She's rubbish, she is; rubbish. You know it, an' I know. If I didn't keep 'er in line like this, she'd be the local bike! I swear—she'd be fucking the whole town! So y'see, I'm only doin' it for you, mate. Someone's got to keep 'er in line, 'aven't they? I tell yer, if it wasn't me it'd be everyone, and the 'ole fuckin' town'd know about it! Now, you wouldn't want that, do yer?'

'No…' admits Trev. (Appearances, remember!)

'Right! So blow yer nose an' cheer up, mate! No-one's gunna know about this! It's just between me, you, and the whore. Right? What are friends for, eh?'

And he gives Trev a friendly slap on both chops.

Twisted Fate are on stage.

The support act for the main event, Twisted Fate are a band from the local secondary school. Year Ten boys, they perform hard rock with caterwauling vocals. ('From the way you were singing, it didn't sound like it was your "fate" you'd got twisted!' one teacher had remarked after a school concert performance.)

The Boat House is your typical pub venue: just one big room with bar at one end, stage at the other, crowd capacity about three hundred. As expected, there is a strong turn-out this evening, the audience ranging from aging rockers with ragged voices and long grey hair, down to the teenage classmates of the support band, with all the Generation Xers and 18-30 demographic indie-kids in between. And it's hot inside—very hot. Being a live music venue, the windows are all closed and curtained, and there's no air-conditioning to compensate for this. But then, isn't this sweat-bath just another part of the authentic live music experience?

You can notice the gradual diminution of motion amongst the audience, from the front to the back of the room. You have the people at the foot of the stage, exclusively young and male, who are throwing themselves around like berserkers; behind them, you have the people dancing just as enthusiastically but less violently (a lot more girls here); and then behind them you have those people who are just vaguely swaying from the hips upwards; and then right at the back, near the bar, you have the people who are not moving at all. (The greybeards are all here. Old rockers never die, they just stand at the back of the room.)

Standing at the back of the third tier, the not-quite-dancing tier, is our Bwidget Pwice, enjoying her first live concert. She's an ardent music fan, but she's never actually been to a gig before. The stifling, sweaty atmosphere, the flashing stage-lights, the music so loud you can feel it... It's all new to her. Standing where she is, Bridget has a very good view of the heads of the people in front of her. Between two of those heads, she can see the bass-player—and if she moves slightly, between the next two heads she can see the vocalist... No! Now she can't see him! Someone has just changed their position and is blocking her view.

Bridget wears a sleeveless top tonight; appropriate, but unusual for her, as she's very self-conscious about the self-inflicted scars on her arms. But Serena has talked her into dressing appropriately for the gig, pointing out how hot it was bound to be, and also that she wouldn't by a long chalk be the only self-harmer amongst the female portion of the audience. Wear those scars with pride, ladies!

Standing behind Bridget, looking very hot and uncomfortable in a buttoned-to-the-top shirt, is Edward. Edward had surprised everyone by declaring his intention of joining Bridget, Damien and Serena, and making one of the party going to the gig. But why? What on earth is he doing here? He's a textbook classical music snob, isn't he? You would have thought Anthony Burgess (even though he's dead) would have been more likely to have turned up.

Bridget had wondered if perhaps Edward is one of those

203

people who like any and all kinds of music, but looking over her shoulder right now and seeing the pained expression on his face, she suspects this is not actually the case.

(The anticipated fourth member of their group was to have been Lucretia—but the Goth girl had gone out for a walk that afternoon and, so far, hasn't come back.)

Bridget got an email from her parents today, sending her their love. And she has had the first of her 'lessons' as well, down in the underground lab, working with Dr Channing.

Bridget had assumed that Channing was the person in charge of the establishment, because that is how she seems; but according to Damien, Dr Newcome, the one male doctor, is meant to be in charge. But the three women doctors hate his guts, and undermine his authority at every turn; and most of the ESPers can't stand him either. Seeing this, Bridget felt a bit sorry for Newcome, but mentioning it to Damien, he told her not to waste her sympathy: 'He's an annoying prick, and on top of that he's a paedo.' And yes, Newcome *does* seem rather fond of Robert and Roberta. That morning he had been playing 'tag' with the twins, apparently a regular activity. He would lunge at them and they would use their teleportation powers to elude him. Peals of laughter all round. (In many ways the twins are wise beyond their years—but they seem to have a blind-spot where Dr Newcome is concerned; they think that his love of romping with them is entirely innocent.)

In the lab, Bridget's first task had been to ignite a can of domestic lubricating oil with the power of her mind. Channing had told her that her mind has an affinity to all things inflammable; she just has to reach out with her mind, connect with the inflammable object, and will it to ignite. Bridget had followed her advice, staring hard at the can of oil, and yes, she *had* felt a connection with it, a link. She had visualised the can bursting into flame, and concentrating her mind, it *had* burst into flame. Success. Channing had told her that with training her mind would be able to reach out to inflammable objects in the vicinity that were not even visible to her; her mind would be able to sense these sources, and with effort, cause them to ignite.

204

Bridget wonders how long it will be before she will be ready to be sent out on a mission. She can see herself as a sort of pyrokinetic secret-agent, blowing up oil refineries and chemical factories and whatnot—and all for Queen and Country.

The end of the first band's set, and everybody pours out into the beer garden for contradictory fresh air and cigarettes. It's gone eight and the sun is starting to set. Trevor is subdued, doubtless still trying to acclimatise himself to the new phase his relationship with Lindsey has entered. The two of them stand silent together, a newly-erected brick wall invisibly occupying the space between them. Jack meanwhile, has other fish to fry. Yes, *they* are back! The boy Damien (aka 'the skinny cunt'), that sexed-up looking girl, Serena, and two other kids they haven't seen before, a boy with glasses and a girl wearing a silly hat. Jack and Mitch are debating what is to be done about this nuisance, these aggravating outsiders.

'Wanna sort 'em out tonight?' questions Mitch.

'Nah,' says Jack. 'Tonight what we do is follow 'em when they leave; find out where they live.'

'Then what?'

'Then we've got 'em where we want 'em.'

'You call that music?'

Bridget, Edward, Serena and Damien are amongst the throng filling the stone-flagged beer garden, the latter two smoking. Bridget is enjoying a pint of ale that Damien has illegally bought for her. This is Bridget's first ever pint; she is already starting to feel its effects.

'Remind me why you're here, Edward,' says Damien. 'You knew it wasn't going to be a classical music concert.'

'I was curious,' replies Edward. 'I wanted to see if I could discover what people like you see in this kind of so-called music.'

'Oh, really? And, pray, what are your findings, Professor? Do tell.'

'It's just rhythmic noise,' is the answer. 'No skill has gone into making it at all. Compared to classical music, it's what one-plus-

205

one is to Euclid. It's completely primitive; mindlessly stupid. It appeals to the most basic instincts. Listening to it just now was like enduring a prolonged assault on my mind and senses.'

'Wock music's not stupid!' protests Bridget, with alcohol-fuelled indignation. 'Wock bands sing about important stuff in their songs. Politics and things.'

'Oh really?' retorts Edward, unconsciously echoing Damien. 'Well, I can read about "politics and things" in books. I don't really care what a bunch of Neanderthal so-called musicians have to say on the subject. If you gave those guitars to a bunch of monkeys, they could make the same noise as that so-called music.' (Edward's starting to over-do the 'so-called' motif here.)

'Jesus Christ,' sighs Serena. 'Y'know, you classical music snobs really piss me off. You're like all so fucking superior about your taste in music. Like you think it makes you better than the rest of us.'

'Well, it shows that we have more refined tastes,' retorts Edward.

'Oh, does it? Well, then; answer this one—who's got the more "refined tastes": the classical music fan who reads Agatha Christie novels, or the rock music fan who reads Proust?'

'That's hardly the same thing—' splutters Edward.

'Oh-ho! She's got you, there!' chuckles Damien. 'Come on, Einstein; answer the question!'

'Well, it… it—'

Even Bridget, her head starting to buzz in full earnest now, joins in the laughter. Crushed, Edward stalks off, muttering something about needing the toilet.

'My willy's on upside down,
My willy's on upside down,
My balls are in the air and my boner,
Points to the ground,
Points to the ground.'

Not exactly the politically aware song-lyric subject-matter that Bridget has been boasting about; but right now nobody really cares, least of all Bridget herself. Switchback are tearing up the stage, and the audience, fuelled by alcohol, have surrendered their individuality to the music, to the moment, and are just one heaving, screaming, furiously sweating mass. And Bridget is right in there with them, high as a kite thanks to a pint of mild ale, and ear-flaps flying as she ecstatically dervish-dances with the best of them.

It's good to just let go and lose yourself in the moment every now and then, especially when you're young.

'What are you on, girl? We saw you out there; you were seriously shaking it! You got some good stuff?'

'Stuff?'

'Yeah; drugs. What're you on: whizz?'

'Oh, no; I haven't taken any dwugs.'

'What, you're just pissed, are you?'

'Yeah! This is… this is my *second* pint tonight!'

'Fuck, girl, you're really pushing the boat out! Have you seen Switchback before?'

'No, no, never! Cuz I tell you what: thish… this is my first ever gig!'

'First ever gig, eh? How about that?'

'Yesh, but… but I'd heard them on the *wadio* before, though. Bitchswack… Switchback… They got played on… on Wadio 6…'

'Yeah, the boys were really pumped about getting that airplay! We know them, see? I go out with Tod, the drummer.'

'Yeah, an' I'm going out with Neil; he's the guitarist.'

'Wow! That's so *cool!* Going out with the… dwummer and the guitawist! And both at the same time…'

'Well, yeah… There are two of us here, y'know. You're not just seeing double.'

'Yes, there's two of you! …And you're… going out with the guitawist… and *you're* going out with the dwummer! Is that right?'

'Other way round, girl. Mind you, we do swap partners now and then.'

'Ooh! That's *wude!* That's like… pwob…iscis sexual… sex!'

'If you say so! …What about you? Those two guys you're

with. Are you going out with… Damien, isn't it? Or is it the one with the glasses?'

'Mm-mm. Uh-uh. I'm not going out with both of them… Either, I mean… But I *like* Damien, though. I like him…'

'Well, maybe tonight's the night you'll get lucky. I reckon you're about ready for it.'

'Ohhh… You think so? What… but what should I say to him? I don't weally know what to say…'

'You won't have to say anything, girl. Just let it happen. So, where do you and your mates live, then? Are you from out of town?'

'Not weally. We're fwom… sort of just outside the town.'

'Just outside?'

'Yes, it's a big house called Vernon Gwange.'

'Vernon Grange? Seriously? You're living there?'

'Yes, we—whoops! I just wemembered! I'm not supposed to tell anyone! I'm not supposed to say we're fwom Vernon Gwange! It's a secwet! So, shh! Shh! Don't tell anyone about it…'

'Don't sweat it. We'll keep quiet about it!'

'Those two girls went straight up to Jack Stone and his chums,' reports Serena.

'Who's Jack Stone?' asks Bridget.

'A native lifeform I've crossed swords with,' replies Damien. 'He set those girls on you just to find out where we lived.'

'Does it really matter if they know?' asks Serena.

'Well, I doubt they wanted to find out just out of idle curiosity,' says Damien. 'Jack Stone's the vindictive type, and what with me winding him up all the time, he probably thinks he owes me one.'

'So what? It's not like they can just walk into the Grange, is it?' persists Serena.

'Yeah!' agrees Bridget. 'The guards'll just shoot 'em! Bang! You're dead!'

'True…' says Damien, a thoughtful look on his face. 'Still, if they did plan on paying us a social call… It could be quite fun…'

Chapter Twenty-Eight
At Night in Vernon Wood

Dodo, at the wheel of her Jaguar, is driving the kids home. Well, that's what it feels like. Trina and Mayumi, occupying the back seat, are undeniably making as much noise as a couple of hyperactive kids; chattering away, girlishly giggling.

This is because they are both completely hammered.

'...And so, Catherine the Great was in a "stable relationship" with a horse!' splutters Trina.

'A horse?' giggles Mayumi.

'Yep. She liked to do it with horses, y'see. Cuz horses; they're hung like... like...'

'Stallions?' suggests Dodo.

'Yeah, thassit! They're hung like stallions! And it was like she had a team of assistants who would lift the thing on and off of her, like a pulley or something, and this one time someone must've let go of the rope, cuz they dropped the thing on her! Bam! And that was how Catherine the Great died!'

Peals of laughter from the back seat.

'An' you know what?' says Trina. 'You know what?'

'What?' asks Mayumi.

'Iss funny... iss funny they never did that one in *Horrible Histories*!'

More laughter.

Dodo doesn't have the heart to tell them that the horse story is apocryphal.

Our three heroines had rounded off their day out at one of Great Yarmouth's public houses, and Dodo, being the designated driver, has had to limit herself to one pint of beer; after that she was on the Coca-Cola. She hasn't minded. It's been an interesting experience from a professional point of view, watching her two friends steadily inebriating themselves, and how, stage by stage, glass by glass, the conversation became progressively more and more merry and less and less intelligent.

Hence the story about Catherine the Great and the horse. But the story is apocryphal. Just a posthumous attempt to besmirch the name of a remarkable woman. Catherine the Great (after she'd got rid of her idiot husband and became Empress) was an enlightened and well-read woman who did a great deal of good for her country. But she undeniably had a 'work hard, play hard' work ethic and a tremendous sexual appetite when it came to the latter. She always craved variety and kept herself well supplied with men. It was one of the functions of her maids of honour to 'audition' potential sexual partners, testing them for size and stamina to determine whether or not they made the grade and were good enough to perform service in the Imperial bed-chamber... Catherine the Great basically used men for sex; and why not? thinks Dodo. Good for her! (But it's very unlikely that she ever felt the need to experiment with horses.)

Thinking of that rapid turnover of sex partners reminds Dodo of an incident from her own past, one which she now looks back upon with profound embarrassment. It was back when she had just started university, studying for her Bachelor's degree in psychology. The eighteen-year-old Dodo was all fired up, overflowing with ambition and self-assurance. She'd decided she was going to make a big name for herself in the field of psychology and nothing was going to stand in her way! And in this regard she had considered her own behaviour and that of her fellow students to be every bit as much valuable research material as were the studies and seminars. And she had hit on the idea for a grand experiment, some 'original research' of her own. Her objective was this: to set about systematically bedding every male in her class, aiming to achieve this goal in the smallest amount of time possible. She was confident of success. And she was right— the experiment was brought to fruition in just three short (but very energetic) weeks. Along the way she had diligently compiled a record of her own thoughts and sensations, as well as her observations of the behaviour of the males—which of them had agreed immediately to the sex; which of them had taken more seducing. Which of them had insisted on wearing a condom; which of them had insisted on *not* wearing one...

A fascinating experiment, but of course, it all blew up in Dodo's face in the end. Experiments of this nature cannot be kept secret, and inevitably, the story got out—and as some of the boys in her class had girlfriends who were *also* in her class, it all ended up a very noisy mess and Dodo found herself hauled before the board of directors for a disciplinary hearing. Some of the committee members were frankly sceptical of Dodo's scientific pretensions, preferring to believe she had been primarily motivated by a hypersexual desire for sexual gratification. And while there were no rules against undergraduates engaging in sexual congress with each other, they did have rules about causing strife and disruption on campus and generally giving the university a bad name. Her opponents just wanted to throw Dodo off the course completely, but in the end the views of the more lenient prevailed, and Dodo was let off with a stern warning.

Today, Dodo looks back on what she did as a manifestation of youthful zeal combined with embarrassing immaturity and, frankly, a great deal of pretentiousness.

(If you're interested, you can read about this episode from Dodo's academic career, set out in graphic detail in her book *Mind and Body*, still available from all the usual online outlets, as well as any surviving high-street retailers—set out in *too much* graphic detail, according to some of the critics, who argued that with the bedroom activity described with so much colourful detail, the book veered from psychology to pornography.)

'What's that thing in Japan?' Trina asks Mayumi.

'What thing?'

'You know; that thing; with the schoolgirls prostituting themselves, 'cept they don't call it prostitution; they call it something else.'

'Oh, that. It's called "paid dating."'

'That's it! Paid dating!'

'What about it?'

'I was just wondering: did you ever do it when you were at school?' eagerly.

'No, I never did that,' Mayumi tells her.

Trina's face falls. 'Didn't you?'

'No.'

'Never?'

'No.'

'What about your friends at school?'

'What about them?'

'Did any of them do it?'

'No.'

'None of them?'

'None of them.'

Says Dodo: 'You know, that whole "paid dating" business was never really the epidemic it was reported as being, when the foreign press first got hold of the story. The girls who do paid dating basically just want to boost their allowance money—the trendy, superficial girls who just want to be able to buy more make-up, clothes and accessories, and who don't mind selling their bodies in order to get the cash. So, you basically had people saying they were all at it in Japan because they thought all Japanese girls were like that, which is a rather unfair assumption to make. And then you had people pointing the finger at Japan's whole schoolgirl-idolising culture, saying it was responsible for creating the market. But the fact is, you can find teenage prostitution in just about any country; but in the case of Japan they were calling it "schoolgirl prostitution" which kind of emphasises the gymslip element. I was going to write about paid dating in one of my books, but when I read all the stuff that had already been written about it, I realised it would be more interesting to write about people's reaction to the phenomenon, rather than the phenomenon itself.'

'Is that when you went to Japan and first met Yumi?' asks Trina.

'Yes, it was,' is the reply.

'It was love at first sight,' says Mayumi.

'That's sweet!' gushes Trina. And then, suddenly becoming aware of their surroundings: 'Here, this is Vernon Wood!'

'Yep, we're nearly home,' confirms Dodo.

'We could stop and see Mark!' suggests Trina.

'Unfortunately, we don't know where he's pitched his tent,' points out Dodo.

'In the same place those other people had their tents,' says Mayumi.

'Yes, but I don't know where that is, because I haven't been

212

there,' says Dodo. 'None of us have.'

'He should have left us a map.'

'He should, really,' agrees Dodo. 'I'd prefer it if I knew where to find him—'

And then the car dies.

'What the fuck?'

Propelled by its own momentum, the vehicle coasts onwards, gradually slowing to a halt. Dodo tries the ignition. Nothing. The dashboard remains in darkness.

'Is it the battery?' asks Trina.

'I'm not sure,' says Dodo. 'But if you'll remember, that policeman's car died on this same stretch of road, just before he had his close encounter with some spacemen.'

'Aliens!' squeaks Trina. 'They've stopped our car! They're going to abduct us!'

'Calm down, you silly mare,' says Dodo. She rummages in the glove compartment and produces her handgun. 'See? I've got this, so we're not helpless.'

'There's a light over there,' reports Mayumi.

Trina looks in the direction indicated. 'Ooh, yeah. What is it?'

Dodo steps out of the car. Above the tree-tops across the road, a green aurora lights up the night sky.

Mark Hunter also observes the light.

He has been concerned about Lucretia. The girl has disappeared. At least, that was how it seemed. One minute she was there, the next minute she had gone. Had she simply ran off while his back was turned? Had she had time to make herself scarce as quickly as that? Quite possibly. And then, from what he knows of the girl, she does seem like the type who might elect to make enigmatic sudden exits while people's backs are turned... But would she have pulled a childish stunt like that right at the moment those strange, unearthly sounds were filling the air?

After ineffectually calling out the girl's name, Mark had run back to his campsite; he had found no sign of her there either. True, if the girl had wanted to pull a disappearing act, she might have gone home by another route; she might, for instance, have headed for the road, and returned to the Grange that way. But what if she *hadn't* left of her own accord? What if she had literally disappeared? That was how it initially seemed. There she was, standing in the middle of the landing-site, the circle of compressed vegetation, with those inexplicable sounds playing in the air above them... Could she have been taken away somehow? Transported? Could the sounds have had something to do with it? Could the spot she was standing on have had something to do with it? And if she has been taken away, taken by whom and to where? That night at the Grange, Mark saw one of the spacesuit creatures apparently teleport itself... Could Lucretia have been teleported; taken onboard some alien spacecraft? The only other person to have reported such an experience was the unfortunate Flora Hodgson with her cliché-ridden abduction story... Mark is fairly certain that the only close encounter Flora Hodgson ever experienced was the one that killed her...

These Mark's thoughts when sky over the treetops becomes irradiated by the green glow. He is far away from his campsite, following one of the nature trails, but he can tell that the aurora is emanating from the landing-site—and from the video footage recovered from the ill-fated Mantell Project, he can guess what might be producing that light. What puzzles him is that the light has just *appeared*; it hasn't dropped from the sky as it had on the night of the Market Stanford Incident. Could the spacecraft be able to teleport itself? To move instantaneously from one location to another? That might explain its successive disappearances and reappearances; it might even explain the fact of their being two landing sites.

And it has to happen while he's nowhere near the place. He sets off running.

(And for anyone who's thinking, 'Oi, hang on a minute! Mark should know that the UFO can just appear out of thin air! He saw that film the Mantell Project took, didn't he?' Well, yes he did, but during the time they were filming it, the Mantell Project trio never actually referred to the fact of the craft having materialised out of thin air. No, they didn't. If you don't believe me, go back to Chapter Seven and see for yourself.)

'It must be that spaceship,' says Dodo.

Mayumi and Trina have joined her outside the car.

'What should we do?' inquires Mayumi.

'I think we should go'n take a look,' answers Dodo.

'But we'll get machine-gunned to death!' wails Trina.

'Alright, then you and Yumi can stay here,' says Dodo. 'You're both pissed as farts, anyway.'

'I'm not staying here on my own!' declares Trina.

'Me neither,' adds Mayumi.

'Then *come on*,' says Dodo, teeth gritted. 'Just keep quiet and keep behind me.'

And off they set into the woods; one television psychologist and part-time spy, accompanied by one steaming drunk Japanese photographer girlfriend, and one scatter-brained intern, also steaming drunk; all boldly setting forth into unknown dangers.

They strike a footpath, and close in on the source of the glow. The light is much more intense at ground level; you can see it through the gaps in the trees. And a sound reaches their ears: a regular mechanical humming.

'What's that noise?' says Trina loudly.

'Keep your voice down!' hisses Dodo.

The sound increases in pitch, the light in intensity as they near the clearing. Dodo leads her friends off the path and they take cover behind some shrubbery.

And there it is, right before them; the source of the light and the sound. A luminous vehicle of some kind; spherical, metallic, radiating a greenish light, humming with power.

'Well, there it is,' breathes Dodo. 'The same UFO we saw on that camera film.'

'A flying saucer...' says Trina.

'Looks more like spinning top,' says Mayumi.

'Who's inside it?' wonders Trina. 'Aliens or just people?'

Maybe we'll find out tonight,' says Dodo.

Aliens or just people... Dodo finds it hard to believe that what she sees could be an experimental aircraft of Earth construction; everything about the thing just seems somehow *wrong*. It doesn't belong here.

She becomes aware of a hissing liquid sound by her side. She looks round and, in the half-light, sees that Trina, knickers down around her ankles, is urinating.

'*Trina.*'

'Look, I was *bursting*,' is the defensive reply.

'There's a time and a place for everything.'

'Well, we're outside. It's not like I'm peeing on the carpet.'

'Gives me idea for next photobook,' says Mayumi. 'Ladies urinating in all different places.'

'Yeah! That'd be great—'

'You two!' remonstrates Dodo. 'This is not the time! Keep quiet!'

Silence falls, save for the continued splashing sound. (Trina really has been holding it in.) Dodo wonders where Mark could be. By all rights he ought to be nearby, observing the UFO the same as they are... Unless he's been reckless enough to try and get inside the thing...! Or maybe even has been *taken* inside the thing...?

And then the craft starts to fade. The green glow, the humming sound—both start to diminish in intensity. At first Dodo thinks that the vehicle is powering down its engines (or whatever its power source might be); but no, the object itself is starting to fade, not just the halo of light surrounding it.

Dimmer and dimmer grows the craft, and then it fades to nothing. Darkness and silence take possession of the clearing.

'What just happened...?' from Trina.

'Beats me,' answers Dodo. 'It didn't take off; it didn't move. Maybe it teleported itself away.' She stands up. 'Come on, you two; let's see if we can find Mark.'

Stepping out from the thicket, they move cautiously along the periphery of the clearing, Dodo walking in front with her gun at the ready. She hears the sound of movement ahead. Is it Mark? No, it isn't. Dodo flattens herself against the nearest tree, urgently motioning the others to do the same. Two figures emerge from the shadows before them; two humanoid figures in spacesuits, each of them carrying some kind of weapon—like a rifle but of no identifiable design.

They pause on the periphery of the clearing for a moment, and then turn and move off, away from the three watchers, deeper into the woods.

'Okay, you can relax now,' says Dodo.

'Spacemen!' says Trina.

'Yes. Just like the one that attacked Mark.'

'Are we going to follow them?'

'No…' says Dodo, ruminating. 'Not with you two in tow. Anyway, I want to find Mark first. He ought to be here. What's just happened here is the whole reason he's camped out in the woods—so why isn't he here? Let's check out his camp.'

'But we don't know where it is,' Trina reminds her.

'I do now,' says Dodo. 'Mark said the clearing he was setting up his tent in was just to the north of the UFO landing site: *that* is obviously the landing site, and *this* way is north; so we go this way.'

They strike off in the direction indicated and sure enough they soon light upon a clearing in which a collapsible tent is pitched.

'He's not here,' announces Dodo, looking inside the tent. 'Where is he…?'

'Maybe he's in another part of the woods,' suggests Trina.

'I'm more worried that he might have been on board that spaceship or whatever it was,' says Dodo. 'I don't know what to do…'

And then the sound of machinegun fire tears into the night.

Dodo springs to her feet. 'You two stay here. Stay together and keep out of sight.' And with this, gun in hand, she runs into the woods, following the direction of the gunfire.

Mark is still some distance from the landing-site when he sees the green glow above the treetops begin to fade. He stops in his tracks, watching the glow slowly expire. Like Dodo he wonders if the craft producing the light is just switching off its lights, powering down.

Well, he'll know when he gets there.

He sets off again, and rounding a curve in the trail, finds himself suddenly confronted by a humanoid figure. Mark pulls up short. He hadn't heard a sound; nothing to warn him that he wasn't alone. One of the spacemen; he can see that much. It just stands there, a few yards ahead.

With hunched posture and awkward steps, it starts to move

217

towards him, arms outstretched. Mark deliberately raises his gun, aiming at that impenetrable visor.

'We've met before, haven't we?' murmurs Mark. 'At least I think it's you, unless there's more than one of you maniacs around here. Want to finish what you started last time, eh? Well, I'm not going to let you get your mitts around my windpipe this time: I'm going to shoot you if you don't stop. I don't know who you are or where you came from, but surely you must be able to understand that I'm pointing a gun at you? You can see that, can't you...?'

Regardless of whether it understands it is being menaced by a weapon, the figure still continues forward.

'Well, don't say I didn't warn you...' Mark's finger tightens on the trigger.

But then more newcomers enter the arena. This time Mark does hear the approaching footsteps. So does his assailant. Two more spacemen appear on the pathway, dressed like the first but armed with rifles. The first spaceman stops his advance towards Mark, and turns to face the newcomers.

If there is any communication between the three spacemen, it is non-verbal, because not an audible word is exchanged, as Mark looks on. Are they having some kind of telepathic conversation? Or are they just silently facing each other like combatants waiting to see who will make the first move?

And then, whether as the result of any unheard dialogue or not, the second two spacemen clearly come to a decision—two rifles are raised and levelled at the first creature. Mark, who also happens to be in the line of fire, dives into the bushes. He hears the rattle of machinegun fire; a short burst. Getting up, he peers through the bushes in time to see the result of the gunfire; the first spaceman, his erstwhile assailant, collapses to the ground. The two assassins close in on the body, looking down at it.

What now? wonders Mark. Are they going to drag the body away?

The spacemen turn to face the spot in which Mark lies concealed. They raise their rifles. It appears the gunmen don't want to leave any witnesses.

Mark flattens himself behind the trunk of the nearest tree. He expects a fusillade of gunfire. Nothing happens. Mark waits a few moments, then risks a peep out onto the track.

The two spacemen are still standing there, guns pointed in his direction, but they are motionless, and starting to fade away. Even more surprisingly, the prostrate form of the dead spaceman is likewise disappearing. Even as Mark watches the three of them fade into nothingness, leaving no sign that they were ever there.

And then the silence is broken by a new sound, this time coming from deeper within the woods. The sound of someone moving at great speed; and coming in his direction.

Now what?

Fixing his eyes on the direction the sound is coming from, Mark soon sees a swiftly-moving form detach itself from the shadows. Holstering his pistol, he moves to intercept the newcomer. He barrels into the figure, attempts to restrain it. His opponent reacts with surprising force, and the next second they are both on the ground, fighting desperately.

But then Mark recognises a familiar perfume.

'Dodo!'

'Mark!'

They help each other to their feet.

'I suppose this is where one of us ought to say, "We really must stop meeting like this,"' says Mark.

'I'm glad you're okay,' says Dodo, kissing him on the mouth. 'I heard machinegun fire and I thought you might be the target, so I came running.'

'I was the target and I wasn't,' replies Mark. 'But what were you doing here in the first place?'

'We were on our way back from Yarmouth, and were passing by when the car conked out on us. We could see a light coming from the landing site and we decided to come and have a look.'

'You say "we" but I don't see Mayumi and Trina.'

'That's because I left them at your campsite. Let's walk while we talk; they'll be wondering what's happened to me.'

They set off back towards the campsite, Mark recounting his recent encounter.

'Then it looks like your theory about those spacemen was right,' observes Dodo. 'That the ones with the guns were after the strangler.'

219

'That's what it looked like,' agrees Mark. 'They tracked him down and executed him. What I don't get is why they disappeared.'

'They teleported.'

'Yes, but it didn't look like anything they'd done intentionally. They were about to turn their attention to me, but then they just faded out.'

'Then they were teleported by someone else. Their boss back in the spaceship—Which reminds me: *that* just faded out as well; the spaceship did.'

Dodo describes what she and the others witnessed at the landing site.

Mark is surprised. 'So the *ship* can teleport as well! ...I wonder if that's what had happened when those Mantell Project kids saw it... You know, that could explain a lot: why the ship disappeared after it originally landed; and then the presence of that second landing site across the road... Which reminds me of something: our spaceman strangler claimed one more victim, unfortunately—poor Flora Hodgson. I only got the news after you three had set off this morning.' Mark describes the crime-scene. '...Maybe last night the UFO materialised at the other landing site; the light from it would have been clearly visible to Flora from her bungalow... She must have gone out across the fields to see what it was, and probably walked straight into her murderer... Yes, that would explain everything except why she didn't have any clothes on...'

'Her psychiatric assessment might explain that one,' says Dodo.

'And you say you didn't actually see those two spacemen emerge from inside the UFO?'

'Nope. They came from the direction of it, but after it had already faded out.'

'Strange...'

Dodo shrugs. 'Maybe the door was just round the back from where we were.'

Shrill screams pierce the night.

'That's the girls!' exclaims Dodo, breaking into a run.

Mark follows suit and they rapidly close in on the campsite.

The screams, becoming cries of Dodo's name, draw closer, and then the running forms of Mayumi and Trina appear from the darkness ahead. To Mark it first seems as though the girls are running a three-legged race; shoulder to shoulder, supporting each other, hobbling along awkwardly—but then he sees that the problem is actually that Mayumi has her underwear and shorts twisted around her knees, and she is being more dragged along by Trina then moving under her own impetus.

Seeing Dodo and Mark, the girls stop running and panting for breath, utter cries of relief. They both look distressed, and a lot more sober than they did a few minutes ago.

'What's wrong? What happened?' demands Dodo.

'They're after us!' pants Trina.

'Who is?' asks Dodo.

'There doesn't appear to be anyone chasing you,' says Mark, his eyes on the direction they came from.

'Good! Then we must've lost them!' says Trina.

'Lost who?' asks Dodo.

'Aliens!' says Mayumi.

'Yeah; aliens!' confirms Trina.

'Where?' urgently. 'Where did you see them?'

'Back at the campsite!'

'Okay, just relax and tell me what happened,' instructs Dodo. 'And Mayumi, why've you got knickers and everything halfway down your legs?'

'I was urinating,' is the reply. 'I'm all wet.'

'Well pull them back up anyway, sweetheart,' says Dodo. 'You can have a bath when we get home. Now, just tell me what happened.'

While Mayumi makes herself decent, Trina takes up the story: 'We were back at the camp, waiting for you to come back, and Mayumi said she needed a pee. So we went round the back of Mark's tent—'

'We?' interrupts Dodo. 'Why did you have to go with her?'

'Well, you told us to stick together,' answers Trina. 'Anyway, we were in the middle of a conversation, cuz we were working out stuff for Yumi's next book—'

'Never mind that! You'd gone behind Mark's tent…'

'Yeah, and Yumi squatted down to have a tinkle and I squatted down next to her so we could talk. We were saying how unfair it is for us girls; peeing, I mean; cuz y'know, guys, with their cocks to pee with, can do loads of things we can't; like peeing right up trees and drawing pictures in the snow and—'

'Never mind what you were *talking* about!' says Dodo, exasperated. 'Just tell me what *happened*.'

'I was just getting to that bit,' responds Trina defensively. 'If you're going to keep interrupting me—'

Dodo draws a deep breath. And then: 'I apologise. Please proceed with your narration.'

'Okay.' She looks at Mayumi. 'Where was I?'

'Drawing pictures in the snow,' supplies Mayumi.

'Oh yeah. And that's when we saw the aliens!'

'Where were they?' asks Dodo.

'Right in front of us! It was like they just popped up out of nowhere!'

'And how many of them were there?'

'Two! A matching pair!'

'Two... Do you think they were the same two we saw before?'

'Nooo!' says Trina, stretching the word for emphasis. 'They weren't *those* aliens. They were the other ones! The grey ones with the big black eyes!'

Dodo and Mark trade glances.

'And what were they doing?' asks Dodo. 'How far away were they?'

'I told you: they were right in front of us! We were like right at the edge of the clearing; there were a load of weeds and stuff in front of us; and the aliens popped up just on the other side of them! They were crouching just like we were, and they were gawping at us with those big creepy eyes of theirs! And while Yumi was watering the flowers, the perverts!'

'And what happened next?'

'Well, then we ran for it. We got up and scarpered. Yumi had to get up and leave the stage in the middle of her performance!'

Mayumi nods her head in confirmation. 'I think I got some on you,' she says.

'Yeah, you did,' says Trina. To Dodo: 'And then we came

looking for you.'

'While screaming like a couple of idiots,' adds Dodo, bringing the story to a conclusion.

'That was to let you know where we were,' explains Trina.

Dodo looks at Mark. 'It's all happening tonight, isn't it?'

'Yes... But those damned grey aliens,' sighs Mark. 'Why do they keep popping up like that? They just don't fit into the picture.'

'They don't fit into *your* picture,' says Dodo.

'Well, yes,' agrees Mark. 'Let's get back to the campsite—although I'm not expecting those greys to be still around when we get there. Whenever they've appeared, they never seem to stick around for long.'

The quartet set off.

'What about that idea of yours that the greys might be illusions, whipped up by one of the ESPers at the Grange?' says Dodo.

'Ah, yes, I'm glad you brought that up. I ran into Lucretia this afternoon and I asked her about that one. She said it wasn't them—that none of the ESPers at the Grange have that kind of ability.'

'And do you believe her?'

'Yes, I don't think she was lying to me,' says Mark. 'And she was someone else who disappeared on me, as well.'

Mark relates the incident to the others.

'So, do you think she was teleported? Abducted?' asks Dodo.

'I just don't know. Either she just bolted while my back was turned, or something took her away...'

They gain the campsite. Trina and Mayumi take to the scene of their First Contact; as predicted, there is no sign of the little grey men.

'Christ. Suddenly I can't stop yawning,' says Trina, stretching noisily.

'Me too,' says Mayumi, hugging Dodo. 'Tired.'

'That'll be the early-evening drinking catching up with you,' Dodo tells her. 'I think we'll postpone that bath when we get home. We'll just clean you up and then straight to bed.'

'Yes,' concurs Mayumi.

'Oh fuck, and we've got to walk it, an' all,' says Trina, remembering the stalled car.

'The car might be okay now,' argues Dodo. 'And anyway, it's not far.'

'Yes, apparently it's proximity to UFOs that can cause car engines to suddenly die,' affirms Mark. 'They're usually okay once the disturbance is over.'

'Well, I'm going to take the kids home; what are you going to do? Are you coming back to the cottage as well?'

'No, I'll stay on here. I'll come with you as far as the car, though.'

The party make their way to the road. As anticipated, the Jaguar's engine starts first time. The female contingent drives off, while Mark returns to the campsite.

Chapter Twenty-Nine
The Old School Tie: Rachel Farrow

Rachel Farrow. Mark Hunter's—unofficial—girlfriend during his secondary school years. His first girlfriend, but not his first lover. Rachel has been mentioned more than once in this chronicle, we've seen her briefly with Dennis Shrimpton in an earlier chapter, and now we join her for breakfast. The scene is the kitchen of her house: bowls of cereals, buttered toast, cups of coffee. Also present, Rachel's husband, David Randall.

David Randall! Rachel went and married David Randall? This would have likely been Mark Hunter's reaction on hearing about this domestic arrangement (which he isn't going to.) Mark remembers David as the rather annoying boy who—like the generality of geeks—couldn't open his mouth without being sarcastic and/or scornful. (The worst kind of person in the world to be sitting watching television with!) I would love to be able to say that David has changed a lot since then, but that would be a blatant lie—because he hasn't changed at all. So why has Rachel married the guy?

It is a question she often asks herself.

Rachel was always a well-fleshed girl, but now, in her maturity, she is distinctly running to fat. Her hair-style is still the same pudding-basin she has affected since childhood (albeit with the dark hair now threaded with silver), and she still wears glasses. Her husband, seated opposite and also bespectacled, is as lank and thin-faced as he has always been, just older.

David is holding forth. Since her marriage, Rachel has discovered a new facet to David's character, something in addition to the sneering and sarcasm: to wit, a propensity for self-pitying whining and complaint. Today it's about work.

'...And I know he sits at my desk when I'm not there!'

'Well, tell him not to,' says Rachel, transferring a spoonful of milk and corn flakes to her mouth.

'Oh! "Tell him not to." Very helpful. And how, precisely, do I do that?'

'Just go up to him and say the words.'

'Oh, yes. "Just go up to him and say the words." Couldn't be easier, could it? *You* try going up to him and saying the words, if you think it's so easy.'

'It's not my bloody desk, is it?'

'Oh! "It's not your bloody desk, is it?" How very considerate. Shows how much you care about me. Yes, very understanding. Full of wifely sympathy, aren't we?'

'Well, what do you want me to say, for Christ's sake?'

You can take this conversation as a typical sample.

David is actually Rachel's second husband. Her first husband had been one Simon Bryce, also her peer at school. If Mark would be surprised to learn Rachel had married David, he would be even more surprised to learn that she had also been married to Simon. Simon hadn't even been a member of their little outcast clique at school. He wouldn't have fitted in. Simon had been one of those boys, the vast majority in fact, who always spent their school breaks playing football. The sporty type. And not even the sporty type who was also good academically. Rachel had only really become friends with Simon after their school years were over; and then, one day, perhaps from having nothing better to do, they had gone and got married. The divorce had followed in due course, along with the legacy of one son. (The son was now

225

twenty and only visited his maternal parent when he wanted money.) A long period of being blessedly single had followed this, until Rachel had finally agreed to marry David, someone she had always remained friends with. However, subsequent to this marriage, and now that they have come to be living under the same roof, this friendship has started to show signs of wear and tear. David is an insecure husband—a jealous, emotionally-retarded and constantly-complaining husband. Rachel's patience is taxed to the full just in living with him. She's managed this for seven monotonous years now.

So why doesn't she leave him? Rachel has considered this privately, but David, surmising without being told that she might have thought of leaving him, has pre-empted her by threatening her with violence if she should dare to do such a thing. No, not violence towards her—he has threatened her with violence against *himself.* 'I'll kill myself if you leave me! I will! And it'll be your fault!'

Stalemate. Rachel knows that this kind of emotional blackmail is actually a form of abuse against herself; but even so, she hasn't wanted to call his bluff—and anyway, sometimes splitting up just seems like way too much hassle. In other words, Rachel stays with her husband for the same reason millions of other discontented couples stay together...

David rises from the table. 'I'm going now. Some of us have to work.'

'Yes, *I* work, as well. My shift doesn't start till this afternoon.' (She works at a local baker's shop.)

'Oh, yes. And what will you be doing until then? Chatting with all your internet friends, I suppose.'

'And what if I am?'

'Oh, yes. Very nice. Flirting with men. Gossiping with women. Complaining about me. Nice, loving wife you are. You care more about your online friends than you do about me!'

'For God's sake, David!'

'"For God's sake, David!" That's all you can say, isn't it? That's your answer to everything. And why? Because you know I'm right! I ought to confiscate that laptop of yours.'

'Just you try!'

226

'You see! You admit it! You can't live without it, can you? All your little internet friends...'

And then he is gone, and blessed peace descends upon the house.

He is right, of course. Rachel *does* feel a closer bond with most of her online friends than she does with her own husband. With the people you meet, and see from day-to-day you are all too aware of their imperfections; online friends are people who present themselves to you simply as text on a screen; you can judge them only by their words; your imagination fills in the gaps.

Her husband gone, she sets about washing up the breakfast things. She looks at her hands as she slips the yellow gloves over them; thinking that they look all of their forty years, wondering why she couldn't have taken better care of them when she was younger...

Of course Rachel still remembers Mark Hunter—you don't forget your first boyfriend and the person you lost your virginity with. (It's always nicer when they're the same person!) She usually remembers him at times like this; when she is vainly regretting the things she did and didn't do in her life. She remembers him as someone she had a happy time with; and she remembers him as the one partner—unlike her two husbands and a couple of other boyfriends—she never really argued with. She can't recall that he ever lost his temper... And that lovely smile he had...

But then he'd buggered off to London for some reason Rachel can't now remember. That's the thing Rachel really regrets—how different things would have been if only he hadn't gone away...

They'd stayed in touch by letter for a while, but then he had stopped writing to her... Or had she stopped writing to him...? Yes, maybe it was when she'd started going out with Simon...

Having done the washing up, Rachel decides to indulge herself with ten minutes online before getting down to the housework. Rachel likes to keep their modest semi-detached spick and span, and knows that if she left it David it would never get done. David might look like the kind of husband who would take charge of the housework, but he's not; he's lazy. So Rachel does the housework, but she does it for her own satisfaction and not for his.

Rachel goes into the front room, picks up her laptop from the coffee table and sitting down on the settee, she opens the device and presses the power button.

Rachel does not consider online communication to be false communication, as some people say it is; she would call it *new* communication; digital communication for the digital age. The critics say that you shouldn't just live online; that the only real communication is face-to-face real-world communication. When you speak to someone face-to-face, you see and you hear the immediate reaction of that person to whatever it is you have just said to them; and you in turn have to react immediately to that reaction. Online communication can be conducted piecemeal: you say your piece, you post it, and if the other person's not online at that moment, you have to wait for their response. This form of communication can allow you time to measure your words, to mull over your responses before actually making them.

This 'new' communication can have its drawbacks. It can allow the more shy and socially-awkward a means of being able to communicate with more honesty and eloquence than they are able to do it in face-to-face situations (although this in itself could be considered an equivocal virtue, as it really only enables these people to bypass their communication issues, instead of actually addressing them. I remember seeing an example of this in an anime; where a girl sent a text message in reply to a question asked to her by a person who was standing directly in front of her!) But it can, on account of its indirect and semi-anonymous nature, also encourage some people to be much more argumentative, inconsiderate, and even threatening, than they would ever dare to be in the real world.

For Rachel, as for millions of other people, social networking is a very necessary escape from a dull and unsatisfactory domestic life. And it is for this very good reason that her husband is excluded from her online circle of friends.

Rachel logs onto Facebook. She hasn't replied to Annette's last message yet... Rachel has a healthy circle of friends on Facebook, most of them people she has never actually met face-to-face. Some of them are women, some of them are men. But the

228

person Rachel feels closest to is Annette. Annette is a woman from Preston, married like herself, and with whom she has built up a strong rapport; they unburden themselves freely to each other, sharing all their complaints and problems, offering each other sympathy and advice... Annette seems such a caring, insightful, warm-hearted person; Rachel would like to meet up with her one day... Arranging it would be difficult; David would never agree to coming here to stay for the weekend... But Christ, it's not like Annette's her secret lover or anything! She's just a friend; maybe even her *best* friend; there ought to be nothing wrong with them just getting together over a weekend or something...

Rachel goes to Messenger, and clicks on Annette's message thread.

And she stares at it in disbelief. Seconds pass, her mind refusing to accept the information her eyes are relaying to it. It's impossible... It can't be... It just can't be...

But there it is, in stark and irrefutable digital text:

You cannot reply to this message. The sender has blocked you.

And Rachel feels like her whole world has just come crashing down around her shoulders. She shakes, her insides heave; she actually comes close to soiling herself.

Rejected, betrayed, annihilated.

Maybe it's a mistake; an error. She clicks on Annette's Facebook page; the page cannot be found. Rachel has been blocked; locked out.

Just a couple of clicks, and Rachel has lost the person she thought was her best friend. But why? What did she do wrong? What did she say to make Annette do this to her? It just doesn't make sense... She scrolls through her recent conversation with Annette, and in her doubting and distressed state of mind sees a dozen things in her messages that Annette might have taken the wrong way. Rachel has always known that there is far more room for your words to be misunderstood when they are just words on a screen, when the other person at the other end cannot hear the inflection of your voice or see the expression on your face; she's

229

known that, but so has Annette. Christ, they've even talked about that very subject! So why has she done this? Why has Annette taken something Rachel said to her so amiss that she can't even talk it out with her; that she has to immediately go and sever all ties with her? And she had already *replied* to Rachel's last message...! She hadn't sounded like anything was wrong. It just doesn't make any sense...

What Rachel doesn't know, and will never know, is that she hasn't actually done anything wrong at all. She hasn't written anything that has unintentionally enraged her correspondent. Annette has blocked her out of petty spite and revenge for a wrong that had nothing to do with her at all. Last night Annette had suffered just the same thing Rachel is suffering now. She had gone online and found herself suddenly and unexpectedly blocked by a friend she had considered to be *her* best friend. And from the subsequent whirlwind of feelings that had assailed her, had emerged the desire to revenge herself, to revenge herself by making someone else feel as bad as she herself felt right then... And so she had picked on Rachel. Rachel was the Facebook friend she knew would be most afflicted by being blocked by her—and so she had gone ahead and blocked her.

Another downside to the 'new' communication. Unfriending (a new word invented by social media which needs to be added to the dictionary if it hasn't been already.) Unfriending, and its implacable sibling, Blocking. The rejecting, shunning and severing of all ties with an online friend abruptly and arbitrarily, in a way in which, out in the real world, nobody but thoughtless children would treat a friend.

And to maliciously block someone with the sole intent of inflicting misery... An ultimately pointless act of smallminded malice. By the very definition of blocking, you will never actually know how the other person reacted; you can never actually see it; you can only gloat over a conjured up mental image; an image as fictitious as the original friendship was...

Finally, and as with Annette, Rachel finds her tumult of conflicting emotions resolving themselves into a feeling of intense baffled rage... And she soon finds a fitting target for that rage. His name is Vincent; a man with whom she has (had!) been enjoying a flirty conversation; nothing too explicit; just light-heartedly flirtatious; all within bounds. But as all too often happens in these situations, the male protagonist has gone and stepped *out* of bounds. Vincent has just sent her a completely pornographic message—an obviously masturbatory one judging by all the spelling mistakes. Intended to arouse her, in her current state of mind, the loaded words merely sicken Rachel. She immediately blocks him.

And oddly enough, it doesn't make her feel any better after all…

Chapter Thirty
Mavis Shagwell Calls the Shots

It is set to be a blistering day; a globally-warmed, Greta Thunberg kind of day. Up to thirty-seven degrees this afternoon in some parts of the country; a severe weather warning has been issued. Here in Market Stanford it's set to peak at thirty-five.

Mark Hunter, sitting in his tent reading *Sentimental Education*, feels very hot and grubby, and that he would like nothing more than to have a nice long soak in the bath. He could, of course, nip back to the cottage. It wouldn't take long, and he could grab a shower and a change of clothes and then come straight back here…

He's still concerned about Lucretia. She still hasn't turned up. What has become of the girl? Has she been whisked away by some unseen force? Or is she safe and sound back at the Grange? Dodo had seen the alien spaceship just fade out of existence; *he* had seen—what he assumes to be—its occupants do the same thing. Was that what had happened to Lucretia? Or had she simply run away while his back was turned and he's busy worrying about nothing? The only way to find out for sure would be to walk up to the Grange and make inquiries about the girl. But to do that, might be to walk into a lion's den. Mark has already made one entirely unofficial visit to the Grange, and he was caught on security camera. Those shotgun wielding guards might

231

have been primed to keep an eye out for him.

Wait a minute. Instead of going himself, how about an official visit from the police? Yes! He could ask Mavis Shagwell to pay the Grange a visit, and about Lucretia's wellbeing… At least then he would know for sure if the girl is actually missing or not. Yes… he'll have to give the police station a buzz and ask her…

'Hello?' comes a familiar voice.

Mark crawls out of his tent. Mavis Shagwell stands there before him, glowing as usual, neat and tidy in her crisp black uniform, seemingly unfazed by the hot weather.

'Hello, there!' greets Mark. 'It's funny; I was just thinking about you this very minute.'

Mavis looks pleased. 'Were you?'

'I was. So, to what do I owe the honour of this visit? Has something happened?'

'Yes… There's been… another incident…'

'Another incident? A sighting?'

'Yeah, a sighting…'

'And does it involve the grey aliens or the spacesuited variety?'

'Erm… The grey ones…'

She seems rather hesitant, thinks Mark. 'So, what's happened?'

'Honestly, I think I'd better take you there and show you, if that's alright with you.'

'That's fine with me. Where has this incident occurred? Inside Market Stanford or out of it?'

'It's in town.'

Mark grabs his jacket and follows Mavis to her squad car, parked on the lay-by. They climb in and set off.

'So, what's happened, then?' asks Mark, enjoying the blessed cool air of the car's air conditioning.

'Well, it's something very odd…' replies Mavis, unsure.

'Well, we've had a lot of "odd" around here lately,' says Mark. 'Can you be more specific?'

'It's hard to describe,' says Mavis. 'It'll be best if I just take you there…'

'Take me where?'

'To where it happened…'

'And where's that?'

'A house… A house in town…'

'A house, eh? And who lives there?'

'Just a feller… He can tell you about it better than I can…'

'Okay… And this definitely involves the grey aliens, does it?'

'Yeah…'

'No-one's been hurt or killed, have they?'

'No, no; nothing like that…'

Mark sits back in the passenger seat. Mavis Shagwell seems determined to be mysterious about whatever has happened…

Changing the subject, he tells her about Lucretia and his concerns for safety.

'Well, we haven't had any missing person's report,' Mavis tells him.

'Yes, but even if she is missing, the people at the Grange might choose not to report it,' says Mark.

'Funny lot there, are they?'

'Very. Which is why I want to find out for myself if she's still there.'

'No problem with that. I can go and ask them soon as we're finished up here.'

They are driving through the town now.

'So… this incident: when did it occur?'

'Last night.'

'When last night?'

'Quite late.'

Mavis steers the car into a close of semi-detached houses.

'I know this street,' says Mark. 'These houses were only being built when I was a kid. I remember we used to play 'wars' on the building site, running around, climbing up onto the scaffolding and everything… These days you'd expect a building site like that to be fenced in and padlocked, but it wasn't like that back then… Still, they didn't like us kids playing there. A local copper came to our school one day; he was going to show us a film about the dangers of playing on building sites, but he couldn't find the right film or something; so as a substitute he showed us a film about the dangers of playing on farms…'

The squad car pulls up before one of the houses.

'Here we are,' says Mavis.

'Which one?'

'Number seventeen. Come on.'

They walk up to the front door, but instead of knocking, Mavis produces a key and lets them both in unannounced. Is this man they're seeing unable to come to the door for some reason? wonders Mark. He can't be hurt; Mavis said no-one's been injured. A disabled man? Or perhaps traumatised by the incident?

Mark is ushered into a comfortable living room. There is no-one there.

'Where is he, then?'

'Just sit yourself down on the sofa,' says Mavis.

Obediently, Mark sits himself on the sofa.

'I can see you're determined to be mysterious about this,' he observes.

'Just gimme a sec…'

Mavis moves over to a desk placed in a corner of the room, and flips open a laptop computer. She switches it on. Mark watches her, increasingly confused. Something online she wants to show him…? Or has someone grabbed a screenshot of that alien writing…?

But Mavis, having finished on the laptop, returns to Mark without it, planting herself on the rug, directly in front of him. She looks eager, expectant.

And then the music crashes in. 'The Stripper' by the David Rose Orchestra; the most iconic striptease soundtrack of all time; most people know the tune, even if they can't put a name to it. The music just cries out 'striptease performance'; you couldn't use it for anything else.

And Mavis Shagwell clearly intends to put the music to its correct use.

First, she throws her hat across the room, and shakes loose her long blonde hair, its silky abundance tumbling around her shoulders and over her face. Now she kicks off her shoes (no socks underneath), and, moving in time to the music, shrugs off her uniform jacket, swinging it in the air before tossing it aside. Turning her back to Mark, she next slowly pulls down her trousers, swinging her hips and thrusting out her buttocks as she

234

does so. Stepping out of these, she turns to face Mark again; off comes the tie, and then, button by button she undoes her blouse; this is likewise thrown aside. Now she stands in her underwear: a lacy black bra and knickers set that you would not expect a policewoman to be wearing to work. Still moving her body to the music, she reaches behind, unclips her bra, pulls back first one shoulder-strap and then the other. The bra comes off; she twirls it round her finger before throwing it aside. And then, presenting her rear to Mark once again, she slowly peels off her knickers, bending low so that her vagina peeps out at him from between the buttocks. She arranges herself on the rug to complete the removal of her knickers, kicking them aside just as the music reaches its climax.

And then—silence.

Mavis, nude, reclining on the rug, legs spread wide as she leans back on her elbows, looks at Mark. Mark looks at Mavis. Her pubic hair is as fair as the hair on her head; not the beige colour you often find on blondes. Mark has seen many a striptease act in his time, in many different parts of the world (look; he's a spy, okay? It comes with the territory), and he has to concede that this presumably amateur performance he has just been witness to has been very well executed. But—

'What… what precisely does this have to do with grey aliens…?' he asks.

'Nothing,' is the frank response.

'So, let me see… Your story about their being an incident of some kind last night was of the cock and bull variety, and this house you have brought me to is actually your own…'

'Yes, and yes,' replies Mavis, looking at him intently.

'I see… So, you've just brought me here to show me your striptease performance. Perhaps you're rehearsing it for some station-house party, and you'd like my feedback…? Well, I shall be happy to oblige: I can honestly say that your performance was extremely well executed, your choreography flawless, and the overall effect highly stimulating. If you want to be graded, I will happily give you a full ten points out of ten. Okay? …But now, having done this, I think I'd really better be getting back to my own business. We've all got our jobs to do, haven't we? So, don't worry about driving me, I can find my own back.'

So saying, Mark rises from the sofa. But upon this, Mavis, from her recumbent position suddenly pounces like a tiger, and Mark finds himself seated again, the naked law-enforcement officer pinning him down.

'You're not going anywhere,' she tells him, breathing hard, staring at him with smouldering intensity through eyes partially clouded by stray locks of hair.

'Oh,' says Mark. 'Is... the performance not over, then?'

'No, it isn't. We haven't got to the best part.'

'And what part would that be?'

'The part where I mount you and fuck every last drop of cum out of you.'

'I see...' says Mark. 'It's like that, is it? Well, before we commit ourselves to anything we might later regret, and although I do think you're a lovely girl, Mavis, let us consider that we have only known each other a few days, and during that time I'd say we've spent not much more than an hour in each other's company, all told... So perhaps we're being a tad hasty here...?'

'No. I've thought this through carefully,' says Mavis. 'I want you. I want you to fuck me like I've never been fucked before.'

'Ah, but you can't be entirely sure that that's what you want, can you?' cautions Mark. 'After all, fleeting acquaintance... I'm sure you're not in the habit of throwing yourself at men you've only just met...'

'No, I'm not,' agrees Mavis. 'But you're different.'

'And how am I different, exactly?'

'You're a spy.'

'Well, yes I am, but—Ah! I think I see the problem here. Film and television has no doubt accustomed you to the idea that us men of the intelligence community are all virile, insatiable womanisers, but actually—'

'Oh, shut up and kiss me, you handsome monster.'

And she crushes her lips against Mark's, forcing her tongue into his mouth.

'Frrr iff thrumthn iff gtt tllyu.'

Mavis extracts her tongue.

'Sorry; what was that?'

236

'I said: there is something I have to tell you.'

'What is it?'

'Well, you see… I'm impotent.'

Mavis grabs Mark's inner thigh, smiles triumphantly.

'Oh yeah? Then what's this crawling down your leg? Funny place to keep your gun.'

Mark sighs.

'Well, the body may be willing but the mind rebels… And so I will have to bid you a good day!' And so saying he pushes Mavis from on top of him, dislodging her with some force. *She* lands in a heap on the rug and *he* bolts for the door. He finds it locked and with no sign of the key. He turns round; Mavis faces him, nipples erect, panting and eager.

'Be violent with me!'

'I'll do no such thing!'

All other exits blocked, he hares up the stairs. Mavis charges after him. *Of course* Mark ends up in the bedroom, and *of course* he falls onto the bed, and *of course* Mavis jumps on top of him, pinning him down.

'Now stop running and start fucking. Put a baby inside me, you beast!'

'Please,' protests Mark. 'I've been camping; I haven't bathed; I'm…'

'I don't mind. I like the raw smell of a man. It drives my senses wild.'

Through the open window comes the sound of a car pulling up in the drive.

'Shit,' says Mavis. She springs from the bed and over to the window. 'Shit, shit, shit!'

'What's wrong?' asks Mark.

'It's Frank.'

'Who's Frank?'

'Me husband.'

'Your husband?' squawks Mark. 'You mean you're married? What were you thinking of, woman? This is no way for a married woman to be conducting herself!'

She looks at Mark. Her lust has evaporated as though it was never there; she just looks helpless and alarmed. 'I didn't know he'd be coming home for lunch. What should we do?'

'Well, the first thing you need to do is put some clothes on—'

'Right!'

Not waiting to hear more, she darts out of the room.

'Not downstairs!' protests Mark, his voice a strangled cry.

But Mavis is already running down the stairs, intent on retrieving her police uniform from the living room. She doesn't make it. Mark hears the front door open and a male voice saying: 'What the hell are you doing?'

Time to make myself scarce, decides Mark. He springs from the bed and goes to the window. Opening it to its full extent, he climbs out backwards onto the ledge, lowers himself and drops. He lands on the lawn, springs quickly to his feet. The front door bursts open and a very angry man appears.

'Hold it right there, you bastard!'

Now Mark knows that he is perfectly innocent of any wrongdoing, but he also knows that appearances are dead against him; and in that split-second in which he has to make the choice of whether to stay and calmly state his case to the irate husband, or whether discretion would be the better part of valour, he opts for the latter and is off like a shot.

Chapter Thirty-One
Endless Summers: Scene Five

Brave New World by Aldous Huxley. A Penguin Modern Classics edition from nineteen sixty-three (coincidentally the year of the author's death.) The cover illustration by Denis Piper shows the identical faces of a group of male and female Alphas, with superimposed over them the letters 'O' and 'T', presumably symbolising the male and female genitals. The back-cover blurb erroneously announces that the setting of this dystopian novel is thousands of years into the future—in fact it is only six-hundred. The price, printed on the front cover of the paperback book, is three shillings and sixpence, which Mark knows means seventeen-and-a-half pence in new money.

Mark carries the book as though it is contraband, concealed, carefully wrapped up in a blue-and-white striped Tesco carrier bag, as he wends his way through the streets of his home town one sunny afternoon. The book is a secret; and a clue to another secret; a name written in pen on the front endpaper—a name that no-one must see.

Mark has changed since we saw him last. He is now a boy with a secret; he is a boy leading a double-life—in fact, leading the life of a spy(!) He has been sworn to secrecy by the owner of the book he's carrying; the woman who has transformed his life. No-one must know about Marianne, and her secret summer school; if anyone was to find out, the instructress would have to disappear; the lessons would be terminated; teacher and student would never be able to see each other again. Mark, being the eager and devoted student that he is, doesn't want this to happen; his respect and admiration for his mentor amounts to complete, unquestioning veneration; and so he has kept his word; he will never tell a soul.

Even his friend Clyde Waring doesn't know anything about it, although Mark cannot entirely conceal the fact that he is changing, developing under Marianne tutelage—and he knows that Clyde can sense this change, even if he doesn't understand it. No longer tethered, the boys are starting to drift apart, Mark's life following a much more rapid current, while poor Clyde just gets left further and further behind. The boys still meet, but they are too old now to play those imaginary games they used to play; they either watch TV together, or go for rambles or bike-rides.

In addition to secrecy, another spy trait Mark is starting to pick up is the old 'eyes in the back of the head;' to wit, to be aware, when it is necessary, of whether he is being observed or followed. And the time for exercising this caution are times like this, when he is on his way to his summer school lessons with Marianne. He must not allow himself to be followed to destination; not by Clyde or anyone else.

That destination is an old bungalow on the edge of town; rustic and picturesque, surrounded by hedges and with apple trees blooming in the garden; a dwelling made to be seen as Mark has been seeing it these past weeks: basking under a summer sun, an

239

idyllic pastoral image.

With a final look round to make sure he is unobserved, Mark opens the gate, crosses the front garden and knocks on the front door.

'You've finished the book then?' asks Marianne, turning on to her side, elbow on the pillow, hand supporting her head.

'Yes,' says Mark. 'I read it really quickly, it was so good.'

'Good,' says Marianne, stroking his smooth, hairless chest. 'I'm glad you enjoyed it. Care to tell me your thoughts about it?'

The bedroom is small, the furnishings old-fashioned, in-keeping with the bungalow's exterior. Sunlight, diffused by net-curtains, enters through the small, open window, bringing with it the orchard fragrances of the garden. The covers, unwanted, form a crumpled tide line at the foot of the bed, while teacher and pupil lie side by side on the mattress.

'Well...' says Mark; 'I thought it was quite different to *Nineteen Eighty-Four.*'

'Yes, people often compare those two books; that's why I wanted you to read them together. So, tell me: in what ways would you say *Brave New World* was different to *Nineteen Eighty-Four*? Give me an example; something that struck you while you were reading it.'

'Well, I suppose they're different because in *Brave New World* the people were happy. Except for Bernard.'

'Why do you think they were happy?'

'Well, because they had all been conditioned from when they were born—no, from *before* that—to be happy. In the *Nineteen Eighty-Four* it was all spies and informers and secret police and the people always scared they might be doing something wrong. But they didn't need all that in *Brave New World*, because nobody really did anything wrong. They liked things how they were.'

'So, do you think *Brave New World* was a nice place compared to the world in *Nineteen Eighty-Four*?'

'Well, I suppose it was nice for the people who lived there, but I wouldn't want to like it. It was just sex all the time for the Alphas; they didn't really talk or think about anything else.'

'That's right,' concurs Marianne, reaching a hand down to

Mark's testicles. 'In that society, they had completely separated sex from reproduction, so sex had become entirely a recreational activity, and the people had been conditioned to see it as the *only* recreational activity. And as you say, it was a very shallow world, where people never stopped to think about things. Bernard was an exception of course, but it was suggested that someone made a mistake during his incubation process which had led to him being born—or *hatched*, I should say—a square peg... What did you think of the Savage Reservation?'

'Well, the Alphas called them savages, but really I think they were people who lived more like we do; just normally. John Savage was more like us.'

Marianne gently fondles Mark's testicles. He is very advanced for his age in this area, she has told him; way ahead of the rest of his body.

'I can tell you've really been thinking about this. That's good. Always keep an active and inquiring mind. Right from the start, I knew you would be able to read the books I wanted you to read; I knew your mind was ready for them—and you haven't disappointed me.'

She leans in and kisses him.

'My precious boy...'

Mark smiles at this praise. Pleasing Marianne, earning her approval, means the world to him.

'What's the future really going to be like?' he asks her. 'I mean, do you think it'll be like *Brave New World* or *Nineteen Eighty-Four*?'

'There's a question! What *I* think is that right at the moment, we seem to be heading more in a *Nineteen Eighty-Four* direction. We've got the Cold War still going on; we've got the threat of the Bomb; we've got lots of countries spying on each other all the time; a lot of people feel threatened and unsafe. And there are lot of places in the world, a lot of countries where people can't say the things they want to say, they can't speak freely; and in some of those places if they say the wrong thing they can be arrested by the authorities; even if they think they're talking secretly and amongst friends, there might be an informer...'

'We've passed that year now,' says Mark. '1984, I mean.'

241

'Yes, but the year doesn't really matter,' Marianne tells him, now gently teasing his flaccid penis. 'George Orwell wrote the book in 1948, and he just chose the year 1984 by swapping round the last two numbers. But yes, you're right that Orwell was thinking of a much nearer future than Aldous Huxley was in *Brave New World*... When you start your new school next month, you'll see that your curriculum has a strong bias towards the sciences. That's because Margaret Thatcher wants to raise a generation of scientists...'

Margaret Thatcher has come up in their lessons before. Marianne has talked a lot about women, about how they used to be held back, kept at home and prevented from making careers for themselves; so he at first had thought that she would have been all in favour of Britain having a woman prime minister—but boy was he wrong! Marianne does not like Thatcher at all, and she has given Mark compelling reasons, explaining very clearly why he shouldn't like her as well (regardless of the fact that his parents both vote for her.)

'...So, if you consider all this, and think about all the advances in eugenics, artificial insemination, the genetic 'improvement' of human beings... Yes, I think that maybe in the long-run, we could end up in more of a *Brave New World* situation—ah! Your recovery time is beautiful, Mark. I think it's time for another practical lesson...'

Mark is a very diligent and submissive student with regard to both his academic studies and with his 'physical education.' Marianne is his mistress (in the genuine rather than popular meaning of the word) and whatsoever she commands, he obeys. If she tells him to be gentle, he is gentle; if she tells him to be forceful, he is forceful. He does whatever she tells him to, and never presumes to take the initiative and do anything he has not been asked to do. He does whatever she tells him to, and he carries out her instructions with all his heart and soul and with the student's desire to earn the praise and approval of his teacher...

With face pressed to the humid, pungent crevice of her buttocks, lips glued to the distended sphincter of her anus, Mark draws out

242

the last of the semen so recently deposited within that forbidden orifice. ('Forbidden' in the sense that it was technically still a no-entry zone back then—not legally accessible.)

Lesson over, they both subside onto the damp sheets. Marianne sees the tears streaming down Mark's face, and she smiles, knowing these tears signal only his overwhelming joy. She hugs him close to her, kissing his scented lips.

'Oh, my darling,' she says, her voice a soft whisper. 'That was another A-plus. I'm so proud of you...' She strokes his hair. 'My darling student prodigy...'

They lie there for a minute in happy silence and contentment.

'Now...' says Marianne, still speaking softly. 'Let me tell you about the next book I want you to read. I'll go'n get it in a minute; it's called *Swastika Night*, and it's by a writer called Murray Constantine. It's a very neglected book this one; not as famous as it should be I only discovered it myself more or less by accident; but I liked the book so much I wanted to know more about the writer; and doing some digging, I found out that Murray Constantine was actually a pen-name for a female writer called Katherine Burdekin. She wrote *Swastika Night* in the late 1930s, so it came after *Brave New World* but before *Nineteen Eighty-Four*; and although most people have forgotten it, it's just as important as those two books.'

'Is it another dystopia?'

'Yes, it is. It's set in a future where the Germans and their allies won the Second World War, and in this future the world is divided into two empires, the German and the Japanese. There have been a lot of "What if the Axis Powers had Won the War?" books written, but this one is different, because it's much more about gender than just about fascism and imperialism. You see, in this society men completely control everything; they rule by force because in this world all the most violent and aggressive male tendencies have come to be looked on as virtues. Women have been "reduced." That's what they called it: "The Reduction of Women." Their status has been reduced to zero. They have no human rights, and they're just used as breeding machines.'

'They just have babies?'

'Yes. From birth the women in this world are conditioned to

perceive themselves as being less than human; they are made to see themselves as being contemptible, physically hideous creatures, cursed from birth for not being men.'

'So, do some of the women rebel?'

'Actually no; that doesn't happen. You see, the women have been so down-trodden for centuries that they can't imagine for one minute that things could be any different for them; and they're denied any education, so they've never learned to think for themselves. You see, history has been suppressed and rewritten in this world, so neither the women or the men know that things were ever any different. It's a man in the story who starts to discover the truth about the past and how women were once treated differently; and he learns it from a book, which shows that George Orwell must have been influenced by *Swastika Night* when he wrote *Nineteen Eighty-Four*. The Big Brother figure in *Swastika Night* is Hitler, who has been made into a God.'

'So, is there a Church of Hitler?' asks Mark, smiling.

'There *is* a Church of Hitler,' confirms Marianne, returning the smile. 'And it's a swastika shaped church!'

She reaches out to stroke his buttocks.

'When I was doing my research,' she continues, delicately squeezing; 'I discovered that Katherine Burdekin had previously written a book about a future in which women ruled the world, and it was men had been reduced in status; they weren't treated badly like the women in *Swastika Night*; in fact, they were quite happy with their lives; but they were only half-educated, and kept separate from the women except for breeding purposes. This book was rejected by Burdekin's publishers, but I was able to read the manuscript; that's how I know about it. And so, because this book was rejected, she wrote *Swastika Night* instead—which was making the same basic point as the other book, but by showing the opposite extreme; and this one was accepted by her publishers.'

'Why wouldn't they publish the first one?' wonders Mark.

'Well, I think to answer that one, you also have to ask: why did they publish the second one? And the answer would be that *Swastika Night*, being the much darker and more pessimistic book, was a much more stimulating read. We're drawn to worst-case scenarios—in our fiction, anyway! We wouldn't want them to happen in real life; but it's good to give some thought to what *might* happen, if we're not careful.'

'Could *that* happen, then?' asks Mark. 'I mean, what they've done to women in this book?'

'"The Reduction of Women?" Hmm... Well, there are some people who say that human evolution is a one-way street; that anything that's changed for the better can't go back to being how it was before—But then, the people who "reduced" women in that story were fascists, and another word for fascist is reactionary; and that means they *want* things to go backwards; they *want* to reverse any changes in society that they see as bad. And even now, Mark, in the world today things aren't perfect. There are places in the world where they are very bad. There are places in the world where women don't have many rights at all; where men exert control over them in all kinds of ways; even mutilating their bodies. Here...'

She takes Mark's hand and guides it between her thighs, pressing his fingers to her clitoris.

'That's it. Stroke my clitoris.' Mark obeys. 'You may find it hard to believe, but there are places in the world where women are forced to have their clitorises removed. They call it female circumcision, but genital mutilation is a better name for it. They do this because to them the clitoris serves no purpose; it doesn't enhance a man's sexual pleasure, and it plays no part in the reproductive process. For these people, the clitoris is only there for women to pleasure themselves and each other, and these people don't want women to be pleasuring themselves or each other. They only want women to have the vaginal cavity for their own pleasure, and ovaries for her to produce their offspring. And so they remove the clitoris, leaving the woman scarred and mutilated and robbed of her dignity. So you see, women are already being "reduced" in some parts of this world, and if reactionism takes hold, it could spread... Keep going...'

Mark obeys, watching Marianne's face as she reaches her climax: seeing the knitted brows, the eyes tight shut and the mouth wide open, teeth bared in that grimace of intense

245

pleasure—and then the lingering sigh of release…

Her face resuming its placid look, Marianne takes Mark's hand, wet with her emission; she draws the hand up to her face, and starts to suck her salty effluent from his fingers, taking each finger lingeringly into her mouth, one after the other.

'Are you a spy, Marianne?' asks Mark.

The question, so suddenly put, makes her laugh. 'A spy?' she says. 'Where did that one come from?'

'Well, I thought because you're so secret about yourself and everything,' explains Mark. 'I thought you might be a spy.'

'I'm a teacher,' says Marianne. 'I've already told you that.'

'I know, but I thought you might be a spy as well, and I thought you might be teaching me to be a spy.'

'Hmm… Teaching you to be a spy… And what if I was? Would that be okay with you, Mark? Would you like to be a spy when you grow up? Do you know much about spies?'

'I watch the *Man from UNCLE* films,' says Mark.

'Oh, the *Man from UNCLE* films! Then I've got nothing more to teach you, have I?' She laughs, then kisses him fondly. 'Oh, Mark, my sweet… What I'm teaching you… You can be whatever you want to be; a spy if you like; whatever you want to be; anything in the world…'

Chapter Thirty-Two
Thrilling Cellars

Over the course of his illustrious career Mark Hunter has been imprisoned in many rooms in many basements. It is something of an occupational hazard in his line of work. In many buildings in many countries around the world he has found himself incarcerated in basement dungeons by people of many different races, creeds and colours. It has occurred to Mark more than once that he could write a travel guide on the subject, Ian Fleming style: *Thrilling Cellars*.

There is a certain basement cell in Paris which Mark recalls with particular fondness: Dodo and himself had spent several

246

hours incarcerated in this cell on that fateful night the two of them had first met. She looked very nice in that nurse's uniform, and the escape plan had worked beautifully.

His current prison isn't much to talk about; whitewashed walls, itchy blanket, not much room to move about…

After putting a couple of streets between himself and the Shagwell domicile, Mark slows to a walk, incidentally passing a fat, bearded man in whom he completely fails to recognise his childhood best friend Clyde Waring.

For not the first time in his life, Mark finds himself reflecting on how everything seems to happen to him. True, he had had little experience upon which to accurately gauge the personality of Mavis Shagwell, but even so, her behaviour today had rather taken him by surprise. He had no idea she felt that way.

Running away, he adjudges, was the best option open to him. True, he had been completely guiltless in what had transpired, but the only way he could have convincingly cleared his good name to Mavis's husband, would have involved dropping Mavis herself right in it. Yes, he was right to exercise discretion. Having said that, it occurs to Mark that by leaving Mavis to do explaining, the only way she can really be able to exonerate herself would be by dropping *him* right in it.

Oh, well. He doesn't want to cause Mavis any more domestic trouble than can be helped; she just let herself get carried away by the moment. Well, if that's what it takes, he's willing to take the fall for her and assume the role of the over-sexed spy from London who tried to seduce the naïve country policewoman… At least, as long as she *does* say it was an attempted seduction, and not an attempted rape!

Mark guides his steps towards the edge of town and back to the cottage. He wants to get cleaned up before returning to his post in Vernon Wood. He finds the cottage empty. The car is in the drive, so the girls have obviously gone off on foot somewhere. After eating a quick lunch, Mark goes up to his bedroom, disrobes, and then takes himself to the bathroom to have a much-needed shower. He is still in the middle of this, he hears sounds that indicate the others have returned; someone coming up the stairs. Well, a towel around the waist will be enough to make him decent in the event of bumping into anyone while crossing the landing.

His ablutions completed, he extinguishes the shower, and pulls back the frosted glass screen.

A woman stands in the bathroom doorway, and she is neither Dodo, Mayumi or Trina. She is a woman in her late thirties with long dark hair and wearing an unbuttoned lab coat over her clothes. She is also pointing a gun at him.

'Step out of the bath,' she orders. 'Slowly.'

Mark steps slowly out of the bath.

'Hands in the air.'

Mark raises his hands in the direction indicated.

'That gun's mine, isn't it?' he says.

'Yes; I found it in your room,' is the reply. 'You shouldn't leave things like this lying around.'

'You're right,' says Mark. 'That was very careless of me.'

'It was. So now we're both fully cocked.'

'I'm feeling a lot more half-cocked right at the moment, to be honest.'

A smile curls the woman's lips. 'Yes, I do have you at a disadvantage. But let's get down to business; My name's Dr Channing; but I suspect you know that, don't you?'

'And why would I know that?'

'Well, we have met before. And I know who you are, Mark Hunter of MI5. I know all about you—and your associate, Professor Dupont. Incidentally, where is she?'

'Out,' says Mark. 'But she could be back any minute.'

'I see. Well, to refresh your memory, the first time we met was on Monday night at the Four Bells pub in Market Stanford...'

'Yes, now you mention it, I do remember seeing you then, but we were never introduced.'

'...And the second time we met was the following evening when you illegally entered Vernon Grange, and where you were nice enough to drag me out of a lift and throw me across a corridor.'

'Ah, yes, I'm sorry about that,' says Mark, smiling contritely. 'I was in something of a hurry at the time. I can understand your

248

annoyance. Would that be the reason you're here?'

'Not entirely,' replies Channing. 'I've lost some property of mine; and I have reason to suspect that you may have come into possession of it.'

'And what is this property you've mislaid?'

'Her name's Lucretia.'

'Ah.' So she *is* missing.

'I believe you've met her, yes?'

Mark shrugs as best he can with his arms raised. 'Yes, we did speak briefly that night at the pub…'

A tight smile. 'And what about the night after that, at the Grange? The girl denies it, but I have a strong suspicion she was instrumental in you and your friend escaping from us that night.'

Another awkward shrug.

'Couldn't say, really…'

'So, where is she now?' demands Channing crisply.

'I wish I knew,' is the truthful reply.

'She went out for a walk yesterday afternoon at roughly 2 p.m. She hasn't been seen since then; not by us, anyway. Have you seen her?'

'I have,' admits Mark. 'But it's rather a long story. Could I at least put my arms down?'

Channing looks at him for a moment. And then, as if coming to a decision: 'No. I've got a better idea; we'll adjourn this conversation until we've moved to somewhere we're not likely to be interrupted. Listen carefully: I'm now going to allow you to walk back to your room and put your clothes on; I shall be behind you and keeping you covered with this gun all the time. We'll then go downstairs and out to the van that's waiting for us on the road outside. And I recommend you don't try anything, Mr Secret Agent; no sudden, violent moves. Even if you were to get past me, there are three of my men downstairs, armed with shotguns.'

'Oh, I see. You've brought some of your guards with you,' says Mark, shelving his plans for jumping Dr Channing.

'Correct.' She backs out of the room onto the landing.

Mark, hands still raised, slowly follows.

Dr Newcome is very proud of his office. He feels that it suits him very well. He is proud of his cumbersome antique desk, and the leather-upholstered chair that supplies it; he is proud of the fitted mahogany bookcases with their shelves ranked with the gilt embossed spines of the uniformly-bound books; he is proud of the Persian rug, the antique chiffonier, and the Dutch landscape; he is proud of the ormolu mantel clock, the vintage globe drinks cabinet and the swordfish letter opener on his desk… But most of he is proud of the fact that as director of the institute, he is the only one with a spacious, ground floor office with a bay window looking out into the gardens; while Doctors Caxton, Clavering and Channing have to make do with much smaller office spaces down on the basement level, white-washed and spartan in common with all the rooms down there.

When nothing urgent requires his attention, Dr Newcome likes to just sit behind the desk of his office, like he is now, survey with approval everything around him, like an admiral on the bridge of his ship, and generally basking in the glow of his own importance, of being the top-dog at Vernon Grange.

At this moment, the door opens and in walks Mark Hunter, escorted by Dr Channing, one of the Grange's sharp-clawed cats, covering the spy with a gun.

Dr Newcome's good mood evaporates.

'You could try knocking, Dr Channing,' he says, getting up from his desk.

'I've brought back Mark Hunter,' says Channing, ignoring the criticism.

'I can see that,' says Newcome. 'Why have you brought him back?'

'Because he has information about Lucretia's current whereabouts.'

'Excuse me—' begins Dr Newcome.

'I never said I had any information about her *current* whereabouts,' says Mark to Channing.

'Excuse me—'

'You did! You said you'd seen her!'

'Excuse me—'

'Yes, but that was *yesterday*. I don't know—'

'EXCUSE ME,' says Dr Newcome loudly.

Mark and Dr Channing look at him.

'What is it?' asks the latter impatiently.

'Where did you get that gun?' inquires Dr Newcome.

'The gun? It's his.'

'And how did you manage to get it off him?'

'It wasn't *on* him. He happened to be taking a shower when we arrived at the cottage. I was able to surprise him.'

'Give it here.'

'What?'

'The gun: give it here.'

'Why should I?'

'Because I'm ordering you to. Give it HERE.'

Frowning, Channing steps forward and deposits the gun on the desk.

'Careful!' exclaims Dr Newcome. 'You'll scratch the woodwork!'

He picks up the automatic, examines it.

'Careful; it's cocked,' warns Channing.

'I *know* that,' says Newcome, who knew nothing of the kind until that moment. 'You can leave us now, Dr Channing. *I* will question the prisoner.'

'I'd prefer to stay here and participate in the questioning,' says Dr Channing.

'Well, I'd prefer that you *didn't* stay, so you can leave us now, Dr Channing.'

'But—'

'You can leave us now, Dr Channing,' pointing the gun at her.

Channing glares at Newcome, lips pursed. She then turns abruptly on her heel and stalks out of the room, making a point of slamming the door behind her.

Dr Newcome turns a smiling face to his guest.

'Take a seat, Mr Hunter; and we can have a nice, quiet chat.'

'By all means.'

Mark sits himself on one of the chairs facing the desk, while Newcome slips back into his own chair. He continues to examine Mark's gun with interest.

'What type is this?' he asks.

'It's a Walther PPK,' answers Mark. 'And if you don't know

251

about guns, I would suggest you put it down; as your colleague just warned you, the safety is off, and you've pointed the thing at yourself at least twice.'

'I know about guns, Mr Hunter,' says Newcome. 'I don't require your advice.' Nevertheless, he carefully places the gun down on the blotting pad in front of him.

Thinking it will look good, he sits back in his chair, and elbows on the armrests, regards his guest over steepled fingers with a contemplative smile.

'So, Mr Hunter...' he says. 'You're a spy.'

'Yes, I am,' agrees Mark.

'And you work for MI5.'

'I do indeed.'

'And you've come here to spy on Vernon Grange.'

'No, I haven't.'

Newcome considers a brief chuckle is appropriate, so he chuckles briefly. 'Oh, come now, Mr Hunter. Let's not play around; we're both intelligent men.'

Well, one of us is, thinks Mark.

Newcome leans forward, picks up his cigarette box, and opening it, offers it to Mark.

'Cigarette?'

'Thank you,' says Mark, swallowing the urge to say, 'Yes, it is.' He takes a cigarette and Dr Newcome produces (with understandable pride) his gold-plated Venus de Milo petrol lighter and lights Mark's cigarette and then one for himself.

Newcome sits back in his chair and takes a deep drag, then slowly exhales a funnel of smoke into the air.

'Now, Mr Hunter,' he resumes. 'You say you're not here to spy on us. Well, we happen to have CCTV footage positively identifying you as being one of three persons who broke into these premises on the night of Tuesday last. Do you deny that you were here?'

'If by Tuesday last you mean the Tuesday just gone, no I don't deny it.'

'Tuesday last *is* the Tuesday just gone,' says Newcome, brows knitted. 'There hasn't been any other Tuesday since then, has there?'

252

'No, but when people say "Tuesday last" they usually mean the Tuesday of the previous week,' explains Mark.

'No, they don't,' insists Newcome. 'Anyway, you were here. You admit it. So that proves you came here to spy on us.'

'Actually it doesn't,' says Mark. 'The reason I'm here is to investigate the Market Stanford Incident, as it's called; the UFO sighting, and all the other phenomena that have occurred recently…'

Newcome smiles, feeling himself back on safe ground. 'Come now, Mr Hunter. That won't do, will it? If you were investigating the UFO sightings, why would you break into Vernon Grange?'

'Because I believed—erroneously as I now know—that this facility might be connected with the UFO sightings. I knew this to be a Vallotec facility, and that you had something important enough that you needed armed guards to protect it; this and the Grange's close proximity to the centre of the unexplained occurrences made me suspicious.'

'And so you thought we were hiding little green men in the basement,' smiles Newcome. He shakes his head sadly, knowing it to be the ideal moment for this. 'Come now, Mr Hunter; you can't expect me to believe that little fairy tale. I mean to say, we're both men of the world…'

Once again, I think you've miscounted.

'You knew that our research was in the field of extra-sensory perception,' proceeds Dr Newcome; 'and you knew that we had acquired test subjects—you wanted to spy on us and find out what we're doing, didn't you? Well, our research is completely orthodox and on the level, and our test subjects are all volunteers. And that's it, Mr Hunter. So, if you've got any crazy ideas that we're using our ESPers as industrial spies, or for carrying out acts of sabotage and even the odd assassination, I can assure you that you are gravely mistaken.'

So that's what they're doing, muses Mark, while Dr Newcome smiles triumphantly.

Mark has been cooling his heels for several hours now in his latest Thrilling Cellar. His cell here at Vernon Grange is a very spartan one: just a pallet bed, a wooden chair, a toilet and hand

253

basin. Given the dimensions of the room, there isn't really room for anything else.

These several hours of isolation and with only his own thoughts for company have actually been blissful, weighed in comparison with the interminable interview with Dr Newcome that had preceded them. It had taken more than half an hour of verbal sparring before the subject that was the whole reason he'd been brought to the Grange in the first place—i.e. the disappearance of Lucretia—had even been brought up; and even then only because Mark himself had reminded him about it…

At length, Dr Newcome had—thankfully—managed to chain-smoke himself into a coughing fit, and thus his 'interrogating the spy' performance had come to an end, and Mark had been escorted down to his Thrilling Cellar.

And now evening draws on, and Mark lies on his bed, hands behind his bed, deep in thought.

He hears footsteps approaching along the corridor outside. They stop at the door, a key turns in the lock, and in walks a woman with grey hair cropped very short, and wearing the ubiquitous lab coat over her clothes. Mark hasn't met her before, but recognises her from Lucretia's description as Dr Caxton, one of the Four Doctors of Vernon Grange. The door being closed from without, she stands there, hands in pockets, studying the recumbent agent with unfriendly eyes.

'I want to have a word with you,' she says.

'Of course,' replies Mark. 'I think I can guess what about.'

'You know who I am?'

'Unless I'm mistaken, you must be Dr Caxton. Lucretia told me about you.'

'Good.' Caxton seats herself on the straight-backed chair, primly crosses her legs. 'Let's talk. And in case you have any ideas about harming me, there's an armed guard in the corridor outside.'

'I promise you I won't make any attempt to escape,' Mark tells her. He smiles faintly, adding: 'At least, as long as your visit lasts. I make no promises about the future.'

'Your word is good enough for me,' says Caxton. 'Lucretia seemed to like you, and she's usually a good judge of character.

What have you done with her?'

The question, thrown suddenly, causes Mark to pause. 'Well, hasn't Dr Newcome told you what I told him?'

'Yes, he has.'

'Well, there you have it,' says Mark 'I told him the plain, unvarnished truth. There's not really much else I can add to it.'

'So, you maintain that Lucretia vanished into thin air right before your eyes?'

'It was right behind my back, but yes.'

Dr Caxton exhales something between a sigh and a bitter laugh. 'I always wondered if she would just disappear on me like that, one day.'

'You did?' queries Mark, bemused.

'Yes. You've spoken to her; you must know what she's like. She goes off travelling, journeying to places in her mind and out of her body. She's always come back again; but I can't help feeling that one day her mind might just float off so far away that she'll drag her body along with it; just wink out of existence…'

'Well, she *has* disappeared without a trace, but I don't think it was of her own volition, if that's any consolation. She was taken; taken by some external force.'

She looks at him. 'What, by those aliens, or whatever they are, that are haunting Vernon Wood? That's not very encouraging, is it? One of those spacemen killed a guard here, strangled him to death.'

'Ah yes, well he's out of the picture now, the strangler; she's not in any danger from him.'

'Yes, but who has taken her, and where have they taken her, and why did they take her.?'

'I don't know. I can only tell you what happened: there were strange sounds in the air; alien sounds; we were both at the UFO landing site; Lucretia was standing right in the centre of it; I don't know if that's significant…'

'And she disappeared without a trace when your back was turned…'

'Yes.'

'And you didn't do anything about it.'

'Well, what could I do? At first I wasn't even sure if she *had*

255

disappeared; I thought she might have just run off and come back here. I've looked around for her; but I've had a lot on my plate since yesterday, and I wasn't able to discover if she was actually safely back here at the Grange, before you people came looking for *me*.'

Caxton is silent for a moment.

'Do you know what that girl's been through?'

'Yes,' replies Mark soberly. 'She told me her story yesterday; not in detail; just the broad outline. I know what you rescued her from.'

'Yes, I rescued her, although I can't really take any credit for it; I just happened to be at the right place at the right time. Serendipity, really: a parapsychologist just running into an ESPer like that. What are the chances of that happening?'

'Not everyone would've helped the girl like you did,' says Mark. 'You stopped and let her into your car—a girl being chased by gangsters. A lot of people would have just driven off. And you didn't know she was an ESPer then, did you?'

'No; not then... I saw a girl in trouble and I helped her. And then...'

'You fell in love with her.'

A bitter smile. 'Love. I'm not sure I'm even capable of feeling that emotion. I'm not sure if she is. I *made* her my lover. But that's not quite the same thing, is it? I made her my lover and I made her dependent on me, and I kept her because she had ESP.'

'Yes, but I think she's more than just a test subject to you, isn't she?'

'Yes... Yes, she's a lot more than just that.'

'And I know from how she spoke of you that you mean a lot to her, as well.'

'That's not surprising, considering what I rescued her from. Yes, she was grateful, and she looked up to me, and came to rely on me, and we were physically compatible... But I feel like I've started to lose my hold on her, since I brought her here to this facility... She's mixing with her peers, as I suppose she ought to be, and me, I'm just one of the staff...'

She meets Mark's eyes. 'Will they bring her back? Whoever it was that took her away—will they bring her back?'

256

Mark shakes his head helplessly. 'I have no way of knowing that.'

'It must be because of her power... The aliens, or whatever they are: they must have been able to sense her power. Perhaps they were able to lock onto it, and drag her away from here...'

'I hadn't thought of it that way,' confesses Mark. 'You might be right, though.'

'Well, no-one else has disappeared, have they?' challenges Dr Caxton. '*You* didn't disappear. It must be because she's special.'

Abruptly, she stands up. 'Thank you for the talk, Mr Hunter. I'll bid you good evening now.'

With a curt nod, she turns, opens the door and quickly exits the cell. The key turns in the lock.

Chapter Thirty-Three
Grid Patterns

'They sell these things in the shops, you know...'

Mark Hunter proffers the cigarettes. She takes one, he lights it for her.

'Are you here to spy on us?' she asks. And he *is* a spy, she thinks. They're all talking about him back at the Grange. She wonders if she should give him a heads-up that they're onto him...?

Brown suit, brown hair, smiling face... Does he look like a spy...? Maybe one of the laid-back, easy-going ones...

That old gas heater...

A rickety old thing on wheels, it's the only heat-source in the room that is her prison and her workplace... A cold, unfriendly room... Just a box with a single bed, chilly white walls, a wardrobe, a plain table with a chair, and on the table a mirror, and make-up and perfume...

She knows when she's not wanted.

The voices of her mum and new dad, raised in argument, float up to her bedroom, where she sits in the friendly darkness.

'You can't even talk to the girl!'

'Well, she's at a funny age...'

'Come off it! Lots of people are her age, and they're not all like that! I tell you, there's something wrong with her!'

'And what am I supposed to do about it?'

'Get her sent to one of those schools for problem kids or something! Anything! Just get her out of here! I feel like I can't even breathe with her around!'

She knows when she's not wanted.

Grid-patterns.

Nature doesn't work in straight lines. Grid-patterns, the framework of the universe are straight lines; therefore, the universe is a construct, not a natural phenomenon. Nature, as we understand it, exists within an unnatural framework; and the big bang was a stray synaptic flash in a vast computer mainframe...

Staring at the river. Thick like oil, speckled with reflected light.

Why this river?

People come from all over—just to throw themselves into this river. The river exerts an allure, an enchantment: it calls out to the lost, the lonely, the despairing.

She starts to climb onto the parapet. A sudden hand grabs her arm...

Staring down the barrel of a gun.

'You work for me, now, bitch!' says the Albanian. 'Your body belongs to me. You're a whore. You're just female meat for men to fuck. No-one's going to rescue you, cuz no-one fucking cares about you! You're a stupid bitch whore and you'll fucking well like it! If you don't, if you give me any shit, I'll put a bullet through your fucking head!'

The man looks dejected, head bent, sitting on the edge of her bed.

'I can't do it...' he says.

'That's alright,' she tells him.

'I thought it would be different, coming here...'

258

'Don't worry about it…'

'You're laughing at me.'

'I'm not laughing at you.'

'You *all* laugh at me. Everyone laughs. Everyone laughed when my wife left me the day after the wedding…'

'I'm not laughing at you…'

'You're *all* laughing at me!'

He launches himself at her, childish fists pummelling her. Finally, her keepers burst into the room and drag the man off her…

It's not another universe. It's like the flip-side of our own. The underbelly that we're never supposed to see. Full of things we were never supposed to see.

But now they've come out to play.

The bath.

One tub of water for twelve girls. Last one gets to wallow in lukewarm filth, hair and skin cells. One cheap razor. Cheap bar of soap that won't lather. One at a time; line up outside the door, naked and shivering; in you go: wash and then dry, one towel for twelve; in and then out like cattle through a cattle-dip…

A different bed. A luxurious bed; a warm and friendly bed. The woman with the short grey hair smiles at her as she smokes a cigarette.

Isabelle Caxton. She has made it all better. She has washed all the filth away. Her body is clean again and belongs to herself.

She snuggles up to the woman, taking her cigarette. Together in their warm nest; the rest of the world locked outside…

They did it the wrong way.

Maybe there is no right way. Maybe you're not supposed to do this at all. Breaking the rules of time…

But they did it the wrong way, and now it's all coming apart. That's why people are starting to see them.

Slap.

'You don't laugh at the fucking clients, you bitch!'

Slap.

'I wasn't laughing at him.'

Slap.

'Don't fucking bullshit me! You were laughing your fucking head off!'

Slap.

'I wasn't laughing at *him*. I was thinking about something else.'

Slap.

'What the fuck do you mean? Thinking about something else when a guy is fucking you?'

Slap.

'I just remembered something funny…'

Slap.

'You remembered something funny?' Slap. 'You fucking useless cunt on a stick!' Slap. 'When a client's fucking you, you fucking pay attention, you fucking bitch!' Slap. 'You don't think; you just fucking do your job, you stupid fucking fuck-meat!'

Slap. Slap. Slap.

'You see further than everyone else,' Caxton tells her. 'We've only got five senses; you've got six.'

'Sometimes I can't take it all in… There's too much…'

'Information overload. Don't try to understand—just let it flow over you; just *feel* it all; absorb it all…'

For every one of us there's one of them.

They have no purpose, these other people; they just exist. Inhabiting this underbelly of our reality—separate but somehow connected.

There's mine now. Just looking at me… Separate, but somehow connected…

For every one of us there's one of them…

Chapter Thirty-Four
The Old School Tie: Clyde, Rachel, & Dennis

'Tonight on *Book Review*, we will be focusing on the science-fiction genre, which is enjoying a surge in popularity, and we are pleased to have in the studio veteran science-fiction writer Michael Moorcock, and one of the most exciting new writers in the field, Clyde Waring. Thank you both for joining us.'

The veteran writer wears a suit, but Clyde sits there in t-shirt and Bermuda shorts, wilfully informal. The presenter, Natasha Shore, looks immaculate as always with her short blonde hair and tailored skirt suit. She directs her polished smile at Clyde.

'Now, Clyde; you've written a science-fiction novel that has become a mainstream success. What's your secret?'

'Well, I think my secret is that I have a very readable writing style, and that I write science-fiction stories that are easy to read; they're not too complicated for people to get their heads around.'

'But yet, you do tackle all the social issues in your books...'

'That's right. Science-fiction is the best medium for tackling social issues. As some people have worked out, the conflict between the C'Fahh and the Drox in my last novel was allegorical of the Arab-Israeli situation in the Middle East...'

'Yes, and you made some very profound observations on that conflict...'

'That's right. Us writers, we look at the world around us, and we notice things that other people don't notice...'

...After the show, in the BBC bar; Natasha approaches Clyde, sliding onto the stool next to his.

'Clyde, I'd like to continue our conversation from the show,' she says, gazing into his eyes. 'But shall we go somewhere more... private?'

And it's back to her place—silk sheets, dim lighting. Natasha takes off her designer suit and her lacy underwear, and joins Clyde in the bed.

'You're so cuddly,' she purrs, cuddling up to him. 'You're like a big teddy bear...'

Clyde, still unpublished, lies on his solitary bed. Clyde often likes to lie down on his bed in the dark, building castles in the air. (He particularly likes to perform his supine castle-building at times like the present, when his neck and shoulders are giving him serious gyp.) Yes, he considers this an essential part of the creative process, just lying there in the dark, letting the ideas come to him... His intentions are noble, but as you can see, his mind often wanders from his stories to fantasies of a slightly different nature; dreams of fame and fortune, success in all things...

But... But tonight, he just isn't in the mood; and the fantasy, before it can become X-rated, starts to swim out of focus; he just loses his grip on it and it dissolves from his mind...

This happens to Clyde quite a lot—his libido just disappears him; slips under the floorboards, and no amount of fantasising can bring it back; or rather, it seems that his ability to fantasise vanishes along with the sex drive, and only when it returns can he start to visualise those erotic scenarios again. The cynical amongst you might cynically inquire what does Clyde need a sex drive for anyway, when he lives a solitary life. Well, people leading solitary lives, be they male, female, hermaphrodite or gender neuter, are still entitled to their onanistic sex lives, to experience the fleeting pleasure of an orgasm every now and then; the same as those with partners. In fact, this type of sex happens to be growing more and more popular, what with the steady global increase in solitary people.

Clyde is a creative writer, so his imagination ought to suffice for him when it comes to sexual arousal, as it does for most women; and for the most part it does suffice—but occasionally, and when the mood takes hold of him, he does need to have recourse to his Guilty Secret. (The upper-case letters are not mine; they exist inside Clyde's mind; part of the 'Guilty' aspect of the Guilty Secret.) The Guilty Secret finds its home in Clyde's bedside cabinet and it takes the form of a couple dirty magazines. Yes, a couple of pornos; they are the Guilty Secret. I can hear your reactions, ranging from 'so what?' to 'disgusting!' (although

262

there probably aren't many people with the latter attitude amongst my regular readership); but ultimately the collective response will simply resolve itself into: 'Well, why doesn't he just go online and look at porn for free instead of spending good money on dirty magazines?'

Well, there's a story behind that one, and it ought to be told: so let us unstick the pages of time, and venture to twenty years, to when Clyde was younger and slimmer and still clean-shaven— this was when he bought the magazines. Yes, the Guilty Secret has been sitting in Clyde's bedside cabinet for that length of time. I'm no expert, but the magazines might even be collector's items by now. All that time, hidden under a pile of more innocuous periodicals, has reposed the Guilty Secret. Clyde's mother, who used to clean his room for him, is now dead, and Clyde lives on his tod, so there's actually no earthly reason why they should still be hidden; but... you know, old habits die hard. So yes, the Guilty Secret has its origins in a time when although the internet existed, the memes had still yet to achieve their goal of installing it in everybody's houses. So there was young Clyde, fresh from sixth-form, and still in the early stages of his solitary, bedroom dwelling existence; when one fine evening, suddenly and with no prior warning, found himself completely overwhelmed by the imperative desire to view explicit images of naked women. The lingerie section of his mum's *Kay's* catalogue just wasn't going to cut it—not this time; only the most explicit erotic images would satisfy this hunger. There was only one solution: he would be compelled to make one of those furtive expeditions to the newsagents under cover of darkness. (It happened to be winter time, so the necessary cover of darkness was available.) At this time there were still several outlets for newspapers, children's comics and pornography to choose from in Market Stanford, and Clyde selected the one that was run by a Pakistani man, not because it was the closest to his place of residence (it wasn't), but because the Pakistani proprietor was a reassuringly impassive, uncommunicative man; not the type to make knowing comments or shoot dirty looks at any patron who happened to be purchasing a dirty magazine. And so, Clyde, saying 'I'm just going out to the shops' to his mum and dad (best to stick to the truth as much as possible), had ventured forth on his mission—the urge was upon him, and would not be gainsaid. He had arrived at the newsagents in good time. He had peered into the lighted interior to scope the joint. He had walked up and down the forecourt a few times. He had turned hurriedly away when a woman had appeared and gone into the shop. He had crossed the road to survey the target from a safer distance. He had walked up and down the pavement a number of times. He had crossed the road again and marched boldly up to the door. He had fled precipitately when a customer had stepped out of the shop. He had walked halfway back to his house. He had stopped in his tracks, berated himself for his cowardice and had gone back to the shop. He had paced the forecourt a few more times (just to be on the safe side.) And then he had walked into the shop. Averting his eyes from the checkout, he had walked to the magazine aisle. He had looked up at the top shelf with its half-concealed display of magazine covers, each one half hidden by the one in front of it. He had looked, and then finally he had reached up and started flicking through the magazines. He knew he could be seen from the checkout, but he considered this to be a good thing, because now the owner would know what this customer was planning to purchase, so it wouldn't come as a complete surprise when he went up to the counter with his pornographic purchase. Clyde had rummaged for some time, looking for a magazine whose cover particularly took his fancy; and then, in a fit of obsessive-compulsiveness, he'd decided if he was going to buy one magazine he might as well buy two, and so he had rummaged for a second one. Now, armed with the sacrifice fit to proffer up to his demon, he had drawn a deep breath, and made his way to the checkout—and wished he hadn't averted his eyes from it when he had first walked into the shop. The impassive Pakistani proprietor had gone and morphed himself into a blonde-haired young woman. A cold hand clutched Clyde's heart. It was too late to back out now; she had seen him. The girl was a stranger to him, but that didn't really make it any better. She was still a girl. Eyes down, bowels clenched, Clyde deposited his purchases on the counter. A quick look up and he saw the girl's eyes burning into his face. She may have just been scrutinising him to determine whether he looked over eighteen,

264

but Clyde had just read unutterable disgust and contempt in those pale blue irises. Then the transaction had been completed, the girl had handed him his change without a word. Clyde had attempted a breezy 'thank you!' just to show that he for one was not ashamed, but the words had come out half strangled.

And this was the origin of the Guilty Secret. He successfully smuggled it past his parents and into his bedroom. Okay, so the buying of it had been something of a nightmare; but why does he consider it a Guilty Secret? Well, the 'Guilt' element arises from the fact that Clyde considers himself to be a feminist, an advocate of female equality, and opponent of anything sexist; and believing that feminist women are universally and without exception anti-porn, he considers himself a hypocrite and a turncoat on account of what he went out and bought that night. Clyde doesn't have any friends, feminist or otherwise, but he often imagines having such friends, female sci-fi fans, and imagines the contempt with which they would dismiss him from their lives upon learning of his possession of the Guilty Secret.

But Clyde is hard upon the Guilty Secret; it has done him a lot of good service over the years. In all that time they have been his only source of masturbation fodder, and the models in the two magazines—apart from one or two he doesn't like because they look too pleby—have become almost like friends to him; he has even invented personalities for them. (The Guilty Secret hails from the dark days before top-shelf magazines made themselves more politically correct by running interviews with the models alongside their photospreads.) For example, Sandra, who looks very posh and is posing in a room full of antique furniture, he imagines to be an upper-class wild child; and Yolanda, a stern and bespectacled Mediterranean woman, is a Greek university professor who just does porn modelling on the side for kicks. Sometimes, Clyde has even based characters in his stories on some of the models.

Even now that he is internet-connected Clyde has rarely viewed online porn—whenever he has felt the need for visual stimulus, it is the Guilty Secret to which he has turned. But right now, he feels so turned off that he knows, even without trying, that the Guilty Secret is not going to raise a reaction from him;

265

not tonight.

Clyde decides to turn to food for solace. This is a typical response with Clyde; the comfort he has always turned top, and which explains his obesity.

Yes, he'll get up and grab himself something to eat.

But this turns out to be easier said than done; as Clyde works his muscles to raise his head from the pillow and himself from the bed, a bolt of excruciating pain shoots, completely unannounced, up the back of his neck. He cries out, the pain is so intense, and subsiding back onto the bed, can only lie there in agony until the pain slowly dies down. What just happened? What the hell is this? In his entire life, he cannot remember experiencing so much pain; it was like every nerve in his neck was screaming... Oh, well. Maybe it was just a one off; a fluke.

It wasn't. He tries to raise himself again, and the pain assaults him again, forcing him back onto the bed.

Now, panic starts to well up in Clyde. He can't get up! He can't get off the bed! If he tries to so much as move an inch that unbearable pain shoots through his neck!

He's stuck here! Stuck lying on his bed!

Alone and helpless...

One of the few people who remember that such a person as Clyde Waring actually exists is by chance walking past his house at this very moment; it is Rachel Farrow, on her way to the convenience store. The old story—they have run out of milk.

She observes the absence of any lights in Clyde's windows. Could he actually have gone out somewhere? No; more likely he's just gone to bed early. She can easily imagine Clyde being the kind of person who would do that, when his mood is low and he feels at a loose end; go to bed early, just to make the day shorter...

Rachel has tried to remain friends with Clyde over the years, but Clyde doesn't always make it easy for her. There have been times when she would knock on his front door and receive no answer. She is pretty sure that Clyde was at home on those occasions—he just wouldn't answer the door. Clyde isn't on any forums or social networking sites that she knows of, so she can't communicate with him that way; he seems determined to isolate himself.

But, passing Clyde's house, he also passes out of Rachel's mind, and she gets back to thinking about her lousy day; being blocked by Annette is still rankling with her, upsetting her thoughts.

Arrived at the convenience store Rachel goes straight to the dairy section and picks out a two-litre carton of milk. Milk is all she really needs, but she finds herself lingering at the cake section. She has been indulging her sweet tooth more and more in recent years, and like most people who do this, she feels guilty about the fact. Back when she was younger, she had used to abstain apart from on rare occasions, and the abstaining didn't feel like much of a sacrifice. But now she has let herself go, and yes, she is getting fatter as a result. Why is it that people start to let themselves go in the weight department as they get older? she wonders. People must just come to a point where they stop caring about their outward appearance; where they start thinking it's not worth their while…

She picks out a packet of caramel cake bars and goes to the check-out.

Outside again, her self-conscious chain of thought moves to her hair. Should she start dyeing it to cover up that grey that's starting to show through…? Or would it be just another pointless vanity; something not worth worrying about…? Getting old… everyone tries to conceal it, cover up; and it's so much worse for women, so unfair on them. Yes, men can go bald, which women don't have to worry about; but those indelible ciphers of age that write themselves on your face—they're the hardest thing to conceal. She knows that most men don't like to read those signs any more than women, when they see them looking back at them in their mirrors; but the fact is a lot of people consider that the lines of age to lend 'dignity' to a man's face, to make it look 'distinguished.' But being 'distinguished' like that is not desirable for the female countenance; a woman is somehow supposed to contrive to make her face look as fresh and faultless as it did when she was eighteen…

Rachel espies Dennis Shrimpton across the street, walking

267

rapidly, like a man with a purpose. Where is he going at this time of night? He looks like he has a definite destination... Hopefully, he's just going to the pub... All those rumours circulating about Dennis—are they actually true? Rachel isn't sure. The rumours are recent; there has never been any talk about Dennis messing around with kids in the past... He might just have been seen talking to kids; he's the kind of person who'd do that; but that can be enough to set people's tongues wagging in this day and age... Rachel has known Dennis all her life, had gone through school with him, and had seen him emerge from the education system a very maladjusted adult; but there have never been any stories like this about him; not until recently...

David has gone round a friend's this evening, which is unusual, because he doesn't have many friends to visit, and doesn't usually like to go out of an evening. Rachel arrives back at her house and lets herself in through the back door. She finds David is waiting for her in the kitchen.

'You're back soon,' says Rachel. 'Did something happen?'

She sees a look of savage triumph written across her husband's features. 'Yes,' he crows; 'you didn't expect me to come back so soon, did you?'

'I know I didn't; that's what I just said.'

'Yes, you thought you could get one up on me, didn't you? "While the cat's away..." Well, I fooled you, didn't I? I outsmarted you this time. You walked straight into my trap.'

'What are you on about?' snaps Rachel. Is this another one of his mind-games?

'I wasn't really going round Tom's house,' David tells her. 'I just walked around the block and came back again. And what did I find when I got here? Surprise, surprise! *You* weren't here. You, who said you'd be staying in.'

Rachel holds up the carrier bag. 'That's because I went to get some milk.'

'Oh, you went to get some milk, did you? How very convenient. Just popped out to get some milk. That's what you *want* me to think; but I know better. You went round *his* house.'

'Whose house?'

'I don't know whose house! Whoever it is that you're having

sex with behind my back!'

'For Christ's sake, David; I've only been out twenty minutes!'

'That's what you say. You could have been out twice as long as that if you went out just after me; that's plenty of time.'

'Plenty of time! Forty minutes?'

'Enough time for a quick one!'

This is the limit! 'Will you listen to yourself, for Christ's sake! David, you're paranoid. You really are. We'd run out of milk and I went to buy some. End of story.'

'And I'm supposed to believe that? Tell me who it is! Who have you been screwing?'

'No-one, for fuck's sake!'

'Liar! Yes, you have! Who is it? Is it Simon? It is; it's him! You're still seeing him behind my back, aren't you?'

'He's remarried, for Christ's sake!'

'Like that would stop you two!'

'Oh, for—Look, you know damn well I split up with Simon because I couldn't stand him! Why would I want to go back to him?'

'You'd go back to him just for the sex, wouldn't you? Just because he's probably bigger than me, and better than me in bed. Is that what it is?'

Rachel heaves a sigh. 'Yes, David,' she says slowly, her voice calm now. 'If you want the honest truth, yes; he was much more well-endowed than you, and he was a damn sight better than you are in the sack. There. Are you satisfied now?'

Spitting unintelligible abuse, David stalks across the room and slaps her round the face.

A pregnant moment.

And then Rachel snaps. This, coming at the end of a particularly shitty day, is more than she can take. She's stronger than her scrawny husband anyway; so he doesn't really stand a chance when she starts laying into him with her fists. She lets it all out—all her pent-up rage, resentment and frustration.

She stops when she has punched David to the floor; he lies there on linoleum, curled up in a ball and sobbing like a child. He looks pathetic. Rachel doesn't feel sorry for him; she just feels disgusted with him and with herself.

269

'For God's sake, David…' she sighs wearily.

After the war will hopefully come the peace negotiations, followed by the reconciliation—so let us leave Rachel and David. Rachel had seen Dennis Shrimpton heading off somewhere, and I think we should follow him, particularly as this will be the last journey Dennis will ever be making on this Earth.

Where is he going? To his allotment! And not because he has the strange urge to do some nocturnal gardening. No, it is a letter that had been pushed through his door that has prompted this outing; a brief letter, written in a childish scrawl, which reads: 'Come to the allotment right now! We got something to show you.'

This was all. No name appended. Who could it be? wonders Dennis. Who has written this letter to him? Obviously children, but which ones? He knows a lot of children. He likes kids.

Could it be them two boys he'd seen at the allotment a couple o' days back? Yeah, mebbe it's them! What've they got to show 'im? Some new toy one of 'em 'as got, mebbe? P'raps one of 'em's got a new bike! Or mebbe it's somethin' they've found. Always findin' things, kids are… He hopes it's not a dead cat!

Children shouldn't be out this late; even if they do 'ave somethin' good to show 'im! 'E'll 'ave to tell 'em about that; tell 'em they shouldn't be out so late!

He arrives at the allotments and makes his way to his patch. There's no-one about. No sign of any kids. But they said to come here right away! So where are they?

''Ullo?' he calls out. 'Where's you 'idin', then?'

Has he been pranked? Is there really no-one here?

He walks up to his ramshackle shed.

''Ullo? Is you there? Stop 'idin' from me, will yer?'

They appear from behind the shed; four dark figures, and most definitely not children, because they're big—very big. First a fist smashes into Dennis's face and then another one and down he goes. And then, when he's down on the ground, they start kicking him; all four of them—kicking him with gusto and like they don't intend to stop anytime soon. You should hear poor Dennis screaming!

270

But nothing lasts forever and the cries grow weaker and weaker as blessed oblivion floods over our Dennis; a blissful state from which he will never emerge.

Chapter Thirty-Five
Jack Stone Loses His Head

Before the property had been taken over by Vallotec, the previous owner of Vernon Grange had been one Jem Croxley. A misanthrope, recluse and collector, Croxley had been just what you might have imagined him to be: a bitter, crotchety old man, living alone in the vast mansion. He had considered his home his castle, and woe-betide anyone who attempted to breach the ramparts! He had once found himself in trouble with the police on one occasion when he had threatened with a gun some kids who had climbed over the walls into his grounds.

One fine night four local lads had broken into the Grange with a view to relieving Croxley of his collection of rare coins. In this they had succeeded, but not without awakening the owner, who, hearing the intruders, had burst in on them armed with a blunderbuss. In response to this unprovoked threatening behaviour, the intruders had beaten Croxley into unconsciousness; strictly in self-defence, of course! *They* hadn't been carrying guns, had they? And yes, it's true that Croxley had subsequently died in hospital on account of this beating—but as I said, he was an old man, so he would have died sooner or later anyway.

Tonight, history is about to repeat itself. For tonight, four local lads—and would you believe it: the very same four!—are, on this stifling summer's night, making another assault upon the precincts of Vernon Grange. But this time it is not for larcenous purposes...

The front gates of the Grange. A nimble figure runs across the road to the gates, and examining them, finds them to be closed but unlocked. He opens the gates and beckons with his arm. Three more figures, one of them armed with a shotgun, cross the road and join the first. They enter the grounds. The gate-keeper's lodge is in darkness. Ahead of them stretches the treelined drive, at the far end of which rises the bulk of Vernon Grange. Not a light shows in the many windows. The four intruders proceed along the drive, keeping under the shadows of the flanking trees.

In case you haven't guessed, our four intruders are none other than Jack, Trevor, Fergus and Mitch. Trevor walks in front, with Jack and his shotgun close behind him. You might almost have thought that it is Trevor himself who is being menaced by that gun, and you wouldn't be far wrong. You see, Trevor is a very reluctant participant in this night's excursion, and Jack is keeping an eye on him to make sure he doesn't chicken out and do a runner.

They had worked out the details that afternoon. Having learned, the night before, that Vernon Grange was the current residence of that smug prick Damien and his friends, Jack Stone formed the resolution to pay said 'smug prick' (previously the 'skinny cunt') a nocturnal social call, in order to 'teach him a lesson.' Discussing their plans at the farm, Trev had declared he wanted nothing to do with it. After what had happened last time, he never wanted to see the inside of Vernon Grange again. Jack however, was equally determined that Trevor *would* form one of the party, and his method of persuasion was to introduce that lumbering hulk Fergus into the argument; and Trevor had been forced to submit to the wily politician and his able adjutant. And so here he is, at the head of the column, as they draw close to the house in the silent stillness of the night. He has a very bad feeling about this...

When they had been discussing their plans at the farm that afternoon, Trev had thought he'd heard sounds coming from inside the barn behind them; the sound of whispering voices. He had gone to look in the barn and had found nothing and no-one; none of the others had heard anything at all and had dismissed his fears. But Trevor couldn't help thinking of those twins and their teleportation act... What if they had been listening in? They would have heard everything. And then they would have told Damien and the others. Those kids are weird; all of them, not just the twins... Jack just thinks they must be a bunch of problem kids on a supervised summer holiday; all he thinks about is getting even with Damien. Jack doesn't reflect; he just does what his instincts tell him.

They stop before the house. In spite of the heat, none of the ground floor windows seem to be open. There's no-one about. Trevor has been half-expecting a trap; expecting the cops to spring out on them; but here they are, standing out in the open, and nothing has happened...

'Door or window?' asks Mitch.

'Let's try the door first,' answers Jack. 'Might not be locked.'

'Yeah; if they're usin' this place as an 'ostel, don't they 'ave to keep the doors unlocked all the time, or somethin'?'

'That's only in France,' says Trevor.

They mount the steps to the portico. Mitch tries the door. It opens.

'"Only in France," 'e says,' grinning at Trevor.

'What if it's a trap?' retorts Trevor.

'It ain't a fuckin' trap,' declares Jack. 'Now get in.'

And he pushes Trev through the doorway.

The first thing Trev notices in the semi-darkness of the hall is the suit of armour. He remembers it being there the last time they had visited the place, standing in the exact same spot. He sees it as a bad omen. That door off to the left led to the room in which old Croxley had kept his coin collection. Trev recalls that night; Croxley bursting in on them in his long nightgown and bobble hat, brandishing his blunderbuss. Fergus had only punched the guy a few times, but a few punches from his fists are enough to pole-axe anyone. And Croxley had croaked... It's bad luck; that's what it is: it's bad luck coming back to this place after what happened last time...

Well, at least there is no sign of a welcoming committee. The air is cool. The place must be air-conditioned...

'Where to now?' breathes Mitch.

'Upstairs, of course,' says Jack. 'That's where they'll be.'

Treading carefully, they climb the broad staircase to the landing.

What now? wonders Trev. Start looking in all the rooms? Check them all until they find the one with Damien?

And then the lights come on.

Trev shields his eyes, blinking as they adjust to the sudden glare.

They aren't alone anymore. There, before them on the landing stand seven kids: Damien, those twins, that sexy looking girl, the younger girl with the silly hat, the poncy looking four-eyed boy, and one other girl. For a moment, Trev thinks this last might be the goth girl, with her hair dyed and not wearing black; but no, the face is different; it's not her.

None of the kids look surprised to see the intruders, and none of them look worried. In fact, Damien, the twins, and that sexy-looking girl have all got big fat grins on their faces. And they're all fully dressed, as well; they don't look like they've just got out of bed.

'You took your time,' says Damien, breaking the taut silence. 'We thought you weren't coming.'

I knew it! is Trev's first thought. In the barn—they bloody *were* expecting us!

Jack levels his shotgun at Damien. 'You knew we was comin'?'

'Yes, Jack,' replies Damien, apparently unconcerned about the gun. 'I knew you was comin'.'

''*Ow* did you know we was comin'?'

'Can read you like an open book, old son. Thought you'd be popping round tonight. Very neighbourly of you to pay us this little visit. Not sure why you brought the gun, though. Or were you planning a midnight poaching expedition? Give us townies a real taste of fenland nightlife?'

'I'll give yer both fuckin' barrels, you little scrote!' grates Jack.

'Jack...! Jack...!' protests Damien, affecting a wounded look. 'Now that's not very friendly, is it? And I always thought we got along so well, us two.'

'Shut yer fuckin' face!'

'It's a menagerie!' bursts out Robert, pointing at the intruders.

'You'd better say "zoo," Robert,' opines Roberta. 'They proberly don't know what "menagerie" means.'

'Yes, you're proberly right about that,' agrees Robert. 'It's a zoo then. The zoo's come to town, to show us the local wildlife!' He points at Jack: 'There's the growling bull-dog...' To Mitch:

274

'And there's the nasty weasel…'

'Are you sure he isn't a stoat, Robert?' questions Roberta.

'No, cuz stoats are 'stoataly' different!'

'And weasels are 'weasely' recognised!'

Robert points to Trevor. 'There's the mouse; the squeaking little mouse…' To Fergus. '…And *that* one's the gorilla!'

Roberta claps her hands. 'That's right! The big, stupid gorilla!'

The twins vanish and reappear right in front of Fergus.

'Ug, ug! It's the gorilla!'

'Big, stupid gorilla!'

A look of baffled rage settles over Fergus's heavy features. He may be slow on the uptake, but he knows when someone's taking the piss. He flails wildly at the twins with his brawny arms—and he finds himself flailing at thin air.

The twins, giggling, are suddenly standing right across the landing.

'Missed us by a mile!'

'Can't catch us, big, stupid gorilla!'

Enraged and even more baffled, Fergus lurches towards his taunting foes.

Another teleportation and Robert and Roberta are now standing on the balustrade overlooking the hallway.

'Ug, ug, stupid gorilla!' taunts Robert.

'Nya-nya-ny-nya-nya!' sings Roberta.

With an inarticulate cry of fury, Fergus charges at his tormentors, who promptly disappear, and Fergus, propelled by his own momentum, pitches straight over the balustrade, plunging headfirst to the floor below. The cry of terror he trails behind him is abruptly silenced when he hits the ground with a loud thump. He lands on his thick skull, which actually might have saved him; but sadly, the weight of the rest of his body coming down on top of it, snaps his neck in two, killing him instantly.

'Oh dear!' say the Twins, peering through the railing of the balustrade. 'The gorilla's taken a fall!'

'He's not moving, is he, Robert?'

'No, I s'pect he's broken his neck, Roberta.'

'I hope you got all of that, Helen,' says Damien.

'Yes, I got it,' replies Helen wearily, pointing her smartphone over the balusters for an aerial shot of the victim.

'Excellent! Should be a winner on YouTube!'

The stupefied (remaining) intruders just stare at them: Damien, the girl, the twins joyful; the four-eyed boy and the girl with the phone bland and unconcerned; only the girl in the hat looks at all upset at what has happened.

Jack Stone struggles to find his voice. 'You... You... You *bastards!*' His face comes to life again, livid with rage. 'You fuckin' bastards!'

He aims the shotgun.

Then he freezes, a confused look clouding his face.

'Wha's wrong?' demands Mitch.

'I can't move...' says Jack, confused. 'Feels like someone's 'oldin' the gun...'

'What you talkin' about? *You're* 'oldin' it!'

'Well it feels like someone else is 'oldin' it!'

'Yeah, that'll be me,' says Damien. He studies Jack thoughtfully. 'You know... I feel a *Village of the Damned* moment coming on. Make sure you get this one as well, Helen. Jack Stone, centre stage.'

Those of you who have seen the film just alluded to (the George Sanders version, of course), will know what comes next: Jack, as though wrestling with some invisible opponent for possession of the gun, struggles with every muscle, with every ounce of his strength; his face red and contorted with the effort. But slowly, inexorably, the shotgun is turned and raised until the muzzle is pressed firmly against the underside of Jack's chin.

Mitch and Trevor just look on, bewildered, horrified.

'Don't... just... stand there...!' gasps Jack. 'Fucking... help me...'

Too late for that.

Bang! And Jack Stone's head disintegrates in a red geyser— and the BNP has lost from its ranks a valuable candidate.

'Well, he certainly lost his head!' exclaims Robert.

'Yes indeed, Robert,' concurs Roberta. 'It was neck or nothing, there!'

'Jesus Christ...!' croaks Mitch, his dazed face liberally splattered with cranial matter. 'Jesus fucking Christ...!'

'Relax,' purrs Serena. She steps forward and takes his arm in her hands. Mitch convulses, screams; his body starts to convulse spastically, and smoke rises from his clothes; his screams become louder, shrill with agony; his face starts to burn, his hair to smoke; for a moment a disturbingly appetising aroma of cooking meat fills the air, but this is soon replaced by the charcoal smell of burnt meat; and then, Serena releases her grip, and Mitch drops to the floor a charred and blackened corpse.

'That was a rather shocking experience,' says Roberta.

'Yes, but at least he got a buzz out of it,' says Robert.

All eyes now turn to look at Trevor, the remaining intruder. And Trevor is quite a sight to see: shaking like a leaf, eyes bulging from their sockets, face drained of colour.

'Look at him,' says Damien, indulgently. 'Dearie me. No need to fill your trousers, old son. We're not going to kill you. The twins here; they like you, so… All you've got to do is keep your gob shut. Nothing happened tonight, right?'

Trevor remains rooted to the spot.

'That means you can go, silly,' Roberta tells him.

'Yes,' adds Robert. 'Be off with you. Shoo!'

Suddenly galvanised, Trevor shoots down the stairs, across the hall and out through the front door. He runs, and he keeps on running and he doesn't look back.

Chapter Thirty-Six
Batteries Not Included

I'm sure you've all been worried about Mark's tent. You're probably thinking that ever since Mavis Shagwell lured him away from it yesterday, it has been sitting there unattended; that anyone could have come along and walked off with it or with the possessions therein. But you would be wrong. The tent is not attended; the tent has in fact been attentively attended to, and by Dodo Dupont. To be brief, she has spent the whole night in it—and not being as materialistic as you obviously are, she has done this much more out of concern for its absent owner, than for the tent itself.

It was an empty shoulder holster that had got Dodo worrying. When they had returned to the cottage yesterday afternoon, Mayumi, Trina and herself, they had found obvious signs that Mark had been there during their absence; signs that he had made himself some lunch and that he had taken a shower. Nothing strange about that. Mark was camping out in the woods, with no washing facilities and a limited supply of food; and as his campsite was within easy walking-distance of the cottage, it made all kinds of sense that he would back, clean himself up, grab some food, and then return to his vigil. Nothing strange about that at all.

But then there was that empty shoulder holster. It was just lying on the bed in Mark's room. Obviously, he had taken it off when he took his shower...

So why hadn't he put it back on?

On the one hand, it seemed such a trivial thing, but on the other it just didn't make sense. Why would he leave it behind? He hadn't left his gun behind; there was no sign of that; only the holster had been left behind... Trina didn't think much of it: she said he'd probably just put the gun in his pocket or tucked it into his trousers belt... But Dodo knew Mark better than Trina and knew that he wouldn't do that—he had a shoulder holster for his gun because he preferred to have his gun in a shoulder holster. Simple as that.

Therefore, the only conclusion Dodo could arrive at was that Mark had for some reason left the cottage in a hurry with the gun in his hand; or, someone else had taken possession of the weapon. Either way, it meant that something had occurred; an incident, an event of some kind. This conjecture was supported by the fact that they had returned to find the cottage door, which they had locked behind them, unlocked.

At first Dodo had tried calling Mark on his phone; but doing this had only revealed that Mark's phone was sitting in the drawer of the bedside cabinet in his room. This in itself was not suspicious; Mark often preferred to go out without his phone. As a rule, spies do not care to carry mobile phones around with them when on assignments; to them this seems too much like planting a tracking device on yourself.

The next thing Dodo had decided to do was to go to the campsite in Vernon Wood. This she had done, accompanied by Trina and Mayumi, and following the short-cut across the fields which Mark had previously described to her. They found the campsite unattended. And so, they had made themselves as comfortable as the hot weather permitted, and waited for Mark to return. They had waited several hours, and Mark had not returned. In the end, as night was beginning to fall, Dodo had announced her intention of spending the night at the campsite. The other two had wanted to stay with her, but Dodo was firm, and had sent them back to the cottage. Apart from the possibility of danger, she knew that with all three of them lying close together in the confines of one small tent and in the middle of a heatwave, was not going to lead to any of them getting much sleep…

As it transpires, even with the tent to herself, Dodo has passed a very uncomfortable night. It is morning now, and already uncomfortably hot, and Dodo, wearing the bra and knickers she has slept in, crawls out of the tent and stretches her cramped muscles. She scratches her thighs, her forearms; in spite of applying the usual preventives, she has still been profusely bitten by hungry insects.

After pausing to water the dandelions, Dodo goes back into the tent and gets out the camping stove, a carton of tepid tap water, and the other paraphernalia for the making of a cup of coffee. It's instant coffee, of course, which Dodo usually detests, but when you're roughing it beggars can't be choosers, and caffeine is still caffeine…

The beverage prepared, Dodo sits herself cross-legged on the grass outside the tent, sipping Mark's coffee from Mark's tin mug, and wondering what could have become of their owner.

As said, she has passed an uncomfortable night, and not just on account of the heat and the insects—she was woken more than once during the night by strange, unearthly sounds filling the air. The first time it happened, she thought it must be that the UFO had materialised again at the landing site nearby; but, on getting out of her tent, she had seen no lights coming from the direction of the landing site, and the sounds weren't coming for that direction either; they were in the sky above her, all around her…

279

She realised these had to be the same unearthly sounds Mark had described hearing two days before, when the girl Lucretia had vanished into thin air...

Could something like that have happened to Mark? Has he been taken away? Spirited away by someone or something?

Her smartphone starts ringing. She picks up the device and sees that her caller is Mayumi.

'Hello, sweetie... Yes, everything's okay with me; still no sign of Mark, though. Has he turned up at the cottage...? No? Okay... The what...? Oh, the two grey aliens? No, they didn't show up this time. Didn't see any of the spaceman aliens, either; just some weird noises in the sky... Yes, like Mark heard... So how are you? Quiet night...? Oh, Trina tried to get into bed with you, did she? Well, I hope you made it clear to her that that kind of thing is only acceptable when we're *both* there... What...? You knocked her out and left her tied up to Mark's bed! What did you do that for...? Oh! You thought that if Mark came back during the night, he'd—No, I don't think he would have done that, sweetheart; but it was a thoughtful gesture, anyway... Hm...? Well, I've been thinking about that; I've decided I'm going to strike camp—I'm going to pack up the tent and everything and come back to the cottage; then we can figure out what we're going to do next... No, that's alright; I'll walk it; it's not far... When? Well, as soon as I've finished my coffee; so I should be with you within the hour... Okay, sweetheart, see you soon... Yes, you can untie Trina now...'

'So, what do you think about cruelty, Mr Hunter?'

'Cruelty? Well, what type are we talking about: Physical? Psychological?'

'Oh, physical. Just physical.'

'Okay; physical cruelty: torture and the like?'

'Yes, that's right. What do you think about it?'

'What do I think about it...? In what way do you mean?'

'Well, for example, do you think it's natural?'

'Is it natural to be cruel? Just for human beings? Or the animal kingdom as well?'

'No, no; just with humans.'

'Well… I suppose it *is* natural; otherwise it wouldn't be such a popular pastime.'

'So, you agree that cruelty is a natural element of human nature, and not a perversion, a distortion of human nature?'

Just where is this conversation going? wonders Mark.

He is enjoying a morning visit from the blonde, bespectacled Dr Clavering, last of the Four Doctors of Vernon Grange to make his acquaintance. He sits on the edge of his bed, while she occupies the chair.

'I agree with you,' proceeds Clavering. 'Just look at human history: it's a history of cruelty. It's a basic urge; we just feel happy when we're inflicting pain on other people. Look all those torture devices they had back in the middle ages; wonderful machines that didn't just inflict pain, but protracted it, by keeping the victim alive as long as possible. Wonderful refinements of cruelty; superlative feats of human ingenuity. Just think of the minds that invented them!'

'We're not as cruel now as we were in the middle-ages,' argues Mark. 'For most of us, our own better natures tell us that it's not a good thing to enjoy inflicting pain on other people.'

'"Our better natures,"' scoffs Clavering. 'Why don't you just go ahead and say "our moral side." *That's* the real perversion: all these codes of ethics and morality, imposing all these checks and prohibitions on natural human behaviour… I'm a Wiccan, Mr Hunter. I believe in nature. I believe in people behaving naturally and with no restraints; just doing whatever your instincts and inclinations tell you to do…'

Mark looks at her closely. A woman in a scientist's lab coat, bespectacled, her blonde hair neatly tied back out of the way. She seems much less commanding than the other two female parapsychologists; quieter in her speech, slightly awkward in her movements… But, what she's saying now…

'You know… I'm not an expert of course, but I always thought there was something in the Wiccan creed about doing what you want as long as it does no harm to others…? I'd say that torturing people would contravene that one…'

Clavering waves a dismissive hand. 'Oh yes, somebody did write something like that… but it's not official… The Wiccan religion has no recognised holy book, no official list of dos and don'ts… It's a very adaptable religion.'

Mark smiles wryly. 'Yes, I think most religions can be "adaptable" in that way. You only have to watch the news to see proof of that one.'

'Exactly!' Clavering sounds delighted at this. 'You've illustrated my point beautifully! Flying airliners into skyscraper buildings; driving lorries into dense crowds of people; inspired acts of cruelty!'

'Well, I can see you have already evolved a personal philosophy that embraces cruelty as a natural and healthy human behaviour.'

'That's right!' affirms Clavering.

'And you weren't really interested in hearing my views on the subject at all, were you?'

'That's right!'

'Because you're already perfectly satisfied that when you have another human being at a disadvantage, and are in a position to be cruel to them with impunity, you should just go ahead and be cruel to them?'

'That's right!'

'And with me being your prisoner, you have me at that kind of disadvantage right now, haven't you?'

'That's right!'

'And that's an electric cattle-prod sticking out of your coat pocket, isn't it?'

'That's right!'

Mark moves to jump from the bed, but Clavering springs to her feet, snatching the cattle-prod from her lab-coat pocket.

'Ah-ah, Mr Hunter. Not so fast!'

She lunges and jabs him with the prod. Mark flinches instinctively, but the expected shock doesn't happen.

Clavering frowns. She jabs him again.

Still nothing.

'Are you immune, or something?' she asks, an accusing look on her face.

'No, I'm not immune to electricity,' says Mark. 'The device is obviously not working.'

282

'It should be. It's new.'

She prods Mark several more times; still with no result.

'Have you got it switched on?' suggests Mark.

'Of course I've got it switched on!' snaps Dr Clavering. 'Why isn't it working?'

'Did you remember to put the batteries in it?'

'Batteries? I just assumed it came with them already installed... There weren't any batteries with it. Let's have a look...'

She inspects the handle of the device. Mark springs from the bed and delivers a sharp uppercut to her jaw. Stunned, she falls back onto the chair—Mark is already out of the room and running. There's no-one in sight in the corridor and he sprints straight for the lift doors. He is almost there when Dr Channing appears through the doors of the sickbay at the end of the corridor.

'Hey!'

Curses!

No time for the lift. Mark takes the emergency stairs. He comes out into the Grange's entrance hall, and heads straight for the doors. Reaching them, he looks back and sees a girl standing at the foot of the stairs; a young girl wearing a blue hat with earflaps. She doesn't speak, makes no move to intercept him, but just stands there looking at him. Mark eyes meet hers—blue eyes staring out of the faultless but expressionless face of a child.

Does she want something? Is she—?

The sound of the lift ascending warns Mark that he cannot be hanging around. A last brief, questioning look at the girl and he is out through the front doors.

It is the last time he will see Bridget Price.

Chapter Thirty-Seven
The Edge of Beyond

'He was a dedicated cynic; especially as a young man.'

Who was a dedicated cynic...? Oh yes; it was Aldous Huxley. Something Marianne said to him once... What was it about...?

HG Wells—that was it; she was telling me about HG Wells' utopian novel *Men Like Gods*; and how it was Huxley's cynical reaction to the book that had inspired him to write *Brave New World*...

'...And it pretty much destroyed the reputation of *Men Like Gods*,' said Marianne; 'which is a shame, really, because it's actually one of his best books... And in fairness to Wells, the utopias he wrote about were always set in parallel universes; they were never meant to be visions of Earth in the future...'

Yes, when the humans came along, they nearly ruined that utopia... Wasn't one of them Winston Churchill...?

History is Bunk in the Year of our Ford, Nineteen-Hundred and Eighty-Four...

Trees.

Trees in every direction, but widely spaced—standing just far enough apart from each other for it to not look right. There is a uniformity to the trees; the same height, the same breadth of foliage...Similar, but not quite identical... And there are no bushes, no bracken or weeds growing between the trees; only a carpet of short grass.

This isn't Vernon Wood.

This should be Vernon Wood.

Mark stands in a clearing in the middle of this unnatural scene. The white tissue-paper sky is wrong as well. The sky was blue a minute ago—now it is hazy, like the sky on that day he met Marianne, met her for the first time under the Lone Ash Tree...

What did he do with her book...?

A moment before the heat had been well-nigh unbearable—an intense, oppressive heat... Now, the temperature is neutral. A vague sound, ethereal, hangs in the air...

Yes! The Sound of the Sky—it had been much louder before, filling the air... This... what he hears now... this is just its lingering echo...

Memory retraces its steps. The sounds, the clearing, the landing site. Running through Vernon Wood...

The heat; it hit him like a solid barrier—coming from the air-conditioned atmosphere of Vernon Grange, it was like stepping into a furnace...

A daring escape. Down the drive, Dr Channing in pursuit, raising the alarm. Tackling the guard at the gate and then out onto the road. Into Vernon Wood, armed guards in pursuit... Back to the campsite; the clearing empty—someone's walked off with his tent!

And then the sounds. They draw him towards the landing site—

And now he is here.

Sentimental Education. The book; it was in his tent. His one memento, his only physical reminder of Marianne—lost, stolen.

The trees, too widely spaced to be natural, stretch off in all directions. All is still, all is silent save for that background noise, a mild tinnitus, barely noticeable. He has been moved; transposed; relocated—moved in space, or time, or both? The atmosphere feels strange, unfamiliar—this is not the world he has come from; this is somewhere else; another place... Marianne said something about parallel universes... And was this where Lucretia was taken to...? This is not the inside of a spaceship... Unless it *is*... Parallel universes, alternate planes of reality, manufactured hallucinations, artificial constructions... Mark has known them all. He's a spy—it comes, like the strip joints, with the territory.

Another question: Has he been brought here by accident or design? No sign of a welcome committee. Mark starts to walk... walks in the direction he was facing when he arrived—that disjointed moment—walks that way because it seems like the right direction in which to walk... The trees... Their odd spacing reminds him of an orchard more than anything else... But these trees look like beech trees; not fruit-bearing trees... The parallel world where Men Like Gods... Like them very much... The Eight Million Gods of Japan... A pantheist nation, obsessed with panties... Is this other world the centre of it all? The Market Stanford Incident... All the other incidents...? Nothing that came from outer-space, but slipped over sideways from other-space...

Something up ahead... Trees thinning out... A barrier, a golden line of demarcation. As Mark approaches, the view unfolds before him—an endless plain of ripe corn, stretching off to the horizon, a golden sea. There are no tracks, ditches, or borders; none of the patchwork signs of cultivation familiar to Mark—just one vast ocean of corn, extending as far as the eye can see; nature, not agriculture. A silent ocean; not a rustle of movement in the perfectly still air...

What is he searching for...? A book... A lost cherished possession... I've lost some property of mine... Who said that...? Channing... Lucretia... Lucretia, the lost property... Sexual property... Corporate property...

A blemish in the landscape catches his eye. There it is... off to the left, way out on that wheaten heathland—a figure... Mark stares at it... It wasn't there before...   The figure remains motionless; a vague grey shape... From this distance he can make out no details, but he feels sure that the motionless figure is facing him, staring right at him...

Mark starts moving towards the figure, moving with purpose, wading through the waist-high corn. The distance steadily diminishes, details coalesce into shape... A grey, humanoid form... Yes, it *is* a grey—two black oval eyes, expressionless, stare at him... Eyes he has seen before, looking at him out of a mirror. The grey aliens; the ones that don't fit the pattern of his theories.

Is this your world? Did you bring me here?

It stands perfectly still as Mark advances towards it... Standing in a field of corn—Flora Hodgson's vril-powered Coming Race...

In this place it is real... It is no fiction; no fabrication implanted into the subconscious; no dreamy fiction of alien abduction; no CIA conspiracy; no MK-altered reality...

But then Mark blinks and the grey man disappears.

When you're not looking; that's when they can disappear—and

when you blink you're not looking; one split-second out of every five, you're not looking…

Mark reaches the spot where the grey man stood and steps out onto a causeway. Wide as a road, but showing no signs of being used as one; a green carpet of turf, bisecting the ocean of golden corn, extending itself, ruler straight, in both directions…

Nature doesn't work in straight lines…

Grid lines…

There's something else… On the edge of the causeway, down there on his left—an object, a construction of some kind, rising above the wheat-ears into the sky.

It looks like a house.

Mark turns his steps towards it, and as he gets closer, it looks more and more like a house—but there's something odd about it… It is all of one colour, and the colour is gold; the same gold as the surrounding sea of corn… It's a straw house, a wicker-work construction—and standing in front of the straw house is a straw car.

Drawing level, Mark stops. The house is made of straw; solid, tightly-woven; a wickerwork house… Rectangular voids representing front door and windows… Above the wicker walls, a wicker roof and a wicker chimney.

And it looks like the cottage—*their* cottage; the holiday cottage… The dimensions of the straw house are identical; a perfect match—and the straw car in the drive is a life-sized model of Dodo's Jaguar. He walks over to inspect it…The replica car appears to be solid; just a shape; no details worked into it… He touches it; he strikes it: a solid construction, tightly-woven… He moves on to the cottage; this construction is not solid; it has an interior. He steps in through the doorway. The interior is a shell; no rooms, no stairs, no upper floor; just one empty space…

Outside again, he returns to the causeway, surveys the replica house and replica car… Why are they here? What purpose do they serve? Just outlines… a rough approximation of their real-world counterparts…

Wait a minute…

He turns round. Across the ocean of corn rises the plantation of beech trees; the place he first arrived… The holiday cottage—the farm track—the arable land—and then Vernon Wood... Yes... Not just the cottage is represented—this whole landscape around him... It is like a simulacrum of the world he came from; a shadow of that world; a still-life world devoid of organic life...

But the rough sketch is incomplete. Behind the cottage the wilderness of corn stretches off in the place where Market Stanford ought to be...

But then, he hadn't seen the cottage until he'd stepped out onto the causeway... And from the trees, he hadn't seen the causeway at all... Perhaps proximity is the key; perhaps these things only become visible when you draw near to them... Or perhaps he carries this semblance of the real world around with him like an aura...

Turning his back on the wicker house, Mark heads back along the causeway... Straw house... Wicker house... A Wicker House for a Wicca witch... The Wiccan Witch of the West...

He's looking for something... A girl... A book... Marianne... No, not Marianne—Lucretia... Lucretia standing in the circle... Disappeared... And himself—standing in the same circle... Disappeared... Brought to this place...

A path of trampled corn ahead... Who made it...? Idiot! *He* did... Yes, chasing that grey shadow from the Shadow Vernon Wood... Go back to Vernon Wood—Vernon Wood the epicentre...

He turns from the causeway, retraces his steps along the avenue of flattened what... No, *not* retracing his steps... Look at the stalks... Crushed by someone moving in the same direction he is moving now... Not retracing his steps—following someone else's...

The path suddenly debouches into a much wider area of flattened ground... A crop circle of vast and intricate design... Companion of those elaborate hoaxes that once deceived a nation; UFO investigators and neo-pagans both claiming them as their own... But this crop circle has an occupant, perhaps also its architect—lying in the centre of the circle, Lucretia... Lucretia; the girl whose mind inhabits the stars... Still wearing her black skirt and blouse, those heavy boots... Lying on her back, the nucleus of her abstract design, arms and legs stretched out, perfectly still...

Mark kneels down beside her... Her eyes are closed, her features motionless... He senses life, touches her shoulder... The eyes open suddenly, fix themselves on Mark.

'Got a cigarette?' she asks.

Chapter Thirty-Eight
From Out of the Rain

A storm is gathering. Ominous grey clouds pile up on the horizon.

Bridget can see them through the window as she lies on the bed in her room.

Downstairs, she'd seen Dr Newcome was being defied and ridiculed by Channing and Caxton as usual. After the women had walked off, Bridget had gone up to Newcome offering what she thought would be welcome words of support and sympathy. But Newcome had rounded on her, fixing her with a look of the most annihilating contempt.

'I don't need sympathy from *you*.'

Lying here in the growing gloom, Bridget thinks about that man—she can't remember his name; that spy she'd allowed to escape this morning. He was an enemy, they'd said—a bad person. But he hadn't looked like a bad person; when their eyes had met, it had seemed to Bridget that he'd looked at her like he'd wanted to help her. That was the feeling she got. She'd wanted to speak to him, only she hadn't known what to say to him; and there hadn't been time, because he was escaping, and he was already gone, out through the front door. She'd felt a strong urge to follow him, to escape with him...

But she hadn't; she'd just stood there, and then Dr Channing had come charging out of the lift, yelling at her for letting the spy escape...

Bridget is in the throes of an existential crisis (although she wouldn't have put it that way herself.) She's just not sure who are the good people and who are the bad people anymore; she always thought she knew; she always thought it was easy to tell who was good and who was bad... But now she's not so sure. That spy; she thought he looked like a good person, a kind person; but she's been told that he's a bad person, an enemy. And those people who broke into the Grange last night; they were supposed to be enemies as well. That she could believe; those people had looked like bad people and one of them had been carrying a gun—but had they had to kill them like that? Was it really necessary to do it the way they had?

But this is supposed to be her world now. She's not a normal person; she's an ESPer. Her place is here, with the other ESPers. This is supposed to be her world, but she doesn't see where or how she's supposed to fit into it...

And then there's Damien.

She thought it was going to happen—that night, after the gig, when she was drunk and ecstatic. She thought it was going to happen—with Damien and her. They'd said she was ready for it, those two groupies at the gig. And she was. And when they'd been driving back to the Grange and they were laughing and horseplaying together, she'd thought it was going to happen. And when they came up here to their rooms, still goofing around, she thought it was going to happen. She'd stopped at her door, and Damien was there and she thought he was going to come into her room with her... But he hadn't; he'd just smiled and said good night to her, and gone off to his own room...

The bubble had burst then, and she'd gone to bed feeling deeply disappointed. And now... and now she's not sure if she even likes Damien anymore.

Mavis would have come round sooner, but there has been an incident this morning: some public-minded citizens—yet to be identified—have taken it upon themselves to assist the turning of the wheels of justice by kicking Dennis Shrimpton, local idiot recently promoted to the status of local child-molester, to death. The police had heard about these rumours, quietly looked into them, and had found absolutely nothing to substantiate them; but give a dog a bad name...

'Oh!' says Dodo. 'You look like you've been in the wars. Did somebody resist arrest?'

Mavis Shagwell, her sunny good looks currently tarnished on account of a black eye and swollen cheek, takes the seat offered to her; Mayumi resumes her own place beside Dodo on the sofa.

'Yeah, it was me husband,' answers Mavis, smiling awkwardly.

Dodo frowns. 'Well, I hope you paid him back in kind.'

'Yeah, you should've whacked him over the head with your baton,' speaks up Trina.

'I let him off with a warning this time.'

'Are you sure he deserved that?' asks Dodo.

Mavis shrugs. 'Well, you know what happened...'

'No, I don't know what happened,' Dodo tells her. 'Should I?'

A surprised look. 'Didn't he tell you, then?'

'Didn't who tell me what?'

'Mark. Didn't he tell you about what happened?'

'As we said, Mark isn't here,' replies Dodo. 'He's gone missing, and we're actually quite worried about him.'

'Oh!' says Mavis. 'Missing, is he? But this happened yesterday lunchtime—you've seen him since then, haven't you?'

'No, we haven't,' states Dodo emphatically. 'We haven't seen him since Thursday night. Are you saying that *you* saw him yesterday lunchtime?'

'Yeah.'

'Where did you see him?'

'First, I went to where he was camping; then I drove him into town.'

'You drove him *here*, then?' demands Dodo.

Mavis looks surprised. 'No. We didn't come here.'

'Oh. Because we know Mark did come here yesterday lunchtime,' says Dodo. 'We were out at the time, but there were signs that he'd been here when we got back.'

'Oh... Yeah, that must've happened after, then,' says Mavis.

'After *what?*' asks Dodo, controlling her impatience. 'Look: please just tell me everything that happened after you picked Mark up in your car.'

And so Mavis tells them—not without embarrassment and completely omitting the striptease act. Dodo and Mayumi are amused at the account of this failed seduction; Trina, not so amused.

291

'So your husband walked in and Mark escaped by jumping out of an upstairs window,' summarises Dodo, smiling at the mental image. 'Well, it was very honest of you to take all the blame on yourself, Mavis, when you got caught red-handed like that. It would have been easy enough to drop Mark right in it; clear yourself that way.'

Mavis looks uncomfortable. 'I'll be honest with you,' she says, smiling awkwardly again; 'that *is* what I tried to do, at first. But me husband wasn't having any of it; reckon he knows me too well.'

'So...' says Dodo; 'Mark must have come straight here after that incident at your place... But then what happened to him...?' She looks at Mavis. 'And you haven't heard anything about him? Nothing's been reported to the police?'

'No, nothing. I didn't know he'd gone missing...'

'Then what brought you here? Or did you just want to apologise to Mark...?'

'Partly that,' says Mavis. 'But yesterday, before everything happened, Mark asked me to do something for him; so I wanted to find out if he still wanted it doing.'

'What was it? What did he want you to do for him?'

'He wanted me to go round Vernon Grange, and ask about some girl he's worried about or something; can't remember her name...'

'That'll be Lucretia,' supplies Dodo.

'Yeah, that was it! Lucretia. Yeah, he wanted me to go'n ask if she were there and if she were alright.'

'He asked you to do that, did he?' says Dodo, pensively. 'Is that where he went...?'

'You think Mark might've gone there?' asks Trina.

'Yes... It's possible...'

Mark and Lucretia, walking through the sea of corn.

'For every one of us there's one of them,' says Lucretia.

'So you're saying these grey aliens are actually our doppelgängers?'

Lucretia draws on her cigarette. 'Yes,' exhaling. 'They're like puppets; they just follow us around and do whatever we do. But normally you can't see them; we're not supposed to. They can see us but we're not supposed to see them; they exist in another reality.'

Doppelgängers. Yes; it makes sense. The explanation makes sense. All those sightings around Market Stanford—each time they appeared, the person involved was seeing *their own* doppelgänger. Most people, himself included, were alone when it happened, so they had only seen one grey alien. The little boy who saw one said that it looked like a child. Mayumi and Trina had seen two. The kids in the spinney had seen a whole group of them. Everyone was seeing their own doppelgänger.

'So they come from this place?' queries Mark. 'This is their reality?'

'*No*. This isn't their world. This isn't anywhere. This is limbo.'

'Limbo?'

'Yeah, it's not one place or the other. You have to be careful here; don't let your thoughts wander, cuz they can wander off too far and then you can lose yourself; lose yourself in your own thoughts. I got lost like that until you found me.'

'I think I've been experiencing the same thing,' says Mark. 'Since I've been here, my thoughts have been running away with me at times…'

'Don't let them,' Lucretia tells him. 'Think about something; something that's right now and important.'

'Okay, I'll try and focus on getting out of this place.'

'Yes; let's both think about that.'

'Speaking of which: how did we get here in the first place? Were we brought here on purpose?'

'Don't think so. The walls between realities are very weak around here. There. People can slip through…'

'And why is this happening? Is it something to do with the greys?'

'No, it's the future people.'

'Future people? What future people?'

'They're the ones that look like spacemen. They've travelled back to this time, but they did it wrong. They did it wrong somehow and they brought their doppelgängers back with them—into our world. They're not supposed to be in our world; they don't belong here; that's why things are coming apart.'

They brought their doppelgangers back with them... The two landing sites...

'You suddenly know a lot,' says Mark. 'Is that from being stuck in this place?'

'Yes. This place is full of echoes,' answers Lucretia. 'They're in the air, all crossing over each other like grid-patterns... I can feel them all, hear them all...' She turns and looks at him. 'Are you staying focused?'

'Yes, I'm staying focused,' Mark assures her. 'I'm focusing on you; that seems to be doing the trick.'

'Yes, it's better when you're not alone in this place,' agrees Lucretia. 'Your mind doesn't wander as much... Now that you're here, maybe we can get back and warn the others...'

'Warn whom?' asks Mark.

'The others—the other ESPers at the Grange; the future people want to kill us. That's the reason they came here...'

A ripple of thunder across the lowering sky.

A flash of lightning briefly disturbs the gathering gloom in the room where Bridget still lies on her bed. She can't figure this out; she needs help; someone to turn to, someone to lean on...

The door opens and in walk Damien and Serena, all smiles. In her current frame of mind, the intrusion irritates her. She doesn't like those two right now. Shutting the door behind them, the pair just stand there, smiling at her.

'What do you want?' asks Bridget, her tone unfriendly.

'Charming,' says Serena. 'Someone's in a bad mood, aren't they?'

'She's just down in the dumps,' says Damien. 'Not surprising, sitting in the dark like this. Here we go.'

He switches the light on.

'I don't want the light on,' says Bridget. She sits up on the bed, crossing her legs, regarding her unwelcome guests with a pouting face.

'We can't have you being a misery-guts,' says Damien

'Yeah, let us cheer you up,' offers Serena.

'I don't want cheewing up. I don't like this place and I don't

294

like you two. I want to go home.'

'You want to go home?' echoes Damien. 'Yeah, that's not an option, is it?'

'Why not?' demands Bridget. 'They can't keep me here.'

'Actually, they can,' says Damien. 'And anyway, where do you plan to go home *to?* Your parents don't want you back.'

'What do you mean they don't want me back?'

'Just what I said. They were just scared of you with that pyrokinetic ability of yours; they just wanted to get rid of you; they didn't want you burning down their house, did they? So you see, they don't want you; you haven't got a home to go to. In fact... you haven't really got anyone you can turn to, have you...?'

'Yeah, you're right. She hasn't, has she? Sad, really...'

Tears gather in Bridget's eyes. 'Shut up!' she snaps. 'You don't know my mum and dad! They'd take me back if they knew I didn't like it here!'

Damien shrugs. 'Whatever you say...'

'Just go away,' says Bridget. 'You've only come here to be nasty to me.'

'Who's being nasty?' retorts Damien. 'We're just trying to make you understand how things are.'

'Well, I don't care, so just go away!'

A rumble of thunder, louder than before. The storm is coming closer.

'Not yet,' says Damien. 'I've got a confession I want to make to you first. You see, I've sort of been misleading you...'

'What about?'

Damien shakes his head, spreads his hands. 'Oh, everything really. About us. About this place. Everything. It wasn't hard to fool you, with your stupid, naïve black and white view of the world. You see, we're not the good guys you thought we were; we're not really the good guys at all...'

'What do you mean?' asks Bridget, her alarm increasing.

'I mean us, here,' says Damien. 'We don't work for the government; we're not fighting for justice and Queen and Country, or any of that bullshit. We work for the people with the money; the corporate machine; the ones with the real power. They own Vernon Grange, not Her Majesty's Government.'

'I don't believe you…' says Bridget. 'The doctors—'

'The doctors wouldn't lie to you? Is that what you were going to say? Sorry, but they did. We've all been lying to you. It's true enough that we go out on missions; we spy on people, we steal things, sometimes we kill people; but we do those things at the behest of our corporate overlords. We spy on their rivals, we steal their rivals' secrets, and we're told to, we kill any of their rivals who are in the way. And it's all done in the name of money, filthy lucre; cuz you can do everything with money; money equals power, and luxury and getting what you want and whenever you want it.'

'But… a company can't make me work for it, if I don't want to…'

Serena laughs out loud at this one, and Damien grins all over.

'You just don't get it, do you?' he says. 'Can't make you. The "company" as you call it, *owns* you. You are bought and paid for, girl. And you know who it was that sold you to the company? Your loving parents. Yep, your Mummy and Daddy sold you, lock, stock and barrel.'

Tears course down Bridget's cheeks. 'I don't believe you…'

'Yes, you do,' Damien tells her. 'I mean, we're all slaves to the corporation here; not just you. Difference is, the rest of us volunteered; we willingly signed away our souls, and we're happy in our servitude. As long as we do our jobs, the rest of the time we get to do whatever the hell we want—we've got more freedom than most of the people who *don't* think that they're slaves. Yeah, we all volunteered—you didn't. That's the difference.'

'Better believe it, girl,' advises Serena. 'You're working for the bad guys now.'

'Oh yeah; which brings me to the last part of my confession,' says Damien. 'The other thing I deceived you about is me. You see, I'm not the nice person I kind of let you think I was. In fact, I'm not a very nice person at all.'

'It's true. He's not,' confirms smiling Serena. 'Nastiest piece of work I've ever met, this lad.'

Damien sighs, shaking his head, as though disappointed with himself. 'True… True… I think I can honestly say I've never done a single good deed in my life; not one…'

Bridget wipes her face with her sleeve. 'But you… you killed that wapist…'

'Did I? Oh yes; Alan…Yes, well, y'see, although that story wasn't a *complete* work of fiction, I did sort of change some of the details. It wasn't that guy Alan who was date-raping those girls: it was me. Yes, I was the one doing it, and *Alan* was the one who found out about it and decided he'd take the law into his own hands; that's why he came at me with the knife… So that part was true enough, although it wasn't really in self-defence. I could've let him live if I'd wanted to…'

Bridget stares at him, appalled at what she hears. 'You… you were the one who waped all those girls?'

'Guilty! Cuz like I said, I'm just not a nice guy.'

'He's the worst,' agrees Serena.

'Yeah… What can I say? I'm completely selfish… I'm always being led by my own uncontrollable urges… I like messing with people's heads… And of course, I'm a big fat liar. Ever since you got here I've been lying to you, pretending to be nice, pretending to like you… But, you know, you're so stupid and gullible, that really you were asking for it…'

'Begging for it,' affirms Serena.

More tears stream down Bridget's face; her lips quiver. 'But why…? Why…?'

'"Why? Why?"' mimics Serena.

'Why have we been leading you on?' says Damien. 'Well, because it was fun. It was fun to see you trusting us the way you did. You really fancied me, didn't you? Followed me around like a puppy dog. Night before last, when you were bladdered, you really wanted me, didn't you? I could tell—everyone could. Wanted me to come into your room and fuck you, didn't you? And cuz I'm such a bastard, I didn't come in and fuck you, cuz I knew you wanted it, *then*. So I'm going to fuck you *now*, instead.'

Serena puts her hands to her mouth in mock horror. 'Damien! You don't mean… you're not going to *rape* the child, are you?'

'Yes. Sadly, that is *exactly* what I'm going to do…'

Bridget springs from the bed, backs away from the two intruders, terrified. She sees them now as they really are—glaring at her with hungry, savage smiles; predator smiles.

Say Damien, 'First, let's get rid of the wrapping…'

He clicks his fingers and Bridget's clothes start to move, pulling and tugging as though they are being buffeted by a gale. She staggers, struggling to keep her balance… And they start to tear, loudly ripping themselves apart, coming away from her body… The torn shreds fly around like confetti. Even her jeans tear themselves apart as though they were made of the lightest cotton… Her socks, her underwear… And Bridget finds herself standing stripped naked—naked except for beloved hat, which, in a gesture of ghoulish irony, Damien has spared.

And now she stands before her tormentors like a slave at a market; instinctively, trying to protect herself, to conceal her nudity, a forearm shielding her breasts, a hand over her crotch.

'Nice bod,' acknowledges Serena.

Damien makes a noise. 'I've seen better. Still…'

He advances towards her.

Bridget shakes her head, crying and sniffling.

'Please don't, Damien…' as though saying his name might somehow help her cause.

Damien raises a hand theatrically, and his psychokinetic force comes into play, grabs her again, spins her round, throws her facedown onto the bed, buttocks raised.

'Yeah, that looks better…'

Bridget fixes an imploring look on Serena. 'Help me…'

'Not me,' says Serena, getting out her smartphone. 'I *love* rape scenes.'

And then the storm breaks. The heavens open up, the rain hurls itself down, and the roar of the thunder drowns out Bridget's screams.

Amongst the most ridiculous things that people say about the weather (and another classic is 'It's too cold to snow!') is when a storm occurs during a heatwave, and people say, 'That's cleared the air!' when in fact the exact reverse of this has been achieved.

Dodo Dupont can avouch for this, because she has been caught in this deluge—and as well as being soaked to the skin, she is also being stifled by the humidity. She is in Vernon Wood, which at the

298

moment feels like a tropical rainforest during the monsoon season. Her hair is plastered to her skull, her saturated jeans and t-shirt cling heavily to her body, with the former in particular doing its best to weigh her down and impede her movements.

And she's gone and got herself lost. With the fierce downpour reducing visibility, she has somehow managed to wander off the footpath, and she's now wading through weeds and nettles, with all sense of direction lost to her.

She could have driven. She could have driven to Vernon Grange, but, in spite of the gathering clouds, she thought it would be a good idea to go on foot, so she could check the campsite once more for Mark, before venturing to step into the lion's den...

She blunders on, constantly wiping the streaming water from her face to keep her vision clear. Dodo is not the vainest of people, not one to care about superficial appearances and the opinion of the world at large—but she just cannot help thinking how can she possibly present herself at the front door of Vernon Grange looking this...?

I don't know if it is that fate decides to interpose at this juncture, in order to teach Dodo a lesson about the vanity of worrying about appearances—but nevertheless it is at this very moment that, wading through some bracken, the ground disappears from beneath Dodo's feet, and she tumbles arse-over-tit (or head-over-heels, if you prefer) to the bottom of a steep declivity, with the end result that instead of just being soaked to the skin, she is now also caked in mud from head to foot.

And the first thing she sees, upon rising to her knees and wiping the mud from her face, is that she is in the company of a corpse. The body lies on its face in the mud, a shotgun at its side. Dodo crawls over to the corpse, turns it over. A man in his thirties, dressed in tweeds and flat-cap. He looks very much like one of those gamekeeper guards from Vernon Grange. A quick examination reveals that he has been shot to death; his torso peppered with bullets. For a moment Dodo wonders if the man fell down here like she did and managed to shoot himself with his own weapon—but on closer inspection the spread of the impact holes bears more the hallmarks of rapid fire from a machinegun, than of pellets from a shotgun. And this suggests the culprit is one of those spacemen from the UFO.

Suddenly alert, Dodo produces the pocket automatic she has brought with her and scans her surroundings. The hollow she has tumbled into stretches off in both directions, curving out of sight. No sign of movement; no sounds other than the ubiquitous rainfall... The corpse is so waterlogged, it's hard to tell for sure, but Dodo guesses the man has been dead for an hour at least; and she certainly hasn't heard any gunfire since she's been here... But the killer or killers could still be around... Beretta in hand, she sets off cautiously along the waterlogged course of the dell, heading in what she hopes is the direction of the Grange.

She comes across a second body, further down the hollow. Another guard from the Grange; shot, just like the first. What were they doing out here? They were security guards; their job was to guard and patrol the grounds of the Grange; the only reason Dodo can think for them being here in the woods is that they were searching for or pursuing someone—and the two most likely candidates Dodo can think of for being pursued or searched for by these guards are Lucretia or Mark.

Emerging from the dell onto level ground, she strikes off cautiously through the trees, moving from cover to cover. She espies a clearing ahead, and reaching it, discovers yet another dead body. The presence of the corpse distracts her, and it's only after glancing around that she sees she has arrived back at the former campsite.

Thank God! At least she now knows where she is.

The dead guard lies on his back; he's older than the other two. Dodo thinks it must be Travers, the head guard. She examines his shotgun; both barrels have been fired. Ineffectually, it seems; there is no other body in sight.

Now that she knows where she is, Dodo decides that her best course will be to remove herself from the environs of Vernon Wood. She throws the shotgun aside and heads towards the nearest trail, a route that takes her towards the landing site. Closing in, she catches sight of something that makes her drop to the ground, and, keeping flat snake her way to the border of the trees. She peers through the foliage towards the landing site, alert, gun at the ready.

300

The UFO stands in the clearing. The same craft from the other night (she vaguely thinks she might be lying where Trina was peeing); an inverted spinning top. The same, but different. Today, it is neither emitting any light or producing any sound; it just stands there in the clearing, smooth, solid, metallic—stark and real against the backdrop of rain-sodden foliage and timber, under the frowning grey sky. It is an intruder, an unsettling presence; it doesn't belong here.

There is no sign of movement, no sign of the craft's occupants. Dodo surveys the scene for several minutes; then she makes a careful retreat, keeping low until, safely out of the craft's line of sight, she joins the pathway and heads towards the main road.

They finally come to the edge of the cornfield. A row of trees stands before them; they pass between them and find themselves in a pasture, guarded on all four sides by these leafy sentinels. In the middle of the pasture lies the incongruous form of a railway carriage—or at least a straw-woven replica of one.

Mark stares at it. The celebrated train carriage in the middle of a field. The legend from Mark's childhood, searched for on many occasions, but never found.

'You know this place?' asks Lucretia. 'You look like you do.'

'I know *of* it,' answers Mark. 'It was like this local legend when I was a kid; that somewhere there was a field with a train carriage sitting in the middle of it. Some of the older boys said they'd been to it, but, my friend and I, we were never able to find it...'

'You've found it now,' says Lucretia. 'Woo-hoo.'

'I wonder...' says Mark.

'What?' asks Lucretia.

'...Maybe the carriage *doesn't* exist in our world,' says Mark, shaping his thoughts. 'Maybe it only exists physically here, in this limbo; and in the real world it somehow became known of as a legend; something that filtered through from this world to ours...'

'Nice idea,' says Lucretia. 'But wrong. If it's here, it's there. Let's check it out.'

They cross the pasture to the wickerwork train carriage. A row of empty windows face them, demonstrating that the carriage has

301

an interior like the straw house, and is not a solid object like the car.

The sounds in the sky, before a background noise, almost subliminal, are becoming louder now; rumbling reverberations like metallic thunder.

'Something's happening,' says Lucretia, staring up at the sky.

'Do you know what it is?'

'Might be the future men, building up their power.'

'You said that before,' says Mark. 'They haven't struck yet because they keep slipping in and out of our reality…'

'Need to build up their power,' confirms Lucretia. 'Then they can attack.'

'Attack the Grange?'

'Yes.'

'And you don't know why? You don't know why they want to kill you all?'

'No. Just know that they do.'

Mark steps up through the doorway and into the wicker rail car; Lucretia follows. Like the cottage, the interior of this reconstruction is just an empty shell; there are no seats, no partition walls. The rumbling in the air increases.

'It almost sounds like thunder,' says Mark.

He looks out the window and sees that they are not alone. A large number of greys have suddenly appeared in the field. They stand at irregular intervals, motionless, surrounding the carriage, staring in at them.

'We've got company,' he murmurs.

Lucretia joins him at the window. 'Lost souls…' she says.

In the common room Helen reaches out and turns on the standard lamp beside her chair. It is becoming too dark to read. Edward sits at the piano across the room, playing Chopin, vying with the sound of the rain pelting on the windows.

Poor, stupid Edward, thinks Helen, looking at him over her book. He had fallen for that girl Bridget—God knows why— almost as soon as she had arrived; a fact he confessed to his fellow telepath, but not to anyone else. And especially not to the girl herself. At Helen's suggestion, he'd gone with Bridget to that rock concert in town in the other night, but then the idiot, instead of doing the obvious thing of ingratiating himself with Bridget by taking an interest in her interests, had gone and let his ingrained cynicism take over and had started deriding the kind of music she liked right to her face! Idiot. Well, she's not going to give him any more love advice; he can sort it out for himself. Not that he'll ever get anywhere; not with his social skills and with Damien on the scene. The girl's obviously besotted with Damien. More fool her. She's going to find out the mistake she's made sooner or later. (Bridget is actually upstairs finding out her mistake with a vengeance, at this very moment.)

Love problems. Love. Stupid, the things people try to pass off as 'love'... The whole thing makes Helen sick. All it is is people in heat, chasing after each other's genitals; fucking like animals... There's no 'love' in that; just a stupid and nasty physical function.

There had been this girl at Helen's school: her name was Denise. Tall, beautiful and elegant; Denise was a top scholar and captain of the hockey team. She seemed to succeed in everything she turned her hand to; and she had such a warm, generous personality; always friendly, always had time for people... To Helen, Denise had seemed a model of perfection. It hadn't been a sexual attraction she felt for the girl—more like hero-worship. Helen can still see Denise as she was back then: standing in the schoolyard on a sunny day, the centre of a group of girls; her golden hair glowing; the way she tilted her head when she smiled... Helen had been a lot shyer back then; she wasn't part of Denise's inner circle of friends; she could only worship her from afar... And then there had been that party—the usual teenage party round the house of a classmate whose parents are away. Helen had only gone to the party because she knew that Denise was going; she thought it might be the ideal opportunity for getting to know her idol—and in a way, it was just that. Searching for the bathroom, Helen had gone upstairs and opened what proved to be a bedroom door—and there was Denise, flat on her back on the tumbled sheets, and a boy on top of her, pounding furiously away at her; Denise, groaning and grunting under this onslaught, writhing her arms and legs, screaming obscene encouragement... Helen's image of her idol had shattered at that moment. That elegant and dignified prize student—where was she now? How could Denise have submitted herself to this? How could she degrade herself like this?

Helen could never look at her the same way again. She felt like she'd finally seen the real Denise; and the other one, the Denise at school, was just a hypocritical imposture.

The sounds of a commotion in the hall outside. Edward stops playing.

'What's going on out there?' he wonders.

Helen shrugs. 'I dunno. I think they're still worked up about that spy who escaped. The guards who went after him into the woods never came back.'

'Do they think they've been killed or something?'

Another shrug. 'The spy didn't have a gun; that's what Channing said.'

'Maybe this is something else. Let's go'n see.'

They go into the hallway, where they find Channing, Clavering and Caxton, standing at the open front door, staring down the avenue. Channing is armed with a pistol (Mark's), and Caxton with one of the guard's shotguns.

'What's going on?' asks Helen.

'We've got intruders at the gate,' answers Channing. 'At least that's what it sounds like; and now we've lost contact with the people at the gatehouse.'

'Is that spy again?'

'I don't think so,' is the reply. 'They reported there were some "funny looking people" outside the gate; and Newcome, being the idiot he is, charged out into the rain to see for himself; after that we lost contact with the gatehouse.'

'What did they mean by "funny looking people"?'

'Well, we don't know.'

'Why don't we go and investigate instead of just standing here?' suggests Edward.

'Because we don't know what we're dealing with,' retorts Channing. 'It might be—'

'Look!' cries Caxton, urgently. 'Coming up the drive!'

They look.

From out of the rain they come, three figures, identical,

304

advancing side by side along the treelined drive, moving at a steady, unhurried pace. Three impossible figures, vivid red and silver, vivid against the drear surroundings. Armed with rifles, they advance purposefully towards the house, intentions concealed behind impenetrable helmet visors.

Helen is the first to break the stunned silence.

'What the hell are they?'

'Aliens,' says Edward, alarmed. 'All those stories must have been true.'

'They *can't* be aliens,' declares Caxton. 'This is some kind of trick.'

'Trick or not, they've got guns and they're coming this way,' says Channing. She steps out onto the sheltered porch, and takes aim at the three approaching figures.

'Stop where you are,' she orders. 'If you come any closer, I will fire.'

The intruders continue to advance. Channing squeezes off a shot, aiming at the central figure. It appears to have no effect. Scowling, she fires again, emptying the clip at the spacemen. She knows she can't have missed her targets, but they don't even flinch; just keep moving inexorably closer.

Caxton steps forward. 'Out of the way; let me try.'

Channing steps aside, and, taking position, Caxton levels her shotgun at the intruders, and fires off both barrels. They have absolutely no effect.

'They've got a forcefield...' comes Clavering's voice.

'Get back!' orders Caxton.

The five of them retreat into the house. Channing and Caxton quickly close and lock the doors, throwing all the bolts.

'Back!' yells Channing. 'Away from the door!'

They retreat to the foot of the staircase.

Robert and Roberta materialise out of thin air.

'What's going on?' inquires Robert.

'We heard shooting,' says Roberta.

'We're being attacked,' reports Channing. 'Where are the others? We need to get everyone together.'

A loud thump against the entrance doors. Another. The doors shake under the impact.

'*Who's* attacking us?' demands Robert. 'Why didn't you just shoot them?'

'They're bullet-proof,' answers Helen. 'They're wearing special suits or something.'

'*Who* is?'

'Aliens!' snaps Helen. 'They're fucking aliens, alright?'

'Aliens!' cry the twins, delighted.

Another impact. A crack appears in one of the doors.

'How are they even doing that?' cries Caxton. 'Those doors are three inches thick!'

Says Channing: 'You two: go'n get the other three down here! They're the strongest ones—we need them right now!'

'But we want to stay and meet the aliens,' protests Robert.

'Yes,' agrees Roberta; 'we've never done a first-contact before.'

'This isn't a game, you little idiots!' grates Channing.

Another impact and one of the doors is torn from its hinges, crashing to the parquet floor. The three spacemen appear, stepping over it and into the hallway.

A blinding flash of lightning, and suddenly a torrential downpour is hammering on the metal roof of the train carriage. Metal. They are no longer in a wickerwork effigy; they are in the real thing. The interior, darker now, is still hollow, but with bolts and grooves on the floor indicating where seats and partition walls had once been fixed. The heat and humidity are stifling.

They have moved. They are back home.

Mark peers out through the now-glazed window. They are still in a field, but the grass now is wild, tangled with brambles. And there is no sign of the greys.

'We're back home,' he reports.

'I know,' replies Lucretia. 'It's gone quiet.'

'Gone quiet? It's chucking it down!'

'Gone quiet here,' says Lucretia, tapping her temple with an index finger.

'Oh, I see. All those signals you were picking up…'

'We should get back to the Grange,' says Lucretia.

'Trouble is, I don't know where it is from here,' says Mark, looking out of the window. The pasture here is bordered with trees, as it was in limbo, obstructing the view. 'We'll just have to start walking until we get our bearings. And we're going to get soaked, as well.'

'I like the rain,' says Lucretia.

Mark isn't surprised to hear this.

They step out into the downpour, and make their way with difficulty across the overgrown field. They squeeze through a gap in the bushes and emerge onto a farm track; they follow this and it very quickly brings them to a main road. Mark recognises the spot as being roughly halfway between Vernon Grange and Vernon village—the scattering of houses that constitute the latter are visible off to the left.

So, the legendary field with the train carriage: only a stone's throw from the main road; as a boy Mark must have driven past the spot in the family car dozens of times; but on foot, across the fields, way beyond the territory he and Clyde had ever dared to venture as boys; way of the beaten track…

They have left Bridget alone. They have left her defiled, bleeding and hurt; but still, technically—as they laughingly pointed out to her—a virgin.

She lies in foetal ball on her bed, head clasped between the right-angles of her arms. She whimpers quietly to herself, sobbing, quivering. Outside the air-conditioned room, the tempest still rages.

A note rises, the staccato sobs extending themselves to form a single doleful sound, an agonised moan that rises in volume, louder, louder, until it becomes a loud shriek of mingled rage and despair ripped from the girl's mouth, horribly contorting her face.

And her body, before so frail, comes violently to life, throwing itself around the bed in frenzy, limbs kicking and punching the air, as she screams and screams…

Bridget has no conscious awareness of it, but something else has been stirred up inside her. Her power has awoken, fuelled by her overwhelming rage, and it has fastened itself on the means of exerting itself; has sought out and connected with the most flammable source within reach of her mind—which happens to be the gas main running directly beneath the Grange…

Mark and Lucretia hurry along the roadside towards Vernon Grange. Having no means of protecting themselves from the downpour, and they are already drenched, soaked to the skin.

The perimeter wall of the Grange appears through the murk ahead. And, as they draw closer, something else; something lying on the ground by the open gates.

They hurry to the spot. The object on the ground is the body of one of the guards. Just inside the open gates are two other fatalities; another guard and a man in white lab coat—Dr Newcome.

'It looks like we're too late,' says Mark, raising his voice over the storm. 'Question is: have they been and gone, or are they still here? Can you—?'

Lucretia has grabbed his sleeve. Mark turns. He follows her gaze further down the road; a figure has appeared from the curtain of rain; mud-caked, trudging towards them.

'Swamp monster,' says Lucretia.

'No…' says Mark. 'It's just Dodo.'

And then the house explodes. A tremendous roar, more powerful than any thunderclap; and the ground shakes beneath their feet. A huge pillar of flame shoots high into the sky above Vernon Grange.

'Get down!' yells Mark, and not waiting for Lucretia to comply he throws the girl to the ground, and himself on top of her. And a deadly hail starts to fall from the sky—a sustained barrage of debris, chunks of all sizes, slamming into the ground around them, like rocks hurled from a volcano.

The deadly hail subsides. Mark, unscathed, helps Lucretia to her feet. He looks down the now rubble-strewn and pock-marked road; sees Dodo rise from her prone position, waving an arm to indicate she's okay.

Mark's eyes return to the house. There's not much left of it now; a few broken walls, fangs of masonry, still standing, while the inferno rages on in what was once the interior of the building, and dense black smoke billows up into the grey sky.

And the rain—just when it might conceivably have done some good, the rain starts to ease off…

Epilogue
Endless Summers: Autumn

Mark would always remember this day.

A rainy, depressing November day. Walking the now familiar route to Marianne's bungalow. It has never rained before on his way to or from Marianne's. He wears his navy-blue parka with the hood up.

Mark is a secondary school student now, but he still continues special studies with Marianne. Being at school just means that these lessons at the bungalow are less frequent than they were during the holidays; usually only happening once a week on Saturday or Sunday.

She's still lending him books, of course; these still form the foundation of their lessons together. This time it is Gustave Flaubert's *Sentimental Education* that he is returning. He holds it in his gloved hand, wrapped up in a carrier bag. A 1970s Penguin edition, translated by Robert Baldick, typeset in Monotype Fournier, the cover illustration Gustave Courbet's 'Man with Leather Belt', 430 pages including introduction and explanatory notes. Mark has enjoyed the book, and of course he couldn't help but think that the hero's love for an older woman echoes his own relationship with Marianne. The book is another one that Marianne bought in her teens, so it has her name written in it.

French literature is the subject of Mark's lessons at the moment; with books by Honoré de Balzac, Emile Zola, and Simone de Beauvoir having already been read and discussed.

As soon as Mark arrives in sight of the bungalow, he sees something is very wrong. There is an estate agent's 'for sale' sign up in the front garden. Mark's heart drops. Is Marianne moving house? She hasn't said anything to him about moving... He comes to the front gate, and looks at the bungalow; there is something odd about the windows—the net curtains have been taken down.

With a horrible sinking feeling, Mark runs through the gate and up to the living room window. Just as he has feared, the room is completely bare, every scrap of furniture has gone.

His mind reels. It can't be... Last weekend—he'd only seen her last weekend. She hadn't said anything about going away. This doesn't make sense. She wouldn't do this; she wouldn't just go off and leave him without saying a word...

Maybe she's left a message for him! A note, or something. He tries the front door. Locked. He goes round to the back of the house. The kitchen door is also locked.

It can't be... It can't be... He looks in through the bedroom window. The room, their classroom, their snug nest, is now barren, denuded of its furniture.

A man appears from round the corner of the house. Thin-lipped and narrow eyed, he wears a trench-coat and smokes a cigarette. He looks at Mark without emotion.

'She's gone,' says the man, without preamble. 'She won't be coming back.'

'Where's she gone?' demands Mark. 'And who are you?'

'Never you mind who I am, sonny,' says the man. 'And where she's gone is none of your business. You won't be seeing her again. Not ever.'

Mark's mind struggles for an explanation; finds one. 'Are you the police? Has she been arrested?'

The man smiles bleakly, blowing out smoke. 'The police don't usually take people's furniture away, do they?' he says. 'She's okay, and she's not in any trouble. That's all you need to know. That's all you're *going* to know. She's no longer a part of your life.'

'She wouldn't just go away without saying anything; she wouldn't just leave me like this...' says Mark, helplessly.

The man drops his cigarette, crushes it under his foot. 'Just get out of here, sonny. It's over. You're done here.'

'No! Not until—'

The man grabs Mark's arm in a painful grip.

'I said go. Or do I have to drag you to the gate?'

Mark relents; he takes his leave, shooting a defiant, frustrated look at the man as he turns the corner. In a daze, he walks down the garden path and through the gate. He looks back at the bungalow. The man has sauntered round to the front garden; he stands there, hands in pockets, watching. Mark turns and walks away, and as he walks, he begins to cry—he cries, and he cries more than he has ever cried in his young life, or ever will again. Marianne had only ever made him shed tears of joy; but now, it is a hopeless despair that wrings the tears from his eyes; the crushing sense of an irretrievable loss; an intense private grief that he can never share with anyone else.

In years to come he will wonder whether Marianne planned this from the start. Did she intend to disappear when she did, with no goodbyes, leaving him the book, her copy of *Sentimental Education* as a keepsake, a memento? Did she plan all this from the start?

He has never been able to find out.

Suggested Further Reading

The Three Trollops	Anthony Clerk
The Trollop of Bullhampton	Anthony Vicar
Trollop Farm	Anthony Orley
Ralph the Trollop	Anthony Heir
The Trollop Estate	Anthony Belton
An Old Man's Trollop	Anthony Love
The Prime Trollop	Anthony Minister
Trollop Parsonage	Anthony Framley
The Small Trollop at Allington	Anthony House
The Eustace Trollops	Anthony Diamond
The Last Trollop of Barset	Anthony Chronicle
The Trollops of Ballycloran	Anthony Macdermot
Doctor Wortle's Trollop	Anthony School
Castle Trollop	Anthony Richmond
Trollop Towers	Anthony Barchester
The American Trollop	Anthony Senator
An Eye for a Trollop	Anthony Eye
The Trollop's Children	AnthonyDuke
Mr Scarborough's Trollop	Anthony Family
Kept in the Trollop	Anthony Dark
The Golden Trollop of Granpère	Anthony Lion
Ayala's Trollop	Anthony Angel
The Trollops	Anthony Bertram
The Trollops	Anthony Clavering
The Trollops	Anthony Landleaguer

Samurai
West

disappearer007@gmail.com

Printed in Dunstable, United Kingdom